The Quilter's Legacy

An Elm Creek Quilts Novel

Jennifer Chiaverini

Simon & Schuster Paperbacks

New York   London   Toronto   Sydney   New Delhi

Simon & Schuster Paperbacks
An Imprint of Simon & Schuster, Inc.
1230 Avenue of the Americas
New York, NY 10020

First Simon & Schuster trade paperback edition April 2011

SIMON & SCHUSTER PAPERBACKS and colophon are registered
trademarks of Simon & Schuster, Inc.

For information about special discounts for bulk purchases,
please contact Simon & Schuster Special Sales at
1-866-506-1949 or business@simonandschuster.com.

The Simon & Schuster Speakers Bureau can bring authors
to your live event. For more information or to book an event,
contact the Simon & Schuster Speakers Bureau at
1-866-248-3049 or visit our website at www.simonspeakers.com.

Book design by Lauren Simonetti

Manufactured in the United States of America

3   5   7   9   10   8   6   4   2

The Library of Congress has cataloged the hardcover edition as follows:

Chiaverini, Jennifer.
The quilter's legacy : an Elm Creek Quilts novel / Jennifer Chiaverini.
p.   cm.
1. Compson, Sylvia (Fictitious character)—Fiction. 2. Quiltmaking—Fiction.
3. Art thefts—Fiction. 4. Aged women—Fiction. 5. Quilters—Fiction. I. Title.
PS3553.H473 Q58 2003
813'.54—dc21   2002030930

ISBN 978-0-7432-3613-3
ISBN 978-1-4516-0610-2 (pbk)
ISBN 978-1-4165-8734-7 (ebook)

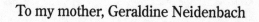

To my mother, Geraldine Neidenbach

Acknowledgments

I owe a deep debt of gratitude to Denise Roy, Maria Massie, and Rebecca Davis for their ongoing support of my work. Thank you for doing what you do so well.

Many thanks to Anne Spurgeon for her research assistance, but most of all, for her friendship.

I am grateful for the unwavering encouragement, faith, and tolerance of my friends and family, especially Geraldine Neidenbach, Heather Neidenbach, Nic Neidenbach, Virginia and Edward Riechman, Leonard and Marlene Chiaverini, Martin Lang, and Rachel and Chip Sauer. Thank you, Vanessa Alt, for playing with Nicholas while I wrote this book.

My husband, Marty, and my children, Nicholas and Michael, have enriched my life with their love and laughter. I could not do it without you.

other unnamed siblings

Anneke Stahl (1838–1880) ----- Hans Bergstrom

Elizabeth Reese ----- David Bergstrom (b. 1859)

Stephen (b. 1859)

Gertrude Drayton-Smith (d. 1927) ----- Charles Lockwood (d. 1918)

Abigail Lockwood (1886–1912)

Albert

Lydia

George

Lucinda

Herbert Drury (d. 1912) ----- Eleanor (1890–1930)

Frederick Bergstrom (1888–1945)

Maude (d. 1918) --- Louis (d. 1918)

Lily --- Richard (d. 1918)

William

Clara (1905–1918)

Harold Midden ----- Claudia Bergstrom (1918–1995)

James Compson (1918–1945) ----- Sylvia Bergstrom (b. 1920) ----- Andrew Cooper (b. 1927)

Agnes Chevalier (b. 1928) ----- Richard Bergstrom (1927–1945)

Joseph Emberly -----

Stacy

Laura

——— Descendants

------- Marriages

Chapter One

Sylvia supposed all brides-to-be considered eloping at some point during the engagement, but she had never expected to feel that way herself, and certainly not a mere few weeks after agreeing to become Andrew's wife. She shook her head as she flipped through the magazines someone had left on the desk—*Bride's, American Bride, Country Bride*—and dumped the whole stack into the trash can. Unless they came out with an edition of *Octogenarian Bride,* she would leave the pleading overtures of the bridal industry to the younger girls. Surely she could fend for herself when all she and Andrew wanted was a small, private ceremony in the garden.

The door to the library swung open, and in walked her young friend and business partner, Sarah McClure, neatly dressed in jeans and a button-down shirt, the glasses she wore only reluctantly tucked into the breast pocket. She carried a small white box in one hand. "Do you have a moment?"

"Yes. I was just doing some light housekeeping." Sylvia gestured to the trash can. "Are you responsible for this?"

"Are you kidding? After you scolded me for offering to take you shopping for your wedding gown?"

"I'm glad you learned your lesson." Sylvia frowned. Who could it have been, then? All of the Elm Creek Quilters had free run of the office. Summer spent more time there than anyone other than Sarah, but she was not the bridal magazine type. "Diane," she declared. "Just yesterday I overheard her say that this will be her only chance to plan a wedding because both of her children are boys. Do you suppose she forgot the magazines or left them deliberately, hoping I would be caught up in the wedding planning frenzy that seems to have captivated everyone else around here?"

"Ask her yourself," said Sarah, smiling. "She and Agnes are coming over to discuss new courses for next season."

"Already? Elm Creek Quilt Camp won't open until spring."

"Would you rather have them work ahead on next year's classes or plan your wedding?"

"I suppose you're right."

"You can't blame us for being excited. After you turned down Andrew the third time, most of us gave up hope that you two would ever get married."

"If you were disappointed, it was your own fault for treating our relationship like a spectator sport."

Sarah laughed. "I wasn't disappointed. I always knew it would happen eventually. In fact, I've been saving something for you for months with this occasion in mind."

She set the box on the table.

"What is it?" asked Sylvia, wary. "I distinctly said we did not want any engagement gifts."

"This doesn't really count."

"How could it not count? It's in a wrapped box; it's quite obviously a gift." But Sylvia smiled and unwrapped it. Inside was nestled a pair of silverplated scissors fashioned in the shape of a heron. "My goodness." She slipped on her glasses and studied the scissors, astonished. "My mother had a pair exactly like these. Where on earth did you find this?"

"In your attic, earlier this summer when we were looking for your great-grandmother's quilts," said Sarah. "You ordered me back to work every time I got sidetracked, so when I found them, I set them aside to show you later. When you found the quilts, I forgot about the scissors in all the excitement."

"In the attic. Then—" The weight and shape of the scissors felt so familiar in her hands that, even with her eyes closed, she could have described the pattern of nicks on the blades. "Then these must be my mother's. I should have known them immediately. Did you know these were given to her by the woman who taught her to quilt? An aunt, or someone. My mother was just a girl when she used these scissors in making her first quilt."

"I thought you might like to use them when you make your bridal quilt."

Sylvia nodded, scarcely hearing. She could picture her mother slicing through fabric with a sure and steady hand, cutting pieces for a dress or a quilt. She remembered sitting beneath the quilt frame as her mother and aunts quilted a pieced top, eavesdropping on their conversation, watching as they worked their needles through the layers of fabric and batting. The weight of her mother's scissors as they rested on the quilt top made the layers bow at her mother's right hand, the depression vanishing and reappearing, accompanied by a brisk snip as her mother trimmed a thread. Those were the same scissors Sylvia and her elder sister, Claudia, had fought over as they raced through their first quilt project, each determined to complete the most Nine-Patch blocks and thereby earn the right to sleep beneath the quilt first. It was a wonder the scissors had not been damaged beyond repair that wintry afternoon, the way Claudia had flung them across the room in frustration when she tried to pick out a poorly sewn seam and jabbed a hole through her patches instead.

"What pattern are you going to use?"

Sylvia looked up. "Hmm?"

"What pattern are you going to use for your wedding quilt?" Sarah regarded her, curious. "You are planning to make one, aren't you?"

"I honestly hadn't thought about it," said Sylvia. "Do you think Andrew expects a wedding quilt?"

"'Expects'? No, I don't think he expects one, but don't you want one? You'll need something for your new bed anyway, unless you're planning to squeeze both of you into your bed or Andrew's."

"Oh, of course," Sylvia said. "You're right. We'll need something."

Sarah's eyebrows rose. "Did you forget about that part? Most married people, you know, cohabit. Unless you were planning on twin beds a discreet distance apart?"

"Our sleeping arrangements are none of your business." Then Sylvia paused. "Actually, I suppose this sounds foolish, but I forgot we would be sharing a room."

Sarah put an arm around her. "I know it's probably been a while, but there's nothing to be nervous about. Especially with Andrew. I'm sure he'll be—"

"No, you don't understand," said Sylvia. "I'm not talking about what you think I'm— You're going to force me to say it, aren't you? Very well, then. Sex. I'm not talking about sex. I said share a room, not share a bed."

"I think you should be prepared to do both," said Sarah carefully. "Andrew might be disappointed if you don't want—"

"I said I'm not talking about sex," exclaimed Sylvia so forcefully Sarah jumped back in surprise. "Andrew and I will be fine in that department, and that's the last I'll say on the subject. My concern is with my room. I haven't shared a bedroom since—well, since James passed. Before then, even. Since he went overseas."

"I see. You're used to having a room of your own. Your own space."

"Precisely." If her bedroom didn't reflect Andrew's tastes and interests as well as her own, he would feel more like a visitor than an occupant. Hardly anyone but herself ever entered the adjoining sitting room, one of her favorite places to read or sew when she wanted solitude. Would she have to shove her fabric stash aside to make room for Andrew's fishing gear? "I don't think there's enough space in my suite for two people."

"Didn't you manage to make room for James when you married him?"

"That was different. I was younger. I didn't have so many things, and neither did James." When Sarah looked skeptical, Sylvia added, "Besides, when James came to live at Elm Creek Manor, I left my old bedroom and we moved into the suite together. That made it our room, not merely mine."

"Why don't you and Andrew do the same? You could move into the master suite on the third floor."

"I couldn't. That was my parents' room."

"But it's just sitting there empty and it's the largest suite in the manor."

"I suppose," said Sylvia, reluctant. But that would not solve the problem. She was content with her room as it was. It was private and it was hers. She did not want to change it or move somewhere else, but what was the point of getting married if they meant to leave things exactly as they were?

Sylvia stroked the heron scissors with a fingertip and carefully returned them to the box. She would just have to get used to the idea. If she told Andrew how she felt, he might think she was having second thoughts about marrying him.

Whatever they decided about the room, they would still need a quilt. Sylvia could no longer sew as swiftly as she had before her stroke, and she did not want a half-finished quilt covering their bed on their first night as husband and wife. She could ask the Elm Creek Quilters for help, or—

"I know just the thing." Sylvia rose from her chair, tucking her mother's scissors into her pocket. "Thank you, Sarah. Your gift has inspired me."

"Where are you going?"

"Up to the attic, to look for my mother's bridal quilt."

Sylvia stifled a laugh, amused by Sarah's baffled expression. It was nice to know that, in spite of their closeness, Sylvia could still surprise her young friend.

Sylvia went upstairs to the third floor, then climbed the narrow, creaking stairs to the attic. Rain drummed on the roof as she fumbled for the light switch Sarah's husband, Matt, had only recently installed. The overhead light illuminated the attic much better than the single, bare bulb it had replaced, but even now the sloped ceiling and the stacks of trunks, cartons, and the accumulated possessions of four generations cast deep shadows in the corners of the room.

Directly in front of her stretched the south wing of the manor, added when her father was a boy; to her right lay the older west wing, the original home of the Bergstrom family, built in the middle of the nineteenth century by her great-grandparents and her great-grandfather's sister. Only a few months before, Sylvia had searched the attic for the hope chest her great-aunt Lucinda had described, the one containing her great-grandmother's quilts. One of those quilts, the family stories told, had acted as a signal to runaway slaves in the years leading up to the Civil War, beckoning fugitives to the sanctuary of a station on the Underground Railroad. Sylvia had found the hope chest and much more, for it had contained three quilts made by her ancestors and a journal, a memoir written by Gerda Bergstrom, her great-grandfather's sister. Within its pages Gerda confirmed that Elm Creek Manor had indeed been a station on the Underground Railroad, but the particular circumstances differed greatly from the idealized tales handed down through the generations.

Despite these new uncertainties, Sylvia still knew much more about her father's side of the family than her mother's. Until that summer she had excused her ignorance as a consequence of growing up on the Bergstrom family estate; naturally her father's family tended to talk about their own. Her mother died when Sylvia was only ten years old, and the few stories her mother had shared about her youth were almost certainly edited for a young girl's ears. Her mother spoke of strict, wealthy parents who raised her to be a proper young lady, and since this was the very sort of well-behaved child Sylvia invariably failed to emulate, her mother's stories seemed like dull morality tales. Sylvia eventually decided that the Bergstrom family was far more interesting than the Lockwoods and paid little attention when that distant look came into her mother's eyes as she remembered events long ago and far away.

The events of the past summer had pricked Sylvia's conscience, and for the first time in her life, she regretted neglecting an entire half of her heritage. Sarah's gift—the silverplated scissors Sylvia had so often seen in her mother's hand—had flooded her mind with images and conversations long forgotten and a warmth of remembered love. Mother had tried to pass on more than quilting skills as she taught Sylvia how to work a needle. If only she had paid more attention to her mother's reminiscences, she might feel as if she had truly known her, and known her family. Now all Sylvia had were her memories and the incomplete list of names, birthdates, baptisms, marriages, and deaths recorded in the Lockwood family Bible.

She surveyed the attic. Somewhere in one of those trunks or cartons were her mother's quilts. Claudia must have stored them up here, for upon Sylvia's return to the manor after Claudia's death, only a few of Mother's most worn utility quilts had been spread on beds in the rooms below, awaiting guests who never came. Her mother's bridal quilt was sure to be among those that had been put away for safekeeping.

"Now, where to begin?" mused Sylvia. The search earlier that summer had focused on a specific hope chest, so she had ignored those that did not fit the description. Still, she had opened enough, just in case, to detect a pattern within the clutter. The newest items were closest to the stairs, as if Claudia or her husband had merely stood on the top step and shoved the boxes inside. Moving deeper into the attic was like stepping back in time, with an occasional object from another era juxtaposing the past and present: an electric lamp missing its shade rested on top of a treadle sewing machine; a pile of Sylvia's schoolbooks sat on the floor beside a carton of clothing from the seventies. For the most part, however, the pattern held true, and since Sylvia had found Gerda Bergstrom's journal in the deepest part of the west wing, possessions from her mother's era ought to be somewhere in the middle of the south wing.

She chose a trunk at random, tugged it into the open, and had just lifted the lid when she heard the stairs creaking. She turned to find Agnes emerging from the opening in the floor. "Oh, hello, dear," Sylvia greeted her. "Did you finish your business with Sarah and Diane?"

"We didn't even get started," said Agnes, touching her curly white hair distractedly. "Once Sarah told me what you were up to, I came right upstairs."

"If you came to help, you're a brave soul. It took me weeks to find Gerda's hope chest."

"Sylvia." Agnes hesitated, removed her pink-tinted glasses, and replaced them. "About your mother's quilt—"

"Oh yes, of course," exclaimed Sylvia, suddenly remembering. "You've seen it—the burgundy, green, black, and white New York Beauty quilt. It was on the bed of your guest room when you visited us that first time." She chuckled at the memory. "We used it for only our most important visitors, but you apparently had no idea how we had honored you. The next morning, when you complained about how cold you had been all night, I wanted to snatch it off your bed and give you a few scratchy wool blankets instead. I would have, except my brother would have been furious."

"I don't remember complaining . . ." Agnes shook her head and began again. "Sylvia, dear, I hope you don't have your heart set on using your mother's bridal quilt."

"I don't plan to, not every day. Just on our wedding night." She sensed Agnes's dismay and amended her words. "I wouldn't damage an antique quilt just to indulge a whim. If it seems too fragile, I'll just display it at the reception instead."

"I'm afraid that won't be possible, Sylvia." Agnes took a deep breath. "The quilts aren't here."

"Of course they are. They must be."

"I don't mean they aren't in the attic. They aren't in the manor. Claudia sold them."

"What?"

"She sold them. All of them, except for the utility quilts."

"I don't believe it." Sylvia steadied herself with one hand on the trunk, then slowly closed the lid and sank to a seat upon it. "Not even Claudia could have done such a thing. Not even Claudia."

"I'm so sorry." Agnes worked her way through the clutter and sat down beside her. "After the family business failed, the money ran out. Claudia and Harold sold off the horses, acres of land, furniture, anything to raise cash. I—I did, too, of course, but mostly to keep them from selling off the rest of the land and the manor with it."

"She sold Mother's bridal quilt?" Sylvia repeated.

"And the others, her other fine quilts." Agnes took Sylvia's hands. "I would have prevented it if I could have. I wish you knew how hard I tried."

"I'm sure you did." Sylvia gave Agnes's hand a clumsy pat and pulled away. She rarely allowed herself to imagine what life in Elm Creek Manor had been like after her angry and abrupt departure, but for Agnes, it must have been a nightmare. Sylvia suspected she owed the survival of what remained of the estate to her sister-in-law. Agnes never spoke of those days, which Sylvia considered a kindness. What she imagined pained her enough.

She never should have run away.

"When Claudia made up her mind, there was no reasoning with her," said Sylvia. "The quilts were hers to do with as she wished, since I abandoned them. It's not your fault she sold them."

"But—"

"It's not your fault." Suddenly the attic seemed dark and confining. "It's mine."

Sylvia left the attic without another word, without looking back. She retreated to the sanctuary of the sitting room adjoining her bedroom. Ordinarily she preferred to quilt in the bright cheerfulness of the west sitting room on the first floor where friends came and went as they pleased, but she was too distressed now to welcome company. She brooded as she worked on her Tumbling Blocks quilt, piecing the diamond-shaped scraps together and thinking about her sister.

The fading light reminded her she had spent too much time alone with her thoughts. Tonight was supposed to have been her turn to prepare supper for herself, Andrew, Sarah, and Matt, but Agnes's revelation had driven all thoughts of eating from her mind. Finally, she set her quilting aside and hurried down the grand oak staircase, across the marble floor of the foyer, and down the west wing toward the kitchen. When camp was in session, they served breakfast in the banquet hall off the foyer, but in the off-season, they preferred the intimacy of the kitchen.

Andrew and Matt were setting the long wooden table for four when she entered. "Glad you could join us," said Sarah as she took a steaming casserole dish from the oven.

Andrew took her hand and kissed her on the cheek. "Are you feeling any better?" he asked in an undertone.

"Who said I was feeling poorly?"

"You shut yourself in your room all day," said Andrew. "That's usually a pretty accurate sign."

"It's nothing," she said, giving his hand a pat and forcing a smile. "I'll explain later."

But Sarah's curiosity would not wait. They were barely seated when she gave Sylvia a searching look and said, "Did you and Agnes have an argument? She came down from the attic upset about something, but when I asked what was wrong, she just shook her head and asked Diane to drive her home."

"We didn't argue," said Sylvia, and told them what she had learned about the fate of her mother's quilts.

"Oh, Sylvia," said Andrew, his brow furrowed in concern. "That's a real shame."

"It can't be helped," she said briskly when Sarah and Matt nodded in sympathy. "What's done is done, and I have only myself to blame. If I hadn't run away—"

"Don't blame yourself," said Sarah.

"Oh, don't worry, dear. I've set aside plenty of blame for my sister, too. I don't understand how she could have parted with our mother's quilts." She waved her hand, impatient. "I've sulked about this enough for one day. May we please change the subject? I'd rather talk about anything else, even the wedding."

"That's good," said Sarah, "because Diane wants Andrew to find out how many of his grandchildren are coming in case we need to set up a special playroom for them during the reception."

"She's moving right along, isn't she?" said Sylvia. "I suspect she'll have my dress picked out soon."

Andrew looked dubious. "I think my grandkids are too old to be interested in a playroom unless it has video games, but I'll ask."

"I suppose we ought to set a date before Diane does," said Sylvia. "Did you find out when the grandkids will be out of school for the summer?"

Andrew shrugged. "I forgot to check."

Sylvia gave Sarah and Matt a knowing look. "What he means is that he still hasn't summoned up the courage to tell his children we're engaged."

"That's not the kind of news you spring on someone over the phone," protested Andrew.

Sarah's eyebrows rose. "You say that as if you don't expect them to be happy for you."

"They will be," said Andrew, "once they get used to the idea."

Sylvia patted his arm. "I love you, dear, and I promise I'll marry you with or without your children's blessing, but I think we should tell them soon, before they hear about it from someone else."

"I want to tell them in person."

"Do you really think that's necessary?"

Andrew nodded.

"Very well. Shall we break the news together?"

"I'd like you to travel with me, but I'll tell them myself, alone. Bob first, and then Amy. Bob knows how to keep a secret, but Amy would be on the phone to her brother within five minutes."

Clearly he had given the matter a great deal of thought. "I'm sure we'll have a lovely visit and they'll be delighted for us," said Sylvia. She smiled encouragingly and squeezed his hand, wishing she felt as certain as she sounded.

The next day, Sylvia attended to her household chores and made mental notes about what she should pack for the upcoming trip. Bob lived in Southern California, which at this time of year meant warm, sunny days and cool evenings. If they left tomorrow, as Andrew wished, and took time to see the sights along the way, they would arrive the following Friday.

After calling his son to arrange their visit, Andrew spent the day working on the motor home, checking the engine and purchasing supplies. He and Sylvia kept so busy that, except at lunch, they barely had time to exchange a word. Sylvia found herself uncomfortably relieved by their separation. She knew she shouldn't take Andrew's concerns personally, but she couldn't help it. If Amy and Bob were going to be unhappy, how would telling them in person change anything? They had no business giving Andrew anything less than their wholehearted support of his decision to remarry.

Just when she had worked up enough irritation to tell him so, Andrew appeared at the door of the laundry room and said, "Sylvia, may I speak with you a moment?"

"You certainly may, but I want to speak first." She closed the lid to the washing machine and was just about to give him a piece of her mind when she saw that Summer Sullivan, Sarah's codirector of Elm Creek Quilts, had followed him into the room. "Oh, hello, dear. I didn't know you were working today."

"I'm not," said Summer, smiling. The youngest of the Elm Creek Quilters, the auburn-haired beauty was also their Internet guru and most popular instructor. "I came over to help you look for your mother's quilts."

"Look for them?" Sylvia barked out a laugh and punched the buttons on the washing machine. "Didn't anyone tell you? They aren't here. They've been gone for more than forty years. Nearly fifty. We'll never find them."

Andrew placed a hand on her shoulder. "You ought to hear what the young lady has to say."

Sylvia frowned at him, but he and Summer looked so hopeful that she gazed heavenward and sighed. "Oh, all right. If you make it quick. I have work to do."

"I'll help you with the laundry after," said Summer, taking Sylvia's hand. With Andrew bringing up the rear, she led Sylvia to the library, where the computer was already connected to the Internet. Summer pulled out the high-backed leather chair and motioned Sylvia into it. "There's this awesome Web site—"

Sylvia raised a hand. "You know I don't do e-mail. I appreciate what the Internet has contributed to our business, but I will not drive another nail into the coffin of the fine art of letter writing."

"No one will force you to send e-mail." Summer guided her into the chair. "This is a Web site. It's different."

"Go on," urged Andrew. "It's important."

Sylvia sat down, slipped on her glasses, and peered at the computer. The title at the top of the screen read, "The Missing Quilts Home Page." Down the left side ran a list of phrases: "Home Page," "Help Find Missing Quilts," "Report Your Missing Quilt," and "Reunions! Quilts Found." Other quilt-related topics followed, including articles about protecting quilts from theft and how to properly document quilts—which had long been one of Sylvia's pet causes.

"Perhaps this is worth a look," she admitted.

Summer slid the mouse into Sylvia's hand. "Use this to move the pointer over the links, and if you want to read the article, click the mouse."

"I have used a computer before, dear," said Sylvia dryly, but she did as instructed. First she read the page about documenting quilts and was pleasantly surprised to discover the author provided a clear and thorough description of the appropriate steps. Next she clicked on the "Help Find Missing Quilts" link. On the screen appeared the names of at least fifty quilts, accompanied by pictures too small to be seen clearly even with her glasses.

"Click on the thumbnail." Summer took the mouse and clicked on the first tiny picture. That took them to a new page, which included a larger photo of the quilt, a list of the quilt's dimensions, colors, pattern, and fabric, and a brief narrative describing how it had disappeared from the quiltmaker's car after an accident. The quilter had been taken from the scene in an ambulance, and by the time she could arrange to have her possessions secured, the quilt was gone.

"How terrible," exclaimed Sylvia. "What kind of person would steal a quilt, especially from someone in such circumstances? It's outrageous."

"Keep reading," said Summer, and used the mouse to direct Sylvia to the previous page.

From there, Sylvia linked to each of the missing quilts in turn and read about quilts taken from summer cottages, vanished from the beds of residents of nursing homes, fallen from baby strollers or left behind at schools, stolen from quilt shows or lost in the mail en route to and from quilt shows, and, perhaps most troubling of all, more than two hundred children's quilts made by a Michigan church group for an orphanage in Bosnia, taken in the theft of the truck hired to transport them to the airport.

"It's tragic," muttered Sylvia, shaking her head. All those precious quilts so lovingly and painstakingly made, separated from their proper owners, perhaps forever. "Please tell me there's some good news."

"Try that Reunions link," said Andrew.

Sylvia clicked on "Reunions! Quilts Found," which linked to a photo gallery of quilts that had eventually found their way home. The stories of their discoveries were comforting, but few.

"They don't find many, do they?" said Sylvia, pushing back her chair and removing her glasses.

"But they do find some," said Andrew. "That red-and-white one was missing for thirty years, and it was finally found."

"My mother's quilts have been missing longer than that."

Summer sat on the edge of the desk. "You'll never find them if you don't look."

"Chances are I won't find them this way, either."

Summer frowned. "You know, you sound exactly the way you used to, before Elm Creek Quilts, back when you first returned to Waterford. Contrary and negative and pessimistic about everything."

"I most certainly do not. Not now and not then. I'm just being realistic." Indignant, she added, "How would you know anything about my temperament back then? We didn't become friends until months later."

"True, but I worked at the quilt shop, remember? When you came to Grandma's Attic to buy supplies and to sell your quilts on consignment, I would overhear you talking to Bonnie. 'I don't know why I bothered to bring this quilt downtown. No one will want it.' 'I have no business buying so much fabric. I won't live long enough to use it up.'"

"Sylvia," protested Andrew.

"I never said any such thing," declared Sylvia, but she remembered, vaguely, entertaining similar thoughts, and it was possible she had given voice to them. "Even if I did, I have changed considerably since then."

"That's a relief," said Andrew.

"Then don't be such a cynic," said Summer. "If you really want to find your mother's quilts, let's look for them."

Sylvia pursed her lips, unconvinced, but wavering. "They were never photographed that I can recall."

"We don't need photos." Summer pulled up a chair beside Sylvia's and took over the computer. "I'll use my drawing software to create illustrations based on your descriptions. You write down everything you remember about your mother's quilts—colors, sizes, any unique identifying marks—"

Suddenly, with a flash of insight, Sylvia remembered: "My mother always embroidered her initials and the year on the backs of her quilts. She wrote with a pen, then backstitched over the writing with contrasting thread."

"Perfect," said Summer, typing rapidly. "That's a start."

"This might take a while." Sylvia glanced at Andrew. Now that she had decided to proceed, she didn't want to delay the search until they returned from California. "I still have to pack if we're going to leave tomorrow."

Andrew smiled and patted her shoulder. "I think this is important enough to delay our trip a day or two."

Sylvia placed her hand over his and thanked him with a smile.

At first Sylvia wanted to concentrate on her mother's wedding quilt, but Summer soon persuaded her that by broadening their search, they increased their chances of finding at least one. While Summer produced an illustration of the burgundy, green, black, and white New York Beauty quilt from notes she jotted as Sylvia described it, Sylvia carried a pad of paper and a pen to a chair beside the fireplace and tried to coax memories of the quilts to the forefront of her mind. Eventually the clattering of Summer's fingers on the keyboard became a distraction, so Sylvia went outside to the cornerstone patio where she could be alone.

She was glad for her sweater. The day was sunny but cool, and the leaves on the trees surrounding the gray stone patio had already begun to turn. The cornerstone patio had been her mother's favorite place on the estate, but Sylvia's memories almost always placed her there in spring, when the lilacs were in bloom. The door leading to the patio had once been the main entrance, back in the day of Sylvia's great-grandparents. The patio's name came from the cornerstone Hans, Anneke, and Gerda had laid in 1858, when the west wing of the manor was built. Sylvia's grandfather added the south wing when her father was just a boy, after the hard work of their immigrant forebears had paid off and the family prospered. Now evergreens and perennials hid the cornerstone from view, but every time Sylvia visited the patio, she recalled the passage from Gerda's memoir that described how her ancestors had built their home upon it.

Sylvia seated herself on a teak armchair, pen in hand, and let her mind wander. Her mother had made so many quilts over the years, most of them simple utility quilts pieced from scraps. Some she had given away to charities sponsored by her church; others had kept Sylvia and her siblings warm throughout the cold Pennsylvania winters. Her mother's skill truly shone, however, in her five "fancy quilts," as Sylvia had always called them. Mother devoted years to their making, and often purchased fabric especially for them rather than selecting from her scrap bag.

The first, the oldest of the five, was a Crazy Quilt of silks, wools, brocades, and velvets, heavily embroidered and appliquéd. Mother had displayed it draped over a small table beside her bed, but since Sylvia was only rarely permitted to enter her parents' bedroom, she remembered little except its dark, formal colors and its heaviness. She closed her eyes and concentrated, willing the vague impressions to clarify.

She wrote down all she remembered: the diamond-shaped blocks covered with crazy patchwork; the appliquéd horseshoe, chess piece, and the silhouette of a woman; the embroidered spiderweb and initials; the one block cut from a single piece of fabric, a linen handkerchief monogrammed with the monogram ALC. The L surely stood for Lockwood, but Sylvia had no idea what the A and C represented, since she had found no A. C. Lockwood listed in the family Bible. Although she could not recall her mother telling her so, she knew, somehow, that while the Crazy Quilt appeared to be the work of an accomplished, experienced quilter, it was one of the first her mother had completed. Her grandmother had disapproved of it.

Sylvia sat stock-still. The idea had sprung into her head from heaven knew where, but Sylvia was certain it was true, albeit mystifying. Why would Grandmother Lockwood have disapproved of such a beautiful piece? It was impossible to believe she had found fault with her daughter's handiwork. Crazy Quilts by their nature were more for show than for warmth or comfort; had Grandmother Lockwood thought her daughter's efforts would be better spent on a more practical project?

Sylvia frowned and tapped the pen on the arm of her chair, wishing she knew.

Eventually Sylvia decided to set that puzzle aside for another time. She turned to a fresh page on the pad, and, although she had already told Summer most of what she knew, she jotted a few additional notes about her mother's wedding quilt. Given the complexity of the pattern and the length of time Mother typically devoted to her showpiece quilts, she had probably begun the New York Beauty by 1904 in order to have it finished for her wedding in 1907. But had she even known her future husband then? She would have been only fourteen. Sylvia wished she knew for certain. She wondered if her mother had dreamed about her wedding day as she hand-pieced the hundreds of narrow fabric triangles into arcs. As she set the quarter-circles into the arcs, she might have imagined embracing her husband beneath the finished quilt. Perhaps she hoped the quilt would grace their wedding bed throughout the years, as she and her husband grew old together.

"Sentimental nonsense," scoffed Sylvia, ignoring a twinge of guilt that perhaps she had wronged Andrew by not indulging in such romantic daydreaming. She reassured herself by noting that her mother probably hadn't, either. Most likely, the New York Beauty was already in progress before Father proposed. Knowing she would not have enough time to start a new quilt from scratch, Mother had simply decided to make the New York Beauty her wedding quilt. It was an option Sylvia would do well to consider.

Sylvia's notes on the New York Beauty filled only half a page, but Summer's computer illustration would supplement them. Summer would need better drawing skills than Sylvia possessed to create a picture that would do justice to Mother's third quilt, a white whole cloth quilt. A masterpiece of intricate quilting, it was so much smaller than the others that Sylvia might have assumed it was a crib quilt except that no infant had ever slept beneath it. Sylvia's memory and the quilt's pristine condition concurred on that point. It could have been intended for a fourth child wished for but never conceived, or even a grandchild, but Mother had completed it several years before Claudia had been born. Sylvia had always wondered why Mother had not given that beautiful quilt to her eldest child, and why she had not embroidered her initials and date on the back, the last, finishing touch she had added to all her other quilts. Perhaps it was not a crib quilt at all, but a stitch sampler where Mother had practiced her hand-quilting and auditioned new patterns. If that were true, Mother might have thought a practice quilt too humble to commemorate the birth of her first child, despite its beauty. Claudia certainly would have been offended if she had learned of it, so perhaps Mother made the right choice.

At the top of a fresh page, Sylvia started to write "Sick Quilt" before she caught herself and wrote "Ocean Waves." Better to call it by its traditional title, since no one else would be able to identify her mother's blue-and-white quilt with the nickname Sylvia and Claudia had given it. Sylvia was not sure how the family custom developed, but whenever children in the family fell ill, Mother would take the Ocean Waves quilt from her cedar chest and allow them to use it on their beds until they felt better. In hindsight, Sylvia assumed the privilege of using the special quilt was supposed to boost the sick child's spirits and thereby hasten recovery, but she recalled that when she was particularly queasy, the arrangement of blue and white triangles resembled an ocean's undulating surface enough to make her feel worse rather than better. She would kick off the quilt rather than look at it, but Grandmother Bergstrom, her father's mother, would replace it while Sylvia slept. Grandmother Bergstrom never admitted it aloud, but she seemed to believe the quilt had miraculous curative powers. Sylvia once asked her mother if this were true. Mother said that Grandmother's ideas were merely harmless superstitions, and Sylvia shouldn't let them trouble her. Then her eyes had taken on a faraway look, and she said that she had prayed for the safety of her family every moment she worked on that quilt, and perhaps an answer to her prayers lingered in the cloth.

Sylvia turned to a new sheet and sketched the Elms and Lilacs quilt, smiling as she worked. The Elms and Lilacs quilt was Sylvia's favorite of all her mother's quilts; indeed, it was quite possibly her favorite out of all the quilts she had ever seen. A masterpiece of appliqué and intricate, feathery quilting, the Elms and Lilacs quilt displayed her mother's skills at their finest. The circular wreath of appliquéd elm leaves, lilacs, and vines in the center gave the quilt its name; a graceful, curving double line of pink and lavender framed it. The outermost border carried on the floral theme with elm leaves tumbling amid lilacs and other foliage, and intertwining pink and lavender ribbons finished the scalloped edge. The medallion style allowed for open areas, which Mother had quilted in elaborate feathered plumes over a delicate background crosshatch. Then an image flashed in Sylvia's thoughts: her mother quilting the Elms and Lilacs quilt in the nursery while Sylvia, Claudia, and baby Richard played nearby.

Sylvia laughed, remembering how her father and Uncle William had struggled to disassemble the quilt frame and carry it up the stairs. The Elms and Lilacs quilt had been a gift for Father on her parents' twentieth anniversary, and Mother had brought it to the nursery so she could work on it unobserved. It was a wonder she finished it in time with Sylvia at her elbow begging to be allowed to contribute a stitch or two. Sylvia hesitated, her pen frozen in midstroke. She vaguely remembered that Mother had, in fact, allowed her to work on the quilt, and Claudia, as well, but something had brought their work to an abrupt halt. Perhaps it was an argument; many a quilting lesson had ended prematurely thanks to the sisters' rivalry. Or perhaps their mother had been too ill to continue for a time. Mother's slow decline had already begun by then, and she had been forced to set aside many of her favorite pastimes. Quilting had been among the last she relinquished. She had quilted until the very end, when she could do little more than sit outside on the cornerstone patio and admire the garden Father had made for her.

Sylvia finished her notes on the Elms and Lilacs quilt with a description of its colors and fabrics and an estimate of its size. She wrote down all she remembered. She had her doubts about Summer's Internet, but the tiniest detail might prove to be the key to locating the quilts and determining their identity. And if, through some fortunate turn of events, the quilts could be restored to her, Sylvia might learn more about the woman who had made them.

Chapter Two
1899

Eleanor stole down the hallway past her sister's room, where Abigail and Mother struggled to open Abigail's trunk. Eleanor heard Mother wonder aloud how the latch had acquired that peculiar dent, but she did not hear what excuse her sister invented. She doubted Abigail would admit she had kicked the trunk when she could not close the latch. Eleanor had been standing on the trunk at the time, helping her sister compress her clothing enough to squeeze in one more dress, more than willing to postpone her own packing and delay their return home.

She raced down the stairs to the front door and darted outside, picking up speed as she ran down the length of the porch. She scrambled over the railing and leapt the short distance to the lawn. The grass was damp on her stocking feet; it must have rained that morning. At the summer house, the morning had dawned clear and breezy, with no hint of autumn.

Eleanor felt a pang that had nothing to do with her bad heart. She missed the summer house already, and it was only their first day back in the city. Mother permitted things in summer she allowed at no other time—dancing, brief games of badminton or croquet, long strolls outdoors. The previous three months would have been perfect if Eleanor had been allowed to learn to ride horseback. Abigail had learned when she was two years younger than Eleanor was now, and Eleanor had hoped and prayed that this would be the year Mother and Father would relent. Every Friday evening when Father joined them at the summer house, Miss Langley had tried to persuade him, but he returned to the city each Sunday without overruling Mother's decision.

A cramp pinched her side. Eleanor dropped into a walk, gasping for air, sweat trickling down her back. Her stockings itched; her long-sleeved sailor dress felt as if it had been woven from lead. Mother dressed her daughters by the calendar, not the weather—"Or common sense," Miss Langley had murmured as she tied the navy blue bow at the small of Eleanor's back—and September meant wool. Her short sprint had left her faint; she blamed the sultry air and her heavy, uncomfortable clothing. She refused to blame her heart.

Everyone knew Eleanor had a bad heart. They called her delicate and fragile and, when they thought she wasn't listening, spoke of her uncertain future in hushed, tragic voices. Eleanor did not remember the rheumatic fever she had suffered as a baby and did not understand how her heart differed from any other. It seemed to beat steadily enough, even when she woke up in the night fighting for breath. If it pounded too fiercely when she ran, it was only because she was unaccustomed to exerting herself. Sometimes she placed her head on Miss Langley's chest and listened, wondering how her own flawed heart would compare to her nanny's. Her imagination superimposed the wheezing of steam pipes and the clanging of gears.

It was Miss Langley's responsibility to make sure Eleanor did not run, or climb stairs too quickly, or overexcite herself, or take a fright. Miss Langley was English, and before coming to America to raise the Lockwood children, she had traveled to France, Spain, Italy, and the Holy Land. Eleanor thought New York must seem desperately dull after such exotic locals, but Miss Langley said every land had its beauties. If Eleanor learned to find and appreciate them, she would be happy wherever life took her.

Eleanor agreed with her in principle, but everyone knew she would never be strong enough to go anywhere, except to the summer house for three months every year. It was a fact, just as her bad heart was a fact.

If Miss Langley had not been occupied unpacking her own belongings, Eleanor could not have slipped away. She regretted deceiving her nanny, since Miss Langley was her only ally in a household that expected her to collapse at any moment. If not for her, Eleanor's life would have been even more limited, since Mother had not even wanted her to attend school. Mother had feared exposing Eleanor to the elements and the jostling of her more robust classmates, even when Miss Langley reminded her that Eleanor's fellow pupils would be from the same respectable families as the young ladies in Abigail's class, well-bred girls unlikely to jostle anyone. When Mother would not budge, Miss Langley ignored the sanctity of Father's study and emerged twenty minutes later with his promise that Eleanor would be permitted to attend school. Eleanor doubted Mother ever learned about that clandestine visit; if she had known Miss Langley had persuaded Father, Mother would have yanked Eleanor from school just to spite her.

The cramp in Eleanor's side eased as she walked. She had fled the house not caring where she went as long as it was away from Mother and Abigail, and now she did not know where to go. They had chattered about the upcoming social season all the way home from the summer house, and Eleanor couldn't endure another word. She was not jealous, not exactly, but she was tired of pretending to be happy for her sister.

She saw the gardener and quickly veered away before he spotted her. Ahead, the stable seemed deserted; by now the horses would have been curried, watered, and fed, and the stable hands would have left for their dinner. No one would think to look for her there, since she could not ride and was not even allowed to touch the horses' glossy coats. Only when no one else could see did Miss Langley let her brush Wildrose, the bay mare Father had given her for Christmas. Mother had called the gift an extravagance unbefitting Miss Langley's position, but her friend Mrs. Newcombe had said Mother could not get rid of the horse without raising uncomfortable questions.

Eleanor slipped inside the stable, took two apples from the barrel near the door, and tucked one into her pocket. "Hello, Wildrose," she called softly, polishing the second apple on her sleeve. She heard an answering whinny from a nearby stall—but no stern questions from a lingering stable hand, no alarmed shouts for her mother. Emboldened, Eleanor approached the mare, who poked her head over the stall door, sniffing the air. Eleanor held out the apple, and when Wildrose bent her neck to take a bite, Eleanor stroked the horse's mane. "I'm sorry we had to come back to the city. You and I like the summer house better, don't we?"

Wildrose snorted, and Eleanor blinked to fight off tears. She would not cry. She might be fragile, as everyone said, but she wasn't a baby, crying over rumors. "Father would never sell the summer house," she said, feeding Wildrose the rest of the apple. "We'll go back every year until we're old, old ladies. You'll see."

Wildrose whickered as if she agreed—and suddenly Eleanor felt a prickling on the back of her neck. She glanced over her shoulder to find Jupiter watching her.

She quickly looked away, then slowly turned again to find the stallion's deep, black eyes still upon her. No one but Father rode Jupiter, and only the most trusted stable hand was allowed to groom him. "That's what the Lord can create when He's had a good night's sleep," Father had proclaimed last spring as he admired his latest purchase. Only Eleanor saw the disapproving frown Mother gave him. She disliked blasphemy.

Father said Jupiter had gained a taste for blood in the Spanish–American War and would rather trample a little child beneath his hooves than take a sugar cube from Eleanor's palm. She fingered the apple in her pocket—and jumped when Jupiter tossed his head and whinnied. She caught her breath and took one soft step toward him. She drew closer, then stretched out her hand and held the apple beneath Jupiter's muzzle.

He lowered his head, his nostrils flaring, his breath hot on her skin. Then he took the apple from her hand and backed away, disappearing into his stall.

Delighted, Eleanor lifted the latch to the stall door to follow—and then felt herself yanked back so hard she nearly fell to the ground. "What are you doing?" cried Miss Langley. She quickly closed the stall and snapped the latch shut. "You know you're not allowed near your father's horse. You could have been killed."

"I only wanted to feed him," said Eleanor, shaken. "He kept looking at me, and I felt sorry for him, since none of us ever play with him—"

"Jupiter does not play, not with you children or anyone else."

"Please don't tell," begged Eleanor. "I won't do it again. I know I should stay away from the horses. I'm delicate."

"Jupiter is a proud creature, and very strong. He is not safe for children. I would have given Abigail the same advice though she is four years older."

"You wouldn't have needed to. Abigail's afraid of him."

"Don't be saucy." But Miss Langley almost smiled as she said it, and she brushed a few stray pieces of straw from Eleanor's dress. "Your father is a formidable man. Don't cross him until you're old enough to accept the consequences."

It had never occurred to Eleanor that anyone might intentionally cross Father. "How old is that?"

"I suppose you'll know, if the occasion ever arises."

Miss Langley took Eleanor by the hand and led her outside.

As they returned to the house, Eleanor looked up at Miss Langley and asked, "Do you really think Father will sell the summer house?"

"I know he does not want to." Miss Langley absently touched her straight, blond hair, as always, pulled back into a neat bun at the nape of her neck. "However, it would be more frugal to maintain only one household."

Eleanor had hoped for something more encouraging, but Miss Langley never lied, and Eleanor knew her father was concerned about debt. She had overheard him say that the family business had never completely recovered from the Panic six years earlier. It would surely not survive another unless he took on a partner.

"If he has to sell a house, I wish he'd sell this one," said Eleanor.

"You might find the summer house rather cold in winter."

"Mother would bundle me in so much wool I'd never notice the cold," said Eleanor, glum, then stopped short at the sight of her mother, holding up her skirts with one hand and approaching them at a near run.

"Miss Langley," Mother gasped. "What on earth are you doing?"

Abruptly, Miss Langley released Eleanor's hand. "Walking with Eleanor."

"I can see that." Mother knelt before Eleanor, held her daughter's face in her hands, and peered into her eyes. "Why would you bring her outside after such a hard day of travel, and without a word to anyone? My goodness, where are her shoes? Have you given no thought to this poor child's health?"

Miss Langley drew herself up. "Mrs. Lockwood, if I may, moderate exercise has remarkable curative effects—"

"Curative? Look at her. Her face is flushed. She looks positively ill."

"She does now. She did not before you arrived."

"Your impertinence might pass for the voice of experience if you had children of your own." Mother took Eleanor's hand. "Use better judgment in the future or you shall convince Mr. Lockwood that our trust in you has been misplaced."

Mother led her daughter away without giving Miss Langley a chance to reply. When they reached the house, Mother told Eleanor to go to her room, finish unpacking, and rest until supper.

Eleanor did as she was told, listening through the closed door for Miss Langley. She had to pass Eleanor's room to get to her own, the smallest bedroom on the second floor and the farthest from the stairs. Although only a wall separated her room from Eleanor's, Miss Langley moved about so soundlessly that Eleanor rarely heard her. Miss Langley must have been able to hear Eleanor, though, for if Eleanor was ill or had bad dreams, Miss Langley was at her side almost before Eleanor cried out. Still, it sometimes seemed as if the nanny simply disappeared once she closed her door on the rest of the house.

Eleanor had been invited into Miss Langley's room only a handful of times. The furnishings appeared neat but not fussy like Mother's parlor. A few framed portraits, which Miss Langley had identified as her parents and a younger brother, sat on a bureau; leafy green plants and violets thrived in pots on both windowsills. Displayed to their best advantage were two embroidered pillows on the divan, a quilt draped artfully over an armchair, and a patchwork comforter spread over the bed. The room was very like Miss Langley herself: no-nonsense yet graceful and elegant.

Eleanor waited and listened, but Miss Langley did not come. Heavy-hearted, she put away the last of her dresses and climbed onto the bed, wishing she had not run off. She lay on her back and studied the patterns the fading daylight made on the ceiling, wondering if she should risk upsetting Mother a second time in the same day by leaving her room to find Miss Langley.

She must have drifted off to sleep, because suddenly Abigail was at her side, her long blond curls swept back from her face by a broad pink ribbon. "Why is Mother angry?" asked Abigail. "What did you do?"

Eleanor wasn't sure if it was more wrong to lie to her sister or to expose Miss Langley's deception, so she said, "Nothing."

"You must have done something, because I know I didn't."

Eleanor sat up and made room for her sister on the bed. "I went outside without asking Mother."

"Is that all? You must have done something else to make her this mad. Come on, tell me the truth."

Eleanor shrugged. Mother didn't know about the horses, so that didn't count.

"You should have just finished unpacking, as Mother told us to." Abigail climbed onto the bed and sat cross-legged beside her sister. "If you would just obey her, you wouldn't get in trouble so often."

"I can't help it. I forget."

"You don't forget. You just don't think you'll get caught." Abigail smiled, showing her dimple. "Maybe I should go downstairs and break some dishes or kick Harriet in the shin. If Mother's mad at me, she might forget what you did."

Eleanor was tempted, especially by the image of Mother's maid howling and clutching her leg, but she shook her head. "It wouldn't work."

"I suppose not."

"I wish we had stayed at the summer house."

"Not me. I hate that place. The bugs, the wind messing my hair—and I hate seeing Father only on weekends."

They saw him so little on weekdays that Eleanor saw no difference between the summer house and home in that respect, but she knew better than to seem to criticize Father in front of Abigail. Eleanor hesitated to say anything negative about him at all, as if her very words would make him appear.

"I bet the walk was your idea," said Abigail airily. "Miss Langley wouldn't dare defy Mother except for you. You have her wrapped around your little finger. She treats you much nicer than she treated me when I was your age."

"She does not."

"It's true. She lets you do exactly as you please because you're the baby and you're . . ."

"What?" Eleanor fixed a piercing gaze on her sister. "Go on, say it. I'm going to die. Right? That's what you were about to say."

"You're not going to die."

"You and Miss Langley are the only ones who think so." But Eleanor knew Abigail didn't really mean it.

Timidly, Abigail said, "You won't tell Mother I told you?"

Eleanor sighed and sat up. "No."

"If it makes you feel any better, I think Mother's more angry with Miss Langley than you."

That was nothing new; Mother became displeased with Miss Langley over the littlest things, while Harriet could oversleep or lose Mother's best gloves and Mother would forgive her. Once Eleanor overheard the cook say she thought it a wonder that Miss Langley had not resigned long ago, but Miss Langley did not seem to mind Mother's tempers as much as Eleanor did.

Eleanor remembered her warning and asked, "Do you think Mother will send Miss Langley away?"

Abigail shrugged. "She might. You're too old for a nanny, anyway."

"Maybe they want her to stay in the family in case they have another baby."

Abigail giggled. "I don't think that's very likely."

"Why not?"

"If you can't figure it out, you're not old enough to know." Then a puzzled frown replaced her grin. "I wonder why Mother said Miss Langley had no children of her own."

"Because she doesn't."

"That's not what I heard."

"What?"

"Promise you won't say anything."

"I promise."

"I heard Mother tell Mrs. Newcombe that Miss Langley had a baby. It was ages ago, when she was just a few years older than I am."

"But she's not married."

"That's why she had to leave England. Mrs. Newcombe said that Mother was a model of Christian charity but that she herself would not trust her menfolk with a fallen woman in the house, however humbled and redemptive the woman might be."

Eleanor did not want to believe it, but Abigail had mimicked the haughty Mrs. Newcombe perfectly. "If that's true, where's the baby?"

"It died when it was only a few hours old." Abigail regarded her thoughtfully. "Maybe that's why Miss Langley is so fond of you. Maybe you remind her of her baby, because you're so frail."

"She would have told me." Miss Langley did not lie, but as far as Eleanor could recall, Miss Langley had never explicitly denied having children. Eleanor had never thought to ask. "Why didn't she tell me?"

"You're just a little girl, and she can't tell anyone. Can you imagine what a scandal it would be if everyone knew the character of the woman who practically raised us? No one would ever want to marry me then." Abigail flung herself back against the pillows. "Sometimes I think you're the lucky one. You don't have to worry about learning to dance and sing and act like a lady. You don't have to worry about your beauty or your reputation or marrying into the best family. You never have to leave home or Father, not ever. Sometimes I think it would be so much easier if I could die young, too."

Eleanor nodded, but her mind was far away, imagining Miss Langley cradling the cooling body of a brown-haired infant daughter. The woman Eleanor imagined did not cry. She had never seen Miss Langley cry.

When Mother's maid, Harriet, came upstairs to tell them to dress for supper, Abigail bounded off to her own room. Eleanor dressed more slowly, wondering at Abigail's enthusiasm. Father expected children to be silent at the supper table and absent shortly thereafter. He might give Abigail an indulgent smile and a pat on the head when she asked to be excused, but nothing more than that. Only when he was in a particularly leisurely mood would he linger at the dinner table to enjoy his cigar and brandy in their company instead of retiring to his study. On those occasions he would reminisce about his childhood or tell them stories about the company.

Father's two passions were his business and his horses. Mother had once remarked that she was fortunate her husband did not decide to combine his two passions, or she might find herself married to a groom or a jockey, or worse yet, a gambler. Father had chuckled and said, "I am content to befriend grooms and jockeys, and yes, even gamblers, since I cannot become one myself."

Mother had sniffed. She disdained "horse people," as she called them, and her mouth set in a hard line whenever her husband announced one would be their guest. "I cannot bear to entertain another one of his pets," she had complained to Mrs. Newcombe when Father invited Mr. Bergstrom to spend a weekend at their home. The horse farmer had brought his son with him, a boy named Fred, only two years older than Eleanor, and he had stayed inside to play with Eleanor when Mother insisted it was too cold for her to go out. Eleanor never had friends visit, and she was grateful to Fred, for she knew how much he had wanted to see Father's horses.

Mrs. Newcombe had consoled Mother with reassurances that no one would think less of her for these strange guests; the Bergstroms had traveled all the way from Pennsylvania, after all, and they must stay somewhere, and besides, everyone knew the invitation had been another one of Father's whims. "No man can completely forget where he came from," she said, patting Mother's hand.

Mother's mouth turned sour, and she declared that it was beneath the Lockwood family to have people who were little better than common laborers sit around the same table where the Astors, the Rockefellers, the Carnegies, and William McKinley himself had dined. It was bad enough that Miss Langley dined with the family rather than in the kitchen with the rest of the help, but the children were fond of her and Father appreciated her international perspective on politics, which he said was remarkably keen, for a woman.

"I am sure it is her international perspective he appreciates," said Mrs. Newcombe dryly, then she and Mother remembered Eleanor, reading in a nearby armchair, and changed the subject.

Eleanor had heard Father recount his self-made success so often that she thought she could have repeated the tale from memory, but she never tired of hearing it. Even before marrying Mother he had contrived to start his own business, a respected department store specializing in women's fashions. When Grandfather died, Father invested Mother's inheritance into buying out several of his smaller competitors and opening a dazzling, modern Lockwood's on Fifth Avenue. True, the Panic had hit them hard, but they would come back, Father said, and had been saying for as long as Eleanor could remember.

She wished she could make her own way as Father had done, but when she told her sister so, Abigail tossed her head and said, "Business isn't for women. Did you ever hear Mother talk about sales or fuss over an inventory? All we have to worry about is marrying a prosperous man and hoping that he is also handsome and kindly. Have you seen Father's friends? They're odious, except Mr. Drury, and Father says he's a fool."

For once, Eleanor pitied her sister. "They're old, too."

"I won't marry one of the old ones," snapped Abigail. "Honestly,

Eleanor. Maybe you can't help being jealous, but you don't have to be spiteful."

Father would not have been pleased to hear his eldest daughter speak favorably of Mr. Drury, his chief competitor and bitter enemy. Mr. Drury had been Father's rival for more than twenty years, ever since Mr. Drury had rejected Father's offer to purchase his company. Even worse, Mr. Drury had responded by snapping up several smaller stores Father wanted for himself. Three times Mr. Drury outbid Father and convinced the seller to sign a contract before Father could make a counteroffer. If Father did not exactly blame Mr. Drury for his current financial problems, he did see him as an obstacle to getting clear of them.

As much as Father loved horses and horse people, Eleanor knew he would never leave his store and become a groom or jockey. He had spoken too often of his struggles to build his company, and he surely loved his work, too, because he often left for the office before the children rose for breakfast and did not return home until supper, after which he retreated to his study until long after Eleanor had been sent to bed. Sometimes he worked so late he fell asleep there. Eleanor knew this because several times she had passed his door at midmorning to find the maids gathering up rumpled sheets from the leather sofa.

On their first night home from the summer house, no guests, "horse people" or otherwise, would join them for supper. When Miss Langley at last rapped on her door, Eleanor accompanied her to the dining room and seated herself only moments before Father entered. "Confounded radicals," he grumbled as he strode into the room. He paused to kiss Mother's cheek before taking his seat at the head of the table. "How was your trip home?"

Mother beckoned for the meal to be served. "We are not confounded radicals, but our trip was uneventful, thank you."

"I was not addressing you, and you're quite right to point out my rudeness. Darling, girls, Miss Langley, welcome home."

"It's good to be back, Daddy," said Abigail.

"I do hope you'll cheer up before eight," remarked Mother. "We have a party at the Newcombes' this evening."

"Good. I need to talk to Hammond about these blasted union organizers."

Mother's smile tightened. "Why can't a party be merely a party? Must you conduct business everywhere?"

"If you want me to keep a roof over these children's heads, I must."

"Are the union organizers the confounded radicals you spoke of?" Miss Langley broke in.

Father dabbed at his mouth with his napkin and held up his other hand to forestall her lecture. "Let's not spoil your first night home with another argument. The men on my loading docks aren't paid any worse than those at my competitors."

"Yes, but they aren't paid any better, either. Your workers built your business. They created your wealth, and they're entitled to share in it."

Mother's laugh tinkled. "My husband is better qualified than you to decide what his workers should earn."

"They do share in it," said Father to Miss Langley. "You seem to think their share should be as great as mine."

"Or greater," said Mother.

"I founded this company. I managed fine without unions, and so shall my successor." He smiled at Abigail. "Whoever the lucky fellow to marry my beauty shall be."

Miss Langley asked, "What will you do if the workers strike?"

"They wouldn't dare," declared Mother, but when Father said nothing, she added, "Surely they aren't talking of a strike."

"Merely rumors," said Father.

"If your informants have heard talk of a strike," said Miss Langley, "it's likely the planning is well under way."

"I won't cave in to threats. First they'll want higher wages, then fewer hours, and eventually they'll demand enough to drive the company into bankruptcy."

"Not if they have a share in the company's good fortune. If their success is tied to yours, not through obligation and fear but ambition and loyalty, your employees will work harder and better than your competitors'. You will attract the best workers, and they will be more productive because they have a stake in the outcome of their labors. The evils of capitalism are great, but not insurmountable. Is it more important that you make enormous profits, or that you treat your workers like human beings?"

Mother's voice was ice. "You have been told repeatedly not to air your radical ideas in front of the children."

"I have to stand firm," said Father to Miss Langley. "I pay fair and honest wages. I don't hire children. I provide for any worker who is injured in the service of my company and I don't fire them if they fall ill. You see how they thank me—they take those agitators' handbills and listen to their speeches. The business owners of my acquaintance already accuse me of weakness on these facts alone. I will not give them more reason."

"If you lead, others will follow," said Miss Langley. "We are moving into a new century. You can either ride the crest of the wave or be swept away by it."

"Stuff and nonsense," said Mother. "Darling, what would Mr. Corville think if he heard you were considering allowing a union to organize at Lockwood's?"

"I am not considering it."

Miss Langley sighed so softly that Eleanor doubted anyone else noticed. She did not understand why Miss Langley provoked Father so, and why he permitted it.

"Finish your supper, girls," said Mother.

Eleanor picked up her fork, her appetite spoiled. She wished they had never left the summer house.

Later that evening, Eleanor and Abigail watched from their hiding place on the upstairs balcony as Father escorted Mother, clad in a new Lockwood's gown and wrap, outside to the waiting carriage. "If all you do is talk business, we're coming home early," they heard Mother say before the door closed behind them.

"If she doesn't want to go, I will," Abigail said. "Father is a fine dancer. I wouldn't care if he conducted business as long as he danced with me now and then."

Eleanor thought that if Mother refused to go, Father would be wiser to take Miss Langley in her place. Miss Langley knew how to talk with important people, and Abigail giggled too much. Mother loved society gatherings as much as Father loved horses, however, so Eleanor couldn't imagine Father could conduct so much business that Mother would refuse to go.

"You'll be allowed to go when you're sixteen," she told her sister.

"That's three years away. I want to go now. Why should I take dancing lessons if I'm only to stay home?"

"To improve yourself?" suggested Eleanor, wearily. It was a response Miss Langley often used with her. At the moment, it seemed especially good advice, and Abigail the least likely person to accept it.

"You're just envious because you want to go, too, and you know Father would choose me instead." Abruptly, Abigail rose. "I never get to go anywhere. I might as well be a nanny like Miss Langley or an invalid like you."

Watching her storm off to her room, Eleanor was struck by a sudden thought: If she lived, and if she were not an invalid, she could become a nanny. Perhaps Miss Langley had been preparing Eleanor for that all along. Eleanor could think of no better explanation for her vigilance in seeing that Eleanor received an education. At last she understood how her defiance of Father would one day come about: He would surely object if one of his children, even his strange youngest daughter, went into service in another household. He would rather Eleanor remain an invalid forever.

Although Abigail insisted she was too old for a nanny, she did not mind Miss Langley's company when the alternative was another etiquette lesson from Mother. As the week between their return to the city and the first day of school passed, Abigail joined them more often in the nursery, and Eleanor was surprised by how quickly she agreed to read aloud to them while she and Miss Langley sewed.

Among the accomplishments Miss Langley had passed on to the Lockwood daughters was needlework. Abigail had no patience for it and her first project, an embroidered sampler, was also her last. When Miss Langley had suggested she attempt a small embroidered pillow next, Abigail had declared that when she married she would hire a woman to do her sewing, as Mother did. Therefore, she had no need to learn any new stitches and no desire to practice those she already knew. Miss Langley merely smiled and said, "Very well. You may practice piano instead."

Abigail disliked playing the piano only slightly less than sewing; the saving grace of music was that people watched and admired her as she performed. Still, she had no choice but to pick up a needle or turn on the metronome, so she left without another word, and before long the sounds of scales and arpeggios came faintly up the stairs to the nursery.

It was Eleanor who had completed an embroidered pillow for Abigail's hope chest, and then a second, and then she started a patchwork quilt for her doll. Mother frowned when she discovered Eleanor piecing together squares of flowered calico and asked Miss Langley if the nanny might not find a better use for Eleanor's time.

"Sewing requires less physical exertion than playing the piano, which Eleanor has shown us she can endure," said Miss Langley. "A small doll's quilt will consume little of her time. Quilting will teach her patience and thrift, and to see a task through to its end."

Mother relented with the condition that in the future Miss Langley limit her lessons to embroidery and the finer needlecrafts. Patchwork was vulgar, the province of the lower classes, who pieced quilts from necessity. For all her frailties, Eleanor was a well-bred young woman. It would not do to have her practice the skills of a common housemaid.

"I suppose a well-bred young woman should never be useful if she can be merely decorative," said Miss Langley after Mother left, but Eleanor wasn't sure if her nanny mocked Mother's opinion of patchwork or her own indulgence in the craft. Heedless of Mother's scorn, Miss Langley enjoyed relaxing in the evening with a needle in her hand and a basket of fabric scraps on the floor beside her chair, piecing quilt blocks as Eleanor read aloud. Miss Langley completed several quilts a year and donated them to a foundling hospital. In a brave moment, Eleanor had told Mother that by making patchwork quilts from scraps, Miss Langley both prevented wastefulness and performed acts of charity, but although Mother admired those traits at other times and in other people, they did not elevate quilting in her esteem.

After Eleanor sewed the last stitch on the binding of her doll's quilt, Miss Langley obeyed Mother's orders and taught Eleanor new embroidery stitches. Eleanor balked and pretended to be unable to learn, but she could not bear to be dishonest with Miss Langley, especially when it made her look clumsy and stupid. She had so longed to make a patchwork quilt to brighten her own room. The patterns with their charming names—Royal Cross, Storm at Sea, Dutch Rose—evoked romantic times and far-off places, and Eleanor longed to learn them all.

She could not agree, either, that patchwork was vulgar, for Abigail had seen a quilt in Mrs. Newcombe's parlor, and Mrs. Newcombe never permitted anything in her home that did not adhere to the most current trends in fashion and good taste. Abigail could not describe the quilt very well, but even the few details she remembered were enough to convince Eleanor it must be a Crazy Quilt, the same type of quilt Miss Langley kept on her armchair. The Crazy Quilt was the one sign of chaos in Miss Langley's ordered world, the one nod to ornamentation for the sheer pleasure of it in a room dedicated to usefulness and practicality. When Eleanor was ill or downcast, Miss Langley would let her curl up beneath the quilt in the window seat in the conservatory, warmed by the privilege rather than the quilt itself, which, in the style of Crazy Quilts, was pieced of more delicate fabrics than traditional quilts and had no inner layer of batting.

Eleanor admired the wild and haphazard mosaic of fabric, so carefree, reckless, and robust. In contrast to the undisciplined pattern were the luxurious fabrics and formal colors—silks, velvets, brocades, and taffetas in black, burgundy, navy blue, and brown. Embroidered borders, initials, and figures embellished the few solid cotton or wool pieces. Eleanor's favorite was the spiderweb in one of the corners. Miss Langley had told her that an embroidered spiderweb was supposed to bring the quilt's owner good fortune, but she had included the design in her quilt because the story amused her, not because she believed the superstition.

Another embroidered outline had often caught Eleanor's eye: two tiny footprints, outlined in white. Eleanor had assumed the little feet had sprung from Miss Langley's imagination, like the spiderweb, but Abigail's tale of Miss Langley's shocking secret made her wonder. She longed to ask Miss Langley whose tiny footprints had been immortalized on the black velveteen, but she feared Miss Langley would deny their existence and forbid Eleanor to see the quilt ever again.

Fortunately, Miss Langley apparently did not take Mother's prohibition against quilting lessons to mean that Eleanor was not allowed to watch her quilt, nor did she refuse to answer Eleanor's questions. But that was in their companionable solitude in the summer house. With Abigail present, Eleanor did not dare show too much interest in her nanny's quilts. Instead, as Abigail read to them from Dickens or one of the Miss Brontës, Eleanor worked on a needlepoint sampler and counted the hours until school began.

On the last Wednesday of the summer recess, Mother and Abigail attended a luncheon at Mrs. Corville's. As soon as Father left for work, Mother announced that Eleanor must play in the nursery by herself while Miss Langley helped Abigail prepare. Stung that she should be sent away like a child, Eleanor hovered in the background while Miss Langley and Harriet bathed Abigail, brushed her golden curls until they shone, and dressed her in a light blue dress with white lace at the collar and matching gloves.

As Mother supervised and fussed, Eleanor learned why this particular occasion was so important: the Corvilles had a fifteen-year-old son. Mr. Corville owned a store a few blocks from Father's, and while it was smaller than his, it was so prosperous that Mr. Corville had opened branches in Boston and New Rochelle. Father had once said that he could never buy out Mr. Corville, but he would not object to becoming the man's partner. Unfortunately, there were rumors Mr. Drury had the same idea, and he also had a daughter Abigail's age, though not as pretty.

"If Abigail marries Mr. Corville's son, Mr. Corville couldn't become Mr. Drury's partner instead of Father's," said Eleanor to Miss Langley after Mother and Abigail hurried out the door.

"He could, but he wouldn't."

Eleanor felt a surge of sympathy for her sister. Abigail did not want to leave home, but she would obey to make Father happy. "I hope she likes Edwin Corville," said Eleanor, dubious. That might not influence the decision, but it would make the inevitable easier to bear.

Miss Langley sighed. "So do I, for her sake."

They went inside to the nursery, where Miss Langley said,

"Since our presence is not required at their silly luncheon, how would you like to spend the rest of the morning?"

Eleanor almost asked for a trip into the city, but something held back the words. Something in Miss Langley's expression told her that the offer was meant to compensate for more than the missed luncheon. She looked Miss Langley straight in the eye, steeled herself, and said, "I want to ride Wildrose."

Miss Langley's smile faded.

"Or Princess," said Eleanor quickly. "Abigail will never know. You could ride Wildrose and we could ride together."

"Eleanor—"

"Don't say no. I know I'm not allowed, but I'm not allowed to do anything. Please, Miss Langley. I'll be careful. Don't say it's too dangerous, because if it's not too dangerous for Abigail—"

"Eleanor." Miss Langley's voice was quiet but firm. "You cannot ride Wildrose or any of the family's horses. We could not go riding without at least a half-dozen people witnessing it. We cannot count on them to keep silent."

Eleanor knew Miss Langley was right. She took a deep breath, nodded, and tried to think of something else.

"I know," said Miss Langley. "You've admired my Crazy Quilt for years. I'll teach you to make your own."

"I don't want to make a Crazy Quilt," said Eleanor. Not today, not when the forbidden lessons had been offered only because what she truly wanted was impossible. "Abigail was younger than I am when she rode for the first time. I'm tired of being treated like I'm sick when I'm not. I don't have a weak heart. I don't."

"I know you don't," Miss Langley said. "You have the strongest heart of anyone I know."

She extended a hand, and when Eleanor took it, Miss Langley pulled her onto her lap. Eleanor clung to her and fought off tears. She would not cry and prove that everyone was right about her, that she was fragile and a baby.

Miss Langley stroked her hair and kissed the top of her head. "Eleanor, darling, don't judge your parents too harshly. They're doing the best they know how."

Eleanor made a scoffing noise and scrubbed her face with the back of her hand.

"Good heavens, Eleanor, please use a handkerchief." She handed Eleanor her own. "From the time you were a baby, your parents were told you would surely die. Try to imagine what that must have been like for them. Some families might have responded by spoiling you, by giving you your heart's desire every day of your life to make up for all the days you would not have. Other families distance themselves from their child so that when that terrible day comes they will be able to bear it. It wounds them a little every day to do so, but they tell themselves that they can survive these wounds. They think only of the size and not their number."

Eleanor sat silently, absorbing her words, but a merciless voice whispered that Miss Langley was only trying to be kind. The simple truth was that her parents didn't love her. How could they, when her poor health made her such a disappointment?

Miss Langley was watching her with such compassion that Eleanor couldn't bring herself to say what she really felt. Instead she said, "I wish my parents had been the kind who gave their child her heart's desire."

"I for one am glad they are not. You would have been insufferable."

Eleanor smiled, and when Miss Langley offered the quilting lesson a second time, she accepted.

To avoid Harriet's prying eyes, they carried Miss Langley's sewing basket outside and spread a blanket in the shade of the apple trees on the far side of the garden. Eleanor hugged her knees to her chest as Miss Langley unpacked needles and thread, her favorite pair of shears, and several small bundles of muslin, velvet, satin, and silk, which Eleanor recognized as scraps Mother's dressmaker had discarded.

Miss Langley had also brought along two diamond-shaped "blocks" for a new Crazy Quilt she had begun. "Most Crazy Quilts use squares as the base unit shape," she said, "but I chose diamonds."

"Then I'll use diamonds, too."

With Miss Langley's guidance, Eleanor carefully cut a diamond foundation and appliquéd a velvet scrap to the center. She then selected a triangular piece of dark green silk and held it up to the foundation, trying it in one position and then another, until she liked the angles and shapes it created. She stitched it in place, sewing over one edge of the velvet in the center. In this fashion she added more fabric scraps, working from the center outward, varying the angles and sizes of the added pieces to create the characteristic random appearance. When the entire surface of the foundation was covered, she trimmed off the pieces that extended past the edges until she had a Crazy Quilt diamond like Miss Langley's, if not quite so perfectly made.

"Shall I begin another?" asked Eleanor, reaching for the muslin to cut a new foundation.

Miss Langley shook her head. "You haven't finished this one yet. Has it been so long since you've seen my quilt that you've forgotten about the embroidery?"

"But I already know how to embroider. I want to learn more quilting."

"You've embroidered on solid fabric," said Miss Langley. "Embroidering a Crazy Quilt is quite another matter. Your stitches will follow the edges of the patches, so you will have to sew through seams, which you have never tried. You also need to learn how to choose the perfect stitch for each piece. A skilled quilter uses a variety of stitches to achieve the desired effect."

"What's the desired effect?"

"That's entirely up to you. Sometimes your embroidery will frame the fabric piece, defining it, highlighting it, but other times the fabric recedes to the background and becomes a canvas for the embroidery."

"Such as when you embroider a picture?" asked Eleanor. "Like the spiderweb in your quilt—or the little baby footprints?"

"Precisely." Miss Langley held out her hand for the muslin.

Eleanor had watched Miss Langley's face carefully, but not a flicker of emotion altered her expression at the mention of the baby footprints. If Eleanor had seen the slightest hint of pain at the reminder of a secret tragedy, she could have asked Miss Langley what troubled her, but Miss Langley gave away nothing.

Reluctantly, Eleanor handed her the muslin. "Why couldn't we do the embroidery later, all at once, after the diamonds are sewn together?"

"We could, and I suppose some quilters probably do. As for me, I find it easier to embroider something small enough to hold in one hand."

Miss Langley traded Eleanor's sewing sharp for a longer, sturdier embroidery needle. Eleanor took it, but couldn't resist adding, "We could embroider this right in front of Mother and she wouldn't even get mad."

"If I didn't know better, I might think you only want to quilt in order to anger her. Or perhaps you're simply pouting. Very well. If embroidery has become too routine for you, I'll teach you a few new stitches."

She did teach Eleanor new stitches—the Portuguese stem stitch, the Vandyke stitch, and the Maidenhair. They were more difficult than any she had previously mastered, and attempting them required all her concentration.

The morning passed. Eleanor would have gladly spent the whole day sewing in the shade of the apple trees with Miss Langley, but as noon approached, her nanny began to glance more frequently toward the house. Then she announced that the lesson was over.

"But Mother isn't home yet."

"Not yet." Miss Langley began packing up her sewing basket. "But she will be soon, and I would like your Crazy Quilt block safely out of sight before then. And you do recall it is Wednesday?"

Eleanor's heart sank. She had forgotten it was Miss Langley's afternoon off. "Do you have to go?"

"I'm afraid so." Miss Langley rose and held out her hand. "Harriet will look after you until your mother and sister return."

Harriet. Eleanor pretended not to see Miss Langley's hand and climbed to her feet without any help. Without a word, she picked up her things and headed for the house.

Miss Langley fell in step beside her. "Now, Eleanor, don't sulk. I'll be back in time to tuck you in."

Eleanor did not care. Harriet would scold Eleanor if she tried to read or play the piano and would probably have her polishing silver within minutes of Miss Langley's departure. Worse yet, Miss Langley surely knew that, but she was leaving anyway.

She stomped upstairs to the nursery and slammed the door, something she never would have dared to do if Mother were home. She sat in the window seat with a book on her lap, listlessly looking out the window. When she heard the heavy front door swing shut, she pressed her face against the window and saw Miss Langley striding toward the carriage house. She had changed into a brown dress and hat with a ribbon, and a well-worn satchel swung from one hand.

Eleanor jumped to her feet, then hurried downstairs and outside. She stole into the carriage house just as the driver finished hitching up the horses, chatting with Miss Langley as he worked. Her heart pounding, Eleanor held her breath and climbed onto the back of the carriage as she had seen the grocer's boy do. With a lurch, the carriage began to move.

Dizzy and fearful, Eleanor tore her eyes away from the ground passing beneath the carriage wheels and fixed them on the house, waiting for Harriet to burst through the front doors and run shouting after her. But the iron gates closed, and the carriage pulled onto the street. She pressed herself against the carriage, both to make herself smaller and less visible to others, but also out of fear that she would tumble from her insecure perch. The short drive to the train station had never seemed longer, but eventually the carriage came to a halt. Eleanor knew she should leap to the ground and hide before Miss Langley descended, but she could not move. She squeezed her eyes shut and took a deep, steadying breath. She would not be afraid. She would not.

The carriage door closed; Miss Langley's shoes sounded on the pavement. Eleanor heard the driver chirrup to the horses, and with a gasp, she jumped down from her seat a scant moment before the carriage drove away.

At once a crowd of passersby swept her up and carried her down the sidewalk. She managed to weave her way through the crowd to the station house, where she looked about frantically for Miss Langley. She was not waiting in the queue at the ticket window, nor was she seated in any of the chairs. Eleanor went outside to the platform, where a train waited. She did not know if this was Miss Langley's train, and it would do no good to ask about its destination, for she had no idea where her nanny went on her afternoons off. Even if she had known, she had no money for the fare.

"Miss Langley," she whispered, and then shouted, "Miss Langley! Miss Langley!"

She called out again and again, until suddenly a hand clamped down on her shoulder and whirled her about. "Eleanor." Miss Langley regarded her, incredulous. "How on earth—" She glanced at her watch and shook her head. "I cannot send you back alone, and there isn't time to take you back myself." She gave Eleanor a searching look. "I suppose if I had allowed you to ride Wildrose as you asked, you would not have been so determined to accompany me. Well, there's nothing to be done now but make the best of it. Stay close, and say nothing of this to your parents."

Eleanor shook her head. Of course she would tell them nothing; she fervently hoped they would never know she had left the nursery. She mumbled an apology as Miss Langley marched her back into the station and bought her a ticket. Miserable, Eleanor wondered what portion of a day's wages Miss Langley had spent on her charge's fare.

Miss Langley took her hand and led her aboard the train. "Sit," she instructed when she found two unoccupied seats across from each other. Then she directed her gaze out the window as if she had forgotten Eleanor was there. Eleanor stared out the window as well, hoping to lose herself in the passing scenes of the city, but she couldn't bear the punishment of Miss Langley's silence.

"Where are we going?" she finally asked, less from curiosity than from the need to have Miss Langley acknowledge her.

"The garment district."

Eleanor nodded, although this told her nothing. She knew little of New York except for the streets right around her father's store.

They rode on in silence, and gradually Eleanor forgot her guilt in her anticipation of the outing. Where would Miss Langley take her? To meet her family? A beau? The former seemed unlikely, as the only relatives Miss Langley had ever mentioned were far away in England, but the latter was impossible. She could not picture her nanny linking her arm through a man's and laughing up at him as Mother did to Father when they were not fighting. Not even Abigail's tale about the baby could change her mind about that.

After a time, the train slowed and they disembarked. As Miss Langley led her from the platform to the street, Eleanor looked about, wide-eyed. This station seemed older than the one closer to home, older and dirtier. The street was even more so. Not one tree or bit of greenery interrupted the brick and stone and steel of the factories; the very air was heavy with bustle and noise. She slipped her hand into Miss Langley's and stayed close.

They walked for blocks. Miss Langley asked her if she needed to ride, but Eleanor shook her head, thinking of the money Miss Langley had already spent. The noises of the factories lessened, but did not completely fade away until Miss Langley turned down a narrow, littered alley and rapped upon a weather-beaten wooden door. On the other side, someone moved a black drape aside from a small, square window. Then the door swung open, and a stooped, gray-haired woman ushered them inside without a word.

"The others are upstairs," she told Miss Langley, sparing a curious glance for Eleanor.

Miss Langley noticed. "You can see the reason for my delay."

The older woman tilted her head at Eleanor. "Shall I keep her in the kitchen?"

"No. I think it will be all right."

The older woman clucked disapprovingly, but she led the way down a dark, musty hall and up a narrow staircase that creaked as they ascended. They stopped at a door through which Eleanor heard a murmur of voices. The older woman knocked twice before admitting Miss Langley. Eleanor followed on her heels, but stopped just inside the room as the older woman closed the door behind them.

The dozen women already there greeted Miss Langley by her Christian name and regarded Eleanor with surprise, wariness, or concern, depending, Eleanor guessed, upon their own temperaments. One ruddy-cheeked woman burst out laughing. Her hands were chapped and raw, her clothing coarse, but so were those of two other women present, and they sat among the well-dressed ladies as if they might actually be friends. Only two of the women did not seem to notice Eleanor's presence: a dark-haired woman in a fine blue silk dress who revealed her nervousness by tinkling her spoon in her teacup in a manner that would have earned the Lockwood girls a reprimand at home, and an elderly lady who sat by the stove in the corner smiling to herself.

Miss Langley apologized for her tardiness and removed her hat. "As you can see, Mary could not leave her little lamb at home today," she added as she took the nearest chair and gestured for Eleanor to sit on the footstool.

"Never mind," said one of the women, who was dressed so much like Miss Langley that Eleanor wondered if she were a nanny, too. "We've started without you."

A deeper voice added, "But we're a long way from finished."

Others chimed in as they told Miss Langley what she had missed. Their friends from upstate needed their help in organizing the demonstration at the capital, but while many of them were eager to assist, others insisted they were wasting their time with state governments and should instead concentrate on reform at the federal level. On the contrary, the others countered, success in one state would ease the way for others.

One debate swiftly flowed into another: Universal suffrage ought also to include coloreds and immigrants, with all impediments such as property ownership and literacy removed. No, they should fight for the rights of white women only unless they wanted to jeopardize the very structure of their society.

"Is that not precisely what we seek to do by seeking the vote for ourselves?" inquired Miss Langley, setting off another debate.

Eleanor followed the back-and-forth, fascinated. These women looked so ordinary but they talked like confounded radicals. Even Miss Langley. If Father could hear them, his eyes would bulge and the little blue vein at his temple would wriggle like a worm on hot pavement.

Then the woman in blue silk set aside her tea. "My husband has spoken to his colleague in Washington."

The voices hushed.

"A certain influential senator has promised his public and unwavering support if we compromise on our demands."

"What's he mean, exactly?" said a dark-haired woman in a thick, unfamiliar accent.

"He would limit suffrage to women who owned substantial property."

The caveat made laughter echo off the walls of the dingy room, and the ruddy-cheeked woman laughed loudest of all. "I'd like to see him tell that to the girls on my floor," she said, wiping a tear from an eye. "They'd drown him in their dye pots."

"We cannot abandon any of our sisters," said Miss Langley in her clear, precise tones. "A laundress may have as much reason as the wealthy woman who employs her. We cannot deny the workers their voice."

The ruddy-cheeked woman applauded but the woman in blue silk looked to the heavens and sighed. "Reason, but no education. Do we want the ignorant masses determining the fate of our nation?"

Miss Langley fixed her with a level gaze. "You sound very much like the men who argue that no woman should vote."

"You care more about your workers than the rights of women."

Voices rose in a cacophony that hushed at a quiet word from the elderly woman in the corner. "Women who own substantial property are so few in number that their votes would scatter like dandelion seeds on the wind." Her voice was low and musing. "No, it must be all women, including colored women, including those who cannot yet read and write or even speak English. Yes, they should learn, and we must see they are taught."

She sipped her tea, but not one of those listening would have dreamed of interrupting. "Our emancipation must be twofold. We must have the vote, but we will not be truly independent until we are independent economically as well as politically."

"Hear, hear," said Miss Langley quietly, as the others murmured their assent.

The elderly woman smiled fondly at her. "And to that end, you must continue your work."

Miss Langley nodded.

The elderly woman went on to say that she hoped they would attend the demonstration, and she would express their concerns to the others in her organization. Then she rose, bid them farewell, and departed, accompanied by one of the younger women in the group.

The meeting broke up after that; Miss Langley spoke quietly with a few of the others, then took Eleanor by the hand and led her back down the creaking staircase and outside. Eleanor pondered the strange gathering as they walked back to the train station, so absorbed in her thoughts that she forgot the cramp in her side and her labored breathing. She was sure she heard Miss Langley tell the ruddy-faced woman something about a union and something more about a strike.

As the station came into view, Miss Langley broke her silence. "You were a good girl, Eleanor." Then she laughed, quietly. "I imagine today was quite an education for you."

Eleanor nodded, but she didn't think she had learned very much because she had so many questions. She had understood enough, though, to realize Miss Langley would be discharged if Eleanor's parents discovered her activities.

"Miss Langley," she ventured as they boarded the train, "who was that woman, the one everyone listened to?"

Miss Langley did not reply until they had seated themselves in an unoccupied compartment. "We call her Miss Anthony. She is the leader of an important organization, and the rest of us were honored by her visit."

"When she said you must continue your work . . ." Eleanor hesitated. "She didn't mean being my nanny, did she?"

"No."

Eleanor waited for her to explain, but when she said nothing, Eleanor asked, "Are you a confounded radical?"

Miss Langley burst into laughter. "I suppose some people would call me that, yes."

Eleanor did not think that was such a terrible thing. Even Mother wanted to vote. Eleanor had heard her confess as much to Harriet, although she would never mention such a shocking thing to Father or Mrs. Newcombe. But she did not understand the rest of it.

She took a deep breath. "You're not the one trying to get a union at Father's store, are you?"

"Eleanor, listen to me." Miss Langley took her hands. "Unions are important and just. Only when all the workers speak with one voice can they hold any leverage against the owners. The influence of power and money are too great otherwise." She gave Eleanor a wistful smile. "But I am not organizing at your father's store. I would be recognized."

"Somewhere else, then."

"Yes, somewhere else."

Miss Langley settled back into her seat, and Eleanor rested her head in her lap. They rode in companionable silence until they reached the station nearest to home. The carriage waited for them outside, and the driver's eyes grew wide at the sight of Eleanor.

"There's a lot of trouble for you at home, miss," he said to Eleanor, then removed his cap and addressed Miss Langley. "The missus has her eye on you. You best pretend we found Miss Eleanor on the way home."

"Thank you, but I shall not lie." Miss Langley smiled kindly at the driver and helped Eleanor into the carriage.

"Maybe he's right," said Eleanor as the carriage began to move. "I could get out a block away and walk home. I could say I was hiding. I could say I was mad about the luncheon."

Miss Langley shook her head. "We will tell the truth and accept whatever comes of it."

Mother met them at the door, frantic. When Miss Langley tried to explain, Mother waved her to silence, ordered the nanny from her sight, and told Harriet to take Eleanor to her room. "You should be ashamed of yourself, giving your poor mother such a fright," scolded Harriet as she seized Eleanor's arm and steered her upstairs. "We thought you had been kidnapped or worse."

"I was fine."

"Ungrateful, disobedient child. It's that Langley woman's influence, I know it."

"Leave me alone," shouted Eleanor, pulling free from Harriet's grasp. She ran to her room and slammed the door. She stretched out on the bed and squeezed her eyes shut against tears. She listened for Miss Langley on the other side of the wall until fatigue overcame her.

She woke with a jolt as the first shafts of pale sunlight touched her window. She ran to Miss Langley's room. The nanny opened at Eleanor's knock, and in a glance Eleanor took in the bulging satchel, the stripped bed, the missing quilts.

Eleanor flung her arms around her. "Please don't go."

"I have no choice."

"I hate her. I hate them both."

"Don't hate them on my account." Miss Langley hugged her tightly, then held her at arm's length. "I knew their rules and deliberately broke them. I made a choice, and I am prepared to accept the consequences. Remember that."

Eleanor nodded, gulping air to hold back the tears. "Where are you going?"

"I have a friend in the city who will take me in for a while, until I can find a new situation. Maybe I'll stay in New York. Perhaps I'll return to England."

"I thought you couldn't go back to England because of the baby."

"What baby?"

"Yours. Your baby."

Miss Langley regarded her oddly. "I never had a baby. Whatever gave you that idea?"

Eleanor couldn't bear to repeat Abigail's tale. "The baby foot-prints on your Crazy Quilt. I thought you traced your baby's foot-prints and embroidered them."

"Eleanor." Miss Langley cupped Eleanor's cheek with her hand. "Those are your footprints, silly girl."

Eleanor took a deep breath and scrubbed her eyes with the back of her hand. Miss Langley sighed, reached into her satchel, and handed her a handkerchief. Eleanor wiped her face and tried to compose herself. "Will I ever see you again?"

"That's up to you." Miss Langley closed her satchel. "When you're a woman grown and free to make your own decisions, I would be very pleased if you called on me."

"I will. As soon as I'm able."

Father's carriage was waiting outside, the rest of Miss Langley's belongings already inside. At first Eleanor was surprised to see it, but naturally Mother would also not have it said that the Lockwoods allowed a woman, even one discharged in disgrace, to struggle on foot into the city, unescorted and encumbered by baggage.

"I'll write as soon as I'm settled," said Miss Langley as she put her satchel into the carriage and climbed up beside it. "Take care of Wildrose."

"I will."

Miss Langley closed the door, and the carriage gave a lurch and moved off. Eleanor followed in her bare feet, waving and shouting good-bye. Miss Langley leaned out the window to blow her a kiss, but then she withdrew from sight, and Eleanor could do nothing but watch as the carriage took her through the front gates and away.

"Come inside," called Mother from the doorway. "Goodness, Eleanor, you're still in your nightgown."

"You should not have sent her away."

"On the contrary, I should have done so long ago. You're too old for a nanny, especially one with no regard for your safety."

Without another word, Eleanor went inside and upstairs to the nursery, where she flung herself on the sofa, aching with loneliness. Only anger kept her from bursting into tears. Every part of this room held a memory of Miss Langley, but they would make no more memories here.

After a long while, Eleanor sat up, and only then did she realize she still clutched Miss Langley's handkerchief. She opened it and traced the embroidered monogram with her finger: An A and an C flanked a larger L. She knew the A stood for Amelia, but she did not know what the C was for.

She was tucking the handkerchief into the pocket of her nightgown when her gaze fell upon the window seat. Less than a day before, she and Miss Langley had concealed her Crazy Quilt diamond beneath it. Eleanor had been correct to suspect they would not continue their quilting lessons, but she never could have imagined the reason why.

She crossed the room and lifted the window seat. There, under a faded flannel blanket, she found her Crazy Quilt diamond—but something else lay beneath it. Wrapped in a bundle of muslin were the rest of the fabrics Eleanor had used the previous day, the two crazy patch diamonds Miss Langley had made, and her favorite sewing shears, the silverplated, heron-shaped scissors.

Eleanor held them in her lap a long while before she closed the window seat, seated herself upon it, and cut a diamond foundation from the muslin. She appliquéd a green silk triangle to the center, then added another patch. She added a second patch, and a third, working toward the edges as Miss Langley had showed her.

Then Harriet entered. "Your mother wants you to get dressed and come to breakfast."

"I'm not hungry."

Harriet waited as if hoping to receive some other reply, but Eleanor did not look up from her work. Eventually Harriet left.

Within a few minutes, Abigail replaced her. "Mother and Father want you to come to breakfast," she said. "So do I. Won't you please come down?"

"I'm not hungry."

"But you didn't have any supper."

"I said I'm not hungry."

"All right. I'll tell them," said Abigail. "I'm sorry about Miss Langley."

Eleanor snipped a dangling thread and said nothing.

Soon after Abigail left, Mother herself appeared. "You're too old to hide in the nursery and sulk. Come down to breakfast this instant." She watched Eleanor sew. "What are you doing?"

"I'm making a Crazy Quilt." Eleanor embroidered a seam of velvet and wool with a twining chain stitch. "I will eat breakfast when I'm hungry, and after that, I'm going outside to ride Wildrose."

"Absolutely not. It's not safe. You know nothing about riding."

"Abigail will show me."

"She will not. I will forbid her. I forbid *you*."

Eleanor smiled to herself and worked her needle through the fabric, embellishing the dark velvet and wool with a chain of white silk thread, each stitch another link.

Chapter Three

Their suitcases and supplies were stowed away in the motor home, Sylvia had the map spread out on her lap, and Andrew had just put the key in the ignition when Sarah ran out the back door waving at them. Agnes had just called and was on her way over with something she insisted she must show Sylvia before they departed.

Andrew pocketed the keys, and he and Sylvia returned inside, where Sylvia put on a fresh pot of coffee. Agnes usually sought rides from Diane, who would likely crave a cup or two this early in the morning.

Sure enough, when Agnes and Diane arrived, Diane barely mumbled a greeting on her way to the coffeepot. Agnes, on the other hand, was bright-eyed and pink-cheeked with excitement. "I found it," she said, waving a thick, battered notebook in triumph. "It was with my old tax returns. Thank goodness I remembered the year."

"Found what?" asked Andrew.

"Nothing that couldn't have waited an hour," groused Diane, heaping sugar into her cup. "Even if it does mention your mother's quilt."

"What?" exclaimed Sylvia.

Agnes beckoned Sylvia and Andrew to the table. "I had forgotten all about this notebook. I started it when Richard went off to war, to keep track of news from home to include in my letters. After he was killed, I continued it for myself, as a place to put down reminders, appointments, and so forth."

Agnes opened the notebook to a page marked with a scrap of blue gingham fabric. "The entry for Thursday, March twentieth, 1947, includes my mother's birthday, reminders to write letters to two creditors, and the name and address of a caller who had come to buy a certain quilt," she said. "Claudia was out, and when I told the woman I had no idea which quilt she meant, she left in a huff and ordered me to have Claudia contact her promptly if she didn't want to lose a sale. I assumed Claudia planned to sell her own quilts. If I'd had any idea she meant to sell your mother's, I never would have given her the message."

"I know you wouldn't have," Sylvia reassured her.

"Wait just a second," said Diane, reading over Agnes's shoulder. "Is that who bought the quilts? Esther Thorpe? From right here in Waterford?"

"Not all of the quilts," said Agnes. "Just the appliqué quilt."

"The Elms and Lilacs quilt?" gasped Sylvia. It was impossible to believe she would ever see any of the missing quilts again, but if Agnes's recollection of her notes was correct, the Elms and Lilacs quilt had been sold to a neighbor.

Then Sylvia noticed Diane shaking her head in dismay, or maybe disgust. "Just my luck. It had to be Esther Thorpe."

"What's wrong with Esther Thorpe?" asked Andrew.

"Nothing's wrong with her, not anymore. It's her family I'm worried about, the people who would have inherited her quilts after her death. Esther had a daughter named Nancy Thorpe Miles, and Nancy had a daughter—"

"Oh, dear," said Agnes. "I see."

"I don't," said Sylvia. "Would someone care to enlighten me?"

"Esther Thorpe was the grandmother of Mary Beth Callahan."

Andrew looked around the table, baffled. "And Mary Beth Callahan is . . . ?"

"My next-door neighbor," said Diane. "And my nemesis."

"Oh yes, of course," said Sylvia. "The one who turned you in to the Waterford Zoning Commission when you built that skateboard ramp in your backyard."

"I didn't build it; my husband did," Diane shot back, then nodded, chagrined. "Yes, that's Mary Beth. The one who has been president of the Waterford Quilting Guild for going on fifteen years now."

"She must be doing a fine job, or the guild members wouldn't elect her each year," Agnes pointed out.

"No, they're just intimidated. She has an incumbent's power plus the grace and subtlety of a bulldozer. If she has your mother's quilt, you'll be lucky if she lets you look at it through the window."

The others laughed. Sylvia knew Diane had her own personal grudges against Mary Beth, and she couldn't deny that Mary Beth might have earned every bit of Diane's enmity, but she did not see any cause for alarm. "We'll stop by and see her on our way out of town," she said. "It's our only lead, and I won't pass it up simply because you two don't get along."

"Don't say I didn't warn you," said Diane. "At least send Andrew in alone if you mean to buy the quilt back. Mary Beth might not recognize him, but she knows you and I are friends. She'll triple her price just to infuriate me."

Sylvia promised to consider it, but she couldn't help feeling a thrill of anticipation at the thought of seeing the Elms and Lilacs quilt after so many years. Mary Beth could triple or even quadruple her price, and Sylvia would pay it—as long as she didn't have to mortgage Elm Creek Manor to do so.

After encouraging Diane and Agnes to stay and help themselves to breakfast, Sylvia and Andrew bid their friends good-bye. Soon the motor home was rumbling across the bridge over Elm Creek and through the leafy wood surrounding the estate.

They reached the main road and drove another fifteen minutes to Diane's neighborhood, a few blocks south of the Waterford College campus. Professors, administrators, and their families resided in the gray-stone and red-brick houses on the broad, oak tree–lined streets, but in the distance, the low, thumping bass of a stereo reminded Sylvia that Fraternity Row was not far away.

Andrew carefully maneuvered the motor home into Diane's driveway, nearly taking out a shrub near the mailbox. Sylvia raised her eyebrows at him, but didn't criticize. "Diane won't miss a few leaves," Andrew said as he set the parking brake.

Mindful of Mary Beth's reputation, they went a few extra steps out of their way to stay on the sidewalk rather than walk on her lawn. Mary Beth herself answered their knock and gave them one quick, suspicious glance before the motor home caught her attention. Her eyes widened, and for a moment she seemed to have forgotten the couple on her doorstep. "If she thinks she can park that monstrosity there—"

"No need to worry," Sylvia broke in pleasantly. "That monstrosity is ours. We parked in Diane's driveway to avoid blocking the road."

"Oh." Mary Beth frowned at Sylvia as if wondering whether to believe her. "I suppose that's all right. I'm not the sort to complain, but we do have an ordinance against that kind of thing."

"Of course you do," said Sylvia. "I don't know if you remember me, but we've met before. I'm Sylvia Compson, and this is my friend, Andrew Cooper."

"Fiancé, actually," said Andrew, offering Mary Beth his hand.

She shook it warily, her eyes still on Sylvia. "Of course I remember you. Every quilter in Waterford knows you."

"Not every quilter, surely." Sylvia made her voice as cheerful as she could, considering Mary Beth's viselike grip on the front door.

"I'm sorry we didn't call first, but we're on our way out of town, and I needed to see you rather urgently."

"If it's about that skateboard ramp—"

"Heavens, no."

"Well . . ." Mary Beth glanced over her shoulder, then at her watch. "I guess I have a few minutes, but I can't invite you in. We just had the carpets cleaned."

"That's quite all right," Sylvia assured her, and decided she did not envy Diane her neighbor. "I recently learned that years ago, your grandmother purchased one of my mother's quilts from my sister. I hoped you might know what became of it."

As Sylvia described the quilt, Mary Beth listened, frowning and chewing her lip. Then suddenly she brightened. "Oh, *that* quilt," she said. "Of course. I saw it when I was a little girl."

"Not more recently than that?"

"No, not since my grandmother died and my mother got rid of all her junk before selling the house." Mary Beth rolled her eyes. "Was *that* ever a chore. It took us a week to sort through her stuff. Grandma called herself an art collector, but she had terrible taste. My mother kept some of the antique furniture and a few other things of sentimental value, but she sold everything else to an auction house. She told my father she was surprised we didn't have to pay them to haul the stuff away."

Sylvia smiled tightly. "I don't suppose my mother's quilt had sentimental value to your family?"

"No. Why should it have? My grandmother owned many quilts. If she had made them, we would have kept them even if they didn't go with our decor, but since she just bought them here and there, and they weren't even valuable antiques—"

"Funny thing is," Andrew remarked, "they might be, by now."

"I'm sure your mother's quilt was very pretty," said Mary Beth hastily, "but we didn't have room enough to keep everything."

"So you got rid of the junk," said Sylvia. "I heard you."

Mary Beth opened her mouth and closed it without a word, pinching her lips in a scowl.

Andrew asked, "You wouldn't happen to know the name of that auction house, would you?"

"Not off the top of my head." Then, reluctantly, Mary Beth added, "My mother might remember. I suppose I could call her and get back to you."

"We'd appreciate it," said Andrew. "Thanks very much for your time."

He prompted Sylvia with a tiny nudge, but Mary Beth closed the door so quickly Sylvia had no time to thank her anyway. She shook her head at the closed door. "Be a dear and remind me of this moment if I ever accuse Diane of exaggerating when she complains about her neighbors."

Andrew chuckled. "I'll do that."

"Junk, indeed." Sylvia took Andrew's arm, but when he headed for the sidewalk, she steered him directly toward the motor home. She hoped that unpleasant woman was spying on them from behind the curtain as they trod on her carefully manicured lawn. Mary Beth was fortunate that Sylvia knew how to control her temper, or she might have marched right through the marigold bed.

Andrew drove west on I-80, pleased they had managed to get an early start despite their detour to Mary Beth's house. "By the time we get home from California, I'll bet she'll have the name of that auction house for you," he said.

"She'd better have it sooner than that," retorted Sylvia. "It's the least she can do, considering how she insulted my mother's quilts."

Andrew agreed, but Sylvia couldn't help wondering if Mary Beth's dismissal of the Elms and Lilacs quilt was a response to its condition rather than its artistic merit. The Bergstroms had taken excellent care of it when it was theirs, but as Mary Beth had so gracelessly pointed out, the quilt had held no sentimental value for her family. Heaven only knew how they had used the quilt. Every quilter of Sylvia's acquaintance had her own horror story of quilts lovingly made and given as gifts only to be dreadfully mistreated by their new owners. As for herself, Sylvia had learned not to look too closely at the dog's bed or the rag bag with the cleaning supplies when visiting the recipients of some of her quilts.

They stopped for lunch outside of Youngstown, then drove on across Ohio. Just west of Toledo, Andrew asked her to check the guidebook for a suitable place to spend the night. Sylvia eyed him curiously but obliged. Ordinarily he preferred to drive well past dusk, especially on the first day when he was fresh, but if he'd had enough driving for one day, she wouldn't press him to continue. Driving wore her out, too, although she wouldn't admit it, since it seemed ridiculous that sitting down in a comfortable seat should fatigue her. Besides, Andrew enjoyed the freedom of traveling by the motor home, and she wouldn't dream of spoiling his fun.

The registration office at the campsite had a phone, so after they had settled in, Sylvia called home. Sarah answered and reported that Summer was working on their submissions to the Missing Quilts Home Page, and her mother's quilts ought to be on-line by the end of the week. Mary Beth Callahan had not called. Sylvia had not really expected to hear from her so soon, but she still returned to the motor home rather disgruntled. Andrew was already asleep on the fold-out bed, so Sylvia changed into her nightgown as quietly as she could. She kissed him on the cheek before turning in herself, but he did not stir.

In the morning, she woke to find breakfast ready and Andrew sipping coffee and reading a newspaper he had purchased at the office. Soon they were on the road, heading west to Andrew's son and his family in Southern California.

As the days passed, they crossed Indiana—with a detour to the

Amish community in Shipshewana so Sylvia could visit friends and shop for fabric—and Illinois. In Iowa they spent a day with one of Andrew's army buddies, then stayed over another night to avoid driving in severe thunderstorms. Sylvia checked in with Sarah every other day, although with camp not in session for the season, her young friend had little business to report. Sylvia wondered if Sarah suspected the truth, that checking in on Elm Creek Quilts was really just an excuse to hear Sarah's voice and to let her know she and Andrew were fine. She knew Sarah and Matt worried about them, two old folks on the road alone. Sylvia might worry, too, if she didn't have absolute faith in Andrew's familiarity with the route and his diligence in maintaining the motor home. "Most accidents happen close to home," she had told Sarah cheerfully the one and only time Sarah had expressed concern. "The farther we go, the safer we are."

She knew her logic was flimsy, but at least Sarah dropped the subject.

Sometimes Sarah did have news when Sylvia called: The new brochures had come back from the printer with an error and had to be redone, Elm Creek Quilt Camp was going to be the subject of an article in an upcoming issue of *American Quilter,* Sylvia had been invited to speak at next year's Pacific International Quilt Festival. Other times, the news from home made Sylvia rather glad she was not there. Judy DiNardo had found the perfect wedding gown in a bridal magazine, Sarah had ordered several catalogs from which Sylvia could choose the invitations, and all the Elm Creek Quilters had taken a tour of the local bakeries to sample wedding cakes. Well, Sylvia was sorry to have missed the wedding cake audition, but she was glad to have avoided the other nonsense.

When Sylvia called from Colorado, Summer answered with unexpected and welcome news: She had received fourteen e-mails from people across the country with leads on the missing quilts.

"Fourteen," marveled Sylvia. "I never thought we'd receive such a response so soon."

"Now will you lose your silly e-mail prejudice?" teased Summer. "I wish you had a laptop so I could forward these e-mail messages to you. Several had photos attached, but you're the only person who can make a positive ID."

"You sound like a detective."

"I feel something like one," said Summer, laughing. "Anyway, since I can't e-mail you, grab a pencil and paper. Most of the tips will have to wait until you return, but you'll pass by some of the locations."

Sylvia fumbled in her purse for something to write with. "Hold on a moment, please."

"There's something strange about these responses, too. Statistically I would have expected the responses to be equally distributed among the five quilts, but ten of them were about the whole cloth quilt."

"That is rather odd. I expected the Ocean Waves and the Crazy Quilt to receive the most, since those patterns are more common and there will be more look-alikes to cause false alarms." Suddenly Sylvia had a thought. "Unless you mean all ten of those e-mails mentioned the same location?"

"Sorry, no. I should have been more clear. Ten unique locations."

"That's not a very good sign." At last Sylvia found a pen. "All right, dear, I'm ready to take dictation."

"First for the good news: One of the sightings of the whole cloth quilt was at a library in Thousand Oaks. That's close to Santa Susana."

"Very close," said Sylvia, delighted. "I recall seeing signs for Thousand Oaks on the freeway near your son's home. My goodness, can you imagine? We might actually come home with one of my mother's quilts."

"Or more, if you're lucky. Have you reached Golden, Colorado?"

"Golden is more than four hours behind us."

"Too bad. Someone claims she saw the New York Beauty at the Rocky Mountain Quilt Museum."

"I knew I should have paid them a visit," exclaimed Sylvia. "I would have, except I didn't want to give Andrew another excuse to stop."

"You can investigate on the way back. I have an antique dealer in Iowa and a family in Indiana you should check out on the return trip, too. The only sighting between you and California is a quilt shop in Nevada." Summer hesitated. "And when I said you'll pass by these places, I didn't mean they're right on your route. You'll have to take a few detours."

"I'd go hundreds of miles out of my way if it meant finding those quilts." As Sylvia wrote down Summer's information, it occurred to her that she ought to prepare herself to go even farther—literally and otherwise.

One of the responses had come from a Las Vegas woman who said she had seen an Ocean Waves quilt fitting Sylvia's description in a quilt shop in a nearby town.

"It's not far out of our way," said Sylvia as Andrew turned off I-15 onto the highway that led to Boulder City.

"It's no trouble," said Andrew. "I don't mind the delay."

"I almost wish you did."

"Hmm?"

"Never mind." Sylvia unfolded the map and put on her glasses.

They followed Summer's directions into the historic Old Town district of Boulder City and located Fiddlesticks Quilts with little difficulty. Andrew dropped Sylvia off in front of the shop and promised to return for her after checking over the motor home at a filling station. "Don't buy too much fabric," he teased as she climbed down from her seat.

"If that's the kind of husband you're going to be, we're keeping separate checking accounts," Sylvia retorted, but she smiled as she shut the door.

She entered the shop eagerly, pausing only to return a saleswoman's greeting. Over the shelves of fabric, notions, and books hung quilts of all different sizes and patterns. Her first glance took in Irish Chains, samplers, and children's appliqué quilts—and one Ocean Waves. Her heart quickened as she made her way through the aisles toward it, but she was still half a room away when she realized this was not her mother's quilt. While the ecru background fabric could have been mistaken for aged white cloth, the other triangles were green, purple, and black as well as blue, and the quilting had been completed by machine. She continued across the room with a sinking heart, knowing a closer look would reveal the same disappointing truth.

"Do you like it?" asked the saleswoman. "It's available as a pattern or a kit."

"It's lovely, but no thank you, dear. You wouldn't happen to have any other Ocean Waves quilts, would you? An antique, perhaps?"

She knew before the woman shook her head what the answer would be. Sylvia thanked her and pretended to study a nearby bolt of fabric as the saleswoman returned to the cutting table. How on earth could anyone have mistaken this modern quilt for her mother's? Even someone unfamiliar with the intricacies of quilting should not have missed the obvious differences. After all, blue was blue, not purple or green or black. Honestly.

She soothed her indignation with a bit of fabric shopping, so by the time Andrew came back, her good humor had returned. When Andrew eyed her shopping bag askance as she climbed into the motor home, she protested, "I could hardly visit a new quilt shop without buying something."

"I guess not. By the look of it, you didn't do too much damage."

"That's because the rest of my bags are around back at the loading dock."

A look of such alarm appeared on Andrew's face that Sylvia burst out laughing. He grinned sheepishly. "You had me going there for a minute."

"Well, Summer's friend from the Internet had *me* going." She told him what the search of the store had yielded. "I had such high hopes for this visit, much higher than warranted, obviously. I hate to think I'll be forced to investigate every single Ocean Waves quilt in the country simply because people can't read descriptions carefully enough."

"They're probably so eager to help, they'd rather raise a false alarm than pass over a potentially important clue," said Andrew. "But if you buy consolation fabric each time we hit a dead end, we'll have to add another wing to the manor to store it all."

Sylvia laughed, and they drove on for a while, lost in their own thoughts.

"What do you say we stop soon?" Andrew suddenly asked.

"For supper?"

"For the night."

"But it's only four o'clock."

Andrew shrugged. "If you don't want to—"

"No, no, that's all right. You're the driver. If you're—" She almost said tired, but she caught herself. Andrew wouldn't like her to believe him so easily fatigued. "—bored, we can stop."

"I didn't say I was bored. Who could be bored with you around?"

Sylvia decided to take that as a compliment—and to be direct with him. If they were going to be married, she had the right to straight answers. "Well, then, what is it? I like a leisurely drive with pleasant company as much as the next person, but you're dawdling, as much as it is possible to dawdle in a motor home on the interstate. Are you feeling poorly? The drive seems to be taxing you more than usual."

"The drive doesn't bother me as long as the weather's good."

"I see. Then the only logical explanation is that you don't want to get to California any sooner than necessary."

"What do you mean?"

"Don't tease me with the innocent act. I know you too well. You're not in any hurry to tell your son we're getting married." She sat back in her seat and folded her arms. "If I didn't know any better, I'd think you were getting cold feet."

"What? After I hung in there all those years, still hoping, still proposing, even though you kept turning me down and ordered me not to ask you again?"

"You probably thought I'd never say yes, so it was perfectly safe to keep asking. It required absolutely no courage on your part."

"I'm not getting cold feet. They aren't even lukewarm. And you're wrong about my driving, too. This so-called dawdling is just your imagination."

"I can tell time and count miles," she retorted, but Andrew just shook his head and smiled. Still, he drove on well into evening before asking her if she wanted to stop for supper. This time she was the one who had had enough of the road for one day, but he seemed more than willing to stop for the night after she suggested it.

It was not her night to check in, but Sylvia called home anyway to report that their search of Fiddlesticks Quilts had turned up nothing. Sarah thought that the search might be made easier if Sylvia had pictures of the quilts to show, so she offered to send several printouts of Summer's computer illustrations to Andrew's son's home.

When Sylvia asked if they had received any more responses to their posts on the Missing Quilts Home Page, Sarah told her that they had—two more sightings of the whole cloth quilt. "Mary Beth Callahan phoned this morning, too," she added. "She gave us the name and address of the auction house that bought the Elms and Lilacs quilt from her mother."

"That's wonderful news," said Sylvia. "And very welcome, too, after today's disappointment."

"Mary Beth said her grandmother also bought quilts at a consignment shop in downtown Waterford. She thought Claudia might have sold some of your mother's quilts through them, too. The shop closed in the sixties, but the owner's son still lives in Waterford. He runs the coffee shop on the square in downtown Water-ford."

"I'll get in touch with him as soon as I return," said Sylvia. "I wouldn't have believed it of Mary Beth, but she turned out to be quite helpful after all. Don't tell Diane or she'll be terribly disap-pointed."

The next morning, they continued their journey at the usual pace, and Andrew gave Sylvia no more reason to suspect him of deliber-ately delaying their arrival. A few days later, they drove through the rocky, sun-browned hills of the Santa Monica Mountains into Santa Susana. They left the freeway and passed neighborhoods of houses with stucco walls and red tile roofs. Sylvia had visited Andrew's son and his family several times before, but she still had not become accustomed to the small lots separated by high fences, and the houses seemed rather crowded together.

Andrew parked the motor home in the driveway of his son's ranch house and sat for a moment before rousing himself and help-ing Sylvia down from her seat. "Don't look so grim or they'll think we have bad news," she teased as they carried their suitcases to the front door. They heard happy shouts from within, and before they could knock, the door swung open.

"Grandpa," cried ten-year-old Kayla as she burst outside, her strawberry blond ponytail streaming out behind her. She flung her arms around Andrew. "What took you so long?"

Andrew gave her a hug so strong Kayla's toes lifted off the ground. "I missed you, too, sweetheart."

"Be careful, Kayla." Andrew's daughter-in-law appeared in the doorway, a red pencil tucked behind her ear as if she had been interrupted while grading papers. "You'll knock Grandpa over."

"No, I won't." Kayla released her grandfather and peered shyly at Sylvia. "We have more oranges so you can pick your own for breakfast, like last time."

"How thoughtful of you to have them ready for me," said Sylvia. "I've never had better oranges than those you grow here. You've spoiled me for anything from the grocery store."

Kayla grinned as another strawberry-blond girl squeezed past her mother. "Hi, Grandpa."

Andrew's eyebrows shot up, and Sylvia suspected hers had, too. When last they saw Angela, she had worn her hair cut short, and it was all her parents could do to get her to wear anything but gym clothes and basketball shoes. In the few months since their last visit, Angela had gained at least two inches in height, had grown her hair past her shoulders, and had discovered lip gloss and nail polish. She wore a silver ring around one of her bare toes, tight white Capri pants with the waistband folded down to expose her navel, and some sort of halter top that had more in common with a bathing suit than any blouse Sylvia had ever worn.

"Angela, that is a sports bra, which means it belongs under a shirt, not in place of one," said Cathy wearily. "And pull up your pants or I'll do it for you."

Grumbling, Angela took Andrew's and Sylvia's suitcases and disappeared into the house. "What happened?" asked Andrew in a low voice as Cathy ushered her guests inside.

"An unfortunate collision of interests in boys and Britney Spears. Honestly, I don't know what to do with her sometimes."

Sylvia figured any young woman thoughtful enough to carry their suitcases without being asked was far from a truant, but she refrained from saying so. She had not raised any children, so it was not her place to offer unsolicited observations.

Cathy led them through the house and out a sliding glass door to the back patio, which overlooked the steep, scrub-covered sides of Wildwood Canyon. Kayla brought them both tall glasses of lemonade—freshly squeezed, with lemons from their own tree, she told Sylvia proudly—and a more modestly attired Angela soon joined them, carrying a flat cardboard mailer. "This came for you yesterday," she said, and handed the parcel to Sylvia.

"Summer's pictures, I presume," said Sylvia, noting the return address as she opened the package. Inside she found computer-generated illustrations of the five missing quilts, ten copies of each. She told Cathy and her daughters about the search, but despite her own pessimistic predictions about the likelihood of finding even one of the quilts, she found herself painting a much rosier picture for her listeners. She managed to recast her disappointment in Boulder City as an opportunity for sightseeing they otherwise would have missed, and made pursuing the other Internet tips seem like an intriguing quest.

Cathy was not convinced. "Isn't that a lot of driving around for something you might not find?"

Andrew shrugged. "We like to travel, so we'd be on the road anyway."

"Maybe now, but it's going to be winter soon. What if you don't find the quilts before then?"

"They've been missing a long time," said Sylvia with a laugh. "I'm certainly not going to quit looking for them after only a few months."

At that, Cathy seemed even less at ease, but she smiled when Andrew teased her and promised they wouldn't risk their lives in a blizzard or any other natural disaster for a quilt.

Sylvia set the pictures aside and admired the view of the canyon as they caught up on the news since their last visit. Kayla's inquisitive sweetness was thoroughly charming, and once Angela forgot her affectations of adolescent disinterest, she became as friendly and engaging as her sister. Sylvia suddenly realized that soon she would be related to these girls, and to their parents. For so many years she had mourned the passing of her family, but once she married Andrew, she would gain another. She would be a stepmother, of all things, and a stepgrandmother. She wondered if Kayla and Angela would call her Grandma or if they would feel that would dishonor their real grandmother's memory. Sylvia thought she would like to be called Grandma, and she wondered how she would go about suggesting it.

When Bob returned home from work, he greeted his father with a joke and a hearty embrace and had a hug and kiss for Sylvia, too. Andrew's son was a taller, sturdier version of his father, with the same warmth and gentleness, the same ready grin. He pulled up a chair, eager to hear about their trip, but before long Cathy reminded him that Andrew and Sylvia were probably hungry after their long drive. Bob promised them a home-cooked meal that would beat anything they could whip up in that motor home. "Would you believe he sold our childhood home to buy that thing?" he asked Sylvia. "All so he could wander the country and make us look bad."

The girls laughed, and Andrew said, "Make who look bad?"

"Me and Amy, of course." Bob crossed the patio to light the grill. "People think we won't take in our homeless father."

"I'm not homeless," Andrew called after him. "My home's in Pennsylvania."

"But, Dad . . ." Cathy hesitated. "That's Sylvia's home, isn't it? And you can't really call your RV a home."

Bob added, "What Cathy means is—well, we know we've been through this before, but it can't hurt to try again. You know we'd be honored if you'd consider making our house your home."

Cathy leaned over to Sylvia and confided, "We hoped you would help us convince him."

Speechless, Sylvia could only raise her eyebrows at Cathy. Before she could fumble for a response, Kayla squealed, "You mean Grandpa's moving in?"

Cathy reached over to settle her down. "We have to discuss it first."

"There's nothing to discuss," said Andrew.

Bob returned to the table and rested his hands on his wife's shoulders, his handsome face creased in concern. "Dad, you know you can't stay on the road forever, and when that time comes, you'll want to be with family."

"Sylvia's home is my home," declared Andrew, missing Sylvia's warning look, "and she's going to be my family, too, as much as you are, so you can stop this nonsense about moving in. I love you very much, but I already have a home and I like it just fine."

Bob and Cathy stared at him.

Sylvia sighed and gazed heavenward, wishing Diane were present to break the shocked silence with a witticism.

Andrew shifted in his seat and reached for his lemonade, but did not drink. "This wasn't how I planned to tell you."

A slow smile of delight spread over Angela's face. "Grandpa, are you getting married?"

Andrew took Sylvia's hand, glanced at his son, and said, "Yes, sweetheart, we are."

Angela and Kayla burst into cheers. They bolted from their chairs and showered Andrew with hugs and kisses. "Can I be a bridesmaid?" asked Kayla. "Please? My best friend was one in her mother's wedding, and she got to wear the prettiest dress."

"Don't ask me. I'm not in charge of the bridesmaids. Ask the bride here."

Kayla turned to Sylvia, hopeful. "Can I? Please? I'll do a good job."

"I'm sure you would," said Sylvia, wanting to add that she wasn't certain she was any more in charge of the bridesmaids than Andrew. Likely that role now belonged to Diane or one of the other Elm Creek Quilters. She wanted to assure the girls that they would play an important role in the ceremony, but at the moment she was more concerned about Bob and Cathy, who sat silent and immobile in their chairs.

"I suppose this comes as a bit of a surprise," said Sylvia.

"Maybe a little," Cathy managed to say.

Andrew's expression grew serious. "Thank you for your good wishes, girls," he said to his granddaughters. "Sylvia and I know this is unexpected, but we also know you care about us and our happiness, and so even if this is unsettling, you're going to be happy for us."

"It's not unsettling," said Kayla.

Bob patted Cathy lightly on the shoulders until she also rose. "Congratulations, Dad," said Bob, rounding the table to hug his father. As Cathy embraced Andrew in turn, Bob hugged Sylvia and lightly kissed her cheek. She thanked him, but as he drew back to allow Cathy to hug her, Sylvia thought she saw tears shining in his eyes. When Bob abruptly announced he was going inside for the steaks, Cathy stammered an excuse and hastened after him.

Sylvia smiled brightly at Andrew. "That went well."

Andrew managed a rueful smile. "Now you know why I wanted to tell them in person."

"Oh, my, yes. The look on your son's face when he heard the news is sure to become one of our fondest memories of our engagement."

"I like the part where they ran into the house better," said Angela. When Andrew and Sylvia looked at her, she added, "What? It's not like I don't know why they're freaking out."

"They're not freaking out," said Kayla, a trifle too forcefully, then asked, "Is everything going to be okay?"

"It will be," said Sylvia, when Andrew said nothing. "Once everyone has a chance to get used to the idea."

They all turned at the sound of the screen door sliding open. Cathy and Bob returned to the patio, their expressions somber, and the steaks nowhere to be seen. "Girls, will you please go to the kitchen and fix the salad?" asked Cathy. The girls nodded and hurried inside.

"Dad." Bob sat down beside Andrew. "I'm sorry for my reaction. Really. I'm very happy for you. For both of you."

"We should have known you two would have other plans," added Cathy, with an apologetic smile for Sylvia. "You've grown so close over the years."

"We also should have known you wouldn't want to move in with us," said Bob. He forced a laugh. "In a way I'm glad. We won't have to give up the computer room."

"But—" Cathy hesitated.

Andrew's eyebrows rose. "But?"

Cathy steeled herself with a deep breath. "This isn't easy to say—"

"Then maybe you should keep it to yourself."

"Dad, have you really thought this thing through?" said Bob. "I mean, you and Sylvia are both in good health now, but what if she—if either of you—well, what if your circumstances change? Have you thought about what that will mean?"

Andrew looked from Bob to Cathy and back, his expression darkening. "Are you trying to say we're too old to get married?"

"No," said Cathy. She and Bob avoided looking at Sylvia. "Of course you're not."

Sylvia heard the inadvertent emphasis on the word "you're," and stiffened.

"Our wedding vows will say 'in sickness and in health,' same as yours." Abruptly Andrew rose. "We're going to make those vows, and keep them, the same as you. Whether you like it or not."

He stormed into the house, closing the sliding door with a bang.

"I wish I could put your minds at ease," said Sylvia. "Your father and I visit our doctors regularly and we're both fit as fiddles. I certainly wouldn't marry Andrew if I thought I would become a burden to him."

"I'm sure your friends at Elm Creek Manor find that as comforting as we do," said Cathy.

By the time supper was ready, Andrew's temper had cooled, but a tension hummed in the air around the picnic table as they ate. Cathy engaged Sylvia in polite conversation about Elm Creek Quilt Camp while the men ate with silent deliberation on opposite ends of the table, looking anywhere but at each other. The girls' eyes darted from one adult's face to the next, anxious. Sylvia felt sorry for them, so when the meal was finished, she began collecting the dishes and asked for their help. She ushered them inside to the kitchen, thinking to give Andrew an opportunity to talk to Bob alone. Within minutes, however, Andrew joined them in the kitchen, shaking his head, his eyes glinting with anger. His granddaughters pretended not to notice.

Together they tidied the kitchen and went into the living room to play cards. Bob and Cathy came in soon after, their expressions somber. Cathy made coffee and served dessert, and the family spent the rest of the evening playing games and chatting politely and cautiously on inoffensive topics. This seemed to relieve the girls but irritated Sylvia, who knew all too well what little good came of ignoring conflicts.

Later, Sylvia and Andrew bid their hosts good night and went to the guest room where Sylvia customarily slept. Andrew barely waited to close the door before dropping his facade of affability. "I thought they might have a problem, but not because of some ridiculous concerns about your health." He sat down hard on the bed, a muscle working in his jaw. "I won't have it. I won't be patronized like that."

"They love you. They worry."

"They can show their concern some other way. We are not too old to get married. After all, John Glenn went into outer space at seventy-seven."

"And after that, marriage would seem easy," said Sylvia lightly.

"Not that Bob would agree. I thought you said he would be the easy one."

"My prediction stands."

"Well, I can't say you didn't give me fair warning, but spare us the wrath of Amy. You do realize there's always the phone, or we could write."

"I'm tempted, but then I'd have to explain why I told her brother in person but not her. No, when you have two kids, you have to keep things equal." Andrew sighed and rose, pulling Sylvia gently to her feet. "You do know it's not you, right? They like you."

"I realize that," said Sylvia. "They just don't think I'm qualified for the position of stepmother."

"None of this changes how I feel about marrying you. I still know I'm the luckiest man in the world."

Sylvia gazed heavenward. "Oh, please, Andrew. Not the luckiest. Perhaps if you had caught me in my prime—"

He put a finger to her lips, then kissed her. "As far as I'm concerned, you *are* in your prime."

After he left for the fold-out sofa in the computer room, Sylvia felt a sudden pang of homesickness, tempered only by the sight of the familiar Glorified Nine-Patch quilt on the bed. She had made it for Bob and Cathy after they had admired a similar quilt featured on an Elm Creek Quilts brochure. Cathy must have known how it would comfort her—and honor her quilt-making skill, since by tradition a family reserved for guests their best and most beautiful quilt.

Still, when she drew the quilt over herself in the darkened room, she wondered if she might not have preferred the sort of comfortably worn quilt one would give to a member of the family. And as she mulled over Andrew's parting words, she wondered what his son and daughter-in-law had said to make him feel he had to reassure Sylvia of his love.

She wondered which one of them most needed reassurance.

✦

Even this far inland, night mists off the ocean flowed into the valleys, so dense that Sylvia could barely make out the fence from the patio door. When Kayla took her outside to pick an orange, Sylvia shivered in her thin cardigan and was glad to pluck a dew-covered fruit from the tree and hurry back inside. Later, at the breakfast table, she peeled the orange and reflected upon the canyon, which on a morning like this would be invisible until a passerby was nearly upon it. She thought of the first Europeans who had come to California, the Spanish missionaries and the farmers and ranchers who had followed, and wondered if any had come to a dangerous end mere yards from where she now sat, believing the landscape ahead of them to be as gentle and bountiful as that which they had already traversed, never suspecting the truth until they stumbled into it.

"Angela," asked Sylvia as they cleared away the breakfast dishes. "Can you drive?"

"Not yet," said Angela. "I can't get my learner's permit until next year."

"Then if I drive, could you direct me to the Thousand Oaks library?"

"Can I come, too?" asked Kayla.

"Of course, dear." She smiled brightly at Cathy. "Now all we need is a car. Would you mind lending me yours? I'm not as handy with the motor home as Andrew."

The truth was she had only driven it once, and that was in the parking lot behind Elm Creek Manor.

"Of course," Cathy stammered out, just as Andrew said, "I can drive you."

"There's no need. The girls and I will play detective. You stay here and catch up with Bob and Cathy." Quickly she sent Angela for the car keys and Kayla for her purse and the envelope of pictures

Summer had sent, then herded the girls out the door before the others could stop them.

"That was close," said Angela as she climbed into the front seat beside Sylvia.

Sylvia nodded and put on her glasses. "For a minute there, I thought they might figure out what I was up to."

"Are we leaving them alone so they can fight?" asked Kayla.

"So they can talk," corrected Sylvia, starting the car. "Just talk."

The morning mists had burned off and traffic was light, so Sylvia felt quite comfortable behind the wheel, especially with two bright girls navigating for her. Twenty minutes later they arrived at the Thousand Oaks City Library. Sylvia had expected another Spanish-style stucco building, but the library was quite modern in design, with an exterior of white stone and dark tinted glass, and unusual jutting angles that reminded her of the Sydney Opera House. When she commented on the architecture, Angela said, "People either love it or hate it. I like it, but Mom says it looks like a stack of books that fell over."

Inside, the building was open and spacious, with a fountain trickling near the sloping front entrance. The girls led Sylvia down into the center of the library to the reference desk, where Sylvia asked for the librarian who had e-mailed Summer. They waited while she was paged, but Sylvia could not keep still knowing her mother's quilt might be hanging somewhere in that building. She went off to search for it, instructing the girls to stay together and to find her as soon as the librarian returned.

Within minutes Angela and Kayla came after her, bringing the smiling librarian with them. Sylvia apologized for not waiting. "It's been decades since I've seen my mother's quilt," she explained with a laugh. "One would think I could control my impatience for five minutes more."

The librarian's face fell. "Oh, I'm so sorry. I thought I explained in my e-mail, but perhaps I wasn't clear. We don't have the quilt in the library."

"You don't?"

"I'm afraid not. We only have the pattern."

"The pattern?" But the whole cloth quilt was her mother's original design. There should not be a pattern. She forced herself to smile through her disappointment. "I'm afraid there must be some mistake. Thank you very much for your time, but I believe we're talking about two different quilts."

"I don't think so," said the librarian. "I'm a quilter myself, and the drawing in the pattern is strikingly similar to the one on your Web site."

"Similar, but not identical?" asked Angela.

The librarian smiled. "Similar enough that I think it's worth a look."

"Yeah, let's at least look at it," urged Kayla, tugging at Sylvia's hand. "What kind of detectives would go home without studying the clue?"

Sylvia could not argue with that, so they followed the librarian to a computer terminal, where she soon brought up archived editions of the *Ladies' Home Journal* on CD-ROM. "Here it is," she said, rising, and motioned for Sylvia to take her seat.

Sylvia frowned at the screen, then drew back with a gasp. "My goodness. It's very like my mother's quilt."

"Here." Angela retrieved one of the drawings from the envelope. "Let's compare them."

Sylvia held the illustration up to the computer screen. The two images were fundamentally the same, with a few minor inconsistencies that could easily be explained by Summer's interpretation of Sylvia's description or gaps in Sylvia's memory. "This quilt is enough like my mother's that one must surely be the source for the other," said Sylvia.

"This magazine was published in October 1912," said the librarian. "When did your mother complete her quilt?"

"Around that same time, but I couldn't tell you whether it was before or after." Sylvia sighed, removed her glasses, and rubbed her eyes. "Of all her quilts, why did she have to leave the date off this one?"

"There may be other clues," said the librarian, and pointed to the screen. "Have you ever heard of the woman given credit for this design?"

Sylvia slipped on her glasses again and read the name. "The name is familiar, but I can't place it. Was she a well-known designer for her era?"

The librarian didn't know, but she offered to make a list of resources Sylvia could investigate. She also printed out a copy of the pages from the *Ladies' Home Journal* for Sylvia to take with her, but despite the stack of papers, Sylvia felt as if she were leaving empty-handed.

"I'm sorry you didn't find your quilt," said Kayla as they drove home.

"Me, too," said Angela.

"Me, too," said Sylvia with a sigh.

"You still found some interesting stuff, though," remarked Angela. "Don't you think this magazine pattern's an important clue?"

"I do, but I'm not so sure I like what this particular clue suggests." She did not remember if her mother or another member of the family had told her that that quilt was her mother's original design, but someone had, and she did not like to think that someone, especially her mother, had lied about its origin. Still, this would not be the first time she had discovered errors in the stories handed down through the family.

"Do you think they're done fighting yet?" asked Kayla from the backseat.

"Talking," said Angela before Sylvia could respond. "Don't worry. They're just talking."

But when they returned home to a stony silence, Sylvia knew something had gone terribly wrong. The adults maintained a courteous front before the children, but as soon as Andrew and Sylvia were alone, he said, "We're cutting the trip short. We're leaving Sunday."

"You can't mean that," protested Sylvia. "We drove too far to go home so soon. What will the girls think?"

"Let Bob explain it to them."

"Don't make the children suffer for your stubbornness. Whatever happened today, let's resolve it before it worsens."

Andrew shook his head, grim. "It's not something I'm willing to resolve in any way that would satisfy them."

Sylvia studied him, heartsick. She could not bear to think she was the cause of any ill will between Andrew and his son. "What would satisfy them?" she asked, and when Andrew did not respond, she knew.

Chapter Four
1907

Mother refused to leave her bedroom, so instead of retreating to her study to enjoy Miss Langley's letter, Eleanor spent the morning with Abigail and the dressmaker. Abigail looked nearly as pale as the white satin of her wedding gown as the dressmaker adjusted the bodice and the drape of the train.

"You will be the most stunning bride New York has ever seen," said Eleanor, but Abigail's face took on an even more sickly cast. Oblivious, Harriet clucked approvingly and reached up to place the headpiece. Abigail shrank away, her eyes locked on her reflection in the mirror.

"We need to check the length of the veil," said Harriet, trying again. "Be a good girl and let me—"

"I don't want it."

"Don't be silly. Of course you do."

Eleanor took the headpiece. "Later, Harriet."

"Your mother said to make sure everything is perfect," said Harriet peevishly. "What would she think if she walked in and saw that we didn't check the veil?"

"I don't think we have to worry about that, do you?" Briskly Eleanor gathered up the length of tulle and satin. "She fought with Father only this morning, and she usually needs at least a day to recover."

Harriet gave her a tight-lipped scowl, but the dressmaker said, "I could come back tomorrow."

"That might be best," replied Eleanor in an undertone. The expression on Abigail's face worried her. For someone who had spent every moment of the past four years planning for her wedding day, Abigail seemed a rather reluctant bride. Perhaps she had no idea what she would do with herself once she was finally married.

Harriet and the dressmaker left, and, like an obedient child, Abigail allowed Eleanor to help her change clothes. "You and Edwin were mentioned in the society pages again this morning," said Eleanor cheerfully, troubled by her sister's strange silence. "They're calling this the wedding of the year. Mrs. Newcombe is absolutely furious, since her daughter—"

"Do you still want to become a nanny?"

Eleanor's fingers froze on Abigail's buttons. "What?"

"When we were children you used to talk of becoming a nanny someday. Do you still wish to?"

Eleanor resumed unfastening Abigail's gown. "That was a little girl's wish. I don't think of it anymore."

"Why not?"

"Because someone must remain home to take care of Mother, and it can't be you since in four days you're going to have a husband to look after, and children, too, before long."

"It's not fair to you."

"Perhaps not, but it's my own fault for confounding our parents by forgetting to die. They have no idea what else to do with me."

"You might have wanted to have a husband and family of your own, but they never gave you that choice." Suddenly Abigail took her hand. "You would like that, wouldn't you? Nothing would be so bad as long as you had that, don't you think?"

Eleanor forced a laugh. "If you're trying to make me jealous, you can save your breath. I'm perfectly content with my books, my horse, and my study. And when Mother finally passes from this earth, I'll live with you and be your children's nanny so you can be a proper society lady and spend all your time dancing at balls with your handsome husband."

"But you would want more than that, even then. This house would seem so big and lonesome with just you and Father."

Eleanor felt a pang. Surely Abigail was not too distracted to realize that Father would have sold their home just as he had the summer house if not for Mother, the necessity to maintain appearances, and his refusal to acknowledge his insurmountable debts. Eleanor could only imagine how he was financing Abigail's wedding. He had called her a "scolding shrew" when she asked him outright, saying only that the long-awaited partnership with the Corvilles would restore their good fortune.

"Father will be fine," said Eleanor. "And I will be fine."

"Father will not be alone, even if you were to leave," said Abigail in a voice so devoid of emotion Eleanor felt a chill. "He will not be without Mother. Nothing afflicts Mother but a terrible temper. She will outlive us all."

"None of us will die any time soon, not even me," said Eleanor firmly. "Unless you slipped poison into the soup, in which case I shall have to warn our guests."

At last Abigail showed a flicker of a smile. "Am I being morose?"

"If not for the gown and the enormous cake Mother ordered, one might think you were planning a wake, not a wedding."

"That won't do." Abigail took a deep breath and looked determinedly into the mirror again. "Father has enough to bear without my jeopardizing my engagement."

"Father? What about you?"

Abigail did not answer.

✦

When Abigail said she wished to rest before their guests arrived, Eleanor went upstairs to her study, pausing first to rap on her mother's door. "Will you join us for supper tonight?" she called. "We will have guests."

There was a long silence, and then, "Horse people."

Eleanor suppressed a sigh. "Yes, Mr. Bergstrom and his son will be there, as well as your future son-in-law and his parents. Won't you please come down?" She paused. "The Corvilles might think it strange if you don't."

A lengthier silence, and then, "If I am not too ill."

"Thank you, Mother. Abigail will be grateful." She hesitated. "Do you need anything?"

"If I do, I will summon Harriet."

"Very well." Eleanor pressed her fingertips to the door, gripped by a sudden ache of regret. Abigail was right; illness was Mother's euphemism for anger. Her bitterness at Father had worsened through the years, increasing at the same pace as their debts and expenses. Lately Mother had feigned illness so often that Eleanor feared her imagined symptoms would become real. By then, no one would believe her.

When Mother said nothing more, Eleanor continued upstairs to her study. Everyone else still called it the nursery, though the dolls and toys had disappeared long ago, and Father's oak desk and second-best leather chair from the summer house had replaced those she had studied at as a child. A basket of fabric scraps sat between the treadle sewing machine and the wooden quilt frame Eleanor had purchased with money saved from birthdays and Christmases. The noise of the two deliverymen porting them up the stairs had roused Mother from her bed, and she had stood silently watching from the doorway of her room. She had learned the futility of complaining about her daughter's quilting.

A burgundy, green, black, and white Rocky Mountain quilt lay half-finished in the frame. Eleanor had intended it as Abigail's wedding gift, but the wedding preparations had kept her too busy to complete it. She had selected the pattern after the couple chose their honeymoon destination—or rather, after Edwin chose it. Abigail, who had never traveled farther west than Chicago, wanted to explore the West by train, journeying through the Rocky Mountains and along the coast of California. Edwin laughed at his fiancée's "little fancy" and told her they would be going to Europe, because every newly married couple of their position went to Europe. Abigail knew this was not entirely accurate, and even if it were, she did not care. She had been to Europe three times and wanted to see something new. Edwin assured her he might take her to the West someday, but not now, and made arrangements for a tour of the great European capitals.

Eleanor, who had never traveled farther west than Philadelphia and who had only dreamed of seeing Europe, found Edwin's condescending dismissal of his bride-to-be's wishes baffling and a troubling sign of how he would make decisions in the future. When she failed to persuade Edwin to change his mind, Eleanor decided to give her sister the only Rocky Mountains she could offer, although she knew a symbol stitched into a quilt was a poor substitute for what Abigail truly wanted. That the quilt pattern was also known as Crown of Thorns was an appropriate secondary meaning Eleanor kept to herself.

Ruefully noting the amount of work left to be completed, Eleanor reluctantly decided that the quilt would have to be an anniversary gift instead. She had already become quite attached to it, however, and by next year, she would not be able to part with it easily.

She curled up on the window seat and retrieved Miss Langley's letter from her pocket. The postmark indicated it had been mailed from Boston, where Miss Langley had lived for the previous four years as the boarder of a certain Mr. Davis. She had not worked as a nanny since leaving the Lockwood family, and she was as vague regarding how she made her living as she was about her relationship with Mr. Davis.

June 12, 1907

My Dear Eleanor,

As you no doubt surmised as soon as you beheld this letter, my parting for England has been indefinitely postponed, much to the chagrin of factory owners throughout Massachusetts. Too much work remains to be done here, and Mr. Davis simply cannot manage without me. I cannot shirk my duty simply to indulge my sentimental heart, which is why I must also decline your kind invitation to attend Abigail's wedding. Do not think for a moment that I decline because your family is unaware you invited me, which, although you did not say so, I assume is true. Please give Abigail my kind regards and tell her I will think of her on her special day.

I will also think of you, dear Eleanor, for I wonder what will become of you when you no longer have your sister's company. I do hope you will reconsider continuing your education. We have fine colleges here in Boston and a scholarly community you would find quite invigorating. You could live with us; we all work to help support the household and share all things in common, and I know you would make yourself quite useful. I cannot believe your father would deny you the tuition. He may have come upon hard times, but he is neither unkind nor imprudent, and he would see the wisdom in sending you to college if his pride were not in the way.

Now, on to your questions. As to the first, yes, I am certain that women will eventually obtain the right to vote. It might not come in my lifetime, but it will most assuredly come in yours. It will come to no woman, however, unless we fight for it. You must do your part as I must do mine.

As to your second question: I agree that you must tell Mr. Bergstrom the truth. Some might say that misleading a man is not as grievous a sin as lying to him outright, but in my opinion, deception is deception. If you are certain, then you do no one any good by allowing Mr. Bergstrom to persist in his misunderstanding. Your integrity is at stake, my darling girl, and I know you will do what is right. Let Abigail throw herself on the sword of filial loyalty if she must, but you have sacrificed too much of yourself already.

I must believe myself still your nanny to lecture you so. Please forgive my ramblings and remember that I am always

Your Affectionate Friend,
Amelia Langley

PS: Thank you for the thoughtful gift of fabric. I shall make lovely warm quilts of the scraps from Abigail's trousseau. Please give her my thanks and tell her many immigrant children will sleep more soundly soon because of her generosity. The white and the rose satin are truly lovely, but I have no idea to what use I shall put them. They would be quite attractive in a Crazy Quilt, but I think my time for making impractical luxuries has passed. However, I am confident I will recognize what useful work they are meant for in time.

Eleanor folded the letter and returned it to the envelope. She could almost hear Miss Langley's voice as she read her words, but that only emphasized how great a divide separated them. Miss Langley could never return to the Lockwood home, and Eleanor was nearly as unlikely to visit Boston. Eleanor was loath to admit it, but they would probably never see each other again.

College, of course, was out of the question. Even if Father did not think education wasted on a woman, he would not go deeper into debt for such a poor investment, especially since the recent threat of another Panic. Even if their financial situation improved dramatically after the wedding, Mother would still need her. Eleanor had been given no choice, as Abigail had reminded her. She ought to resign herself to her future and be grateful that she had lived long enough to see one.

More troubling was Miss Langley's opinion on the subject of Mr. Bergstrom. Now that Miss Langley concurred with Eleanor's opinion, Eleanor had no excuse to delay telling him the truth, although this meant she would never see him again. He and his father traveled to New York from their horse farm in central Pennsylvania only infrequently, but he was one of the few people who did not treat Eleanor like an invalid. She had known him since she was nine years old, and she felt oddly hollow when she thought this weekend's visit would be his last.

He would arrive soon, if he had not already. Eleanor hid Miss Langley's letter in her desk—she had caught Harriet snooping for Mother more than once—and hurried downstairs to her bedroom. She brushed her hair, debating whether to change her dress, and decided she would not. Later she would dress for supper, but the clothing she wore was good enough for a visit to the stable, regardless of who waited there.

Her step quickened as she approached the stable and saw Frederick Bergstrom putting a dark brown horse through its paces in the practice ring under Father's watchful eye. Nineteen, dark-haired, and tanned from many hours outdoors, Mr. Bergstrom sat a horse as comfortably as if he had been born to it, which in a sense he had, for his family raised some of the finest Thoroughbreds in the world, and had for generations. The senior Mr. Bergstrom, who until recent months had always accompanied his son, was nowhere to be seen.

Mr. Bergstrom spotted her and grinned as she approached.

"Miss Lockwood, would you help me convince your father that this magnificent animal is worthy of his stables?"

"If my father cannot tell that by the sight of him, nothing I say will make any difference."

"It's a fine animal," Father conceded, "but not suited for Abigail. This is not a woman's horse. Next time you see your father, I'd like you to ask him why he would send me such a temperamental, high-strung horse for my eldest daughter."

Eleanor had a sharp retort ready, but Mr. Bergstrom said, "I'll ask him, but I already know what he'd answer."

"And what's that?"

He grinned. "Those New York women must be exceptionally delicate if they can't handle a sweet-tempered stallion like Diamond."

"I suppose they are," said Father, chuckling. "The most strenuous activities our refined ladies engage in are dancing at balls and spending my money at the dressmaker's. The harsher environment of your part of the country requires greater strength of your women, a strength, I regret to confess, that has atrophied in our ladies."

"Oh, for heaven's sake," snapped Eleanor, entering the corral. The stallion stepped back and snorted as she took the reins from Mr. Bergstrom. "Pennsylvania isn't the Wild West."

Father eyed her as she began to shorten the left stirrup. "What are you doing?"

"I should think it's rather obvious. Mr. Bergstrom, I would be obliged if you would do the other side."

"Eleanor, don't be a fool," said her father as Mr. Bergstrom complied.

Eleanor gave him a long, wordless look as she gathered up her skirts and climbed on the horse's back. Then she dug in her heels, chirruped, and set Diamond into a canter. As soon as they cleared the gate, they broke into a run.

She ran him the entire length of the estate and back, skirts pulled up past her knees, corset squeezing uncomfortably. The horse's hooves thundered on the grass, but he flowed like silk thread through a needle as they raced over the wooded ground. She slowed him to a steady trot as they returned to the corral, where the two men stood watching her, Father speechless in consternation, Mr. Bergstrom trying to hide his amusement.

He took the reins from her, and she slid to the ground. "He doesn't seem temperamental to me," she said, breathless. Perspiration trickled down her back, her hair had come loose and tumbled in her face, and she desperately wanted to give her corset a yank.

Her father glowered. "Temperamental is a relative quality."

"What do you think of him?" asked Mr. Bergstrom.

"Lovely to look at, remarkable speed, good health," said Eleanor as she inspected the horse. "However, he is not as fine as some of the others you have shown us."

"In what way?"

"I'm sure you know." She stroked the horse's flank as if to apologize for her criticism. "His gait is merely acceptable, as is his endurance." She glanced at her father. "And he is a trifle highstrung. The mare you brought us two months ago was far superior. And . . ."

"What else?"

"I know I've never ridden him, but I'm certain I've seen him before."

"What's the meaning of this?" Father demanded. "Don't tell me you Bergstroms are bringing around horses I've already rejected. Play me for a fool at your peril, young man."

"I assure you," said Mr. Bergstrom in a cool voice, "neither I nor my father has ever shown this horse to you."

"I didn't mean to suggest such a thing," said Eleanor, glaring at her father.

"Fine, fine," said Father. "You can't blame me for wondering if you and your father have grown impatient with my strict standards for horses. I admit it would have been a clever joke if I purchased a horse I had rejected before."

Mr. Bergstrom's expression suggested he did not agree. "That would not have been possible, since as I said—"

"Yes, yes, you have never shown me this horse before. But that is not the only reason. It would not have been possible because I have no intention of purchasing him." He drew out his pocket-watch. "The Corvilles should arrive soon. Eleanor, since you apparently bear this horse a particular affection, I will leave you to help Mr. Bergstrom care for him. Mr. Bergstrom, I look forward to your company at supper."

Eleanor was too humiliated and angry to take notice of Mr. Bergstrom's reply. Father knew very well how he had insulted her by leaving her alone with a young man. If confronted, Father could protest that she was hardly unchaperoned, since her parents, sister, and servants were within the house, but the fact of the matter was that she and Mr. Bergstrom would be unobserved within the stable. She knew what her father meant to tell her: No young man would be interested in attempting anything that might ruin her, and furthermore, her reputation was not valuable enough to preserve from scandal.

She took hold of Diamond's bridle and tugged until the horse followed her into the stable. "It seems you have wasted another trip to New York."

"On the contrary, I'm always pleased to visit your family."

Eleanor busied herself caring for the horse. Mr. Bergstrom fell into place beside her, his every motion assured and gentle. "Is your father well? I'm surprised he did not accompany you."

"He's fine, just too busy to leave Elm Creek."

"What a shame. He'll miss the wedding of the century."

"You're not jealous?"

"Of course not," said Eleanor, regretting her words. "I'll just be glad when all the excitement is over. I'm afraid we're all under a bit of a strain."

Mr. Bergstrom grinned. "I guess that means you have something less elaborate in mind for your own wedding."

Eleanor felt a flash of surprise, then anger, and for a moment she wondered if he were mocking her. "I don't have any plans for my own wedding," she finally said. She picked up her curry comb and went around to the horse's other side.

They worked in silence, and gradually Eleanor's anger ebbed. In the eight years she had known him, Mr. Bergstrom had never once treated her as if she were frail or sickly. For all she knew, no one had told him about her weak heart, and he might truly believe her as marriageable as Abigail. She wanted to apologize, but she did not see how she could without revealing the truth.

All at once, she remembered Miss Langley's letter.

"Mr. Bergstrom." She took a deep breath and plunged ahead. "I have something to confess to you. Something . . . rather unpleasant, I'm afraid."

"You won't dance with me at your sister's wedding?"

"No. I mean, that's not what I had to say. I—I would be pleased to dance with you." If he would still attend after what Eleanor had to tell him. "But I'm afraid my father has no intention of buying any of your horses."

"That's the big secret?"

"I don't just mean today. Not ever. When I think of how many times you and your father have come here and how far you've traveled . . ." She steeled herself. "I am ashamed to disclose this about my own father, but I am even more ashamed that he has deceived you. He wants a Bergstrom Thoroughbred, but he does not have the means to purchase one. He hoped your father would give him a horse as a wedding gift for Abigail, assuming that my father would reward his extravagance with loyalty—that, and the purchase of numerous Bergstrom Thoroughbreds for himself."

"Miss Lockwood—"

"I know what you must be thinking—"

"We gave up on your father as a customer a long time ago."

Eleanor stared at him. "What?"

"For years he's visited our farm and we've showed him our finest horses. For the last fourteen months, we've brought them to him. We're persistent, but not stupid. My father suspected your father was angling for a gift, and the invitation to Abigail's wedding confirmed it."

They had known for months. "Then why . . ."

"Miss Lockwood, do you really think I'd travel all this way so often just to convince a man to buy a horse?"

Eleanor had thought exactly that. "You and your father are known as very good businessmen."

"It's not very good business to bring one horse after another such a great distance except for a proven customer. Most of our customers come to us."

Eleanor let out a small gasp. "I was so upset about my father I never thought of the poor horses."

"Don't worry too much about this one." Mr. Bergstrom slapped the horse's flank affectionately. "He's a Bergstrom Thoroughbred I borrowed from a local customer."

"I knew I had seen this horse before," exclaimed Eleanor, then his meaning sank in. "How dare you lie to us! You deliberately deceived my father."

"I did not lie," said Mr. Bergstrom, emphatic. "I said I had never shown him this horse before, not that he had never seen it. I wouldn't have done it except I knew he wasn't buying."

"I suppose it's foolish for me to defend him after he tried to deceive you." Eleanor let out a shaky laugh. "What would you have done if he had made an offer?"

"I would have told him to take it up with Herbert Drury."

"This horse belongs to Mr. Drury?"

Mr. Bergstrom nodded. "He's one of our best customers. I should have asked someone else, but when Drury offered, I couldn't resist. It was a risk, though. If Abigail had seen—"

"How would Abigail have recognized Diamond when I did not?" asked Eleanor, indignant.

"I assumed she visited the Drury place more often than you. She's frequently there when my father and I visit, and you never are."

Eleanor knew Abigail had befriended the eldest Drury daughter at school, but it never occurred to her that Abigail might have called on her without their parents' consent. As far as Eleanor had known, Abigail had seen the Drury home only once, five years before, when the Lockwoods went to pay their respects to the family after Mrs. Drury's death. Even Father had put aside his animosity that day.

"I don't think my mother and father will be pleased if they learn Abigail has been to the Drury home."

"I won't say a word. Not about Abigail, and not about your father."

Eleanor looked away. "You must think I'm terribly disloyal, Mr. Bergstrom."

"You couldn't be more wrong, Miss Lockwood. And would you please call me Fred? You used to."

"We were children then."

"We've known each other too long to persist with the formality of titles. Every time you say 'Mr. Bergstrom,' I think you're addressing my father."

"Very well. I will call you Fred, if you will call me Eleanor." Hastily, she added, "But only when no one can overhear."

Mr. Bergstrom laughed, but he agreed, and Eleanor realized that she had implied she wanted to be alone with him again. She did, but she did not want him to know it, or to think that she valued her reputation as little as her father did. As soon as they finished caring for the horse, she went back to the house, alone, keeping to a brisk walk in case Fred was watching. Once inside, she hurried upstairs to her study. Only when she had shut the door on the rest of the house did she feel safe, but her heart raced.

She pressed a hand to her forehead and paced the length of the room. As impossible as it seemed that someone could care for her, surely Mr. Bergstrom—Fred—had not meant merely to be kind to the poor invalid. Mere kindness could not explain all he had done simply to have an excuse to visit the Lockwood family. To visit *her*.

"I cannot think about this," she said to the empty room. Pushing Fred from her thoughts, she sat down at the quilt frame and threaded a needle with shaking hands. She popped the thread through the three layers twice before she was able to fix the knot in the batting, then slipped her thimble on her finger and quilted a feathered plume in the background of one of the Rocky Mountain blocks. She waited for the familiar, repetitive motions to soothe her, but her thoughts remained an unsettling mix of pleasure and despair. Abigail, not Eleanor, was the beauty of the family, the cherished daughter who inspired affection in all who saw her. Abigail was the one who was meant to love and be loved, to leave home and have a family of her own—

At a flash of pain, Eleanor gasped and withdrew her left hand from beneath the quilt to find a spot of red on her fingertip. If she had stained the back of her quilt, she would never forgive Fred.

She bit back a sob and flung her thimble across the room. Blinking away tears, she fumbled for her handkerchief and pinched it against her fingertip. Fred's affection for her—if it was affection, and she had not in her loneliness allowed herself to misinterpret his friendship—changed nothing. Her health rendered her unfit for marriage, and Mother still needed her. Whatever Fred's intentions were, Eleanor could not fulfill them.

🐾

By the time she returned to her room to dress for dinner, she had regained her composure and had resolved to distance herself from Fred. She could not bring herself to tell him to stay away, but eventually he would make that decision for himself.

As Eleanor went downstairs, she heard voices from the parlor. When she entered, Fred rose from his armchair near the window and gave her a warm smile, which she could not return. On the opposite side of the room, Abigail and Edwin sat on the divan, their parents and Edwin's two sisters arrayed around them. Mother, who had apparently decided that impressing the Corvilles was more important than nursing her wounded feelings, broke off her conversation at the sight of Eleanor. "Where on earth have you been?" she exclaimed. "You missed Edwin's gift to his bride."

Abigail's hand went to her throat, and only then did Eleanor see the beautiful string of pearls that encircled it. "It's exquisite," she said.

"It is not half as lovely as the woman who wears it," said Edwin, his eyes earnest behind his glasses.

"Well said, young man," said Father gruffly, and Abigail flushed pink.

They were summoned to supper; Abigail murmured something and rose to walk out with Father. In a flash of panic, Eleanor feared Fred would escort her, but to her relief, Edwin fell in step beside her instead. "I brought a gift for you, too," he told her, producing a wrapped parcel from behind his back.

"For me?"

"Of course. You are going to be my sister-in-law, aren't you?" They stopped in the corridor and allowed the others to continue on past them. Eleanor carefully unwrapped the colored paper and discovered a fine leather-bound book. "*Bleak House*," she said, reading the spine. "Oh, Edwin, you know how much I enjoy Dickens."

"It's a first edition." Edwin opened the cover and pointed. "Inscribed by the author."

"How on earth did you find this? Thank you. I believe I'm going to enjoy having you for a brother-in-law."

Edwin laughed and said he certainly hoped so, and they continued on to the dining room together.

As the first course was served, Eleanor did her best to ignore Fred. She made every effort to join in the conversation, but as the meal progressed, she realized only the Corvilles seemed perfectly at ease. Father sat stiff and tense in his chair, and Eleanor had no doubt that if it were up to him, he would have rushed off to find a minister to marry Abigail to Edwin that very hour rather than risk letting the partnership fall through. At the foot of the table, Mother chatted with her guests, so energetic and merry that the Corvilles, at least, seemed thoroughly charmed. Fred gave the appearance of polite engagement, but frequently he looked Eleanor's way, a thoughtful expression on his face. Abigail did not eat a morsel, but sat pensive and anxious in her chair, so distracted that she did not respond to the conversation until prompted.

Afterward, as the men retired to the drawing room and the women went off to the parlor, Fred surprised Eleanor by taking her by the elbow and murmuring close to her ear. "What's wrong? Are you afraid I'll step on your feet when we dance on Saturday?"

"Of course not."

"Then what's wrong? Tell me what it is or I'll follow you into the parlor and call you Eleanor in front of all those women."

She whirled to face him. "You wouldn't dare." Then she thought of Mr. Drury and Diamond. "Please don't. I—I regret that I might have misled you in the stable earlier today. Let me make myself plain: My feelings for you extend no farther than friendship. I hope you will forgive me for any misunderstanding."

"There is nothing to forgive," he said. "Of course, I still expect to dance with you at Abigail's wedding."

"Did you not hear a single word I said?"

He held a finger to her lips. "I heard you, and if you're not careful, everyone else will, too. I traveled a long way to dance with the maid of honor at the wedding of the century, and I'm not going home until I do. That's a promise."

With that, he left her and stormed down the hall to her father's study. His touch lingered upon her lips.

Later, alone in her study, Eleanor stitched on the Rocky Mountain quilt until her eyes teared from the strain. Once Harriet called through the locked door that her mother wished her to come to the parlor immediately, but Eleanor sent her back with her apologies and the excuse that she was not feeling well. Sometime after midnight, someone tested the doorknob but did not knock. Eleanor assumed the others had gone to bed hours ago, so she froze in her chair until she heard footsteps moving off down the hall. She did not know if the would-be visitor was Harriet again, Mother herself, or Fred, but she put away her sewing tools quietly just in case she—or he—had doubled back on tiptoe and waited outside. Only when she was certain she was alone did she steal down the stairs to her bedroom, where she soon drifted off into a troubled sleep.

She woke not long after dawn to soft rapping on her door. "Eleanor," called Harriet softly. "Wake up."

She could not bear to see Fred after what she had said to him. "I don't want any breakfast. I'll come down when the dressmaker arrives."

"Get up and go to your mother at once. She needs you."

At the fear and alarm in the maid's voice, Eleanor bolted out of bed and threw a dressing gown over her nightdress. "What is it?" she asked, opening the door. "Where's my mother?"

"Downstairs. Be quiet or you'll wake the Corvilles." Then Harriet's sharp eyes darted to the floor. "What's this?"

Eleanor looked and discovered a small white envelope. It must have been slipped beneath her door while she slept. She reached for it, but Harriet was quicker. "Someone obviously meant that for me," said Eleanor sharply, thinking of Fred.

Harriet tucked it into her pocket. "It may be your door but it's your mother's house. You can have it if she says you might."

They hurried downstairs. Mother paced in the foyer, wringing her hands. At the sight of Eleanor, fury sparked in her eyes. "You put her up to this, didn't you? Where has she gone?"

Eleanor took in her mother's red-rimmed eyes, the note of hysteria in her voice. "Where has who gone?"

"Your sister." Mother resumed pacing, wringing her hands. "As if you didn't know. She took a horse, the bridal silver, and most of her clothes, but she left the pearls Edwin gave her."

"She also left a note." Harriet handed Mother the envelope. "In Eleanor's room."

Mother quickly withdrew a sheet of Abigail's monogrammed stationery. "Dear Eleanor," she read aloud. "I hope someday you will see that this is best for both of us. Edwin is a good and kindly man. I do not leave because he would not be a good husband, but because I love someone else. Please pray for me. Please forgive me. Your loving sister, Abigail."

"Give me that," said Eleanor, snatching the note.

"Why should she ask *you* to forgive her?" demanded Mother. "She should be begging me for forgiveness, me and her father."

"Where is Father?"

"Searching," said Harriet. "He'll call at the homes of all the young men Abigail knows. If he doesn't find her, at least he'll find out who else is missing."

"You're the only one she saw fit to bid farewell," said Mother. "You must have helped her. You must know the man."

"I don't." Eleanor was at an utter loss for a single likely name. "She has been distracted lately, but I thought she was just nervous about the wedding. I knew nothing of her intentions. You read what she wrote to me; you ought to see that."

Mother stopped short, a hand to her throat. "Merciful God, what if they have run off, but not married?" She inhaled sharply, drew herself up, and resumed pacing. "No matter. In fact, that might be best. We can bring her back. We will watch her so she cannot run off again."

"Mother! Whatever else Abigail has hidden from us, she clearly does not wish to marry Edwin."

"Do not cross me today, Eleanor. I will see them married, and you will keep quiet."

"Even if you could find Abigail and convince her to go through with it, you would be making a terrible mistake. Edwin would eventually learn of the deception. The scandal would force him to divorce her."

"Rumors. He would hear rumors only, and those will fade with time. The Corvilles want this marriage as much as we do. They will ignore what they do not wish to see."

Suddenly the door burst open and Father strode in, his face a thundercloud. Mother reached for him, but he brushed her aside. "We couldn't find her," he growled, "and none of the young men are missing."

Mother groped for his arm. "You were discreet? We cannot have your inquiries stirring up rumors."

"For God's sake, woman, we are beyond fearing rumors."

"Abigail's missing?"

Eleanor turned instinctively, but she knew Fred's voice.

"This does not concern you," said Mother, waving at Fred as if she could shoo him back up the stairs.

Father barked out a bitter laugh. "It is his concern. It was his horse Abigail stole."

Fred and Eleanor exchanged a look, and she knew they shared the same thought. "Did you inquire at the homes of Abigail's girlfriends?" she asked her father.

Mother clasped her hands together, a new hope appearing in her eyes. "Then you believe her letter was meant to send us searching in the wrong direction? Then perhaps there is no other man. Perhaps all will be well."

"Mr. Lockwood," said Fred, "I will need to borrow a horse. I know where we should continue the search."

The men left too quickly for Eleanor to call Fred back. Regardless of the consequences to the family, Eleanor did not want Fred to assist in Abigail's recapture.

Eleanor half expected Mother to take to her bed, but instead she set herself to the task of keeping the Corvilles ignorant of Abigail's flight. Mother hid the letter and the necklace and instructed Harriet and Eleanor to say that Father, Fred, and Abigail had gone riding to see if Abigail approved of the horse the Bergstroms intended as their wedding gift.

Eleanor remained silent rather than lie, but Mother's explanation was enough to satisfy the Corvilles. After breakfast, Edwin and his father went into the city on business and Mother amused Mrs. Corville in the parlor. Eleanor withdrew to her study, but she was too heartsick to quilt, so she sat in the window seat and watched the front gates. Some time later, Edwin and his father returned from their errand; surely when they found Abigail still gone, they would grow suspicious. The Drury estate was close enough that Father and Fred could have made the round trip twice by then. What could be keeping them?

At last, the front gates swung open and two riders on horseback approached the house. She raced downstairs and out the front door just as Father and Fred dismounted and handed off the reins to a stablehand. Father stormed past Eleanor and into the house without a word, more furious than she had ever seen him.

"Was Abigail with Mr. Drury's daughter?" she asked Fred.

"No. She was with Mr. Drury."

For a moment Eleanor did not understand, then the shock of it struck her. She placed her hand on her heart and took a deep breath. "Are they married?"

"They will be before the day is out. Your father and I convinced him it would be prudent to do so."

Eleanor sank down upon the top step. "Oh, Abigail."

Fred climbed the stairs and sat beside her. "She asked me to give you a message. She begs your forgiveness and hopes you will call on her at her new home when the uproar has settled down."

Eleanor let out a bleak laugh. "Once again she asks for my forgiveness."

"She must realize what a scandal she's created. She left you here all alone to deal with the consequences."

"She and Mr. Drury will have consequences of their own to face." But at least Abigail would have a home, and the affection of the man she loved, while the Lockwoods would be ruined. "And poor Edwin. She should have told him. Leaving him like this is cruel."

"I'll tell him."

"No, Fred." She placed a hand on his arm to stop him from rising. "It should be someone from the family."

"I saw your sister at the Drury place often. I should have realized what was happening, but I didn't. Let me at least do this much."

Wordless, Eleanor nodded. Fred went into the house.

Eleanor hugged her knees to her chest and wondered what to do next. She dreaded going inside and facing the ugly scenes that were sure to unfold. She closed her eyes and wished she, too, could leap on a horse and flee to the side of the man she loved.

There would be no wedding, she suddenly realized, no dance with Fred. And now that Father knew of Fred's deception with Mr. Drury's horse, no Bergstrom would be welcome on Lockwood property—if any property remained to the Lockwoods now that the partnership with the Corvilles would dissolve.

She waited long enough for Fred to deliver the unhappy news before returning inside. The door to her father's study was closed, but she found Mother in the parlor conversing in hushed tones with Harriet. They broke off at Eleanor's entrance. "Sit down," commanded Mother, her face drawn but determined.

"Did Mr. Bergstrom—"

"Yes, he told Edwin, and somehow he managed to make the circumstances seem less dire than they are." She sighed and touched her hair. "I suppose I ought to thank him."

Eleanor frowned and sat down. "I suppose you should."

"Oh, do be quiet," snapped Mother. "Today of all days you must try to be pleasant."

The front bell rang. Harriet leapt up to answer it, and returned to inform them that the dressmaker had arrived.

"She came to finish fitting Abigail's gown." Eleanor rose. "I'll dismiss her."

"I told you to sit. Harriet, have the dressmaker wait for us in the conservatory, then fetch Abigail's gown. I will meet you there shortly."

Harriet nodded and fled from the room.

"Eleanor," said Mother. "We must have a wedding."

Eleanor felt the blood drain from her face.

"If Edwin and his parents agree, you will marry him in Abigail's place on Saturday."

"Even if he does agree, which I sincerely doubt, there will be no wedding because I will never consent to it. Edwin loves Abigail, not me."

"He is very fond of you."

"As a sister, and I think of him as a brother."

"Good marriages have been based upon less."

Eleanor stared at her mother in disbelief. "It is incomprehensible."

Mother's voice was acid. "Your father's business is so deeply in debt that without this partnership, we will not survive another year. We will have no home, no means of support."

"Father will find other work," said Eleanor, her voice shaking. "I will find work."

"You? What would you do? Do you think someone would pay you to read books or stitch quilts?"

"Perhaps—perhaps Abigail and Mr. Drury—"

"Absolutely not. We will take nothing from them." Mother rose and grasped Eleanor by the shoulders. "You must fulfill the obligations your sister abandoned."

"I cannot marry. You know this. I'm sure Edwin knows."

"The doctors have been wrong about you before. They thought you would die as a child, and yet here you are, as well and strong as any of us."

"That is not true."

"You are healthy enough for Edwin." Mother squeezed Eleanor's arms painfully. "What would you sacrifice in marrying him? A life alone with your books and your needle? Edwin loves books as much as you, so he will spare you ample time for reading. He will come to accept your patchwork fetish as well. You will have a husband and a home of your own. Don't you want that?"

"Mother—" She did want that; of course she did. But she was not Abigail, and the idea that she could simply step into her sister's place as easily as donning her wedding gown sickened her.

"Think of the alternatives. You may enjoy satisfactory health for years. Do you want to spend them impoverished and hungry?"

Eleanor tore herself away. "It would not come to that. We have friends, relations—"

"You will see how much affection our friends bear us when we are ruined."

"If I marry, it will be for love."

"*I* married for love," said Mother venomously. "And you can see what good it has done me. Never marry for love. Marry for position and security, as your father did. As I should have done. That is the only way you will not be disappointed. That is the only way you will receive exactly what you were promised."

Eleanor could endure no more. She turned and fled from the room, but before she could reach the stairs, Father exited the drawing room and closed the door behind him.

"The Corvilles have agreed," he told her. "You are a very fortunate girl."

Eleanor gaped at him. "How am I fortunate?"

"You have narrowly escaped the shame of spinsterhood. Do you need any other reward for fulfilling your duty to your parents?"

"What of my duty to myself? And what of Mother? For years you have told me it is my obligation as the unmarried daughter to care for her in her infirmity."

"Your obligations have changed. Once you marry Edwin, we will be able to hire a score of nurses to care for your mother."

"You are both mad." Eleanor picked up her skirts and fled to the sanctuary of her study. Once inside, she locked the door and barred it with a chair. She felt faint. She lay on the sofa and buried her face in her hands, anguished. Now she understood the reason behind Abigail's apologies. Abigail must have anticipated how her decision would affect her sister. She had known, and yet she had still run off.

A knock sounded on the door. "Eleanor, it's me."

"Edwin." Eleanor rose and opened the door. Edwin stood in the hallway with his hands in his pockets. "Oh, Edwin, I'm so sorry."

He tried to smile. "Was the prospect of marrying me so horrifying that she had to run off without a word? And for a man twice her age." He shook his head. "I thought she loved me. She never said so, but I assumed she was just being modest. I found it charming. She agreed to marry me, so I assumed she loved me."

"Of course you did," said Eleanor, though she had long known the truth. "Anyone would have."

He nodded and looked off down the hall. "I suppose." He cleared his throat. "I do wish her well. I hope she will be happy with the life she has chosen."

Eleanor's heart went out to him. "That's very generous of you."

"Generosity is a fine quality in a husband, or so I am told."

"Then you've spoken to my father."

He nodded.

"Edwin, surely you don't wish to marry me. I am not my sister."

"I know that, but I am very fond of you. We have much in common—more, I think, than Abigail and I had. I would be a good and faithful husband, Eleanor. I will provide for you and your family, and when the time comes, I will ensure the stability and growth of the business your father founded."

"In other words, you want my inheritance, not me. I thought better of you than that."

"Don't think ill of me for promising to safeguard my wife's fortune. That's all I meant." He reached for her hands, and with some misgivings, Eleanor allowed him to take them. "I've been nearly a part of your family for years, long enough, if you'll forgive me for saying so, to know there are no other suitors. We are friends now, and I'm confident we will grow to love each other deeply in time." He caught her eye and smiled. "I've heard that can happen, haven't you?"

Eleanor thought of Mother and shook her head. "How can I simply step into my sister's role as if I were an understudy in a play? Won't you be ashamed to stand with me at the altar before those hundreds of people because the sister you wanted ran off with another man?"

"Far less ashamed than I would be to notify those same hundreds that there will be no wedding at all," said Edwin. "We both have a duty to our families. It is best for everyone if we marry."

"I lack your confidence."

"Then why not rely upon my judgment? We have nothing to lose and a great deal to gain."

"I usually prefer to rely upon my own judgment," said Eleanor, knowing they had a great deal to lose. But she could not find words to tell him it was out of the question. He had borne too much humiliation that day. She could decline tomorrow, and perhaps, after the immediate pain of Abigail's flight had lessened, Edwin would see their circumstances more rationally. In the light of a new day, Eleanor's refusal would come as a relief.

"I cannot answer you now," she said.

"Of course not. You need time to grow accustomed to the idea, to discuss the situation with your parents."

Eleanor nodded, although she wanted nothing less. Her mother's words still haunted her. Eleanor yearned for a husband, a family, a home of her own—but she did not wish to obtain them under these circumstances. Nor was Edwin the man who had figured in her wistful imaginings.

Still, she had learned to compromise in other difficult situations. All her life, she had been forced to make do with the scraps she was given. She had even managed to piece together some contentment for herself.

"I will give you my answer tomorrow," she told him.

He nodded and quickly kissed her cheek before releasing her hands and disappearing down the hallway. Eleanor shut the door and leaned back upon it, closing her eyes. She wished she could run to Miss Langley's embrace and pour out all her grief and worry as she had done as a child. If Miss Langley were here to offer advice, she would tell Eleanor to do what was right. But what was right?

A knock on the door startled her out of her reverie. "I told you I would give you my answer tomorrow," she said.

"You can't mean you're seriously considering marrying him."

Fred. Eleanor flung open the door and he stormed in. "I have to consider it," she said. "You don't know what is at stake."

"I do know that you aren't property to be bartered between families."

Eleanor turned her back on him before he could perceive how he had wounded her. His words had laid plain what she already knew, that the woman Eleanor Lockwood mattered little in the upcoming nuptials. Her parents said she could not marry—except when they needed a bride to seal a contract. They said she could not leave home—except when saving Father's business took precedence over tending to Mother. They did not care how agreeing to marry Edwin would degrade her, and they craved their own comfort and security more than her happiness.

But she loved them, and she could not bear to be the agent of their misery. "I am not being bartered. It is my decision whether to accept or decline."

"Are you sure?"

"They cannot force me. On the other hand, if my choices are between marrying a decent man and seeing my family rendered destitute, I suppose there is only one choice after all."

"There are other alternatives."

"Such as?"

"If you're going to marry, marry for love. Marry me."

For a moment she couldn't breathe. "What makes you think I love you?"

He spun her around to face him. "Why did you tell me your father never intended to buy my horses?"

"It's not fair to answer a question with—" Then he kissed her, and she clung to him for a moment before pulling away. "I can't. My family needs me."

"Only because Abigail broke her promise, not that I blame her. Your parents will have to make their own way."

"I cannot bear children. Do you still wish to marry me?"

For an instant, pain flashed in his eyes, but he said, "I do. We'll have so many nieces and nephews around that it will be as if we have children of our own."

She did not believe any man would be satisfied with that. "How could I refuse Edwin and then marry you?"

"Because I love you. Edwin does not."

"Love is not the only factor to consider. Edwin cares for me in his way."

For a moment he just watched her. "If that's good enough for you, then there's nothing more I can say."

He went to the door. "Fred—"

"Try on your sister's wedding gown," he said roughly. "Maybe I don't know you as well as I thought. Maybe it'll fit you."

He slammed the door behind him.

Fred's visit had shattered the serenity of her study, so as much as Eleanor longed for solitude, she composed herself and returned downstairs. Mother met her on the landing and steered her to the conservatory, where the dressmaker had been waiting all morning. Numb, she allowed herself to be undressed like a doll. Her corset was tightened, a cloud of white satin was thrown over her head—and there she stood, a pale beauty motionless in the mirror, just as Abigail had been.

"Who would have thought she was so pretty after all," marveled Harriet.

The dressmaker assured Mother the gown would be ready by Saturday morning.

The day passed in a blur. Eleanor was only vaguely aware that Edwin hovered in the background and Fred avoided her altogether. Occasionally she overheard snatches of conversation—her mother and Mrs. Corville quietly discussing how their guests should be informed, her father touting the strength of Lockwood's to Mr. Corville, Harriet asking Mother what she should pack for Eleanor's honeymoon. Not a word was spoken of Abigail, and as she had been the dominant subject in their discourse for months, her absence was conspicuous, and made their talk seem to Eleanor as if they spoke a foreign language.

At supper she discovered Mr. Bergstrom was gone. From the conversation, she learned he had lingered for hours before departing abruptly and without the apologies he owed them for his part in concealing Abigail's true affections. Eleanor could not believe how easily he had left her. She sat at the table without speaking or eating, and when the meal was over, it occurred to her that eventually there would be no distinguishing between herself and her sister.

She passed the evening in the parlor with the women and allowed Mother to escort her to her bedroom afterward.

"Your father and I are pleased you have come to your senses," said Mother as she turned down Eleanor's bedclothes. Eleanor could not remember her ever having done so before.

"I don't know that I have. I still haven't given Edwin my decision."

Mother turned away from the bed and regarded her with something very like pity. "You don't really believe you have a choice, do you?" She strode from the room, and with her hand on the doorknob, she said, "Marry Edwin. How will you pay for your physicians if you are destitute?"

She shut the door.

Shivering, Eleanor sat down on the bed. She saw at once how the rest of the week would unfold. She would go nowhere unaccompanied; she would be watched and threatened and scolded until her wedding day. Her parents could not force her to marry Edwin, but they could make it impossible for her to refuse.

She lay back and stared up at the ceiling. For hours, while night fell and the house grew still, she tried to convince herself to marry Edwin. She reminded herself of her duty, of her illness, of Edwin's promises to make her happy. Fulfilling those needs might be enough. She reminded herself that Fred had abandoned her.

She could not do it.

Mother was wrong. Eleanor did have a choice. Miss Langley would take her in. Somehow Eleanor would find a way to help her parents, but not by marrying Edwin.

She glanced about and spotted the suitcase Harriet had begun packing for the honeymoon. Eleanor hastily added a few more necessities. She snatched up her jewelry box, which contained the valuables her grandmother had bequeathed her and what little money of her own she had managed to accumulate, and tucked it in with her clothes. Hefting the bag, she slowly opened the door and stole into the hall. The darkness seemed watchful and accusing as she descended the stairs. Any moment she could be discovered, any moment—

She stopped short. Once she left that house, she could never return. She could not leave behind every cherished thing.

She hid the suitcase behind a statue on the landing and hurried upstairs again, heart pounding as she entered her study for what she knew would be the last time. There was no time to reason out what she could carry. She pulled the Rocky Mountain quilt from the frame and gathered it like a sack. Into it she bundled her sewing kit, the Crazy Quilt, and the box containing Miss Langley's letters. She could not look at the shelves full of beloved books without wanting to weep. She added the diary she had kept as a child, her first embroidered sampler, a silk shawl that had belonged to her grandmother, and, with a pang, a photograph of her family. Then she slung the awkward bundle over her shoulder and left her beloved sanctuary forever.

Eleanor descended the stairs at a near run, as fast and as silently as her burdens allowed. Already she mourned precious belongings left behind: the smooth stones from the shore near the summer house, the notebook in which she had written the addresses of her school friends, the sewing machine that had brought her so much pleasure. Eleanor pushed the thoughts from her mind and quickened her pace. She reached the door and fled outside—and froze at the edge of the porch in shock.

An automobile was slowly creeping up the drive.

As she stood rooted in place, staring, it slowed and stopped. Fred got out and ran to her. "Are you leaving?"

She nodded, thoughts of Boston and Miss Langley fading.

"Do you need a ride?"

"Yes, thank you," she said. Before the words left her mouth, Fred snatched up her suitcase and bundle and strode back to the automobile. Eleanor hurried after him as he tossed her things inside. He helped her into the passenger's seat before taking the wheel, and in moments, they were under way.

Eleanor did not want to look back, but something compelled her. As they passed through the front gates, she glanced back and saw the house, dark and silent, as if no one lived there anymore.

She shuddered and turned forward. "They will come after me, as they did my sister."

"I hope they won't know where to look. They may think you ran away on your own."

Then Eleanor understood why he had left the Lockwood home earlier that day. "You knew if we were both missing in the morning . . ."

"This way, Elm Creek Manor won't be the first place they look."

"Likely they'll think I ran off to Abigail." Then she shot him a look. "I thought you lived on a horse farm."

"I do."

"Elm Creek Manor is a rather grand name for a farmhouse."

He did not look at her, but even in the darkness she detected his broad smile.

They went to the train station, where Fred and Mr. Drury had agreed he would leave the automobile. Fred purchased two tickets for the next train west and they waited for their train, for pursuers. Eleanor's absence would be discovered by sunrise.

The train arrived first. She and Fred found two seats in an empty compartment and stowed her belongings. Exhausted, Eleanor rested against Fred and closed her eyes.

"Try to sleep if you can," said Fred. "We'll have to change trains in Philadelphia."

"You should rest, too. The conductor will wake us before our stop."

"I couldn't sleep a wink, but I'll try if you insist."

She assured him she did, and she left her seat to take down her belongings. She transferred the items from her bundle into her suitcase, unfurled the Rocky Mountain quilt, and, returning to the comfort of Fred's arms, she spread the quilt over them.

"It's not finished yet," she said, "but I think I have all the needles and pins out of it."

"It's beautiful."

It's our wedding quilt, Eleanor almost said, and realized she had always known it would be.

Chapter Five

Sylvia and Andrew drove east through the foothills of the Rockies toward Golden, Colorado. Andrew had said little about Bob and Cathy since the motor home pulled out of their driveway, as if he preferred to pretend the visit had never occurred. Apparently, despite his concerns about informing his children of their engagement, he had still hoped for a much happier reaction to the news.

She sighed and glanced at her map. The enthusiasm of Sarah and the other Elm Creek Quilters would have to compensate for what Andrew's children lacked, or their wedding would be a dismal occasion indeed.

"We just passed a sign for Golden," said Andrew. "Can you direct me from here?"

"Absolutely." Sylvia had last visited in 1993, when Golden had celebrated its first Quilt Day, but the landmarks were too remarkable to forget. "Just follow the M and the arch."

"Beg pardon?"

In response, Sylvia smiled and pointed out the window to a large letter M on one of the more prominent mountains. "Head that way, and turn south on Washington."

Andrew grinned and complied. "Is that M for 'museum'?"

"I think of it that way, but it's actually for the Colorado School of Mines."

They drove into downtown Golden, a charming place that, in Sylvia's opinion, looked exactly as a Western town should. The distinctive flat-topped mountains in the near distance resembled something straight out of a movie about the Wild West, and Sylvia would not have been surprised to see men on horseback kicking up a cloud of dust as they raced along the slopes.

They passed a statue of Buffalo Bill in the median strip, and just ahead, they spied a sign on an arch over the street. "'Howdy, Folks,'" Andrew read aloud. "'Welcome to Golden, Where the West Lives.' And to think I left my six-shooter at home."

"I want you on your best behavior," scolded Sylvia. "I don't see why anyone here should help me find my mother's quilt if you're going to joke about their town."

"Sorry, ma'am," said Andrew meekly, but his eyes twinkled and he tugged at the brim of an imaginary cowboy hat. "I guess this must be the arch you mentioned."

"It is indeed. The museum entrance is almost directly beneath it. Park wherever you like."

"You mean wherever I can," said Andrew. He twisted around in his seat to view the street behind him. "The kids were right about one thing. Sometimes this behemoth is more trouble than it's worth."

"Only when you have to parallel park."

"And when I have to fill up the tank." Andrew grimaced as he maneuvered the motor home into a place across the street from the museum. "Sometimes I wish I'd settled for a nice SUV."

They left the motor home and crossed the street hand in hand. They entered through the front double doors and paused in the foyer long enough for Sylvia to help herself to some of the pamphlets in the rack of brochures. Andrew sniffed the air. "Sure doesn't smell like a museum. Smells like lunch."

"There's a Chinese restaurant on the lower level. We could stop by for a bite to eat later." She smiled slyly and took his arm. "Or we could try the Buffalo Rose."

"You mean that place a few doors down? From the name, I figured it was a florist."

Sylvia erupted in peals of laughter. "I don't think you should tell them that. It's a biker bar."

"Chinese sounds good," said Andrew hastily. He held open the door and ushered her inside.

Sylvia eyed the gift shop with interest as they passed, but she was too eager to find her mother's quilt to be distracted long. They entered the first gallery and were greeted by two docents, who provided them with brochures about the exhibits and invited them to sign the guest book. "Waterford, Pennsylvania," one of the women said, reading upside down as Sylvia handed the pen to Andrew. "Did you ever attend the quilt camp there?"

"She's one of the founders," said Andrew.

The second woman spun the guest book around, and her eyes lit up at what she read. "You're Sylvia Compson?"

"She sure is." Andrew put an arm around her proudly.

"I love your quilt, Sewickley Sunrise," the second docent said, adding that she had a print of it hanging in her office.

Sylvia and Andrew thanked the docents and moved deeper into the gallery. Andrew trailed after her as Sylvia approached the first quilt, an appliquéd scene of the first moon landing, nearly lifelike in its realism. "I don't think we'll find your mother's quilt here," said Andrew, and read aloud from the brochure. "'A retrospective of the works of Colorado quilter Alexandra Grant, age ninety-seven, who used intricate appliqué and surface embellishment to depict the most significant historical events of her lifetime.' That's some lifetime. Do you think you'll still be quilting when you're that age?"

"God willing," said Sylvia, and moved on to the next quilt, a collage of images from the civil rights movement, fluid and vividly colored scenes of hope and triumph. Hanging next to it, in stark contrast in monochromatic grays and browns, was a three-panel work depicting the World Trade Center, the Pentagon, and rolling hills Sylvia immediately recognized as the countryside of her own beloved state of Pennsylvania. A single bright color illuminated each panel: a brilliant blue sky over the Pentagon, a lush green forest for Pennsylvania, a firefighter in a yellow coat against a background of rubble in Manhattan.

Sylvia could hardly bear to look at it, and at the same time she longed to touch it, to find comfort in the soft fabrics even as the images caused her pain. She reached for Andrew's hand instead. He held it in both of his, and let her linger a moment longer before drawing her away to the next quilt.

Before long, Sylvia lost herself in the beauty of the quilts and the poetry of their stories. Andrew's prediction proved true, however, as Sylvia had assumed it would; not even a novice quilter or a very poor historian would have confused Eleanor Lockwood's pieced New York Beauty quilt with the appliquéd pictorial works of Alexandra Grant. They left the first gallery and went upstairs to the second, although one glance at the sign outside the exhibit indicated they were not likely to find her mother's quilt there, either.

"'Agriculture Quilts,'" Sylvia read aloud. "It's a long shot, but if we have time, I'd prefer to check anyway, if only to be sure."

"Maybe they have quilts in here that aren't part of the special exhibit," said Andrew, escorting her into the gallery. "Besides, if we don't look, I'll spend the whole drive home wondering what in the world an Agriculture Quilt is."

They quickly discovered that Agriculture Quilts were quilts inspired by farming. Some artists had used pictorial quilts to create fabric snapshots of farm life, much as the artist featured in the lower gallery had done for historical events. Others had approached the theme more whimsically, resulting in works such as the Pickle Dish bed quilt pieced from cow print fabrics and the Corn and Beans quilt with the Farmer's Daughter border. Sylvia's favorite was an Attic Windows wall hanging pieced from vintage feedsacks. She peered at the quilt closely to study the fabric, then nodded, satisfied that the fabrics were not reproductions. Genuine vintage feedsack fabrics were scarce and highly prized by some collectors, and whenever Sylvia saw the charming works modern quiltmakers had created from the scraps they had found, she remembered with misgivings how many sacks of horse feed must have come to Elm Creek Manor in her childhood. Her thrifty mother would not have simply discarded them, but since she had not cut them up to make quilts as far as Sylvia could recall, Sylvia had no idea what had become of them.

They returned downstairs. Andrew said nothing, but he still held Sylvia's hand, so she knew he was sorry for her sake that their second lead had turned out no more successfully than their first. "There must be other rooms we haven't seen," said Sylvia, unwilling to give up so easily, not after driving so far and hoping for so much.

They returned to the first gallery, where Sylvia showed the docents Summer's computer illustration of the New York Beauty quilt and asked if they recalled seeing it. To Sylvia's dismay, the women studied the picture and shook their heads. "Are you certain?" she asked. "A recent visitor to your museum says she saw it here. We already checked the galleries, but might it be somewhere else in the museum?"

The docents exchanged a look, and Sylvia could see they were reluctant to disappoint her. "It's not in any of the staff offices," said the first docent, "or in the classroom. Did you ask in the gift shop? We do sell some antique quilts. Your friend might have seen it there, although I know it isn't there now."

Sylvia nearly gasped. "You mean it might have been here—but was sold?"

"Most likely not," said the second docent quickly. "We'll ask Opal. She's been with the museum since its founding. If your quilt has ever been here, she'll know."

Sylvia nodded, but as the docent led them back upstairs to the museum's administrative office, she envisioned a clerk closing a cash register and handing a satisfied customer the New York Beauty in a plastic bag. How on earth would she find it then?

Opal turned out to be a cheerful, curly haired woman who greeted them warmly and listened with interest to Sylvia's explanation about her search for her mother's missing quilts. "Your Internet correspondent says she saw your quilt here?" asked Opal, accepting the picture Andrew handed her.

"She did, but unfortunately, she didn't say when."

Opal studied the illustration, shook her head, and returned the paper to Sylvia. "It's not one of ours. We never sold a quilt resembling this one in our quilt shop, and I know we don't have it in storage."

"Storage?"

"Why, yes. We have more than two hundred and fifty quilts in our permanent collection, and when we aren't displaying them, we keep them in protected storage."

"If you don't mind, could we please look for ourselves?" asked Sylvia. "I don't mean to be a bother, but if there's any chance you might have my mother's quilt, I would kick myself later for not asking."

Opal smiled sympathetically. "Unfortunately, that's easier said than done. Ordinarily, we don't even open this room to the public, but I think we can make an exception for the founder of Elm Creek Quilts."

She led them next door to a locked room. Inside the air was cool and dry, and along one wall Sylvia discovered shelves and shelves of quilts, each wound around a long carpet roll and wrapped in a clean cotton sheet. "Oh, dear," said Sylvia. "I suppose looking at these quilts would be more difficult than I thought."

"I'm afraid so," said Opal. "But I've been through this collection many times, and I know we don't have any in the New York Beauty pattern. I would definitely remember such a striking quilt."

She offered to post pictures of the New York Beauty on their announcements board in case any of their other visitors had seen it. Perhaps, she suggested, Sylvia's Internet correspondent had seen the New York Beauty elsewhere in the area and was mistaken only in regard to the specific location. Sylvia appreciated the thread of hope, however thin, and gratefully gave Opal illustrations of all five quilts.

"Strike two," said Sylvia as she and Andrew returned downstairs.

"Don't get too discouraged," said Andrew. "We make progress with every lead we follow, even if the trail doesn't seem to go anywhere."

"I won't feel like we're making progress until we find one of the quilts."

Andrew chuckled. "Come on. I'll cheer you up at the gift shop."

Sylvia raised her eyebrows at him, but allowed him to steer her into the QuiltMarket. She had enjoyed exploring the museum despite the unsuccessful search, but she wasn't about to tell him so. If he wanted to console her with a present, it wouldn't be right to spoil his fun.

By the time they reached Iowa several days later, Sylvia had read her new book on the Agriculture Quilts exhibit from cover to cover twice, and Summer had received nine more responses from the Missing Quilts Home Page. None of these new sightings were on the route home to Pennsylvania, however, which suited Sylvia just fine. After their disappointments in Boulder City and Golden, she and Andrew had decided that it would be wiser to contact future prospects by phone first to rule out obvious false leads rather than put so many extra miles on the motor home for nothing more than another dead end.

But since they were driving through Iowa, anyway, they saw no reason not to turn north at Des Moines and investigate a promising e-mail message sent by the proprietor of Brandywine Antiques in Fort Dodge. Not only had he seen an Ocean Waves quilt fitting Sylvia's description, he actually had it in his possession.

"He inherited the business from his grandfather," said Sylvia as they paused at a gas station to fill up the tank and purchase a map of the city. "His grandparents used to travel to Pennsylvania to buy Amish quilts, but they bought others, too, and he believes this Ocean Waves quilt might have originated in Pennsylvania."

"Why would they go all the way to Pennsylvania for Amish quilts?" said Andrew. "There are Amish communities much closer."

"Perhaps he had a fondness for Lancaster. I certainly do."

"Well, sure, but you're from Pennsylvania. Why would an antique shop be interested in new Amish quilts, anyway?"

"Heavens, Andrew, how should I know? Perhaps they bought antique Amish quilts. You'll have to ask—" She glanced at her notes. "You'll have to ask this George K. Robinson when we arrive."

Andrew shrugged and said he might do just that.

They located the street on the map and, with slightly more difficulty, found it in the city as well, but the shop itself eluded them. "3057 Brandywine Drive," said Sylvia, checking her notes. "Perhaps I wrote down the wrong number."

"Could be. This strip mall is the entire 3000 block, and I don't see a sign for Brandywine Antiques."

Neither did Sylvia, and they had passed the strip mall three times. Andrew drove the entire length of the street once, and again, scanning every sign and building they passed, but they could not find it. They did discover one antique shop, but not only was it not the one they were searching for, the owner claimed there were no other antique shops in that part of town.

"Of course he would say that," said Sylvia as Andrew helped her back into the motor home. "He doesn't want us to visit the competition."

She didn't really believe that, and she knew Andrew didn't either when he suggested they return to the strip mall and inquire at whatever business occupied 3057 Brandywine Drive. If they didn't know where the mysterious antique shop was, Sylvia could phone Summer and verify the address.

They parked in the strip mall lot and strolled the length of the shops. "I hate to think we made this trip for nothing," Sylvia remarked, when Andrew suddenly stopped in his tracks in front of a Letters et All store.

"This is it."

"This can't be it. This is one of those shipping and mailing services." Then Sylvia understood. "There's no store. It's just a mail drop."

Andrew nodded and pushed the door open.

"But that doesn't make any sense," she said, lowering her voice as she followed him inside. "I don't care how much mail a business receives. It wouldn't be practical to send someone to pick it up each day instead of having it delivered to the store."

"Exactly." Andrew strode up to the queue. "I think you might have been right when you said there is no store."

Sylvia had no time to reply, for the smiling young woman behind the counter beckoned them forward. "May I help you?"

"I hope so," said Andrew. "We're looking for a business called Brandywine Antiques. They gave this place as their address."

The young woman's smile vanished. "They must be one of our mail clients." She nodded to a wall of metal post office boxes on the opposite wall.

"We need to find the shop itself," said Sylvia. "Do you have another address?"

The young woman glanced at a middle-aged gentleman behind the counter. He had not appeared to be listening, but he looked up at Sylvia's question and said, "I'm sorry. We can't give out any personal information about our clients. It's a corporate privacy policy."

"We aren't asking for personal information," said Andrew, "just the address of a business."

"I'm very sorry, folks." He looked past them to the next customer in line. "May I help you?"

Andrew scowled, and the young woman gave them a look of helpless apology. "Come along, Andrew," murmured Sylvia, taking his arm. "We haven't hit our dead end yet."

They left the shop and retraced their steps until they came to a pay telephone Sylvia remembered passing earlier. They searched the weathered telephone book, but Brandywine Antiques was not listed in either the yellow pages or the alphabetical business directory. "I suppose it's time to call home," said Sylvia, digging into her purse for change. "Perhaps Summer said Fort Dodge, Indiana, or Ohio. Or maybe the city—"

Andrew placed a hand on her shoulder. "Hold on. I think I see help coming."

Sylvia followed his line of sight and discovered the young woman from Letters et All hurrying toward them, glancing furtively over her shoulder. "Here," she said, and handed Sylvia a scrap of paper. "The owner of the box gave this as his address. Just please don't tell anyone where you got this. I could get fired."

Sylvia glimpsed a hastily scrawled address. "Are you sure, dear?"

She nodded. "This is the third time senior citizens have asked about him in two weeks. I think he's up to something, and I don't like it."

"Thanks very much, miss," said Andrew. "We appreciate your help—and we can keep a secret."

The young woman gave them a quick smile and dashed back to the store.

Sylvia studied the address. "Well, Andrew? Do you feel like playing detective?"

Within minutes they were back on the road, following their map away from the business district into a residential area. When they stopped in front of a two-story colonial house on a pleasant, tree-lined street adjacent to a park, Sylvia shook her head in disbelief. "I suppose our Mr. Robinson might run the business out of his home."

Andrew snorted, skeptical.

A woman who looked to be in her late forties answered the door-bell, wiping her hands on a dish towel.

"Oh, dear, I hope we didn't interrupt your supper," said Sylvia, giving the woman her most disarming smile.

"Oh no, my son isn't even home from school yet," she assured them. "He's a junior at the local college. Is there something I can help you with?"

"I hope so. We're looking for Brandywine Antiques."

The woman looked puzzled. "Brandywine Antiques? There's a Brandywine Drive near the mall . . ."

"Yes, we're quite familiar with that," said Sylvia. "I don't suppose you know a George K. Robinson?"

Behind them, a car pulled into the driveway. Sylvia and Andrew turned to see a bushy-haired young man in baggy clothes climbing out of a bright blue hatchback.

"I'm afraid I don't," said the woman. "My son might. He has me at my wit's end most of the time, but he does know the neighbor-hood."

"Hey, Mom, did I get any mail?" he called, sauntering up the front walk.

"Two packages on the hall table. Jason, do you know the Robin-son family?"

"Who?" he asked, brushing past Sylvia and Andrew on his way to the front door.

"These nice people who you didn't even say hello to are looking for someone named George Robinson."

"George K. Robinson, to be precise," said Sylvia.

"Or his company, Brandywine Antiques," Andrew added.

Jason froze. "Never heard of him. Or—or it. That company. Whatever you called it."

"That's a shame," said Sylvia. "Brandywine Antiques is supposed to have a quilt that belonged to my mother, and we were willing to spend quite a lot of money for it."

Sylvia and Andrew bid his mother good-bye and turned to go.

"Just a sec," said Jason, with a furtive glance at his mother as he followed them down the stairs. "I do all my business over the Internet, see? You can only buy my stuff through AsIsAuctions dot com. I don't have a storefront yet."

"What?" his mother said. "Since when are you an antiques dealer?"

"You told me to get a job," protested Jason. He turned a pleading gaze on Andrew and Sylvia and lowered his voice. "I'm saving up money to buy a store, but until then, I'm running my business out of the house. Really. What was it you said you were interested in again?"

"A quilt," said Andrew, loud enough for Jason's mother to hear. "The pattern's called Ocean Waves. It's made up of lots of blue and white triangles."

Jason nodded, but before he could reply, his mother called, "You mean that raggedy old thing you got at the Hixtons' garage sale?"

Jason managed a weak grin. "You'd be surprised where great finds turn up."

"Great finds? That's no antique. Mr. Hixton's mother made that quilt, and you know it. I heard her tell you myself."

Jason held up his hands, begging Sylvia and Andrew not to leave. "Let me just run inside and get a contract. Once you sign that, I can show you the quilt."

He hurried back up the stairs, but his mother blocked the doorway with her arm before he could duck past. "Sign a contract before they see what they're buying?" Her eyes narrowed. "Just what kind of business are you running, anyway?"

With his mother's help, Sylvia and Andrew eventually dragged the truth from him.

The young man had indeed been running a business out of the house—a shady business Sylvia considered to be just this side of fraud. He trolled Internet Web sites such as the Missing Quilts Home Page and eBay to find potential customers. With a list of the desired items in hand, he rummaged through garage sales and flea markets until he found similar products. Then he would contact the potential customer with the good news that he might have what they were looking for. "The key word is 'might,'" said Jason, glancing from his mother to Sylvia and Andrew apprehensively. "All my sales were through AsIsAuctions. They clearly state in their service agreement that all items for sale are as is. It's the buyer's responsibility to inspect the item in person if they want. All sales are final, so you can't get a refund unless you never get your product or you can prove the seller lied about it."

"You certainly lied to us about this quilt," declared Sylvia.

"I didn't lie." Jason turned to his mother and quickly added, "I didn't."

Andrew frowned. "You said you believed this quilt might have come from Pennsylvania."

"Exactly. I said 'might.' That also means it might *not* have come from Pennsylvania."

"But you knew for a fact that it did not," exclaimed Sylvia. "And what about your alias, George K. Robinson? There is no such person."

"Everybody uses fake names on the Internet. It's for personal privacy, that's all."

"Young man," said Sylvia, shaking her head, "you have such a gift for double-talk I'm sure you're destined for a career in politics."

Andrew folded his arms and regarded Jason sternly. "If you're such an honest dealer, why did you pretend to know nothing about Brandywine Antiques?"

Jason hesitated. "I didn't want my mom to get mad. I knew she wouldn't want me to run a business out of the house."

"A business I could handle," said his mother sharply. "A scam, on the other hand . . ." She shook her head and gave Sylvia and Andrew an appraising look. "The question is, what are we going to do about this?"

Sylvia was reluctant to involve the police, but she and Andrew were both resolute that Jason should not be allowed to perpetrate his scheme any longer. They also insisted that he make restitution for any past customers he might have deceived and write every one of them a letter of apology.

"Oh, he'll do that, all right," said his mother. "If I have to stand over him while he writes every word."

They all agreed that Jason should be denied access to the Internet at least until his obligations to his customers were fulfilled, and that AsIsAuctions must be informed. If all those measures were followed, Sylvia and Andrew would be satisfied, and they would not press charges.

"Do you think that's enough?" Sylvia asked Andrew as they resumed their journey east.

"Nothing short of shutting down this AsIsAuctions place would be enough for me," said Andrew. "They're just as guilty as he is. But I guess this will have to be enough unless we want to have Jason prosecuted for fraud."

"He's just a boy. I hate to ruin his life when all we lost was a few hours of our time and the cost of gasoline."

"We wouldn't be ruining his life. He did it to himself. And I don't know how we can rely on his mother to punish him when she didn't even know what was going on under her own roof."

The harshness in Andrew's tone surprised Sylvia. "She seemed furious. I'm sure she'll see to it he can't swindle anyone else."

Andrew shook his head. "Remember what the girl from the mailbox place said? This is the third time seniors have asked about

Brandywine Antiques. Jason's targeting old folks, and that shows calculation and contempt. He's a crook, Sylvia. A young crook, but still a crook, and he's just going to get worse. Mark my words."

Sylvia did not know what to say. They drove on in silence until they stopped for the night, just west of the Illinois border.

Two days later they arrived in Silver River, Indiana, just outside Fort Wayne, to pursue the last of Summer's Internet leads between them and Elm Creek Manor. Although he didn't complain, Sylvia knew Andrew just wanted to get the visit over with and go home. She could hardly blame him. Her anticipation had lessened with each dead end. She might have considered abandoning the search altogether if not for a sense of duty to her mother—and if not for her proud proclamations that she would not give up the search until every lead had been followed to its end.

"At least they're expecting us this time," Sylvia said as Andrew drove through town, keeping an eye out for the Niehauses' street. Sylvia had phoned them the previous night, for while it was perfectly acceptable to stop by a museum or antique shop unannounced, she would not dream of intruding on a private residence that way. Mona Niehaus herself had answered the phone, and when Sylvia explained they were in the area, Mona invited them to come see the quilt for themselves. Her description sounded so much like Sylvia's mother's Crazy Quilt that Sylvia allowed herself to hope their luck would take a turn for the better here.

They parked in front of a sky-blue Victorian house with a white picket fence and a minivan in the driveway. In the front yard, a sudden gust of wind rustled the boughs of a pair of maple trees, sending a flurry of brilliant gold and orange leaves dancing to the ground. Dried cornstalks adorned a black lamppost in front of the house, and on the wraparound porch stood a white stone goose dressed in blaze orange and camouflage, a wooden duck decoy propped up against its booted feet. It was such a typically idyllic autumn scene that Sylvia would have been thoroughly charmed if not for their sojourn in Fort Dodge.

"Reminds me of Jason's house," remarked Andrew, echoing her own thoughts.

"Don't be ridiculous," said Sylvia, unfastening her seat belt. "His house was brick, and they had no picket fence."

She spoke mostly for her own benefit, however, and tried to prepare herself for the worst as they climbed the porch stairs and rang the doorbell. A boy of about seven opened the door halfway and greeted them in a very formal manner. When they asked for Mona Niehaus, he said, "She's my grandma." At that moment, a girl about two years younger peeped shyly around the door. "I'll get her."

"Thank you, darling, but I'm right here." The door opened all the way, and a tall, thin woman with salt-and-pepper hair pulled back in a batik scarf stood before them. Silver bracelets jingled as she placed her hands on the children's shoulders and steered them back into the house. "You must be Sylvia and Andrew. I'm so pleased you could come."

She welcomed them into the living room, where the two children played with a jumble of unrelated toys in the center of a woven rug. Sylvia took the seat Mona offered, an overstuffed armchair with legs shaped like lion's feet, and glanced about the room for the quilt. She saw heavily embroidered pillows on the sofa, all manner of candles on the mantel, and framed photographs and other eclectic pieces covering so much of the walls that she could barely see the flowered wallpaper behind them. She saw no quilts.

Mona excused herself and returned with a tray. "Please help yourselves," she said as she placed the tea and sandwiches on the coffee table and hurried back out. In a moment they heard the creaking of footsteps on stairs.

Sylvia and Andrew exchanged bemused looks, but Andrew

shrugged and piled several sandwiches on a plate. Sylvia knew she was too nervous to hold a teacup, so she merely sat fidgeting in her chair, watching the children play. "No, the engine goes in here," the little boy told the girl, handing her a small wooden block, but what sort of vehicle the engine was meant to propel, Sylvia had no idea.

Before long they heard footsteps again, and then Mona returned with something draped over her arm. "This is the quilt I contacted you about," she said, unfolding it carefully. "I hope it's the right one. It would be a shame if you came all this way for nothing."

"We were passing by on our way home from California anyway," Andrew said, but Sylvia merely nodded. Involuntarily, she straightened in her chair and held her breath.

Mona held up the quilt, and Sylvia was struck speechless.

"As you can see, it definitely is a Crazy Quilt." Mona regarded Sylvia inquisitively, awaiting a response. "And it has the identifying marks you listed on the Web site. Although some of the stitches have come out, you can still see an embroidered spiderweb in this corner. Here is the appliquéd horseshoe, and if I'm not mistaken, this patch here is from a linen handkerchief. Do you see the monogrammed ALC?"

"Sylvia?" prompted Andrew.

"That's it," said Sylvia. "That's my mother's quilt."

"How wonderful," exclaimed Mona. She draped the quilt over Sylvia's lap. "I hoped it would be. You must be thrilled."

Sylvia hesitated before touching the delicate fabrics, as if they would dissolve like the memory of a dream. She had not seen her mother's Crazy Quilt in more than fifty years. The colors were not as bright as she remembered, and some of the fabrics had unraveled so that only the embroidery stitches held the quilt together, but she did not remember when she had ever seen anything so lovely.

"Mona," she said, "I am so far beyond thrilled that I don't think they've invented a word to describe how I'm feeling."

Mona clasped her hands together and beamed. "I couldn't be happier for you. And to think, I never would have known to contact you except for my daughter-in-law." She indicated the children with a proud nod. "Their mother."

"She's a dentist," the boy piped up. "Grandma plays with us when she works."

"Yes, and we have a lovely time, don't we?" Mona turned back to Sylvia. "She's a quilter, and she heard about the Missing Quilts Home Page at her guild meeting. When she read the description of your lost Crazy Quilt, she immediately recognized mine."

Sylvia felt a pang at Mona's last word, though she was right to use it. The quilt did belong to Mona. "I'm very grateful you contacted me," she said. "I'm also quite curious. How did you come to own it?"

"By a very circuitous route," said Mona with a laugh. "This quilt has had an eventful life since leaving your household.

"On your way through town, you passed a lovely old brownstone called the Landenhurst Center. It was refurbished into an office building during the eighties, but back in the sixties and seventies, it was a theater for the performing arts. A lovely place, too—velvet curtains, ornate paintings and carvings, two balconies, and private boxes for the local gentry—but the acoustics were far from ideal and the roof leaked, and after the new civic center opened, its time had passed.

"The founders of this theater, Arthur and Christine Landen-hurst, were rising stars in vaudeville at a time when vaudeville was going the way of the buggy whip. They traveled from town to town performing their comedy act on a variety of stages—nothing terri-bly grand, of course, but fame and fortune seemed only the next performance away. They had both been married to other people, people who were not performers and thus did not understand them at all, or so Arthur and Christine thought. They fell passionately in love with each other, and one night, after a particularly successful performance in front of a scout from a New York theater who promised them they could be headliners, they ran off to New York, where they divorced their spouses, married each other, and eagerly anticipated their coming stardom.

"Not long after their arrival, they discovered that the theater this scout worked for was not one of the most prestigious. According to the story, it was one of the seediest in the city. Christine and Arthur needed a year to get out of their contract, and almost another year to find a better one, but that, too, was short-lived. Both tried to find work on Broadway, never managing to get more than bit parts, but they persisted, until one day they realized they were ten years older and not one step closer to becoming headliners than the day they had arrived in New York.

"They must have realized their big breaks might never come, for when Christine was offered a role in a traveling production, she took it, and Arthur accompanied her. Eventually he won a part in the cast, too, and together they toured throughout the East Coast and parts of the Midwest, enjoying every minute on stage, but hating the travel and the unpredictability of their profession.

"They were heading West after a performance in Harrisburg, Pennsylvania, when the train was delayed for repairs. The entire company found themselves stranded in a small town with nothing to do but wait and try to enjoy the unexpected time off. Arthur and Christine decided to explore the quaint shops downtown, which is where they found your mother's quilt."

Mona reached for the quilt, and Sylvia reluctantly allowed her to take hold of one edge. "They bought it, of course," said Mona, regarding the quilt with amused fondness. She nodded to the patch cut from a linen handkerchief. "Actors are notoriously superstitious, and when they saw the monogram—the same as their own, ALC for Arthur and Christine Landenhurst—they saw it as an omen of change. I imagine they were ready to give up the road anyway, but finding this quilt gave them the push they needed. So they resumed their journey with the company and waited for another sign.

"The production was in its final week in South Bend when the sign finally came. A childhood friend of Arthur's had driven all the way from Fort Wayne, where he was a college professor, to see the couple's performance. As it happened, this friend was in a position to offer Arthur a job as a drama teacher. Arthur accepted, and so he and Christine moved to Fort Wayne."

"Arthur became a drama professor at the college?" asked Andrew.

"Well, not exactly. The job was at the local high school. But there Arthur discovered a love for teaching, as did Christine, who became a music instructor and vocal coach. Eventually they joined the college faculty, and wouldn't you know it, their acting careers finally took off. They both made numerous appearances in university theater productions, and later, they became quite popular hosts of a local television variety show. They founded the Landenhurst Theater here in Silver River, where they made their home, and they were very well regarded as patrons of the arts and pillars of the community."

"They sound like very interesting people," said Sylvia. Suddenly she didn't mind quite so much that they had owned her mother's quilt. They had purchased it honestly enough, and by its appearance, they had cared for it properly.

"That explains how it ended up in Silver River, Indiana," said Andrew, "but not how you became its owner."

"Oh yes. Please go on," said Sylvia. "Are you related to the Landenhursts?"

"No, but my husband was acquainted with them. Arthur Landenhurst died in 1984, and Christine passed away two years later. They had no children, and except for a modest percentage for the general scholarship fund at the college, they left their estate to a trust to help fund the Landenhurst Theater in perpetuity. Most of their possessions were sold to establish this trust, but others— their substantial collection of costumes and musical scores, for example, autographed photos and scripts from actors they had met, various items that seemed to have little fiscal worth but could be used as distinctive stage props—those remained in the theater, in the safekeeping of the theater board.

"Regrettably, after some time, the theater ran into financial problems, which were augmented, I'm sad to say, by the board's poor management of their finances. The board held an auction of the Landenhurst's remarkable collections in an attempt to shore up the trust, but they held off their troubles for only a few more years." Mona sighed and gathered up the quilt, and Sylvia forced herself not to cling to it. "The theater sold to a business development group. At first there were some sporadic protests from local preservationists who wanted the building to remain a theater, but even they realized it would cost a fortune to bring it up to modern standards." Mona stroked the quilt. "I have wonderful memories of that theater. Now all that remains is its name, most of its original exterior, and those belongings of the Landenhursts that were sold at auction."

"The Crazy Quilt was one of those?" asked Sylvia.

Mona smiled. "Yes. It was a prop in numerous plays over the years—*Little Women* and *Arsenic and Old Lace,* among others. It was also used in *You Can't Take It with You,* in which my eldest son appeared. He went on to become a theater major at Yale, and now he's a director."

"I can see why you wanted to keep this quilt as a memento," remarked Andrew.

"Well, everyone around here knows the legend of how the Landenhursts came to Silver River, but only a few know the story of this particular quilt, or I suspect the bidding would have gone far beyond my reach."

"How did you happen to hear the story?" asked Sylvia, with a sudden fear that Mona's tale might be no more than hearsay.

"My late husband was a lawyer," said Mona. "He was also, at one time, a member of the theater board. When Arthur and Christine up-dated their will to create the Landenhurst Trust, my husband met frequently with them and their counsel. They shared quite a few sto-ries of how they came by certain items of great sentimental value." She gave Sylvia a long look of understanding. "I suppose the only person who valued this quilt more than they did would be you."

Sylvia tried to smile. "In my case, 'sentimental value' would be an extreme understatement."

"That's why although I might own it, it truly belongs to you. To me it will never be more than a beautiful object d'art, a fond remem-brance of pleasant occasions and two people I greatly admired. To you, every piece of fabric, every stitch, every thread contains a memory of your family, of your mother. This quilt is a part of you in a way it will never be a part of me, however attached to it I might have become." She smiled. "That's why you are the only person I could conceivably sell it to."

Sylvia felt a catch in her throat. "You would let me buy it?"

Mona appeared to consider it for a moment, and then she shrugged. "For what I paid for it, and oh, perhaps a little something extra."

"I expect you to make a fair profit, of course." Sylvia worried far less that the price would be out of her reach than that Mona might change her mind.

"That's not what I mean," said Mona. "Did I mention my daughter-in-law is a quilter?"

Sylvia and Andrew began the last leg of their journey home, their spirits light. Sylvia rarely let the quilt out of her hands. She could still hardly believe that Mona had been willing to part with it for the few hundred dollars she had spent at the Landenhurst auction and the promise of a free week at camp for her daughter-in-law. "I hope you offer classes in making Crazy Quilts," said Mona wistfully as they parted. "Perhaps you can encourage her to make me a replacement."

"I'll do my best," promised Sylvia, although they both knew nothing could replace this particular quilt.

As they drove east to Pennsylvania and Elm Creek Manor, the precious quilt on Sylvia's lap, she could laugh at all her worries of the past few weeks. Her disappointment over the earlier false leads suddenly seemed insignificant. Even Bob's and Cathy's lack of enthusiasm for the news of their engagement no longer troubled her quite as much as before.

Cradling her mother's legacy in her arms, she renewed her resolve to search out the remaining four quilts wherever the trail would take her. Now that she had found one, nothing could dissuade her from pursuing every lead. Nothing could diminish her high hopes, not after the impossible had come to pass.

Nothing, she thought, until they arrived home at Elm Creek Manor and found Andrew's daughter waiting for them.

Chapter Six
1912

Eleanor sat alone in her study on the third floor of Elm Creek Manor. The unfinished quilt in her lap was too small to warm her, but she scarcely noticed the chill. If she acknowledged a discomfort as trivial as the cold, she would then have to feel all the other pain. Far better to allow her fingers to grow numb in the draft from the open window. Far better for her to grow numb everywhere.

She stroked the quilt, though she barely felt the soft cotton beneath her hands. She should have set it aside, as she had two years earlier when her hopes had last been shattered. This time, although her morning nausea had almost certainly revealed her secret weeks before she and Fred had told the family, she had waited until nearly halfway through her time before taking up the quilt again. Within a month she had quilted nearly every feathered plume, every wreath of elm leaves, every crosshatched heart, every delicate ribbon in the quilt's pure, unbroken white surface before she lost the child she had so longed to cuddle within its soft embrace.

She would set the quilt aside again, and complete it when she again had reason to do so. If she ever again had reason.

She heard the door open. "I felt a draft all the way down the hall," said Lucinda. "Why on earth is that window open?"

Because Eleanor longed for some scent of spring on the air to remind her of the promise of life. Because she no longer had any reason to take extra precautions regarding her health. Because she might see Fred, and he always reminded her that although God had denied her a child, he had given her a husband who loved and cherished her. He had brought her into a loving family, and that ought to be enough.

Instead she said, "I wanted some air."

"Then you should have accepted Fred's invitation to walk outside with him this morning rather than let all this winter chill into the house."

"Winter's over, Aunt Lucinda."

Lucinda was her father-in-law's youngest sister, only four years older than Eleanor herself, but the Bergstrom family firmly believed in using the honorific. In the five years she had been married to Fred, Eleanor had grown accustomed to their habits.

"In Pennsylvania, April does not necessarily mean the end of winter." Lucinda crossed the room and shut the window firmly, then grasped Eleanor's hands, warming them in her own. "We've had snowstorms in April that rival any in the heart of winter."

"I know. All the more reason to stay indoors." Eleanor tucked her hands into the folds of the quilt. "You forget how long I've lived here."

"No, you forget." Lucinda's voice was gentle, but resolute. "You could not be more a part of this family than if you had been born into it. You do not grieve alone. Don't shut yourself away up here, away from everyone who loves you."

Eleanor choked back the threat of tears. "To think, in my parents' home, I was so eager to turn the nursery into a study. Now I would give anything to turn this study into a nursery."

"If you mean to stay up here until such a need arises, you will be waiting a very long time. That sofa is much too narrow for both you and Fred."

Eleanor was so shocked she forgot to stifle a giggle. "Only you would joke at a time like this."

"It's a pity more people don't realize that jokes are most necessary precisely at times like this." Lucinda took Eleanor's hands again and pulled her to her feet. Eleanor felt only the slightest dull ache in her abdomen. "Come downstairs and quilt with us. If not for you, then for Clara."

Eleanor gently folded the little quilt and nodded. For reasons she could only guess, Fred's seven-year-old sister admired her and imitated her in nearly everything. Eleanor knew that all she did in these dark days would teach Clara how to respond when, inevitably, her own life was touched by sorrow.

She was about to leave the quilt behind when Lucinda said, "Bring it. It's too beautiful to go unfinished."

Wordlessly, Eleanor tucked the quilt under her arm and followed Lucinda from the room. Lucinda would not raise her hopes with false promises that someday her quilt would cuddle a little one, and Eleanor found her frankness reassuring in its familiarity. She would take her comfort wherever she could find it, for she now knew that while she had defied her childhood doctors by living far beyond their estimates, their predictions about her ability to withstand the rigors of pregnancy had thus far proven all too true.

Lucinda slowed her steps so Eleanor could easily keep pace with her as they descended the carved oak staircase in the front foyer of the manor. Her home for the past five years was nearly as grand in its own way as anything she had seen in New York, and its pastoral setting and German flavor only enhanced its beauty. It seemed ages ago that she had assumed her Freddy lived on a humble horse farm. Her parents still believed it, based on what Eleanor could interpret from her mother's brusque responses to the letters Eleanor still dutifully sent them.

They had just reached the bottom of the stairs when Eleanor heard rapid footsteps coming from the west wing. Clara burst into the foyer and dashed across the black marble floor. "Louis went for the mail," she said, breathless, and to Eleanor, added, "You have two letters. One is from New York and the other's from France!"

Eleanor would have been delighted to hear of the second letter had the first not filled her with foreboding. The letter from France must be Abigail's; she and her husband had been touring the Continent for the past month. The letter from New York was equally as certain to be from her mother, and almost as certain not to be a letter at all, but a news clipping—a society page account of a gala event where Edwin Corville and his wife had danced and dined with foreign royalty, a business report of Corville's lucrative expansion throughout the Eastern seaboard. Mother rarely added anything in her own hand except in spite and unless the article discussed Drury-Lockwood, Incorporated, which was, if Mother's caustic notes were to be believed, a misnomer.

"We'll meet you in the west sitting room," said Lucinda, drawing a disappointed Clara away. The girl had never ventured farther from home than Philadelphia, and she loved to hear stories from far-off places. She seemed to believe Eleanor had visited the locales she had only learned about from books, no matter how often Eleanor told her the truth.

Alone, Eleanor sat down on the bottom step and decided to open her mother's envelope first, to dispense with whatever insult it contained. Fred said she ought to discard them unopened, but Eleanor could not bear to risk destroying a letter of forgiveness, should it one day come.

She withdrew a newspaper clipping and read only enough of the article to learn that Mr. and Mrs. Edwin Corville had been blessed with a baby boy. Her heart pounded as she read what her mother had appended to the bottom with bold strokes of black ink: "What has your husband given you but shame and grief? What have you given him?"

Eleanor crumpled paper and envelope and, resisting the urge to fling them aside, tucked them into her pocket. She would put them on the fire at the earliest opportunity. She would not have Fred see them for the world.

How foolish she had been to hope that her mother's anger

would lessen with the years. Did she send the same hateful letters to Abigail? Abigail had never mentioned any, but of course, Mother had no need of letters when she could make her anger apparent in person. Abigail had written of at least a dozen society engagements where Mother and Father had departed as soon as she and Mr. Drury arrived. Abigail wrote little more of their parents, even when Eleanor asked for news, filling her letters instead with tales of her life as mistress of the Drury household.

April 2, 1912

Dear Eleanor,

By the time you receive this letter, Herbert and I may be on our way home. Do not worry; my health and that of your niece or nephew is quite good, but my condition is becoming too noticeable for me to enjoy our tour of the Continent much longer. I do not mind cutting our trip short as much as you might think, as I will find much to console me in decorating the nursery.

Paris was beautiful, as lovely as I remembered. I can almost hear you laugh at that, since my last visit occurred in the height of spring, a season that, as I write this, has only just begun to appear. You will say that my view of this romantic city has been colored by my delight in my husband and my anticipation of our child. Well, all I have to say to that is . . . you are absolutely correct. I find more joy in a sky full of rain now than I ever did on the balmiest summer day before I married. I have no doubt you know exactly what I mean. You are the only person in the world who understands what it was like to live in that cold house. If not for you, I never could have borne it. And this may sound contradictory, but if not for you, I also could not bear being shut out of it forever.

If you had any idea how much I worried about you and ached to hear from you when you left home, you would forgive me every thoughtless thing I ever did to you. I know you have long ago forgiven me for abandoning you when I left home. I suppose that came easily to you, since if I had married Edwin, you probably never would have married Fred! If only Mother and Father would follow your example. Father gets a good living from Herbert. One would think he would be grateful, but of course that is not Father's way.

Please promise me you will come to see me when the child is born. Five years is too long for sisters to be apart when modern conveniences have made travel so safe and comfortable. Bring Fred if you like; Herbert is fond of him, and I would like to know him better. If you wish to avoid Mother and Father, that is easily done; our parents avoid engagements they suspect I might attend. Will gifts tempt you? If so, know that I have a liberal allowance and spent it freely on the Champs-Elysées. If you want your gifts, I insist that you collect them from me yourself.

I have so much to tell you about our travels that I have no patience to put it into a letter, so you must come to me so I can tell you everything. There is one incident I must share now, however, because it amused and yet so affronted me that I hardly know what to make of it. In Germany we attended a ball to honor a certain count who had been awarded a great honor by the Kaiser—I do not recall the name of either the count or the honor, and I make no apology for my ignorance because both were in German. I do not believe even you comprehend a word of that language, although on second thought, perhaps you have acquired fluency living with Fred's family.

At this ball, I was introduced to an old dear from a very respected and influential English family, good friends of the

Drurys, who told me she was very pleased to see me again. I knew we had never met, but rather than offend her by saying so, I merely smiled and steered the conversation elsewhere. She spoke to me quite kindly whenever our paths crossed that evening, and when Herbert and I were about to depart, she clasped my hand and said, "I was so sorry to hear your mother passed. I was very fond of her."

You can imagine my shock upon discovering in this manner that our mother had perished—and now I realize that I may have given you that same fright! Eleanor, dear, our own mother is alive if not well; the "mother" the Englishwoman mourned was Herbert's first wife. The dear lady thought I was his daughter! I wanted to laugh although I was mortified, for my condition was apparent then if not so obvious as now, and since she did not know Herbert was my husband, she must have wondered if I had one at all! Still, her remark was innocent and not offensive, unlike those of many Americans we have encountered in our travels, who seem to find my condition scandalous even when they know full well Herbert and I are man and wife.

How much more I would enjoy confiding these secrets to you in person than through the post. Do promise you will come and see me when the baby's arrival is imminent. If gifts will not tempt you, then perhaps you will think instead of what a coward I am and how I dread the travail that awaits. If you could be by my side, lending me your strength as you always have, I think I shall be able to endure it. You may think me cruel to play to your sympathetic heart so, but if guilt shall speed you to my side, then I must be cruel!

I am not accustomed to writing such long letters, and my hand has grown weary, so I must close. Tomorrow we are off to England, where I shall be certain to collect a vial of earth from the home of Jane Austen, as you requested. You do ask for such silly things. I think I shall buy you a tea service as well, though you did not ask for it. You will never see it, of course, unless you return to New York. Please do ask Fred if you might come.

So tomorrow to England, and after a week, from Southampton to home. Would you be so kind to have a letter waiting there for

Your Loving Sister,
Abigail

Eleanor smiled as she returned the letter to its envelope, warmed by Abigail's happiness but well aware of how it cast her own sorrow into greater relief. She wished she could unburden herself to her sister, but Abigail had scolded her after she lost the first two babies and would certainly be even more vehement if she learned Eleanor had not abandoned her hopes for a child. In Abigail's opinion, Eleanor knew the doctors' warnings and ought to heed them. "If Fred loves you as much as you say," she had written, "I cannot believe he would demand a child of you if it might cost you your life."

Eleanor had hastened to assure her that Fred had never made any such demand, but the news of her first pregnancy had so delighted him that she knew he longed for a child as much as she did. He had responded to her subsequent pregnancies with guarded optimism and comforted her tenderly when they ended in grief. This time, however, he had also gently suggested that they resign themselves to their childless state rather than risk her health again.

She wondered if she could ever resign herself. She longed for a sympathetic friend in whom she could confide, someone who might advise her. She would have turned to Miss Langley, but her former nanny agreed with Abigail regarding Eleanor's yearning for a child.

Moreover, she was not especially receptive to any talk of Fred, since although she approved of Eleanor's decision to flee her parents' home, she could not hide her disappointment that Eleanor had married instead of pursuing her education. The only other women Eleanor knew well enough to confide in were members of Fred's family, and somehow, even sharing her worries with Lucinda seemed a breach of his confidence.

She gathered up the unfinished quilt, slipped Abigail's letter into her pocket, and tried to close off her grief in a distant corner of her mind as she went to join Lucinda and the others. She passed through the kitchen on her way to the west sitting room, and Mother's news clipping quickly turned to ash on the fire.

Fred's mother, Elizabeth, looked up and smiled encouragingly as Eleanor took her usual chair by the window. Maude and Lily broke off their conversation and studied their needlework intently, giving Eleanor only quick nods of welcome. In a surge of bitterness, Eleanor wondered if her sisters-in-law feared they might suffer her same unhappy fate if they acknowledged it. Even Elizabeth, the most superstitious woman Eleanor had ever met, did not believe that.

Clara left her mother's side and seated herself on Eleanor's footstool. "Would you like me to thread a needle for you?"

Eleanor smiled and thanked her. She let Clara borrow the heron-shaped shears Miss Langley had given her and slipped her thimble on her finger.

"I'm pleased you're going to finish your quilt," said Maude. She had married the second eldest of the Bergstrom sons, Louis, the previous spring, and with her first anniversary approaching, she had decided to learn to quilt to make an anniversary gift for her husband. Elizabeth had encouraged her to choose a simple Nine-Patch, but after seeing a picture in the *Ladies' Home Journal,* Maude had fallen in love with a stunning appliquéd Sunflower quilt designed by renowned quilter Marie Webster. Privately, the other women of the family agreed she would be lucky to finish even a small fraction of it in time, but no one wanted to discourage her newfound interest in their beloved craft, and since Maude did not want to settle for a simpler block, they decided to let her go her own way.

"Perhaps she will learn better, learning from her mistakes," Elizabeth had said with a sigh.

"Perhaps," Lucinda had agreed, "and perhaps this quilt will be a gift for their tenth anniversary instead of their first."

Eleanor had joined in the laughter. It had been so much easier to laugh then, when she had just begun to feel life stirring within her womb and every stitch she put into the soft, white whole cloth quilt was another prayer for the health and safety of the precious child she carried.

Eleanor gazed at the quilt. "I don't like to leave work unfinished." In a flash of inspiration, she added, "I've decided to give this to my sister when her child is born."

"You can't do that," said Lily in dismay. "You've worked so hard on it, and you're going to need it yourself someday."

Eleanor smiled fondly at her sister-in-law, her earlier bitterness forgotten. Lily's characteristic optimism was as welcome as Lucinda's frankness. "Perhaps I will," she said, "but my sister has such a good head start that her child will definitely be born first, and I have no quilt for him. Or her. The only other quilt I have under way is the Turkey Tracks—"

"Absolutely not," said Elizabeth, not even looking up from her work. "Under no circumstances should a child be given a Wandering Foot quilt."

Lucinda caught Eleanor's eye and grinned. "She said Turkey Tracks, not Wandering Foot."

"You know very well that they are one and the same." Elizabeth looked up from her work and realized they were teasing her. "Suit yourselves, then," she said, shrugging. "If you want to condemn a poor innocent child to a lifetime of restlessness and wandering, then I can't stop you."

"Quilt or no quilt, I would not be surprised if the child has a bit of wanderlust," said Lucinda. "It seems to run in the family."

The other women laughed, and even Eleanor managed a smile.

Later that evening, after she prepared for bed, she read Abigail's letter again, hungry for news of their parents. Mother was alive if not well, Abigail had written, but Eleanor had read enough similarly derisive comments to know that the remark pertained to Abigail's general opinion of their mother and not to her current health. She was not surprised to hear that their parents still avoided Abigail in society, or that Abigail still seemed genuinely astonished that their parents did not appreciate how she had resolved their financial difficulties. Within months of marrying Abigail and the dissolution of any possible agreement with the Corvilles, Mr. Drury had purchased Lockwood's and had assumed responsibility for Father's debts. He had made Father a vice president, and in an overture of reconciliation that Eleanor had found remarkable at the time, he had kept the Lockwood name in the title of the new company. Since then, as she pieced together the scraps of information her sister let fall, Eleanor had come to believe that Mr. Drury's ostensible generosity had masked one last stab of revenge against his former rival. As best as Eleanor had been able to determine, Father had been given very little work to do, and although he received an impressive salary, he had no influence whatsoever. Sometimes Eleanor wondered if Father would have preferred to go into bankruptcy with his pride intact, but she knew her mother never would have allowed it. It was bad enough that their position in society had been irreparably damaged by the scandal; they should not also have to endure financial ruin.

Eleanor had pen and paper in the nightstand; she could write to Abigail and ask outright how their parents fared, and satisfy both her curiosity and Abigail's request for a letter at the same time. She would have, except she knew Abigail would ignore her questions or respond so breezily that she might as well not have bothered.

She climbed into bed and blew out the lamp, pulling the Rocky Mountain quilt over her. She and Fred had slept beneath it every night of their marriage, even when it was not yet complete. Lately she had fallen asleep beneath it alone more often than not.

She was not sure how many hours later Fred inadvertently woke her as he pulled back the covers. When she stirred, he kissed her and murmured an apology. "It's all right," she said as he lay down beside her at last. "I'm glad you woke me. I haven't seen you all day, except at supper."

"I'm sorry. I've been busy."

"Doing what?"

"You could come outside and see for yourself tomorrow."

"Or you could simply tell me, if you weren't so stubborn."

"Oh. So I'm the stubborn one." He kissed her gently and shifted onto his back, settling against the pillow. He let out a long sigh.

Eleanor knew he was exhausted, but she could not let go just yet. "I heard from my sister today."

"Is she well?"

"She is. She and Herbert are returning from Europe soon." She steeled herself. "She wants me to come when her child is born. I thought I might go. If I can be spared."

She did not mean if Bergstrom Thoroughbreds could do without her. Although everyone was expected to contribute to the family business, the others would divide up her work so that her absence would be little noticed. She meant if Fred could spare her, if the man who had sworn never to leave her side would willingly or eagerly let her go so far away.

"That would be in the middle of August?"

"Unless the child is early. I thought I should be prepared to leave at the beginning of the month, if necessary."

"That's not a good time for me to be away."

"Well, no," said Eleanor, surprised. "I assumed I would go alone. Perhaps Clara could accompany me."

"My sister's a level-headed girl, but she's still just a child," said Fred. "I was thinking of someone who might look after you."

"I'm perfectly capable of looking after myself."

"I know you are," he said quickly. "Well, Clara would be thrilled, and she's a good helper. How long will you be gone?"

She had not decided. "A month, perhaps more."

"That long?" He drew her into his arms. "Maybe I can get away for a few days and visit you in New York."

"That would be nice."

"We could see your parents, if you like."

"I don't think we would be welcome."

"Would they turn us away at the door?"

"I doubt they would even let us pass through the front gates."

He stroked her hair and held her close. "Then we'll leave them alone."

Clara was as thrilled by the upcoming trip to New York as Fred had predicted, and Elizabeth readily granted her permission to accompany Eleanor. The women of the family agreed that at such a time as Abigail would soon face, no woman fortunate enough to have a sister wanted to be without her. "Or without her mother," added Lily, and blushed, remembering too late the state of affairs among the Lockwood women.

"I cannot imagine my mother would be much comfort," said Eleanor, smiling to show Lily she had not taken offense.

"Then you must go, as much as we will miss you," said Elizabeth. "Have you ever assisted in childbirth?"

"No, but fortunately Abigail won't need to rely entirely upon me," said Eleanor with a laugh. "A doctor and at least one nurse will be present. I don't plan to do anything more than comfort my sister and be one of the first to cuddle the newborn."

"Even the best doctors sometimes overlook important remedies," said Elizabeth. "Or rather, they dismiss them as silly folk tales. If you do arrive in time for the delivery, remember to place a knife beneath your sister's bed. That will cut the pain."

"Cut the pain?"

"Will any sort of knife do, or does it have to be a special knife?" inquired Lucinda. "What would happen if you used a spoon instead?"

"Tease me if you must," retorted Elizabeth, "but there was a knife beneath my bed for every child I bore except for Louis, and his birth was by far the longest and most painful."

"Of course it was," said Maude. "He was nearly ten pounds."

"He's your husband, so your children will probably be large, too. You'll be begging for a knife then, and it would serve you right if I made you do without."

"I'll put a knife under your bed for you, Maude," said Clara loyally, but after glancing at Eleanor, added, "Maybe it doesn't help, but it couldn't hurt, either."

Clara spent the next several days in the library, reading everything she could find about New York City. Within a day she had composed an impressive list of all the sights she wished to see, and Eleanor was pleased to discover that many of her favorite museums and landmarks were included.

"We'll have plenty of time for sightseeing," Eleanor promised one evening later that week as the women of the family gathered in the west sitting room for a last bit of quilting before bed. "Unless I can't finish this quilt in time and have to sneak away to complete it while Abigail tends to the baby."

"A whole cloth quilt is the perfect choice for a baby's first quilt," said Elizabeth. "Its unbroken surface suggests purity and innocence. Whole cloth quilts are well suited for newborns and for brides."

"What does it matter, as long as the quilt is pretty?" asked Lily.

"It matters a great deal," said Elizabeth. "Think of the symbolism, the omens in a quilt. What would you think if a bride pieced her wedding quilt in the Contrary Wife or Crazy House or Devil's Claws pattern? It would be far better for her to choose something like Steps to the Altar or True Lover's Knot."

"You're absolutely right," said Lucinda.

Elizabeth regarded her with surprise. "Why, this is a novelty. You agree with me?"

"Of course," said Lucinda. "Can you imagine, for example, if a bride chose Tumbling Blocks? That pattern is also called Baby Blocks, and everyone would gossip about why she had to get married."

"Lucinda," said Elizabeth over the others' laughter, "if you weren't my dear husband's baby sister, I would give you the scolding you deserve."

"Don't let that stop you." Lucinda shrugged. "What do I care what pattern a bride chooses for her wedding quilt, so long as it isn't yet another floral appliqué with bows and birds and butterflies and—oops. Sorry, Maude."

"This isn't my wedding quilt," said Maude primly, struggling to put a sharp point on the petal of another Sunflower block. "And while I might add a few butterflies if I am so inclined, you won't find any birds or bows here. Not that I'd let you influence me. If it's good enough for the *Ladies' Home Journal,* then it's good enough for me, and it would be good enough for you, too, if you weren't so prideful."

"Who's prideful?" protested Lucinda. "I like the *Ladies' Home Journal.* I like it even more now that they're going to publish Eleanor's whole cloth quilt pattern."

"What?" exclaimed Eleanor.

"Now look what you made me do," Lucinda complained to Maude. "It was supposed to be a surprise."

"It is a surprise," said Eleanor. "Believe me, it is."

Maude shook her head. "This must be another one of Lucinda's jokes."

"Not at all," said Lucinda. "I thought we could all use a bit of cheering up around here, so I copied Eleanor's pattern and sent it to the editor. It's such a beautiful, original design, so I thought, why not share it with the world?" She smiled kindly at Eleanor. "I didn't know if you would have the heart to finish your own quilt, and it seemed a shame not to have someone, somewhere completing it."

Eleanor reached out and clasped her hand. "That was thoughtful of you."

"Not really. I just wanted to brag about my famous niece."

Clara said, "Eleanor's going to be famous?"

"Of course," said Lucinda. "This is the *Ladies' Home Journal*, after all. Eleanor's name will be right up there at the top of the page with the picture of her quilt, just like Marie Webster and that Sunflower quilt Maude is making."

"Will her picture be there, too?"

"I don't think I want my picture in a magazine," said Eleanor, a nervous quake in her stomach. "Or even my name."

"Why not?" asked Clara.

Eleanor forced a laugh. "I suppose so no one will know where to send their criticism. Can't they show my quilt without mentioning me?"

She regretted her words when she saw the disappointment in their faces. "I suppose I should have asked your permission first," said Lucinda. "But I'm sure they would let you use merely your initials, or a pseudonym, if you prefer."

"Aren't you proud of your quilt?" asked Clara. "I think you should be."

"I am proud of it," said Eleanor. "And I'm very grateful that Lucinda thought enough of my quilt to send it to the magazine. And I'm thrilled that it's going to be published. However, I would prefer to be all those things and anonymous, too."

She saw from the looks they exchanged that they did not understand, but they let her be. Elizabeth would think her too modest; Maude would think it false modesty and another sign of her pride. Lucinda and Lily would respect her decision, but they would wonder why she had made it. Dear, insightful Clara would probably figure out the reason before anyone else, perhaps before Eleanor herself.

She wondered what Fred would think.

Fred worked through supper and missed Lucinda's announcement to the rest of the family. The other men congratulated Eleanor and agreed that publication in a national magazine was quite an accomplishment, although her father-in-law looked bemused and remarked that he thought quilters did not like others to duplicate their unique designs. "My mother, especially, was adamant about not copying other women's quilts," said David. "Though I remember my Aunt Gerda once whispered to me that my mother had done her fair share of copying when she was a new quilter."

"Everyone learns to quilt by copying other quilters' patterns," said Lily. "Just like painters learn by studying the old masters."

Louis and William guffawed at the comparison, earning themselves frowns from the quilters at the table. Those for William were milder because he was only a few years older than Clara; Louis, however, knew better, as his wife's steely glare made clear. Eleanor hid a smile and wondered if Maude would now consider adding a few Contrary Wife blocks to her Sunflower quilt.

"Perhaps copying another quilter's work without permission is wrong," said Eleanor, "but duplicating her quilt with her consent is another matter entirely. I wouldn't allow my quilt to appear in a magazine if I didn't want other quilters to make it."

In fact, now that the shock of Lucinda's surprise had passed, she was becoming more excited about the thought of opening a magazine and seeing a picture of her quilt inside. She knew, too, that Abigail would be all the more thrilled by the gift, knowing that her baby's quilt had been featured in a national magazine. Eleanor's desire for anonymity would be thwarted in New York, at least, for Abigail was certain to tell everyone she knew.

For a very brief moment, she considered sending her mother a clipping with a note pointing out that none of Mrs. Edwin Corville's quilts had ever received such an honor, but given her mother's distaste for quilting, that would only prove how low Eleanor had fallen.

After supper, she finished quilting the whole cloth quilt and trimmed the batting and lining even with the scalloped edges of the top. For the binding, she cut a long, narrow strip of fabric along the bias rather than the straight of the grain so that the binding would ease along the curves and miters of the fancy edge. Fred came in as she was pinning the binding in place, hair windblown, hands dirty from working outdoors, but he had only stopped by to say hello, so there was no time to tell him her good news. He kissed her on the cheek and told her he wouldn't be late, then left the room as quickly as he had entered.

Later that night, Fred roused Eleanor just moments after she doused the lamp. "Come with me," he said. "It's done. Let me show you."

"Show me what?" she asked. "A new fence? That addition to the stable you and your brothers are always talking about?"

"No, something much better." He pulled back the quilt and took her hands. "At least I hope you'll think so."

Curious, she climbed out of bed and dressed for the chilly spring night. Quietly, Fred led her into the hallway past his siblings' rooms, and as they descended the stairs, Eleanor was struck by a sudden remembrance of another night five years earlier and another flight of stairs she had stolen down in the darkness. Eleanor wondered if Fred ever thought of that night and wished her family had awakened and prevented her from leaving with him. She did not doubt his love for her, but he would have had children if he had married any other woman.

He led her across the foyer, into the west wing of the manor, and paused at the west door. This had once been the front entrance of the Bergstrom home, before Fred's father had added the grand south wing with its banquet hall and ballroom. Fred took both of her hands in his and watched her expectantly. "Are you ready?"

"Of course," she said, but as he opened the door, she dug in her heels. "Fred, no. It's so late. It's too dark and cold now. You can show me in the morning."

"Eleanor." His voice was gentle, but commanding. "You're coming outside."

With no other choice, she took a deep breath and stepped outside—but instead of bare earth, her foot struck smooth stone. A patio of gray stones nearly identical to those forming the walls of the manor lay where rocky soil and sparse clumps of grass had been only weeks before. Surrounding the expanse of stone were tall bushes and evergreens, enclosing the intimate space completely except for one opening through which Eleanor spied the beginning of a stone trail winding north.

"That path leads to the gazebo in the gardens, and to the stables beyond them," said Fred. "The lilac bushes don't look like much now, but when they flower in the spring, this place will be so pretty—you'll see. We'll have flowers before then, though." He gestured to the freshly turned earth lining the patio. "Those are dahlias and irises, and these over here are gladiolus. They'll come up before September."

"I love lilacs," she said, slowly turning and taking in the patio. It felt enclosed, sheltered. Safe. "Dahlias, too."

"Look over here." He knelt and pointed to the northeast corner of the manor. "That's the cornerstone of Elm Creek Manor. The entire estate was founded on this very spot."

"'Bergstrom 1858,'" Eleanor read aloud, and as Fred continued to describe the features of the garden he had created just for her, Eleanor could picture in her mind's eye how lovely it would be in midsummer when the bulbs bloomed, and how the evergreens would bring a spot of color to the landscape even in the depths of winter. A year hence, the lilacs would fill the air with their fragrance.

"I'll make some chairs next," said Fred. "I also thought about putting some benches along the two sides, or maybe along the house. What do you think?"

"Why, Fred?"

He pretended not to understand. "So we can have some place to sit."

"No, Fred. Why? Why did you do all this—for me?"

"Because I love you, and I can't stand to see you making the house into your prison. I would make you a thousand gardens if that's what it took to get you to come outside again."

She stared at him. "I have no idea what you're talking about."

"Don't you? Eleanor, you haven't set foot beyond the foyer since the day we lost the baby. You've wondered why I wouldn't tell you what I was working on all this time. I had hoped your curiosity would compel you outside. Two months ago, you never would have watched from the windows instead of coming out to see what I was doing."

"I've been tired." Her voice shook, and she turned away from him. "I'm still recuperating."

"I'm not asking you to work with the horses yet, just to leave the house for a while." He spun her around to face him. "Eleanor, it's not your fault. You heard what the doctor said. You didn't do anything to harm the baby."

"But I did. I did. I should have rested, I should have taken care of myself—"

"You took excellent care of yourself."

"No. No. I didn't. I came outside, I took walks, all for selfish reasons. I wanted to see the new colts, or I wanted to play in the snow with Clara . . . I should have stayed inside, in bed or by the fire—"

"Nothing you did hurt the baby. My own mother rode horseback and worked the farm when she—"

"But your mother had never lost a child. I had, so I should have known better. After I lost our first two babies, I should have done everything—everything—to make sure I didn't fail you again."

"My God, Eleanor, you didn't fail me." He reached out for her, but she avoided his embrace. "You nearly died. Do you think I could ever be angry with you after that? Do you think I care more about being a father than about spending the rest of my life with you?"

"I'm so sorry, Fred."

"Listen to me. You didn't do anything wrong. Maybe we aren't meant to have children. If that's true, we still have each other, and that's all I ever wanted."

"Fred." She steeled herself. "I told you before we married that I did not think I could bear children. You said it didn't matter, but it does. If you want to divorce me—"

"Never." For the first time, she heard a trace of anger in his voice. "Don't ever say that again. Did you marry me only to become a mother?"

"I—" No. She had thought only of him, of choosing her fate instead of letting her parents and Edwin Corville determine it for her. But the assumption that she could not have children mattered less to her as a girl of seventeen than it did now that she had built a life with the man she loved. "I married you because I loved you."

"The reasons we married are reasons to stay married. Please don't ever suggest we divorce unless it's what you truly want."

"It will never be what I want."

She buried her face in his chest and wept as she had not when she lost the last baby, for she had been too stunned for tears, too unable to comprehend that God could visit this same terrible grief upon her a third time.

Fred held her and murmured words of comfort, but his voice trembled, and she knew he also wept.

"Life goes on, Eleanor," he said. "I know it sounds trite, but it's true. Life goes on not only for us, but for our family."

She nodded. A faint hope kindled in her heart. Life went on—Fred's siblings would have children. Abigail's child would enter the world by late summer. Life would go on, and she and Fred would be a part of those lives.

"We've already been through the most difficult, most painful times we will ever face," he said. "From this point forward, we don't have to fear anything, because we've already survived the worst."

"I hope you're right." She prayed he was right.

Less than a week later, she sat on the smooth stone of the cornerstone patio enjoying the first truly warm, sunny day of that rainy spring. She sat with the women of her family chatting and planning for the summer, for the summer and beyond. She put the last stitch into the binding of the whole cloth quilt and held it up for the others to admire. They praised her, and Eleanor felt warmth returning to her heart as she imagined cradling her little niece or nephew within its soft folds.

Clara sat by her side, working on her most difficult quilt yet, and Eleanor was so engrossed in helping her with the appliqué and answering her questions about New York that a few moments passed before she realized that the others had fallen silent. She looked up to discover Louis whispering into his mother's ear; Elizabeth suddenly went pale, and her hand went to her throat.

"What is it?" asked Lucinda as Louis raced off down the stone path toward the stables.

Elizabeth pressed her lips together tightly and fumbled for her handkerchief, lowering her head so none of them could meet her gaze. Louis rode into town each day for the mail and the papers; he must have brought home terrible news. Clara's face was full of worry. Eleanor stroked her hair reassuringly and tried to resume their conversation, but Clara was too distracted to respond.

Eleanor grew faint when, barely minutes later, Louis returned with Fred. Both men's faces were grave, but behind Fred's eyes she saw a pain she had not seen since her last baby died.

"What is it?" she tried to ask, but the words dried up in her throat.

"Eleanor." Fred knelt beside her and took her hands in his. They felt almost unbearably warm against the ice of her skin. "Your sister sailed from Southampton on the tenth, isn't that right?"

"Yes." She looked from him to Louis and back. "They're probably still at sea. Why?"

"Do you remember the name of her ship?"

"I—I don't recall. I would have to check her letters. Why? What has happened?"

"Two nights ago, a ship sailing from Southampton to New York struck an iceberg and sank in the North Atlantic. Only a few hundred souls were spared."

"No. No." She shook her head. "That could not be Abigail's ship. She wrote me—Herbert told her it was a marvel of engineering. It was designed to be unsinkable. It could not be Abigail's ship. Mother would have sent a telegram." Despite their estrangement, Mother would have sent word, Eleanor repeated silently to herself, though she knew such things took time, and if the accident had only just happened, there would be passenger lists to be sorted out, next of kin to notify— Abigail. Abigail and her baby.

"Eleanor." Fred's voice called to her, quietly insistent. "Was her ship called the *Titanic*?"

"I don't remember." She did not want to remember. She could not believe it; she would not believe it. She took a deep breath and closed her eyes to clear her head of dizziness. It swept over her, crowding out her resolve to forget the name of her sister's ship for as long as possible, and in the space between breaths she went from believing that Abigail's ship was not the one that sank to praying that Abigail had been among the handful of survivors. Women and children were always the first into the lifeboats; surely a woman in Abigail's condition would have been among the very first even of these. Surely Mr. Drury, with his wealth and influence, would have seen to Abigail's safety.

In the days and weeks that followed, Eleanor would read reports of women who refused seats in half-filled lifeboats rather than leave their husbands behind. She would hear rumors that near the end, survivors had witnessed a beautiful, golden-haired woman sitting on the first-class deck, staring out at the sea with unseeing eyes, one hand absently stroking her swelling abdomen, her husband weeping on her shoulder.

Eleanor prayed for a miracle she knew would not be granted.

The family gathered in the parlor on the day the passenger manifest they had requested finally arrived. With it was the list of survivors. Abigail and her husband were not among them.

"Why did she not leave when she had the chance?" said Eleanor. Fred's arm was around her, sustaining her; the whole cloth quilt lay upon her lap. She had scarcely let it from her grasp since first learning of the disaster. The papers from the White Star Line lay on the floor where they had slipped from her fingers.

"Her love for her husband was too great," said Lily in a soft voice. "She could not bear to be parted from him."

"Not even for their child?" Eleanor could not believe it of Abigail;

she could not bear to believe it. Perhaps Abigail refused to take her place in the lifeboat because she did not fully comprehend the danger. Perhaps she thought her child more at risk on the open sea. Perhaps by the time she understood, it was too late. "I know my sister," said Eleanor firmly, though her voice trembled. Instinctively, she clutched the quilt to her chest. "She would not have chosen death with her husband over her child's life. Never."

"Will you let go of that thing?" shrilled Elizabeth. Before Eleanor could react, Elizabeth had crossed the room and snatched the quilt away. "I will throw this wretched thing on the fire. You should have destroyed it after you lost the first baby."

"Give that back to me."

"I won't. Don't you see? Every baby you intend it for has died. It's bad luck."

"Mother," said Fred, rising, "this quilt had nothing to do with any of these tragedies."

"Elizabeth, you don't know what you're saying." David's voice was calm, but firm, as he addressed his wife. "Return the quilt to Eleanor at once."

Elizabeth clenched her teeth against a low moan, but she did not struggle as Fred and David pried the quilt from her white-knuckled grasp. Eleanor examined the quilt for rents and folded it with shaking hands. Her heart pounded, and a sudden flash of pain left her breathless.

"Destroy it or I will," Elizabeth choked out. "I swear to you, no grandchild of mine will ever sleep beneath that quilt."

"Be quiet, Elizabeth," commanded Lucinda. To Eleanor, she murmured, "Get the quilt out of her sight until she comes to her senses."

Eleanor nodded and fled upstairs to her bedroom to hide the quilt, knowing the light of day would not shine on it while Elizabeth lived. The risk that she would destroy Eleanor's only remembrance of Abigail's child was too great. Her heart ached as she buried the quilt at the bottom of her cedar chest, blinded by tears. Oh, Abigail. How could she have spurned the lifeboats, knowing that her death meant the death of her child?

The pounding ache in her heart subsided, and a fire kindled within Eleanor as she locked the trunk and wiped her eyes, her resolution stronger even than that which had compelled her to leave her parents' home forever. She would have a child, and she would live for that child. And Abigail's name would not be forgotten.

No telegram from her parents ever came.

Chapter Seven

"She knows," said Andrew as he and Sylvia watched through the windshield as Amy approached the motor home.

"I'd imagine so," said Sylvia dryly. "I thought you said Bob can keep a secret."

"He can. I don't understand it. He promised me he wouldn't tell."

"Did you remember to get that same promise from Cathy?"

Andrew drew in a breath and winced. "Put your seat belt back on. We're getting out of here."

"I'm afraid it's too late for that." Sylvia rose, shouldered her tote bag with the Crazy Quilt and library printouts inside, and nudged Andrew to his feet.

Amy met them halfway to the house, her arms crossed, her mouth a thin, worried line.

"Amy, dear," said Sylvia. "I suppose it's too much to hope that you've come all this way to congratulate us."

In lieu of an answer, Amy reached for one of the suitcases her father carried. "Let me help you with that."

Andrew set one of the suitcases on the ground, but he continued on to the manor without a word for his daughter. Sylvia gave Amy an apologetic look and fell in beside him.

Amy trailed after them. "Dad, I want you to be happy. I want to be happy for you, but . . ."

"But what?"

"This isn't a conversation I wanted to have in front of Sylvia."

Sylvia did her best to conceal her annoyance. "Pretend I'm not here."

Amy frowned and shrugged as if to say Sylvia had been fairly warned. "Dad, we all know you care about Sylvia."

"I don't just care about her. I love her."

"Of course you do. We understand that." Amy reached for his hand, but Andrew merely opened the back door and waved her inside. "But we wonder if you've thought about what marriage would mean."

"Considering I was married to your mother for more than fifty years, I think I have a good idea."

"I think maybe you have a selective memory," countered Amy. "You and Mom were very happy for a long time, but think about those last three years. Dad, we can't bear to see you go through that again."

Andrew took the suitcase from her and set the pair down with a heavy thud in the hallway. "You mean when your mother had cancer."

"You never complained, but we know how difficult it was to care for her." Amy glanced at Sylvia, then quickly looked away. "Do you really want to put yourself through that again?"

"Sylvia does not have cancer."

"No, but she's already had one stroke and could have another any—"

"All right. Enough," said Andrew. "Sylvia is in excellent health, and so am I, but even if that were to change tomorrow, I would still want to marry her. That's what marriage is about—in sickness and in health, remember?"

"You've already grieved for one wife. You shouldn't have to mourn a second time."

"How do you know that I will? For all you know, Sylvia will outlive me."

Amy gave Sylvia a guarded look. "Maybe she will. We all would love for you to have many, many years together. But the end is going to be the same."

Andrew shook his head. "And it's the same end you and Paul are going to face, and Bob and Cathy. Does that mean you shouldn't have gotten married? If being by your mother's side throughout her illness taught me anything, it showed me that nothing matters but sharing your life with the people you love. Your mother had a great love of life. I'm ashamed that in her memory, you want me to curl up in a corner and wait to die."

Amy flushed. "That's not what I meant—"

"Listen—and you can pass this along to your brother—I don't know how many years I've got left, and neither do you. I'm going to spend them with Sylvia with or without your approval."

"Dad—"

"I love Sylvia, and my feelings aren't going to change. I'm going to mourn her whether she's my wife or my friend, so she might as well be my wife." He strode down the hall, but paused at the door. "I'm going to get the rest of our gear and check the engine. Amy, you're a good girl and I love you, but you ought to know better. You're welcome to stay as long as you like, but I expect you to treat Sylvia with respect. Your mother and I didn't raise you to be rude to people when you don't get your own way."

Amy's cheeks were scarlet as she watched her father depart.

Sylvia sighed and reminded herself it would be unwise to take Amy's reaction personally. Andrew's children would be just as difficult if he were engaged to a woman half her age—in fact, in that case, they might be even more upset. She doubted, however, that telling Amy to count her blessings would help matters.

"Amy dear," said Sylvia carefully. "I have no intention of becoming a burden to your father. Yes, I did have a stroke several years ago, but my doctor assures me I am in good health. However, should that change, I have resources enough to ensure that the burden of my care will not fall upon your father. Sarah and Matt are like my own children, and they will see I am looked after."

"It's not just the caregiving. It's the emotional toll of losing you that we're most worried about."

Sylvia raised her eyebrows. "So you would prefer for him to lose me now? I'm sorry, dear, but that's not living. Your father and I have each lost a beloved spouse. We know—better than you, I think— what we're risking. We also know what we stand to lose if we let fear paralyze us."

"We understand all that," said Amy so quickly that Sylvia knew they didn't understand at all.

"Then let's not have any more of this nonsense." Sylvia smiled sympathetically to show she did not hold Amy's words against her. "I'm sure you mean well, but we've made our decision, and I'm afraid you're going to have to live with it."

In answer, Amy regarded her in silence for a moment, then turned and left through the back door. Sylvia went into the kitchen and sank down upon the bench, deeply troubled. Amy had always been so kind to her—a bit chilly when they first met, perhaps, but she had certainly seemed to warm to Sylvia as they had become more acquainted over the years. Sylvia had even taught her to quilt. She never would have expected Amy to look upon her as if she were the enemy.

She roused herself and rose to fix herself a cup of tea. She must not blow Amy's remarks out of proportion. Amy might not relent easily or soon, but eventually she would see reason. Right now she was still dealing with her surprise, and perhaps some hurt, too, at hearing the news secondhand. After they had some time to adjust, the children would accept their marriage for Andrew's sake. What alternative did they have?

"Sylvia?"

Sylvia started at the sound of Sarah's voice. "Oh, hello, dear."

"Welcome home." Sarah hugged her warmly. "I heard the end of Amy's rant. I was stuck on the phone when you pulled into the driveway or I wouldn't have let her tear into you the minute you got out of the motor home. I'm sorry."

"It's not your fault. I suppose I should have been prepared for something like this after the way Bob and Cathy took the news."

"How can you prepare for something so bizarre?"

"I suppose I could have been more delicate. Telling Amy she would just have to live with it was too blunt."

"You were more polite than she was." Sarah reached into the cupboard for Sylvia's favorite mug and set it on the counter. "To hear her tell it, you and Andrew are a hundred and ten years old and hooked up to life support."

"I hate to imagine what kind of nonsense she's filling his head with at this moment," said Sylvia. "For someone who's so concerned with his health, she doesn't seem to mind sending his blood pressure through the roof. I do hate to see him at odds with his children."

"You haven't done anything wrong," said Sarah firmly. "His kids just need an attitude adjustment. Be resolute, and they'll cave in long before June."

"June? What's in June?"

"Your wedding."

"Oh. I see. So you've set our wedding date, then?"

"Not me. Diane. She had to coordinate it around the Elm Creek Quilters' vacations. She and Gwen almost came to blows before they settled on June nineteenth."

Sylvia looked heavenward. "Well, thank goodness I'm finding this out now. It would have been quite embarrassing not to know until the invitations are sent out. I assume I will be invited?"

"Sure. Bring Andrew, if you like."

"Thank you. I will." Sylvia dried her hands and returned the dish towel to its hook. She glanced out the window and saw Andrew checking under the hood of the motor home while Amy made an impassioned argument by his side. She wondered, briefly, if Andrew regretted asking her to marry him, but just as quickly pushed the thought aside.

Rather than dwell on Andrew's children any longer, Sylvia showed Sarah the Crazy Quilt and told her the story of its journey from Elm Creek Manor to the Indiana home of Mona Niehaus. Sarah admired the quilt, then led Sylvia upstairs to the library, where the responses to Summer's Internet inquiry awaited.

Twelve more e-mail messages and four letters had arrived since Sylvia had last spoken to Summer. While Sarah booted up the computer, Sylvia opened the first envelope and skimmed enough of the letter inside to learn that the writer had purchased a whole cloth quilt at an estate sale. The writer had enclosed two snapshots, one of the quilt draped over a chair, and the other a closeup of the central motif.

Sylvia was so surprised she had to sit down, and the nearest place was the arm of Sarah's chair. "This is it," she exclaimed, holding out the letter to Sarah. "I know the stitches don't show up very clearly in this first picture, but the detail shot proves it, and so does that scalloped edge. No one but my mother used that particular design."

Sarah hesitated. "Before you get too excited . . ."

"What?"

Sarah rose and beckoned Sylvia to take her seat at the computer. Sylvia complied, curious, as Sarah leaned over and clicked the mouse to open the e-mail file. The first message appeared on the screen, and Sylvia gasped. Following a few paragraphs of text there was a picture of another whole cloth quilt, identical to the one in the photo Sylvia held except for a slightly darker hue of fabric and a different pattern of wear and tear.

Sylvia sank back into her chair. "I see."

"I'm afraid that's not all."

One by one, Sarah opened seven more e-mail messages, each with another photo of a whole cloth quilt attached. Sylvia saw quilts draped over bassinets and held up by proud owners, quilts in pristine condition and quilts with water stains and tears, quilts that had aged from white to every shade of ecru and cream—but each was quilted in the same pattern of feathered plumes, entwining ribbons, and crosshatched hearts, and each boasted the same scalloped border.

"I don't need to look at any more," said Sylvia as Sarah tried to hand her a small stack of letters. She tossed the unopened envelope she still held on the desk. "I don't even want to open this one."

"Mind if I do?" asked Sarah. Sylvia waved at the envelope dismissively, so Sarah picked it up. "This one is about the Ocean Waves quilt. They sent a picture."

Her hopes renewed, Sylvia took the photo, only to slap it down on the desk after a glance. "For goodness' sakes. I have this same fabric in my own stash. It's from the late nineties, no earlier, and my description specifically said my mother made her quilt during World War I. Is it too much to ask for people to read carefully?"

"Maybe they hoped you wouldn't be too particular," said Sarah, her eyes on the letter. "She'll sell this one to you for six hundred dollars, or custom make you one in the size and fabric of your choice."

"I wouldn't give her six cents for it. That's not the quilt I'm looking for, and if she read Summer's Internet post, she knows it. She's just trying to make a sale."

Sarah reminded her of the other messages that did not include pictures; they might yet prove to be worthwhile leads. Thanks to Mary Beth Callahan, they also now had the name of the auction house that had purchased the Elms and Lilacs quilt, which just the day before Sarah had discovered was still in business in Sewickley, Pennsylvania. Mary Beth's tip about the now-defunct consignment shop in downtown Waterford was also worth investigating, Sarah said, as were the rest of the e-mail messages.

"So we're down but not out," said Sylvia, and she agreed to see the remaining responses. Two people had written to say they spotted the Crazy Quilt in their states; those claims, Sylvia could safely disregard without further investigation. One e-mail message located the New York Beauty quilt at the San Jose Quilt Museum, while another writer's apologetic note explained that she knew she had seen that exact quilt at a museum, but she could not remember which one.

Those leads seemed more promising, especially when coupled with the mistaken sighting of the New York Beauty at the Rocky Mountain Quilt Museum. Perhaps this most recent writer was not the only one to have forgotten which museum possessed the quilt. Fortunately, one of Sylvia's closest friends was a master quilter living in San Francisco. Sylvia knew Grace Daniels would be happy to investigate this lead for her, and since Grace was also a museum curator, Sylvia could rely on her expert evaluation of whatever she found.

Since the computer was already turned on, Sylvia used the Elm Creek Quilts account to send Grace an e-mail explaining the quest and asking for her help. "I hope Grace receives this," she said as she sent her note off into cyberspace, already feeling misgivings that she was trusting a matter of such importance to something as ephemeral as electrons rather than the comforting solidity of paper and ink. "If you don't hear back in a few days, I'll call."

"She'll receive it," Sarah assured her. "In the meantime, let's check out a lead closer to home."

They went downstairs and met Andrew and Amy in the west hallway. Sarah could not possibly have missed the anger sparking between father and daughter, but she summoned up some cheerfulness and told them about their errand into downtown Waterford. "You're welcome to come with us if you like," she said. "We can get a bite to eat at the coffee shop while we talk to the owner."

Amy began, "I don't think—"

"Sure," declared Andrew. "Let's all go. I have an errand of my own downtown."

Amy's mouth tightened, but she went upstairs for her purse and returned wearing lipstick, her hair brushed neatly back into her barrette. She offered to drive her rental, but Sarah declined, explaining that they would have more room in the company car.

The company car was actually a white minivan emblazoned on both sides with the Elm Creek Quilts logo. During the spring and summer it was so often in use shuttling campers back and forth from the airport or on shopping trips into Waterford that its reserved parking place was rarely occupied except overnight.

Amy kept her attention on the passing scenery as Sarah drove through the woods and into Waterford proper. They turned down a service alley and parked behind a row of stores lining the main street that separated the downtown from the campus of Waterford College; Elm Creek Quilter Bonnie Markham had three spaces reserved for Grandma's Attic employees, but since these days only she and Summer, and occasionally Diane, worked at the quilt shop, she let her friends borrow the leftover space.

They stopped by the quilt shop to say hello to Bonnie before continuing around the corner and up the hill to the square, a green with benches and a bandstand bordered by shops, restaurants, and city government buildings. The Daily Grind, a coffee shop next to the small public library, was a favorite with students and professors; lone figures hunched over coffee cups at tables strewn with papers and books, crumpled napkins, and plates of half-eaten muffins and biscotti.

They joined the queue. When Sarah reached the front of the line, she placed their order, gave her name, and asked to speak to the owner. "He's expecting us," she said. The clerk nodded, disappeared into the back, and returned with the message that Norman would meet them at their table.

Like the rest of his staff, Norman wore a green apron over his jeans and flannel shirt, and his thick black hair and beard gave him a wild look tempered by a good-humored smile. He pulled up a chair beside Sylvia as Sarah made introductions. At nearly six and a half feet tall, he towered over them even sitting down, but what captured Sylvia's attention most was the thick ledger he carried under one arm.

"I called my dad in Florida," said Norman to Sylvia, opening the ledger. "He remembers you and your sister, and he's positive Claudia sold some items through the store in the postwar years, but he doesn't remember the specific transactions."

"I expected as much," said Sylvia. "It was a very long time ago, and he had so many sales."

Norman grinned. "Not too many, unfortunately, or the shop wouldn't have closed. Then again, if it hadn't, he wouldn't have started his second business, and I'd much rather run a coffeehouse than a consignment store." He carefully turned to a page near the back of the ledger. "My father kept good records, and there's a lot of information here once you decipher his shorthand. See, here's your sister's account."

Sylvia slipped on her glasses and read her sister's name, printed in small, neat handwriting on the title line. The same handwriting filled nearly three quarters of the page, which was divided into five columns. Norman ran his finger down the first and stopped at one of the last entries. "These are the dates items were left with the shop, and these apparently random combinations of letters and numbers are my father's descriptions. See this QLT? That's his code for quilt, and believe me, that was one of the easier ones to figure out."

"What about the rest of it?" asked Andrew. "What's the BLUW/L stand for?"

"BLU indicates that the item was blue. The W means white. The information after the slash usually refers to the item's size or its era."

"A large blue-and-white quilt," said Sylvia. "That could be the Ocean Waves. Did your father keep more detailed records so we could confirm this? Did he take any photographs of the items in his inventory?"

Norman shook his head. "Only if the clients requested an appraisal, and they typically only did so for valuables or antiques because of the additional expense. If your sister had asked for one, there would have been a note."

Sylvia pursed her lips and nodded. Claudia would have done so if she had thought an appraisal would raise the price, but if she had understood the quilts' true worth, she never could have sold them. Sylvia gestured to the check mark in the third column beside the code for the blue-and-white quilt. "I assume the check mark indicates the item was sold?"

"It does," said Norman. "A dash instead of a check means the client reclaimed the item before it sold. In the fifth column, the two numbers separated by a slash are the price of the item and my father's commission, and the fifth column is the date the item left the store."

Sylvia had already guessed as much, and she studied the entry with a pang of regret. Fifty dollars. Claudia had parted with their mother's Ocean Waves quilt for fifty dollars, and nowhere on that page did Sylvia see any indication of who had purchased it.

"Why are there blank spaces for some of the items where the checks or dashes should be?" asked Amy. "What happened to the things that didn't sell and weren't reclaimed?"

Sylvia and Andrew exchanged a look, surprised to see her taking an interest.

"If the third column is empty, the item was still in the shop when my father retired," said Norman. "He tried to contact his clients so they would pick up their goods, but not everyone responded. He donated what little inventory remained to charity." He pointed to the last entry on the page. "Which brings me to this."

Sylvia, Andrew, Sarah, and even Amy leaned closer to get a better look at Claudia's last transaction with the consignment shop. On November 22, 1959, she had placed another quilt with Norman's father, one identified as QLT W/S.

Sylvia sucked in a breath and sat back in her chair. A small, white quilt. The whole cloth quilt. And the third column was blank.

"Do you have any idea what charity your father donated his inventory to?" she asked.

"He gave to several—Goodwill, St. Vincent de Paul, a few other local groups that aren't even around anymore, but he didn't keep a record of how the items were distributed, just one receipt from each organization with an amount for his tax deductions."

"May I?" Sarah asked, reaching for the ledger. Norman slid it across the table. She paged through it and eventually shook her head. "Did your father keep a separate record for his accounts receivable? This book tells us how much he paid out and to whom, but not what his customers paid the shop."

Norman winced. "One of my father's failures in the business was that he was always more interested in the contents of the store's shelves than its cash register. He was so disinterested in actually selling anything that I think he would have been happier running a museum." He rose. "I can show you the rest of his records, such as they are. I don't think he'd mind."

He led them behind the counter and through the kitchen into a small, cluttered office. Floor to ceiling bookshelves stuffed with books, magazines, and coffee mugs lined one entire wall, while the others were plastered with movie posters. Someone had taken a pen to them, Sylvia noted, contributing mustaches, eye patches, and blackened teeth as well as dialogue balloons with rather more colorful language than filmmakers typically included in their advertising. A dusty computer sat on a small desk, but there was no chair, and the desk calendar was set to April of the previous year. She and Sarah spotted the filing cabinet bursting with papers and exchanged looks of dismay; looking for records in this place would be nearly as bad as searching the attic of Elm Creek Manor. But Norman merely said, "Excuse the mess," took a key from the desk drawer, and led them back down the hall.

He unlocked the door to a narrow storage room and shoved it open as far as it would go, which was barely enough room for him to reach inside and flip on the light. Sylvia peered past him, noted the several large filing boxes that had impeded the door's progress, and wished they were searching the office instead.

Norman glanced down at her and chuckled. "Not all of this stuff is my dad's." With effort, he shoved the door open wider and squeezed his torso through the narrow opening. "Most of this is for the coffee shop."

"I hope you don't ever get audited," said Sarah, taking in the scene. "You'd need a team of accountants to sort out this mess."

"What?" Norman seemed genuinely bewildered as he looked from her to the room and back. "Oh. Yeah, I guess it's a little untidy, but I know where everything is."

Andrew looked dubious. "All I see are piles of paper."

"But each pile has a purpose." Grinning, Norman hauled four filing cartons into the hallway and lined them up along the wall. "You'll wish my dad was that organized before you're through."

He removed the first carton's lid, and Sylvia heard Sarah stifle a groan as they took in what appeared to be nothing more than a box of the street sweepings after a ticker-tape parade.

"Accounts receivable, I presume?" asked Sylvia, accepting Andrew's assistance as she knelt beside the carton.

"Accounts receivable and miscellaneous," affirmed Norman. "With the emphasis on miscellaneous." Then he apologized and explained that they would have to search on their own, for he had to return to work. He encouraged them to look as long as they liked and offered the use of his photocopier to duplicate any documents that would aid them in their search.

"I hope no one has any plans for the afternoon," said Sarah after Norman left.

Andrew hesitated. "I still need to run that errand."

"Well, there are four of us and four boxes." Amy seated herself on the floor beside another carton and removed the lid. "We shouldn't need more than a few hours."

Behind her back, Sylvia and Andrew exchanged speculative glances, then Andrew shrugged and made his way to the last carton. He patted his daughter on the shoulder as he passed.

Sylvia sifted through the first few layers of paper in her carton, uncertain what she ought to be looking for and doubtful she would recognize it when she found it. Sarah advised them to look for anything with Claudia's name on it, of course, but also bank records or store receipts for purchases made on the date the Ocean Waves quilt was sold. If Norman's father had not written the item code on the receipt, they could still identify the quilt by comparing the total on the receipt to the price listed in the ledger.

Their work was painstakingly slow, and working on the floor added to their discomfort, but within the first half-hour Andrew made a fortunate discovery: an envelope containing receipts for donations to five local charities, dated the same year Norman told them the shop had closed. "We'll phone them as soon as we get home," said Sarah, placing the envelope on a nearby shelf for safekeeping. "I admit it's not likely they still have the whole cloth quilt, but they might know where it ended up."

"Not unless their records are much better than Norman's father's," said Amy as she thumbed through a stack of canceled checks bound by a stack of rubber bands. Wisps of hair had come loose from her barrette, and she absently tucked them behind her ears as she set the checks aside.

Despite the exasperation of the unnecessary labor Norman's father had inflicted upon them, as she sorted through the contents of her carton, Sylvia began to sympathize with him. She had only rarely visited his store as a young woman and its closing had passed her by unnoticed, but the ledger and those haphazard files revealed a man happy in his work, one who had cultivated a close relationship with his customers. He had often scrawled notes on claim tickets, reminders to set an item aside for a customer who would particularly appreciate it or to inquire about the health of an ailing relative. One note brought tears to Sylvia's eyes. "Tell her no more quilts," he had jotted in black pencil on the back of the claim ticket stub for the Ocean Waves quilt. "Hate to sell them. Should keep."

Someone, at least, had recognized that the true measure of the quilts' worth was not in what price they could fetch but in the story they told of the woman who had so lovingly crafted them. But did the ambiguous message mean that Norman's father would like to keep the quilts for himself, that Claudia ought to keep the quilts because she hated to sell them, or that he hated to sell them because he believed Claudia ought to keep them in the family? Sylvia knew her sister's selfishness well, and yet part of her longed to believe that Claudia had sold off their mother's legacy only because she had no other choice. If Sylvia could never reclaim those precious heirlooms, their loss would be easier to accept if she knew Claudia had not parted with them easily.

Their search gleaned one other tantalizing clue, and Amy was the one who discovered it: a canceled check whose date and total matched the ledger entry for the Ocean Waves quilt.

A thrill ran through Sylvia as she examined the check, crumpled from its long storage, the ink of the signature fading, but with the printed name and address of the account holder still legible. Even Sarah's warning that they ought to examine the ledger in the unlikely event that a second item had sold that same day for the exact same amount did not weaken her confidence that this was the check that had purchased her mother's quilt.

"It's more than fifty years old," said Amy. "That woman may no longer live at that address."

"I'm certain she doesn't," said Sylvia. "I know this woman, or rather, knew her. She was my mother's age."

"Were they friends?" asked Sarah.

"Whatever else Gloria Schaeffer may have been, she was no friend to our family. You may recall, Sarah, that I told you how Claudia and I were kicked out of the Waterford Quilting Guild during World War II because of silly rumors that we Bergstroms were German sympathizers. It was utter nonsense, of course, but Gloria thought our presence disrupted the harmony of our meetings, and since she was guild president . . ." Sylvia shrugged. "I figured if they didn't want me, I wanted no part of them, but Claudia took our dismissal hard. What I don't understand, though, is what Gloria Schaeffer would want with a Bergstrom quilt."

"Maybe she didn't know it was your mother's," suggested Andrew.

"Unlikely. My mother and Gloria were both founding members of the guild. They would have seen a good deal of each other's work, both complete and in progress."

"Maybe she wanted to help Claudia financially," said Sarah. "Out of guilt for what she did."

Sylvia admitted it was possible, but perhaps she still harbored some resentment for that long-ago offense, for she could not believe Gloria would wish to assist any Bergstrom. More likely, Gloria had taken a perverse glee in the downturn in the family's fortunes and could not resist parting them from one of their treasured heirlooms.

"Gloria had two sons," said Sylvia, setting the canceled check aside with the charity receipts and the Ocean Waves claim ticket stub. "Assuming Gloria is no longer among the living, one of them may have inherited the quilt." They would be in the phone book, if they still lived in Waterford.

Several hours and cups of coffee later, they finished wading through the detritus of the consignment shop without finding any more clues to the whereabouts of the missing quilts. Still, with Gloria Schaeffer's last known address in hand, Sylvia felt somewhat optimistic, despite her growing concerns about the whole cloth quilt, of which they still knew very little.

Sarah photocopied the relevant documents while the others returned the cartons to the storage room. Then they found Norman out front and thanked him. As they left the coffee shop, Andrew glanced at his watch. "It's four-thirty. If we hurry, we can take care of that errand before the office closes."

"Goodness, Andrew, I completely forgot." Sylvia turned up the collar of her coat and tucked her arm through his. "If I had known we would spend so much time at the Daily Grind I would have suggested we take care of your errand first. Where to, then? The bank? The hardware store?"

"The county clerk's office," he replied, "and it's not my errand. It's our errand. Don't tell me you forgot."

"I'm afraid I did," said Sylvia, smiling at his eagerness.

"How could you forget? What were we talking about ever since the Ohio border? What did we say we'd take care of as soon as we got home?"

With dismay, Sylvia remembered. "Oh, let's worry about that another day, shall we?" Her arm in Andrew's, she began strolling down the sidewalk toward Grandma's Attic and the van. "After all that work, I have absolutely no interest in waiting in a long line."

Andrew stopped short. "There won't be a line at this hour. Besides, we're right here."

"Sylvia's right," said Sarah. Sylvia doubted she had caught on, but she could usually sense Sylvia's moods and must have realized there was a problem. "Anyway, it's my turn to make supper, so I need to get home."

"This won't take long," said Andrew. "All we have to do is fill out a form and show our IDs. It's not that hard to get a marriage license."

Amy looked at her father, expressionless.

"Andrew, please," said Sylvia quietly. "Let's go home."

"The county clerk's office is right across the street. We're here, so we might as well stop by. If there's a long line, we'll come back another time."

"You had to do this now," said Amy. "You couldn't wait until I went home."

"You mean sneak around, as if I'm doing something shameful? I'm proud that Sylvia's marrying me, and I'm not going to hide that from anyone."

"Andrew, please," murmured Sylvia.

"I'm not asking you to hide."

"What, then? Should I pretend that we're not getting married rather than offend you?"

Amy threw up her hands. "Listen, Dad, you do what you have to do. Just don't pretend you're not baiting me, and don't expect me to stand around and watch while you do it."

She stalked off. Andrew glowered, and Sylvia started to follow her, but Sarah caught her by the arm. "I'll stay with her," she said quietly. "We'll meet you at the van."

Sylvia agreed and watched as Sarah hurried down the sidewalk after Amy. Amy paused when Sarah approached, and they exchanged a few words before continuing on together. Neither one looked back.

"Are you coming?" asked Andrew after the pair rounded the corner and vanished from sight.

Sylvia nodded.

Andrew was right in one respect: The county clerk's office was not busy at that hour, and they waited only a few minutes before their number was called. They filled out the proper form, paid the forty dollar fee, showed their driver's licenses, and accepted the clerk's congratulations when he told them they could pick up their license in three days. Soon they were back outside on the sidewalk in the fading daylight. Sylvia returned Andrew's kiss when he told her how happy he was, but she shivered in the cold and tucked her hands into her pockets instead of taking his arm.

They walked in silence toward Grandma's Attic. "Well, that's one more task to cross off our list," said Andrew.

"True enough."

He gave her a sidelong glance. "But?"

"But we could have put it off until later."

"Don't tell me you're siding with Amy."

"The very fact that you would make this an issue of choosing sides tells me you know you're in the wrong."

"What?" He placed a hand on her arm to bring her to a halt. "You're the one insisting we have to go on about our own lives without worrying about their concerns."

"Yes, but that's altogether different from flaunting our decision in your daughter's face. We could have come downtown any day, and you know it. Why did it have to be today, especially after Amy was so helpful sorting through those dreadful files? She was trying to give us a chance, and I think if we had given her more time, we might have won her over. But now . . ." She shook her head and resumed walking. "Now we're worse off than before."

After a moment, Andrew caught up to her. "I wasn't trying to goad her. Honest."

Sylvia could manage only a shrug. She wasn't sure she believed him.

Sarah and Amy were not waiting in the van when Sylvia and Andrew arrived, but they appeared fifteen minutes later carrying shopping bags from Grandma's Attic. Sylvia was thankful that Sarah had attempted to distract Amy until tempers cooled, but there was no mistaking Amy's lingering anger. She barely looked at her father or at Sylvia as she climbed into the van, and she made only monosyllabic replies to Sylvia's attempts at conversation. As they pulled up behind Elm Creek Manor, Sylvia heard Amy quietly offer to help Sarah prepare supper. Sylvia quickly volunteered herself and Andrew, but Amy frowned, and Sarah told her that they were entitled to a rest after their long trip. "You have some phone calls to make, too," she pointed out.

Andrew wanted to unpack, so Sylvia went alone to the library, welcoming the relief of solitude after the tension that had marred their homecoming. She seated herself at the desk that had been her father's and flipped open the phone book to the business pages. She found numbers for Goodwill and St. Vincent de Paul easily, but Lutheran Outreach and St. Michael's Society were not listed. There was a St. Michael's Catholic Church, so Sylvia hoped for the best and dialed.

The young woman who answered the phone had never heard of St. Michael's Society, but she offered to ask around and call Sylvia back. Sylvia thanked her and hung up, and then, although she was reluctant to tie up the line, she called Goodwill. As she had feared, they told her it was highly improbable that they would still have her mother's quilt after so many years. "But you never know," said the woman on the other end of the line, and offered to search for it. This time Sylvia said she would hold, and about ten minutes later, the woman returned to report that the only quilts currently in their possession were pieced or appliquéd, and since they did not maintain detailed records of individual purchases, there was no way to know who had bought the quilt, or when. She promised to call Sylvia if any whole cloth quilts were donated to their collection site in the future. Sylvia appreciated her helpfulness and her sympathy, but as she recited her phone number, she doubted the woman would ever have reason to call it.

Her luck was no better at St. Vincent de Paul, except to rule out one possible destination for the quilt. The man who took her call noted that back when Norman's father would have made his donations, their branch had handled only large durable items like furniture and appliances, and customarily had advised donors to take items such as clothes and bedding to other charities, such as Goodwill and Lutheran Outreach. Sylvia said that she had spoken to Goodwill but could not locate the Lutheran Outreach; the man told her that they had closed down in the early seventies, and that as far as he knew, no one affiliated with the organization remained in Waterford.

Disappointed, Sylvia thanked him for his time and hung up; she was crossing St. Vincent de Paul off her list when the phone rang. The young woman from St. Michael's Catholic Church had called back to report that the parish priest knew of St. Michael's Society, a community service and social justice organization founded in the early 1960s by a group of Waterford College students. For nearly fifteen years, they had served impoverished families, especially single mothers of young children, throughout the Elm Creek Valley, and eventually had become an official organization of the college and was still in existence under a different name. "One of the founders is the emeritus director of Campus Ministry," said the young woman, and since he was also one of their most active parishioners, she didn't think he would mind if she gave Sylvia his name and number.

To Sylvia's delight, he was home when she called, but while he seemed to be a thoroughly charming man and his tales about St. Michael's Society were intriguing, he had no information on the whereabouts of the whole cloth quilt. "All donations were either passed along to needy families or sold to raise money to purchase necessities," he explained.

Sylvia's heart sank, but she persisted, inquiring whether the campus organization might have some record of the donations from the consignment shop. No such records existed, she was told, and he regretted that he could not help her.

Sylvia assured him he had been very helpful, and hung up the phone with a sigh. She fingered the list of crossed-off names and phone numbers for a moment before tossing it on top of the responses to Summer's Internet posts. She studied the pile before beginning to leaf through it, and as she worked her way through the letters, each promising her the whole cloth quilt, frustration and disappointment stole over her. Last of all, she examined the printouts she had obtained at the Thousand Oaks Library, and as she did, she forced herself to accept two unavoidable conclusions she had been trying her best to ignore ever since the discovery of the pattern.

The Mrs. Abigail Drury identified in the magazine as the designer must have created the whole cloth quilt pattern. What Sylvia had always thought of as her mother's original design was nothing more than a reproduction of someone else's work. That surely explained why Mother had neglected to embroider her name and the date on this quilt alone, out of all those she had completed over the years.

Worse yet, since the pattern for the quilt had been published in such a popular magazine, hundreds if not thousands of quilters must have stitched quilts indistinguishable from her mother's. Even if Sylvia purchased every one of these she could track down, she would never be able to determine which one, if any, had belonged to her mother.

No matter how long she searched, the lovely whole cloth quilt would remain forever lost to her.

Later, at supper, she did not share her realization with her friends, because she could not bear to hear them agree with her conclusion. As the meal ended, Sylvia rose from her chair with relief, longing for a good night's sleep. She noticed, too late, that Amy alone had remained in her chair. "If you don't mind," she said quietly, fingering her water glass, "I have something to say."

Sylvia shot Andrew a warning look, but he knew enough to keep quiet until Amy had a chance to speak.

"I'm leaving in the morning."

"Why?" asked Andrew. "Honey, I'm sorry about this afternoon. I didn't intend to taunt you."

"It's not just that." Amy caught Sylvia's gaze and held it. "With all due respect, what you're doing is wrong. You're asking too much of my father, and I simply can't support your decision to marry. Under those circumstances, I no longer feel comfortable accepting your hospitality."

"Please stay," urged Sylvia. "In the morning we'll have a good talk and sort this thing out."

"What's to sort out?" Amy shook her head and rose. "I don't approve of your marriage. I can't. Please don't ask me or my family to witness it."

"Amy, please—" Andrew reached out for her, but she waved him off and hurried from the room. He turned to Sylvia, stricken. She took his hand in both of hers, dumbfounded and heartsick, and utterly at a loss for what to do.

Chapter Eight
1918

With Claudia squirming on her lap, Eleanor tore another long strip from the faded sheet and rolled it into a tight, neat bundle. Claudia crowed and grabbed at it, knocking it from Eleanor's hand. It bounced across the floor, unrolling in a long, narrow streamer that ended at Lucinda's feet.

"I swear she unrolls one bandage for every two you finish," said Maude. "Why don't you just set her on the floor, for heaven's sake?"

Eleanor spread Claudia's Four-Patch quilt on the rug and gently placed Claudia on it. No one argued with Maude anymore, and not even Lucinda retorted when her tongue grew too sharp. Louis's death had left Maude bitter and angry, as if he had not died in a muddy trench in France but had abandoned her. She seemed to believe he could return to her if he wanted to.

Eleanor could almost understand it; even now she found it difficult to imagine handsome, mischievous Louis choking on mustard gas. But she *could* imagine it, so she had come to believe it. Her heart went out to Maude, who could not, and to poor Lily, who could imagine her own husband's death too vividly. Richard had been the first of the brothers to enlist and the first to die, barely three days after his arrival at the French port of Bordeaux. He had gone off to war so proudly, so eager for adventure. Lily had not wanted him to become a soldier, but she could not deny him the chance to distinguish himself when he wanted it so badly. Soon, as patriotic fervor swept over the nation, his elder brothers found their own reasons to battle the Hun. First the Waterford Chamber Orchestra announced they would no longer perform any works by Bach or Beethoven. Then Waterford College suspended the teaching of the German language. Then Eleanor was turned away by the cobbler who muttered that he would not work his craft for any friend of the Kaiser.

Eleanor did not care what an ignorant cobbler said or did. She could not bear for her darling husband to sacrifice himself to pride. She begged him not to go; she implored him not to leave her now that their longing for a child seemed likely to be fulfilled at last. But he was resolute. "No one must ever doubt the loyalties of the Bergstrom family," he had said as he and Louis went off to enlist. "We are not German, but American, and we will fight for America."

Louis died within weeks of Richard. The family prayed for Fred's safe return and thanked God that William was too young to fight and that Clara was a girl. These children, at least, could be protected. They would be safe, and so would Claudia, the only Bergstrom grandchild to remain at Elm Creek Manor after Lily took her boys back to her own family and the home of her youth. Eleanor missed Lily's gentle innocence and the laughing, tumbling happiness of her sons. She did not expect they would ever return.

When Claudia realized her mother no longer held her, she waved her limbs frantically in protest, her face screwing up in scarlet fury. "Hush, my angel," murmured Eleanor, stroking her downy hair. Clara joined them on the floor and playfully dangled a strip of fabric within the baby's reach, bringing it close and then far. Claudia squealed with delight when she managed to seize the end in her tiny fist.

Eleanor returned to her chair, hungry for the joy that watching her beloved little girl brought her. Claudia was nearly five months old and had never seen her father—might never see him.

That was why Eleanor rolled bandages instead of escaping into the solace of quilting. What if Fred were wounded and perished for the lack of a single bandage? What if he faltered from hunger and cold when he most needed strength? She knew, logically, that nothing she did could directly preserve her husband. Her bandages would go to other wounded; the sugar she did not buy would feed other doughboys. And yet she knew, too, there was connection in the greater whole; she sensed it as she doggedly rolled bandages and bought Thrift Stamps and war bonds and conserved every scrap of food and fabric. She could not wield a gun, but she would do all she could to put wind in the sails of the Allied victory and hasten her dear Freddy's safe return home.

"I think Claudia looks like Fred," said Clara suddenly, picking her up. "They have the same eyes."

Lucinda snorted. "She has the Bergstrom chin, but other than that, she's the very image of her mother."

"What did Fred think when he saw her picture?" asked Elizabeth. Like Maude, she was clad all in black, but she had faced the death of her two sons with more resignation than Eleanor thought she could manage in her place.

"He thought she resembled me," said Eleanor, and felt heat rising in her cheeks. Along with the photograph of the baby, she had sent a picture of herself holding up her most recent quilt. She had chosen the Ocean Waves pattern for the ocean that separated them, blue and white fabrics for the crashing storm he faced abroad and the churning sea her life seemed without him. "Hurry home and help me use this, darling," she had written on the back, blushing as she imagined how his buddies would tease him. The photo did not do the quilt justice, but he had written back that it was her most magnificent creation next to the baby. In fact, he liked it so much that when he returned, he might stay beneath it for a month straight, assuming she would keep him company. After all, he had written, they needed to get started making Claudia's baby brother.

Eleanor had implied that no one would use the quilt until his return, and knowing that the idea held special meaning for Fred, it was difficult to look across the room at Elizabeth without embarrassment. Fred's mother was nursing a head cold, and she sat in her favorite chair with the Ocean Waves quilt draped over her, sipping lemon tea sweetened with honey. To ward off a sore throat, she had wrapped her neck with a poultice of her own invention. It smelled like burnt licorice, but Eleanor had no desire to learn its true ingredients. Lucinda decried Elizabeth's remedy as useless for anything but frightening away unwelcome guests, and David slept in a spare bedroom whenever she wore it, but Elizabeth insisted that it worked.

Elizabeth made no such testimonials for Eleanor's Ocean Waves quilt, but she seemed to place at least as much faith in its curative powers. She asked for it whenever she felt unwell, and had done so ever since she had fallen asleep beneath the unfinished quilt as Eleanor sewed on the binding and woke released from a day-long headache. To believe that a quilt could heal the sick was ridiculous, maybe even blasphemous, and perhaps Elizabeth realized this, for she never proclaimed the powers of the quilt as she did her various poultices and charms.

Ordinarily, Eleanor tried to humor Elizabeth's superstitions, especially now, with the war and the losses of Richard and Louis to put her harmless eccentricities in perspective. But what if Elizabeth fell ill in the night and came to Eleanor's and Fred's bedchamber for the quilt at the very moment they were beneath it endeavoring to give Claudia a baby brother? Elizabeth might not be deterred by a locked door if she thought her health was at stake.

Heat rose in Eleanor's cheeks that had less to do with embarrassment than with the scene she imagined Elizabeth interrupting. She lowered her head and tried to appear focused on the bandage she was rolling, but Lucinda's sharp eyes missed nothing. Lucinda appeared about to speak, but at that moment, the front bell rang.

"I'll get it," said Eleanor, rising and hurrying from the room with only one quick glance over her shoulder to reassure herself that Claudia was content playing with Clara. By the time she returned, Lucinda would have found someone else to tease.

As she had hoped, Frank Schaeffer, the postman, stood at the front door. "You should not have come so far out of your way," Eleanor scolded him cheerfully. "One of us would have come to the post office eventually."

"It's no trouble at all," Frank assured her, as he always did. "By the time you got around to it, the pile would have been so deep I would have had to help you haul it home anyway."

He handed her two letters, but even before she scanned the envelopes, his sympathetic look told her neither had come from Fred. Despite his thick shock of gray hair, Frank was barely a year older than Fred and widely regarded as the best marksman in the Elm Creek Valley. His greatest shame was that, as a sleepwalker, he had been declared unfit for military service. Privately, his wife Gloria had told Eleanor that she never imagined she would praise God for her husband's most irritating habit.

"I'm sure you'll hear from Fred soon," said Frank. "He's probably too busy to write much."

"I'm sure that's it," said Eleanor, though her stomach clenched when she thought of all the horrors that could prevent him from writing. She bid Frank good-bye with a forced smile and a reminder for his wife that their blocks for the guild's charity quilt were due in two weeks.

She read the return addresses on her way back to the west sitting room, her pace quickening in delight. The first letter was from Lily; the family would be overjoyed to hear from her. The second was from Miss Langley.

She gave Lily's letter to Elizabeth to read aloud, but months had passed since she had last heard from her former nanny, and she was impatient to learn the reason for her silence. Promising herself she would read Lily's letter later, she quietly tore open Miss Langley's envelope and withdrew two sheets of ivory writing paper.

September 6, 1918

My Dear Eleanor,

Please accept my apologies for my long delay in responding to your letter, but as you will learn, my recent circumstances have rarely been conducive to the sort of quiet contemplation required for thoughtful writing, and when they were, I chanced to be bereft of paper and ink.

I do fear my confession will shock you. Eleanor dear, please do sit down and hand the baby to someone else.

I did not write to you sooner because I was in prison.

You will assume my arrest resulted from my activities organizing the union among the mill workers. A sensible deduction, since the factory owners often use their influence with local law enforcement to harass those who strive for the liberation of the laborer, but incorrect. Instead I was prosecuted for a more villainous crime: speaking my mind too frankly where unsympathetic listeners could overhear.

You are aware, of course, of the law making seditious utterances a crime. I, too, could not claim ignorance of the law as an excuse, although the passionate enthusiasm of the crowd at a labor rally did make me forget it for a moment. It seemed natural to me to divert from denouncing one great wrong to demanding an end to a second, but evidently some among my audience will more readily decry a greedy factory owner than a cruel war.

I was arrested the day after the rally and charged with criticizing the war policies of the United States government. I was convicted, as was to be expected given the current climate of this nation, and was sentenced to a year in prison and deportation. That was the worst part of it, that I should be exiled from my adopted land when so much work remains to be done.

So that my mind would not grow despondent and dull in idleness, I endeavoured to make the best of my confinement by establishing a law library within the prison and organizing a literacy program. Perhaps my imprisonment was a blessing in disguise, for I had not understood the shameful state of the penal system until I was myself subjected to it. I resolved that if I were somehow able to remain in this country after my release, I would fight to reform the prisons as I had fought to improve its factories.

You are a bright young woman, and I am sure you have already perceived some ostensible contradictions in this account. Clearly this letter was posted in Boston, while I ought to be either in prison or in England. As it happens, I did not serve out my year-long sentence, nor was I deported. These remarkable consequences came about through the agency of Charles Davis, who has been my dear friend and comrade for years, almost ever since I departed the Lockwood household. Faced with the prospect of never seeing me again, he proposed marriage, and once assured that unlike many of his sex he would remember we would remain equals after we wed, I consented.

The parole board was greatly impressed by this apparent reformation and domestication of my character, and as I had been a model prisoner, and as no one had been injured nor any property damaged by my speech, I was released after only six months. Moreover, now that I am married to an American, I cannot be so easily deported.

The parole board admonished me to be on my best behavior, which I agreed to do, although I am sure we would define that differently. Thus, upon regaining my freedom, I resumed my union activities. I now forgo criticism of the war except among friends, though I hate to see our Freedom of Speech so abused. I did not forget the promises I made to myself during my incarceration, either, and I have returned to that same prison as a teacher. When I see my students struggling proudly with their lessons, I cannot help wondering how they may have never seen the inside of a prison if only they had been granted a solid education in their youth. I do not romanticize these inmates; many of them have committed abhorrent, unspeakable crimes. Yet while living among them I learned that desperation and fear drove them to these terrible acts far more often than greed or rage did, and they might have chosen another path if it had been made clear for them.

Unfortunately, my enlightenment came with a price, and I do not speak of my temporary loss of freedom. Eleanor dear, I am so sorry I could not be present at the birth of your daughter as I had promised. My only consolation is knowing that you were surrounded by women who love you, and I am sure they were a great comfort. I am pleased little Claudia likes the quilt, and I am very glad I finished it early and sent it to you before the tumultuous events of the past few months could have interfered.

I so longed to see you, and still do, which makes this next part the most difficult to write. Eleanor, you must not come to Boston. There is an illness spreading throughout the city, and although the authorities claim the matter is well in hand, I have my suspicions that the situation will worsen before it improves. Apparently the sickness first appeared in the Navy barracks at Commonwealth Pier, and even now it seems to afflict primarily sailors and soldiers, but yesterday, a friend who is a nurse at Boston City Hospital told me they have admitted civilians afflicted with the same disease. The bewilderment and fear in her expression when she confided the details of her cases filled me with considerable alarm. The onset of the illness is sudden, intense, and cruel; I will spare you a description of the symptoms, as my friend's yet haunts my nightmares and I do not wish to burden you with it.

I do not tell you this to alarm you, only to convince you to stay away until this illness has run its course. Perhaps you will still be able to visit this autumn, before the weather worsens, or perhaps I could visit you. That might be better in any case; I am sure my husband and my pupils can spare me, and I would so enjoy seeing the places and people you have described in your letters. Otherwise we will have to wait until spring. Chin up! We have waited nineteen years; we shall survive another few months.

Please take good care of yourself and give sweet Claudia a kiss from

> Your Affectionate Friend,
> Amelia Langley Davis

"Eleanor?" said Clara.

Eleanor looked up from the letter, startled. "What is it?"

The others were watching her, concerned. "You're as white as a sheet," said Elizabeth, and coughed into her handkerchief. "Is it bad news?"

"I'm afraid so," said Eleanor, quickly composing herself as she returned the letter to its envelope. "Miss Langley—or I should say, Mrs. Davis, for she has married—has asked us not to come."

"Why not?" asked Maude. "Not that I ever thought you should go. The baby is much too young to travel so far."

"There has been an outbreak of illness in Boston." Eleanor fingered the envelope, a fist clenching in her belly. "It sounds a great deal like the three-day fever Fred said afflicted the soldiers overseas in the spring, but . . ."

"But what?" asked Lucinda sharply.

Eleanor smiled and shrugged. "I was going to say more virulent, but you know how Miss Langley exaggerates."

Miss Langley did not exaggerate, and Lucinda had heard enough stories about Eleanor's nanny to know that. Lucinda gave her a long, steady look before glancing down on the floor where Clara played with Claudia. "Mrs. Davis, you mean," Lucinda said, taking up another strip of cloth.

"Mrs. Davis. I must remember that, although it will be difficult after so many years of calling her Miss Langley."

Eleanor scooped up Claudia and held her close.

A week passed with no more visits from Frank Schaeffer, which meant no letters from Fred. Eleanor wrote to her husband nearly every night, a few paragraphs telling him about her day, about Claudia. Maude scolded her for wasting paper and postage on so many letters instead of writing one longer letter once a week, but when Eleanor thought of the hazards her fragile letters would pass through, she decided that sending many separate envelopes would increase the chances that at least one would reach Fred.

Frank still had not returned to Elm Creek Manor by the following Saturday afternoon, the date of the Waterford Quilting Guild's monthly meeting. Eleanor drove into town with Lucinda and Clara, who at thirteen was too young to be an official member but had been granted special permission to attend meetings. Eleanor and Lucinda were two of the four founders of the guild, after all, and even the fussiest members tolerated Clara's presence rather than offend Elizabeth and risk being excluded from the quilting bees at Elm Creek Manor, which were a welcome diversion during the long Pennsylvania winters.

Eleanor had made sure they left home early so she could mail her letters before the meeting. Clara had filled an entire book of Thrift Stamps and was eager to exchange it for a War Bond, so while Eleanor ran her errand, Clara and Lucinda went to the bank.

At the post office, Eleanor joined the line to buy stamps, her thoughts drifting to Fred. She wondered if he was still in France. It was not like him to be silent so long between letters. He must not be able to send mail from wherever he was. If he had been killed, she would have been notified by now.

As she waited, she was at first only distantly aware of the hushed, worried voices around her until snatches of conversation broke through her reverie:

" . . . hundreds by now, and more dying every day . . ."

" . . . dropped dead, right on the street corner . . ."

" . . . Spanish flu, but I say it's German in origin . . ."

"I beg your pardon." Eleanor touched the shoulder of in the man in front of her in line. "What did you say?"

"It's nothing, miss," the man said, and the man with whom he had been speaking nodded. "Nothing for you to worry about."

"You said people are dying."

"Well, yes, I suppose I did." The man hesitated. "They're calling it the Spanish flu."

"Influenza?" Eleanor was not quite sure she believed him. She and Elizabeth had both had influenza in the spring. Only the very old and the very young died from it. "Hundreds are dead from influenza?"

"Yes, miss, but as I said, you shouldn't worry. It's all happening very far away from here."

By force of habit, Eleanor placed a hand on her heart to still its pounding. "Boston isn't that far away."

A long look passed between the two men before the first said, "I was speaking of Philadelphia."

"You could have been speaking of any city east of here," a sharp voice broke in from behind them. Eleanor turned to find a stout woman with her arms full of parcels. "My daughters in New York City say the undertakers are running out of coffins."

Eleanor's heart leapt in alarm; the two men exchanged uneasy glances. "It's true," the woman insisted. "That why I'm sending my girls my best remedies as quick as can be. Wish I could go there and tend to them myself, but this time of year my rheumatism troubles me terribly when I travel."

Eleanor nodded in sympathy, but as the sharp-voiced woman went on to describe her various concoctions, her thoughts raced to Miss Langley—Mrs. Davis—in Boston, to her parents in New York. She must send word to them right away and invite them to wait out the illness in the safety of Elm Creek Manor before they succumbed to it themselves. Mr. Davis, too, of course, and any of their friends who wished to take precautions.

She murmured her excuses to the woman and left the line, retrieving paper and pen from her purse with trembling hands. By the time she finished the letters and rejoined the line, the woman and the two men had left. Others had taken their places, but the newcomers continued the anxious murmurs: The disease had spread as far west as St. Louis; no, it had halted at the Mississippi; no, it ravaged the nation from coast to coast. It was an affliction caused by unsanitary conditions and overcrowding, which is why it afflicted soldiers and the poor. It was simply the same flu they saw every season, nothing to fear. It was a deadly germ released on the Eastern seaboard by spies put ashore from German U-boats.

Eleanor finished her errand and fled.

Outside, Lucinda sat on a bench reading the paper while Clara read over her shoulder. "Lucinda," Eleanor began, and hesitated. She did not wish to alarm Clara. "It seems the sickness has spread beyond Boston."

"It was never confined there." Lucinda folded the paper and tucked it under her arm. "It's everywhere, or it will be soon."

"But the paper says the doctors have it 'well in hand,'" said Clara.

"I know, dearie. I was reading between the lines." Lucinda rose and strode off in the direction of the public library, where the quilting guild met.

Eleanor and Clara hurried to catch up with her. "There's no flu in Waterford," said Clara, a question in her voice.

"Not yet there isn't," said Lucinda. "As far as we know."

Clara looked up at Eleanor, anxious. "Don't worry," Eleanor said quietly, placing an arm around Clara's shoulders. "It's just the flu."

The meeting had already begun when they arrived, ten minutes late, so they quietly found places in the back. Gloria stood at the podium calling for nominations for the next year's slate of officers. One of the women in the front row called out, "Since she's not here to object, I nominate Eleanor Bergstrom as president."

There was a murmur of assent. Gloria grinned at Eleanor and shrugged as if to say she was powerless to object. "Wait," began Eleanor. "I—"

"I second the nomination," declared another.

"But I've already been president," protested Eleanor. "Twice."

"And you did a wonderful job. That's why we all want you back." Gloria regarded the two dozen quilters inquisitively. "Any other nominations?"

The women shook their heads, and a few turned around to smile at Eleanor, who suppressed a sigh.

"It looks like you're running unopposed again," called out a friend of Elizabeth's.

Over the ripple of laughter, Eleanor said, "At least keep the nominations open until next month. Perhaps someone who isn't here today would like to run."

"Everyone's here," the guild secretary noted. "Everyone comes on nomination day."

"That's because if they don't, they'll find themselves president," said Eleanor, but she smiled to show she would be glad to resume the office.

The rest of the guild's business was quickly concluded, for

everyone was eager to work on the charity quilt. Each woman had pieced a block in her favorite star pattern using red, white, and blue fabrics; in the Bergstrom family, where several quilters shared the same dwindling supply of precious fabric scraps, necessity had compelled them to adapt their patterns to make the best use of the available materials, but Eleanor was proud of the results. The five blocks representing the Bergstrom family were among the prettiest presented at the meeting, but what mattered most was that when the quilt was completed, the guild would raffle it off to raise money for the county chapter of the Red Cross.

The women pushed two tables together and placed all the blocks upon it, each contributing her opinion as to the most pleasing arrangement. The blocks were shuffled, considered, and rearranged until all but Gloria and Lucinda were satisfied, and their disagreement came down to the placement of two particular blocks. Lucinda wanted to exchange a LeMoyne Star block in the center of the quilt with a Sunburst block along one of the edges, explaining that the more intricate design would make a better central focal point. Gloria insisted that the two blocks should remain exactly where they were.

"She cares more about herself than the quilt," said Lucinda in an undertone only Eleanor could hear. Then Eleanor realized the LeMoyne Star block was Gloria's.

"If she cares about it so much, let her have her way," Eleanor murmured back. "Honestly, what does it matter?"

Lucinda's eyebrows rose, since Eleanor never settled for less than perfect where her own quilts were concerned. Still, Lucinda gave up the battle, and the women separated into smaller groups of friends to stitch the blocks into rows.

Eleanor expected the conversation to focus on this mysterious outbreak of disease in the East, but instead the women chatted about more ordinary things closer to home. Hungry for news, Eleanor introduced the subject herself, but no one volunteered anything she had not already heard at the post office. The general consensus seemed to be that the illness could not be as dire or spread as swiftly as rumor had it, and that they were fortunate to live in a pleasant little hamlet like Waterford, where they were spared the evils of the cities.

But the rumors did not die out, and swiftly the voices of authority gave them credibility. State health officers advocated the wearing of gauze masks. Eastern governors warned their Western counterparts to start making coffins. All the while, the disease stole closer, creeping along the highways and rivers. Thousands of cases reported in Philadelphia, hundreds more in Harrisburg. The first case in State College. And then the first case in Grangerville, only ten miles down the state road.

Hours after this announcement came, an emergency meeting was called at the town hall. Eleanor, David, and Lucinda attended, along with so many others that the meeting was moved to the Lutheran church on Second Street. As they squeezed into a pew, Lucinda remarked that this was the most unruly crowd in the church's history. David chuckled, but Eleanor was breathless from anxiety and unable to smile at the joke. Her eyes locked on the mayor as he entered and went to the front, followed by three men: Robert Cullen and Malcolm Granger, Waterford's two doctors, and a third man Eleanor did not recognize. He was tall and slim with a neatly trimmed black mustache, and he sat slightly apart from the two doctors, who were engaged in an urgent, whispered conversation.

The room quieted as the mayor took the pulpit. A portly, jovial man, he thanked them for coming and got straight to the point: No cases of Spanish influenza had yet occurred in Waterford, and he meant to keep it that way. A collective sigh of relief went up from the crowd, and as the murmurs rose into a crescendo of questions, the mayor raised his hands for silence and announced the formation of the town's first Health Committee. The two doctors had agreed to serve on it, and the third man, a professor of social sciences at Waterford College named Daniel Johnson, would direct their activities as Health Officer.

The mayor stepped down and was replaced in turn by each of the members of the Health Committee. The elderly Dr. Cullen took the pulpit first and somberly described the symptoms of the disease to a suddenly silent room. Once infected with the influenza germ, the patient's descent from robust health to incapacitation was sudden and savage. Raging fever. Racking coughs producing green pus and blood from the lungs. Gushing nosebleeds. Delirium. Pneumonia. Bluish or even purple skin, followed within hours by death. If anyone suspected the onset of these symptoms, they must report to his clinic at once.

"What will he do for us once we get there?" asked Lucinda in an undertone, but David said nothing and Eleanor could only shake her head.

Malcolm Granger spoke next. As he approached the pulpit, Eleanor took comfort in the reassuring presence of her own physician despite the scattered throat clearings and shuffling of feet that greeted him. Doctors from the Granger family had served the people of Waterford respectably since before the Civil War, but none had been as controversial as the youngest Dr. Granger, who was praised as a modern thinker by some and disparaged as a dangerous fraud by others. No one questioned his ability to set a broken bone or deliver a baby, but his ideas about disease aroused skepticism even among his own faithful patients. Eleanor trusted him, not because his ancestors had cared for Bergstroms since their arrival in America, but because under his care she had given birth to a healthy daughter. Furthermore, while Dr. Granger acknowledged that her heart did appear to have sustained damage, he also said that neither he nor any physician could truly know if it would cut her life short, so she would do well to discount any dire predictions and instead embrace each day as a gift. His advice brought tears to her eyes each time she recalled it, so it was little wonder she had become one of his most loyal defenders.

Dr. Granger addressed the treatment of the disease. The germ of influenza was thought to be a bacterium, perhaps Pfeiffer's bacillus, perhaps something else. Until a vaccine could be developed, the only treatment was rest, fresh air, cool baths and compresses to reduce fever, and fluids to replace those lost in the body's natural responses to the affliction. Make the patient comfortable and pray for the best, he told them, and remember that since the disease seemed nearly always fatal, the best remedy was prevention.

A rumble of protest and disbelief followed Dr. Granger to his seat, and Eleanor wished he had not spoken with his characteristic bluntness and brevity. He had spoken for less than half the time Dr. Cullen had, and he had left his listeners with little hope.

"And just how are we supposed to keep from getting sick?" a man shouted from somewhere in the crowd. "It's knocking strong young soldiers flat on their backs. What chance do we have?"

Amid the chorus of agreement, the Health Officer rose. "I believe I can address that."

He took the pulpit and regarded his listeners coolly. As his gaze swept over the crowd, over Eleanor, she had the sensation of tallies made and percentages calculated, a feeling reinforced when he began to speak. Professor Johnson had observed bubonic plague in San Francisco and other epidemics both at home and abroad, but if the reports were true, this Spanish flu was more virulent and more deadly than anything he had experienced. The only way to prevent Waterford from succumbing as Boston and Philadelphia and New York had was to make sure the germ of influenza never entered the town.

As of four o'clock that afternoon, he declared Waterford under quarantine. No one not currently within the city limits, whether stranger or lifelong resident caught away from home, would be allowed to enter until the danger of contagion had passed. All citizens must wear gauze masks or handkerchiefs over their noses and mouths. All indoor public gathering places, including schools, restaurants, taverns, and churches, were closed until further notice.

At this the grumbling rose to a roar. "We can't close down the churches when we need them most," called out a man to Lucinda's left.

Near the back of the room, a young man with a jauntily loosened tie stood and shouted, "What of the students? If there's a crisis, our families may need us. You can't expect us to stay in our dormitories instead of going home."

Professor Johnson waited for the shouts of affirmation to fade. "The quarantine functions in only one direction," he said. "You may leave any time you wish, but you may not return."

The mayor hurried to the podium, raising his hands for quiet. "These measures are only temporary."

"How temporary?" a woman shouted. "My son works for the railroad. Are you saying he can't come home?"

"That's precisely what I'm saying," the professor said. He looked to the rest of the Health Committee for support. A muscle in Dr. Cullen's jaw tightened. Dr. Granger nodded.

The mayor withdrew a handkerchief from his pocket and mopped his brow. "Listen. I don't like it any more than you folks, but we have to take drastic measures if we want to stay alive. We've all had news from friends to the east. Do you want your neighbors dropping dead on the streets? Do you want coffins stacked chest-high on our sidewalks? Do you want your loved ones flung into mass graves because there aren't any more coffins? Well, I don't, and since I'm the mayor of this town, what these gentlemen have decided stands."

He flung his handkerchief on the floor and stormed out.

The people were shocked into silence for a heartbeat before their voices rose in a cacophony of anger and alarm. Eleanor took a deep breath and felt Lucinda's hand close around hers as her father-in-law urged them to go. Rising, they steadied one another in the rush for the doors, barely keeping their feet. Outside, the crowd quickly dispersed, and among the men and women hurrying home, Eleanor spotted several who had already knotted handkerchiefs over their faces. Only their eyes were visible, wide and frightened above the white cloth.

The following morning, more than thirty people reported to Dr. Cullen's clinic fearing they might have contracted the Spanish flu before the quarantine was enacted, but after examining them, the doctor declared that not one suffered from anything worse than a bad case of nerves and a head cold. The next day, half their number appeared and were sent home with the same diagnosis. On the third day, only a handful came, and on the fourth, none. Two mask slackers were fined fifty dollars apiece. The newsstand parted with its last out-of-town newspaper. A week passed, and it seemed that thanks to the foresight of the Health Committee, Waterford might be spared.

The next time Eleanor went into town, the streets seemed unusually quiet, the shops nearly empty, filling her with a sense of unease that the beautifully mild October day could not dispel. She completed her errands and, ignoring the inner voice that urged her to hurry home to baby Claudia, she found herself wandering through town. Before long she realized she had been searching for news, only there were few passersby and little conversation to over-hear, and that much muffled by masks. Some people wore gauze masks like her own, given to her by Dr. Granger, others wore bright scarves or fine white handkerchiefs. Eleanor's mask moved as she breathed and made her feel as if she could not fill her lungs completely.

She wandered down by the riverfront. The wharf was almost deserted, and the few boats tied up at the docks looked as if they had been there a while. She walked to the end of the nearest dock and read the sign nailed to a piling: WARNING! THE TOWN OF WATERFORD IS QUARANTINED. ENTRY FORBIDDEN BY ORDER OF THE MAYOR.

She walked on, leaving the riverfront and the downtown behind until she had reached the only road bearing east out of Waterford. The heaviness in her breasts warned her she had been gone too long; Claudia needed her. Yet she continued until she found the sign posted by the road, identical to the one on the dock but for the additional line printed in smaller letters: FOR PITTSBURGH AND PARTS WEST, TAKE DETOUR FROM GRANGERVILLE 5 MILES BACK.

A westbound automobile or carriage would have little choice but to turn around and take the detour, for two overturned wagons blocked the road in a spot bordered by deep ditches. A traveler on horseback could circumvent the barrier if he were a skilled rider, and a man on foot would encounter no difficulty at all. The people of Waterford would have to pray that the word quarantine would be interpreted to their advantage, and that all who read the sign would assume that the sickness was worse within the town than without.

Eleanor stared at the sign, catching her breath, her hand on her heart. On other days she could have hoped for a ride back into town, but no one passed now.

The signs were working.

By mid-October, churches resumed Sunday services in defiance of the law. Masks disappeared. Merchants and their customers wondered when the quarantine would be lifted; how would they know when the danger had passed if they did not? Someone should venture out to Grangerville and investigate. Everyone thought so, but no one wanted to be the envoy in case he would not be allowed to return home.

Eleanor hungered for news, news of the sickness, of the war, of Fred. The Bergstroms resumed their normal activities out of necessity, but they rarely left the farm and had few callers. Sometimes their nearest neighbors would come to see if the Bergstroms had any news, bringing little of their own to report, and twice Gloria Schaeffer had shown up in tears to beg Elizabeth to allow the quilting guild to meet at Elm Creek Manor. The Health Committee had banned gathering in public places, not private homes; the Bergstroms had room enough to comfortably accommodate the whole guild and they were unlikely to attract attention here on the outskirts of town. Gloria argued that they needed to work on the charity quilt, but Eleanor suspected Gloria was simply desperate for something to distract her thoughts. She was frantic with worry for her husband, who had been delivering the town's mail to Grangerville when the quarantine signs went up.

The Bergstroms needed no such distractions, for the farm and Bergstrom Thoroughbreds kept them so busy they rarely had time to think of anything but the tasks before them. Sales had dropped off with the start of the war, but with his oldest sons gone, David needed the help of everyone else in the family just to take care of the horses. Eleanor spent most of her days rushing from the nursery to the stable and back, so that at night when she finally crawled into bed, she was too exhausted to lie awake worrying. She ached for Fred every moment she was awake, so sleep was a blessing.

She and Clara were weeding the garden while Elizabeth played with Claudia on a blanket nearby when she heard a horse coming up the road. She sat back on her heels and shaded her eyes with her hand.

"Who is it?" asked Elizabeth.

"I don't know," said Eleanor, and then suddenly she recognized him. "It's Frank. Merciful God, it's Frank! It's over!"

She scrambled to her feet and ran toward him, laughing and shouting his name. He pulled up and grinned down at her. "I knew

I'd get a warm welcome here, but I didn't think it would be this warm."

"I can't tell you how good it is to see you," she gasped, trying to catch her breath. "When did you return?"

"Just this morning." He reached into his bag and pulled out a letter. "This is my first stop. I haven't even been to the post office yet."

"Thank you, Frank. God bless you for this." She took it from his hand with a laugh, her joy dimming only slightly when she read the New York postmark. Now that mail had resumed, she would surely hear from Freddy soon. "When did they lift the quarantine?"

"You mean those signs? They're still up. I guess we won't be seeing any strangers in town any time soon."

Eleanor went cold. "The quarantine is still in force?"

"Well, sure, as far as Gloria knows, anyhow. She hasn't left the farm much. Says there hasn't been any reason." He studied her, puzzled. "Those signs aren't for me, Eleanor. They're for strangers."

"They're for anyone who wasn't in Waterford at the time."

"But I live here," he protested. "And I was in Grangerville all that time and didn't have so much as a sniffle."

"Frank, please don't go into town."

He laughed as if she had told a joke, but when he realized she was in earnest, he spoke to her as if she were a child awakened by nightmares. They were safe in Waterford, he assured her, as safe as any place on earth.

Frank Schaeffer was the first to fall ill. Gloria was the next, and then the other postal clerks, and then, it seemed, nearly everyone.

Soon every bed in Dr. Cullen's clinic was occupied by a feverish, coughing man or woman who only hours before had seemed whole and strong. Dr. Granger raced from house to house, caring for those too sick to come to the clinic. His father came out of retirement at eighty-five to assist him on his rounds, though neither man had any remedy to offer their patients. There was no cure for influenza.

Rumors spread, ignited by fear. A father of six had ridden for help when his oldest child could not be roused from unconsciousness; he returned home with a nurse to find all six children and his wife dead. An ailing husband and wife had tried to drive into town to the clinic; their horse arrived pulling the wagon bearing their corpses. Everywhere Professor Johnson went, the people of Waterford begged him to lift the quarantine so that doctors from the cities might aid them, bring them medicine. "Every doctor who can hold a thermometer is already in service to the sick elsewhere," he told them. "And there are no medicines for anyone to bring."

But there had to be something; the alternative was unthinkable. In the absence of medicine from the doctors, the people of Waterford developed their own: plasters made of mustard and turpentine. Quinine and aspirin. Vinegar scrubs. Tobacco smoke. Poultices of every description. None worked. Nothing prevented Spanish influenza from sweeping through Waterford like fire through straw.

When every chair and even the hallway floors of Dr. Cullen's clinic overflowed with the sick and the dying, Professor Johnson turned the primary school into a makeshift hospital. Lucinda and Eleanor were among the volunteers who set up cots and sewed muslin partitions from old sheets. Then, at Dr. Cullen's request, they joined the teachers working in the kitchen preparing meals to be delivered to the bedridden. They worked late into the night before returning home to Elm Creek Manor, almost too exhausted to eat the meal Maude had kept warm for them, and too drained to describe the horrors they had witnessed passing by the sickrooms throughout the day.

The following morning, Eleanor could hardly bear to leave Claudia in the care of Elizabeth and Maude as she and Lucinda returned to the school. They took the wagon, leaving the strongest horses for David and William, who at Elizabeth's urging spent the days helping their stricken neighbors. They rode from one farmhouse to the next, calling out from a safe distance to ask whether the people inside needed anything. Sometimes their neighbors needed food; often David and William heard a weak voice call out that the cows needed to be milked and the livestock fed. They returned home after dark as exhausted as Lucinda and Eleanor, reluctant to report which of their neighbors had died overnight.

On their fourth day in the kitchens, Dr. Granger strode in; later Eleanor learned that he had just returned from the Waterford College infirmary where he had found more than fifty students, the doctor, and the two nurses all dead from influenza.

His mouth set in a grim line, his eyes shadowed and glittering, he tore into the cupboards and pulled out a large stockpot. "Mrs. Bergstrom," he called, without looking in her direction. "To me, please."

Eleanor quickly washed her hands and dried them on her apron as she joined him. "How can I help?"

"Find me herbs that will smell and taste like medicine when mixed with this." His voice was low as he withdrew four tall bottles of liquor from his overcoat. He set the bottles on the counter and filled the pot with water. "I have some bottles in the clinic. They will need to be brought here and boiled."

Eleanor nodded and sent Lucinda for them. By the time Lucinda returned, Eleanor and Dr. Granger had cooked up a dark, vile-smelling brew that resembled the worst medicine Eleanor had ever seen. "But it is not medicine," she said as they poured the mixture into bottles. The other women were studiously ignoring them, but she kept her voice to a murmur nonetheless.

"If they believe it is medicine, it may help them." He raked his hair out of his face, and only then did she see that his eyes were feverish, his face flushed. "You are wasted in the kitchen, Eleanor. You and Lucinda will be more useful tending to the sick."

"But we are not nurses," said Eleanor faintly.

"You are the closest thing we have to them." He corked the last of the bottles and carefully filled his pockets with them. The rest he placed in the cupboard. "Ask for Dolores Tibbs in the clinic. She is in charge of the nurses now."

Eleanor nodded. She knew Dolores well; the librarian was the fourth founding member of the Waterford Quilting Guild. Dr. Granger rushed off without another word, and Eleanor watched him go, her hand on her heart.

"Eleanor," said Lucinda. "I don't think I can."

Something in her voice made Eleanor turn sharply. Lucinda was pale and shaking, her teeth chattering. She clutched the counter as if it alone kept her upright.

Eleanor pressed a palm to Lucinda's forehead; her skin radiated heat. "We must go after Dr. Granger."

Lucinda nodded in reply. Eleanor helped Lucinda to a chair, then raced through the school searching the sickrooms for Dr. Granger, Dr. Cullen, anyone who might help. A white-faced girl too young to be a nurse interrupted her duties long enough to say that they had no more beds left and that Eleanor would be better off taking Lucinda directly to Dr. Cullen's clinic rather than waiting for a doctor to return. Eleanor hurried back to the kitchen, pulled Lucinda to her feet, and helped her outside, past classrooms hung with blackboards and cheery pictures that now looked down on the dead and dying.

When they reached the clinic, they could not approach the front door for the crowds of afflicted men and women trying to enter. A man stood in the doorway at the top of the stairs shouting that they were too full to accept new patients, and that anyone who could make it that far should go to the Waterford College gymnasium, where Dolores Tibbs was arranging another hospital. "I can make it, Lucinda murmured. So Eleanor turned and half-carried her back down the hill toward the campus, trying not to think of what would become of those who could not walk so far or had no one to take them.

Inside the gymnasium, volunteers were arranging cots in rows, and where they had run out of cots, they had placed mattresses on the floor. Patients filled the makeshift beds as soon as they were available. At the back of the room, dozens of sufferers waited to be examined. Some sat slumped against the wall, others lay upon the floor alone, as if fearful relatives had abandoned them there and fled. One young mother cradled a baby and a young boy in her lap. She called desperately for a doctor, but her children were motionless in her arms, and the scurrying volunteers could not stop to comfort her.

Eleanor stared at the scene in shock before swallowing hard and scanning the room for Dolores. She spotted her among the crowd at the back, bending over a patient, calling out orders, gesturing and pointing. Eleanor knew Dolores would not hear her over the din, so she made her way to her friend's side, still bearing up Lucinda. "Dolores," she began. "Dr. Granger—"

Dolores glanced at her and turned to another patient. "You'll need to wait in line by the door."

"Dolores—" Eleanor stumbled as Lucinda slumped against her. "Dr. Granger sent me to help you."

Dolores looked over at Lucinda quickly. "Then get your friend into a bed and come back."

Eleanor nodded and half-carried Lucinda through the rows of mattresses, looking about for an open bed. Just then, two men passed her carrying a body draped in a sheet. Eleanor looked back the way they had come and found an empty mattress on the floor two rows down. Swallowing hard, she hurried to claim it and helped Lucinda onto it.

"I'll be back soon," Eleanor promised, and raced back to Dolores. Dolores did not seem to recognize her, so Eleanor repeated her offer to help.

Dolores studied her and nodded. "You're new, you're still fresh. You can help with triage. Most of these people would be better off at home, but they won't listen when you tell them that, so save your breath. Send those whom we can still help to a bed. Leave the rest here."

"Wait," said Eleanor as Dolores turned to go. "How will I know which is which?"

"Check their feet. If they're blue, the person won't make it."

Eleanor nodded, but Dolores had already spun away.

Eleanor hurried back to Lucinda. Quickly, before fear could stop her, she removed Lucinda's shoe and stocking, and forced herself to look. The sole of her foot was pink and healthy.

Swiftly she returned stocking and shoe. "Come on," she said, grunting from the effort as she pulled Lucinda to her feet. "You're going home."

"Don't be stupid," said Lucinda faintly. "I can't risk carrying this illness home to the family."

Eleanor knew that, but she also knew if Lucinda stayed in that makeshift hospital, she would die. "There are too many patients here and not enough nurses. Dolores herself said people like you would be better off at home." She draped Lucinda's arm over her shoulder and breathed a sigh of relief when Lucinda walked along beside her, supporting much of her own weight. "When we get home—"

"No. You're needed here. The horses know the way home, and Elizabeth can care for me."

As they left the gymnasium, Eleanor reluctantly agreed, and they made their way back to the wagon. Eleanor warned her always to always wear her mask and to allow only Elizabeth to care for her, to limit the risk to the others. She watched Lucinda ride off, slumped with exhaustion but steady in her seat, and hoped it would be enough.

Then she raced back to help Dolores.

She did not know how long she worked before another volunteer helped her, stumbling, to a chair to catch a few minutes of sleep. One day blurred into another. She knew many of the sick at least by sight, while many others were unfamiliar and young, probably students of the college. She could not think about friends and neighbors left by the wall and strangers directed to beds; she could not give special consideration to anyone, except for children and mothers carrying babies. She did not care if they had to be carried to their cots, they were assigned them.

Once she passed Dr. Granger administering his concoction to a middle-aged man. She had to turn her face away when he swallowed the bitter liquid and gazed up at the doctor, his eyes shining with gratitude. Too busy to acknowledge her, the doctor swiftly moved on to the next patient, but something compelled Eleanor to follow. "Dr. Granger," she said. "Will the Health Officer lift the quarantine and send for help?"

"Professor Johnson was buried this morning. In the trench." Dr. Granger's voice was hoarse, his gaze haggard. "There is no help to send for, Mrs. Bergstrom. We have only ourselves."

He hurried away. Eleanor stood there dumbly nodding, her ears ringing. The trench. She had heard whispered rumors about the mass grave, but she had not wanted to believe them true.

"Eleanor." She felt a hand on her arm. "Eleanor, dear."

Slowly she turned. Elizabeth stood beside her. "You must come home at once," she said. "We need you."

Eleanor felt a fist close around her throat. "Lucinda?"

"She lives yet, but others fell ill even before she returned to us." Elizabeth put her arm around her daughter-in-law and guided her to the door. "My husband. Maude. Clara. William."

"Claudia?"

"We must hurry," said Elizabeth, her anguish like a knife in Eleanor's heart.

Eleanor felt as if she tended her family at a dead run. First to Claudia to try to get her to nurse, then to Lucinda to change her bed linens, soaked through with perspiration, then back to Claudia to coax her to sleep in her cradle, then to the kitchen to prepare a sustaining broth, and then back to Claudia. Always back to Claudia.

Maude was the first to die. Two days after Eleanor's return, her sister-in-law slipped away before the sun rose. Through the frenzy of nursing those who yet lived, Eleanor watched Elizabeth with a sort of detached amazement as she arranged for her daughter-in-law to be buried on the family estate. Maude was her son's widow, and Elizabeth would not see her interred in a mass grave with strangers.

David, Clara, William, and Claudia hung on. Once Clara came out of her delirium enough to beg Eleanor for the Ocean Waves quilt, and she was inconsolable until Eleanor found it, draped it over her, and assured her it was there. Eleanor sat beside her and stroked her sweaty hair until she drifted off to sleep.

That night, Claudia screamed in pain until she was too exhausted to do more than whimper. She lay so limp and silent in her cradle that Eleanor's last bit of control finally shattered. She broke down in sobs and gathered her child in her arms, but Claudia did not even blink at the tears that fell upon her hot skin. Eleanor carried her into her own bed and lay beside her; Claudia took her nipple in her mouth but had no strength to suckle. "You will be all right," whispered Eleanor, kissing her, knowing that Claudia would probably not survive the night. She murmured soft words of comfort, all the while silently praying: Please, Lord. Please. You took all of my babies but Claudia. Please don't take her from me now. I will never again ask you for more children. I will never again ask you to spare my dear Freddy. Please Lord. Take whomever else you want, take me, but let my child live.

Eleanor fell asleep to the rhythm of her desperate prayer. She woke late the next morning to find Claudia breathing beside her, the Ocean Waves quilt spread over them.

She sat up, startled. Claudia let out a soft cry and rooted for her, so Eleanor lay back down and gave her the breast. Claudia never opened her eyes as she nursed, and fits of coughing forced her to spit out more milk than she swallowed, but she did not cry as she released the nipple and drifted off to sleep. Eleanor pressed a hand to Claudia's forehead; she felt cooler, if only slightly.

Carefully Eleanor gathered up the Ocean Waves quilt and stole from the room, whispering a prayer as she closed the door. She met Elizabeth in the hallway on her way to Clara's room. She looked haggard, but she must have seen something in Eleanor's face to give her hope, for she asked, "How is the baby?"

"She nursed, and I think her fever has broken," said Eleanor. She saw no point in saying how little Claudia had drank, or how weakly she had suckled. "You should not have let me sleep so late. How are the others?"

"I let you sleep because you needed your rest. David is sleeping. William asked for something to eat. Lucinda drank some broth, but I had to force her. Clara . . ." Elizabeth shook her head. "Clara is the same."

"I'll tend to them while you rest."

Elizabeth nodded, but stopped Eleanor before she went two paces. "Where are you going with that?"

"To Clara." Eleanor indicated the quilt in her arms. "She asked for it yesterday. Thank you for returning it, but I don't need it."

"I didn't bring it for you." Elizabeth took the quilt, and Eleanor was too surprised to stop her. "Claudia may still need it."

"Surely you don't believe the quilt will cure her."

"You yourself said her fever broke," Elizabeth countered. "What does it matter to you what I do? I've heard you say my superstitions are harmless. The quilt will not harm her, even if you don't believe it will help."

"I don't believe it, but what if Clara does? She asked for this quilt for a reason. What if you've taken her hope from her?"

"Clara herself insisted I give it to Claudia. She said the baby needs it more than she does."

Eleanor heard the note of hysteria in her mother-in-law's voice and could not bear to prolong the argument. "If Clara asks, we must give it back to her at once," she said. Elizabeth nodded distractedly as she hurried off to Claudia, the quilt in her arms.

Clara never asked for the quilt. Within hours she sank into an unceasing, feverish sleep in which she screamed and cried and babbled nonsense. Then, suddenly, she grew still. While Eleanor tried to rouse her, Elizabeth fled from the room and returned with the Ocean Waves quilt. Weeping, she flung the quilt over the bed and threw herself upon her daughter's silent body, moaning her name.

Finally Eleanor had to gently pull Elizabeth away.

William insisted that he be the one to dig his sister's grave. Though his legs wobbled beneath him when he rose from his sickbed, Elizabeth was too heartsick to object. She had not left Clara's side since fleeing to retrieve the quilt. "Too late," she whispered, rocking back and forth on her chair and staring straight ahead at nothing.

When the time came to bury her, Eleanor gently asked Elizabeth if she felt well enough to join them and say a prayer over the grave. Elizabeth did, but she said not a word until the end, when she fixed Eleanor with an icy stare. "My daughter gave her life for your daughter," she said. "Never forget that."

She took Claudia from Eleanor's arms and returned to the manor.

Slowly David, William, and Lucinda recovered, and as they did, the absence of their loved ones became a tangible pain. Elizabeth held Claudia almost constantly, and Eleanor, remembering how Elizabeth had already lost three of her children and might yet lose her eldest son, could not bear to take the baby from her.

No word came from Waterford. In the bleakest hours after

Clara's burial, Eleanor sometimes wondered if all there had perished, if they alone had survived the plague.

"Someone needs to go into town," said David, still in his sickbed.

"I'll go," said his son. At fifteen, William seemed a shriveled old man with sunken cheeks and hollow eyes.

Elizabeth grew frantic and insisted that none of them must leave the manor, especially William, who was still too weak to sit a horse. They placated her, but they knew that eventually, someone must go.

The thought of news from town reminded Eleanor of a letter she had never opened. Frank Schaeffer's appearance had so unsettled her that she had forgotten all about the slender envelope that had brought him, and the contagion, to Elm Creek Manor. She found it where she had left it weeks ago, a relic from a different age. She hesitated before opening it, gripped by the sudden fear that she would unleash more disease upon her family like Pandora lifting the lid to her box of evils.

Within the envelope Eleanor found a single clipping from *The New York Times,* her father's obituary. He had died in September of influenza.

Days passed. When still no one came to Elm Creek Manor, Lucinda insisted that Eleanor, ironically now the strongest of the family, go into town. Even Elizabeth did not object.

Eleanor rode alone. She did not wear her mask; she did not know what miracle had protected her and Elizabeth when all around them had fallen ill, but she assumed it protected her still. She did not stop at any of the other outlying farms and passed no one on the road or working in the fields. She saw no one at all until she reached Tenth Street. The people she encountered waved excitedly, smiling and laughing. They wore no masks. She wondered at their rejoicing. Perhaps they were merely happy to be alive.

From far away she heard voices crying out in joy. When she rounded the corner of Main Street, she saw that the square between the library and town hall was filled with people. From everywhere came the sounds of celebration—music, raucous cheering, firecrackers, voices raised in song and laughter.

Someone called to her; she searched but could not find the speaker in the crowd.

"Eleanor!"

Then she saw the frantic waving; it was a woman from the quilt guild. Eleanor knew her name but could not call it to mind; all she could think of was the Starburst block the woman had made for the charity quilt.

"Eleanor!" the woman shouted again, crying tears of joy. "Did you hear? It's the armistice! The war is over!"

The war was over.

Freddy was coming home.

Chapter Nine

November was one of the busiest months of the year for Elm Creek Quilts, rivaled only by the first month of the new camp season. Although summer probably seemed a long time away for their campers, Sylvia and her colleagues were already deciding what classes and seminars to offer, assessing their staffing needs, printing up brochures and registration forms, and running new marketing campaigns. Sylvia wondered why they bothered to advertise since hundreds of registration forms had already arrived, but Sarah insisted the investment would pay off later. Sylvia shrugged and decided to have faith in Sarah's and Summer's judgment. She couldn't argue with their success, and besides, the activity kept her friends from talking about wedding gowns and bouquets day and night.

When she could spare time from Elm Creek Quilts, Sylvia continued the search for her mother's quilts from behind her father's oak desk in the library. The flood of letters and e-mails in response to Summer's post on the Missing Quilts Home Page had slowed to only one or two a week, but Sylvia followed each trail until she was sure it had reached a dead end. Unfortunately, virtually all the newest leads did so, for whenever Sylvia called or wrote to verify certain details, her questions brought forth new information that confirmed the quilt in question could not be her mother's.

Other leads that had once seemed promising had faded away. Even her friend Grace Daniels, the quilt historian from San Francisco, responded to Sylvia's e-mail with bad news.

TO: Summer.Sullivan@elmcreek.net
FROM: Grace Daniels <danielsg@deyoung.org>
DATE: 10:10 AM PT 6 Nov 2002
SUBJECT: Your Quilt Investigation

(Summer, please print out this note for Sylvia.)

Sylvia, I'm sorry it took me so long to get back to you, but I'm afraid I have bad news. I checked the San Jose Quilt Museum as you requested, but they do not have any New York Beauty quilts on display or in storage. I also called my contacts at the New England Quilt Museum and the Museum of the American Quilter's Society with the same result. We'll keep spreading the word and eventually some better information will surface.

I wonder if you might want to modify your inquiries to include the alternate names for the pattern. As you probably know, the New York Beauty did not acquire that name until the 1930s, when its pattern was included in the packages of a certain brand of batting. Until then, it was known as Rocky Mountain, Rocky Mountain Road, or Crown of Thorns.

I'll talk to you soon, and remember, don't give up!

Grace

PS: You really ought to get your own e-mail address.

Sylvia had never heard of the alternate names for the New York Beauty pattern, but when she searched her memory, she was forced to admit she could not think of a single occasion when her mother had referred to her version as anything but her wedding quilt. Sylvia's earliest memory of the name was a time several years after her mother's death, when Great-Aunt Lucinda showed Sylvia's father a similar quilt in a magazine and remarked how appropriate it had been for Sylvia's mother to choose that pattern for her bridal quilt, as she had been a New York beauty herself. Tears had come to her father's eyes, and he had agreed.

Sylvia doubted that adding the alternative names to the description of her mother's missing quilt would help where an illustration had failed, but with so little else to go on, she decided it wouldn't hurt to try.

The only clues that still gave Sylvia any hope were the check Gloria Schaeffer had used to buy the Ocean Waves quilt, the name of the auction house that had purchased the Elms and Lilacs quilt from Mary Beth Callahan's mother, and—despite Grace's disappointing reports—the few responses that placed the New York Beauty quilt in a museum. Although none of these responses named the same museum, Sylvia still believed she could not afford to dismiss them. She theorized that the quilt was or had been part of a traveling exhibit, which was why those who spotted it did not agree on the location, and why none of those museums now had the New York Beauty in its possession.

The one quilt Sylvia had abandoned her search for was the whole cloth quilt. Without her mother's embroidered initials and date, and with so many virtually identical quilts in existence, Sylvia reluctantly had to admit that identifying her mother's version would be impossible. Why, then, did the name of the quilt's designer sound so familiar? At first she assumed that she must have seen other examples of Abigail Drury's work, but Summer searched the Waterford College Library's databases and Sylvia pored over her many quilt books and magazines without finding a single mention of her name besides the October 1912 issue of *Ladies' Home Journal*. It seemed unlikely that a quilt designer of her considerable talent would have published but a single pattern in her entire career.

The frustration of this unsolved mystery urged Sylvia on to likelier prospects. The auction house in Sewickley kept excellent records, including who had purchased the Elms and Lilacs quilt and when, but it also had a strict confidentiality policy and would not release the name of the current owners without their permission. After a few anxious days, the auction house called back to inform her that the owner's niece, who had inherited the quilt upon her aunt's death, had agreed to take Sylvia's call. The niece traveled often, so Sylvia left several messages on her answering machine before finally reaching her, only to learn that the niece had sold the Elms and Lilacs quilt two years before.

"I hated to give it up," the young woman said. "Unfortunately, in her will, my aunt left the quilt to me and my husband. Ex-husband. She never thought we would split up or she would have left it to me alone. Our divorce negotiations dragged on for months longer than necessary just because he would not give up that quilt."

"He must have been very fond of it."

"Not at all. He preferred the duvet. He just wanted to hurt me."

"I suppose you're better off without him, then."

"You have no idea. Eventually I just couldn't deal with the struggle anymore, so I offered to sell the quilt and divide the money. He considered that a victory since I would lose my quilt. We agreed to have an independent appraiser from some organization, the Association of Quilters of America or something—"

"The National Quilters Association?"

"Yes, that sounds right. Would you believe she said the quilt was worth three thousand dollars? I'll never forget my ex's face when he heard that. He practically danced around the room with dollar signs in his eyes and cash registers ringing in the background." The young woman sniffed. "But he wasn't laughing long.

"I offered to find a buyer for the quilt, and since in addition to being a jerk my ex is also lazy, he agreed. I took it to the quilt shop in downtown Sewickley, but they were having financial problems and weren't buying quilts. From there I went to two different antique stores. One offered me a thousand and the other, two."

"But you knew it was worth much more."

"That wasn't the point. So I took it to Horsefeathers."

"Where?"

"The Horsefeathers Boutique. It's a funky arts and crafts store in downtown Sewickley. The owner is a local artist and you would not believe the stuff she makes. I showed her the quilt, she oohed and ahhed and agreed it was beautiful—and offered me thirty dollars for it."

"That's all? Did you tell her about the appraisal?"

"No, I told her it was a deal. I handed over the quilt, she gave me the cash and a receipt. Then I drove right over to the apartment my ex was sharing with his new girlfriend and gave him his fifteen bucks."

Sylvia closed her eyes and sighed. "I suppose I can understand why you did that, but it sounds like a bitter triumph to me."

"So it wasn't my proudest moment. At least I showed him he couldn't walk all over me and get away with it. He knew I loved that quilt, and that's why he took it from me."

"If you cared for it so much, why didn't you buy it back after the terms of the divorce negotiations were satisfied?"

"I couldn't. That quilt became a symbol of everything wrong in our marriage." Suddenly her tone shifted. "This doesn't mean you'll never find your mother's quilt. It might still be at Horsefeathers, and if not, they'll know who has it."

Unless it had changed hands once again. "I'll try to contact them right away. Thank you very much for the information."

"No problem. Oh, one more thing."

"Yes?"

"When you make out your will, don't leave something to a couple when you really just mean for one of them to have it. And if you know anyone who's getting married, your grandchildren or whatever, make sure they have a great prenup."

"Thanks," said Sylvia. "I'll be sure to keep that in mind."

Sylvia had lived in Sewickley for many years, but she had never heard of the Horsefeathers Boutique, and she would have sworn there was a toy store at the street corner the young woman had described. Still, she knew better than to rely upon her memory alone, and sure enough, when Summer searched on-line, she found a phone number and address for the store. When Sylvia called, the owner was not available but the sales clerk said the Elms and Lilacs quilt sounded familiar. Sylvia decided to take this as a good if ambiguous sign. She left her name and number and asked for the owner to call her at her convenience.

Following the trail of Gloria Schaeffer's check proved easier. Gloria's old phone number was no longer in service, as Sylvia had expected, and the house and land had been razed decades ago to make way for a shopping mall. Fortunately, one of her two sons still lived in Waterford and was listed in the phone book. When Sylvia called, she reached Philip Schaeffer's wife, Edna, a friendly woman close to her own age. She seemed fascinated by Sylvia's tale of the search for her mother's quilts and explained that the two sons had divided up the quilts they had inherited from Gloria. "My husband and I don't own any quilts that sound like your Ocean Waves quilt, so it must have gone to his brother, Howard," said Edna. "He lives in Iowa now, but he and his family are coming here for Thanksgiving. I'll ask him to bring the quilt if he still owns it, but I'm afraid I can't promise he'll sell it to you."

"I understand," Sylvia assured her, and they made plans for Sylvia to stop by on the Friday after Thanksgiving. She could not expect everyone to part with their quilts as readily as Mona Niehaus had. The Schaeffers had owned the Ocean Waves quilt for more than fifty years, longer than the Bergstroms themselves.

They likely considered it one of their own family heirlooms by now. After the disappointment of the whole cloth quilt, Sylvia would be satisfied just to see the quilt again and to know it was treasured.

As Thanksgiving approached, Sylvia waited for Andrew and his children to decide how they would spend the holiday. Sometimes Sylvia and Andrew joined his children and their families at Amy's home in Connecticut, but on alternate years, Sylvia invited everyone to Elm Creek Manor. She enjoyed those celebrations the most because Sarah's mother and Matt's father also joined them for the weekend, and the other Elm Creek Quilters always found time to stop by for some coffee and pie. This year was supposed to be Sylvia's turn to play hostess, which Sylvia considered especially fortuitous because she knew she would have few opportunities to make peace with Andrew's children before the wedding. Welcoming them into her home would, she hoped, show them how much she cared about them and their father.

But as the days grew colder and shorter, and the first light snow fell, Andrew said little about the upcoming holiday. When Sylvia pressed him, he would say that they had not had a chance to discuss it, or that his children had not made up their minds. Finally Sylvia insisted that he call them and make a decision, because in a few days she would either need to buy a turkey or pack her suitcase and she would appreciate a little advance notice. Andrew apologized and went off to the parlor to phone them, but returned shaking his head.

"They're not coming?" asked Sylvia.

"Not this year. It's too far to drive round trip in four days and they don't want to fly. Since they know it wouldn't be fair to ask me to choose between them, they thought it best if we all spend Thanksgiving at our own homes."

Sylvia heard Amy's voice echoed in Andrew's words. "I can't believe Bob is afraid to fly," she said. "If your children want to get together with you at Amy's, I'll stay home. I don't want to rob you of a holiday with your family."

"Absolutely not." He put his hands on her shoulders. "Like I told Amy when she was here last month, you're my family."

He kissed her, and Sylvia knew he meant what he said, but she felt sick at heart thinking about the widening divide between Andrew and his children. She thought of his grandchildren and wondered how the holiday plans would be explained to them. She wondered what excuses they would invent for Andrew's absence, year after year, if the disagreement grew into estrangement.

A shadow darkened their Thanksgiving feast that year, and not even the presence of Sarah's mother and Matt's father could lift it entirely. Sylvia knew that Andrew missed his family; he glanced at the clock throughout the day, as if imagining what his children and grandchildren were doing at that moment. He left shortly after dessert to call them, but he returned a mere fifteen minutes later to say that they were well and that they gave Sylvia and her friends their best regards.

Privately, Sarah tried to reassure Sylvia that the disagreement would not last long. The chill must be thawing already, or Andrew wouldn't have phoned Amy and Bob at all. "By Christmas everyone will be on good terms again," she said, giving Sylvia a comforting hug. "You'll see. We'll invite everyone here and have a wonderful time. We'll wine and dine the adults and slip the kids candy when their parents aren't looking. Before long they'll start to see the advantages of having you as a stepmother."

Sylvia had to laugh. "You're absolutely right. Why didn't I resort to bribery long ago?"

She was joking, of course, but although she wouldn't admit it to a soul, she might have tried to win them over with gifts if not for her pride—and her certainty that it wouldn't work. Nothing Sylvia could do or say or give could change the facts that she was seven years older than Andrew and had once had a stroke. It would be easier to persuade his children to give the marriage their blessing if they merely disliked her.

The next morning, Sarah drove Sylvia to Edna and Philip Schaeffer's house, a red-brick ranch with two large oak trees in the front yard and four cars parked in the driveway. Three young children ran through scattered leaves on the lawn, shouting and laughing, while an older boy, rake in hand, called out orders they ignored. The four watched with interest as Sylvia and Sarah got out of the Elm Creek Quilts minivan and approached the front door. "Hewwo," called the youngest, a boy not quite two.

"Hello, honey," Sarah replied, waving. The little boy grinned and hid behind the eldest girl.

"You could have one yourself, you know," said Sylvia as she rang the doorbell.

"Please. You sound just like my mother." Sarah rolled her eyes, but she smiled as she spoke, with no hint of the resentment that used to surface whenever her mother was mentioned. Their relationship had been strained for years, but they had reconciled while both women helped Sylvia recover from her stroke. She should take comfort in their example, Sylvia told herself. If Sarah and Carol could find a way to accept their differences, surely Andrew and his children could. She just hoped they wouldn't require an unexpected calamity to push them forward.

A woman who looked to be in her mid-eighties answered the door. "You must be Sylvia Compson," she said, opening the door and beckoning them inside. "I'm Edna Schaeffer, as you probably guessed."

Sylvia thanked her for allowing them to interrupt her holiday and introduced Sarah. "Did your brother-in-law have a safe trip?" she asked, surreptitiously scanning the room for the quilt.

Edna's face assumed an apologetic expression that had become all too familiar to Sylvia since she had begun the search. "He did, thank you, but I'm afraid he didn't bring your mother's quilt with him."

"I see," said Sylvia.

"I'm sorry, dear." Edna patted Sylvia's arm sympathetically. "It's a long story and he wanted to tell you himself, or I would have called and saved you the trip over. Howard's been looking forward to seeing you."

"Has he?"

"Oh, my, yes. Phil has, too, but don't worry. I'm not the jealous type." Edna smiled and led them into the living room, where two older gentlemen and several younger men and women sat talking and watching a football game on television. The two older men stood as the women approached. "This can't be little tagalong Sylvia," boomed the taller of the two. "What happened to all those dark tousled curls?"

"I'm afraid they're long gone." Smiling, Sylvia shook the men's hands. "And I beg your pardon, but I was never a tagalong."

"That's not what Claudia told us," said the other man, his voice a quiet echo of his brother's. He had to be Philip, the younger of the two Schaeffer boys. He had always been more bashful than Howard.

"My goodness, that's right. I had forgotten you two were in the same class." Sylvia pursed her lips and feigned annoyance. "I suppose I shouldn't be surprised that she told tales on me."

"I was sweet on her," said Phil, with an embarrassed shrug and a glance at his wife, who patted his arm and laughed. "I hung on every word she said, but she only had eyes for Howard."

"Until Harold Midden came to town," said Howard, shaking his head. "Claudia used to kiss me behind the library after school, but once she met Harold, she tossed me out like yesterday's trash."

"She didn't," said Sylvia, shocked. "She told us she went to the library to study."

Howard shrugged. "We sometimes fit in a little studying afterward. Anyway, I always knew it wouldn't have worked out between us in the long run."

"Why not?"

Edna gestured to two chairs near Sylvia and Sarah. "Why don't we all sit down and hear the whole story?"

"Our mother wouldn't be pleased if she knew we were telling you this," said Phil ruefully as they seated themselves.

Sylvia, who had learned that some of the most important stories began with the revelation of a secret, sat back and smiled to encourage him to continue.

"I guess you know our mother disliked yours," said Howard.

"Why, no, I never knew that," said Sylvia, looking from one brother to the other in surprise. "I knew she didn't care for me and my sister, but neither did the entire Waterford Quilting Guild or they wouldn't have let her kick us out."

"Didn't your mothers found the guild together?" asked Sarah. "They must have been friends at one point."

"You never knew our mothers were enemies and we never knew they were friends," said Phil. "We grew up hearing how awful the Bergstroms were, how selfish, how they had cost our father his life."

"What?" exclaimed Sylvia.

"Now you can see why I knew my relationship with Claudia would never go anywhere," said Howard. "Mother would have fainted if I had brought her home."

"That probably added to Claudia's appeal," teased Edna.

"Let's get back to your father," said Sylvia. "Why on earth did your mother blame mine for his death?"

Howard and Phil exchanged a look before Howard said, "Well, first let me say that even as boys we knew our mother and her friends were jealous of your mother. We knew why, too. Your mother was the prettiest woman in Waterford, and she was so gentle and kind that of course every man and boy in town had a crush on her. She wasn't from around here, either, and that made her seem mysterious and exotic."

"Exotic?" said Sylvia. "My mother? She was from New York, not the other side of the world."

"To people who had never left the Elm Creek Valley," said Phil, "New York might as well have been the other side of the world."

"We were like all the rest," added Howard. "We admired your mother, but we felt guilty about it because we knew we were betraying our mother."

"She always thought our father liked your mother a little too much," said Phil. "Not that she ever thought he cheated on her—"

"Not with my mother he didn't," declared Sylvia. "My mother was devoted to my father. She would never have considered such a thing."

"Our father felt the same way about our mother," said Howard. "At least that's what our other relatives told us. I was just a boy when he died, and Phil here was just a baby."

"How did your father die?" asked Sarah.

"In the influenza epidemic of 1918," said Howard.

"So did several members of my own family," said Sylvia.

Phil grimaced and nodded. "We were well aware of that. Mother never let us forget it. You see, as soon as the people of Waterford realized that the disease was coming closer, they quarantined the town."

Sylvia nodded. Her great-aunt Lucinda had told her stories of those terrible weeks when nearly the entire family had been stricken, and Great-Aunt Maude and young Aunt Clara had died. Claudia, too, had nearly lost her life, although no one but Aunt Lucinda ever spoke of it.

"The town stayed free of the disease for a while," said Phil. "But it didn't last, and our father was the first to catch it."

"And the first to die," said Howard. "He was the town mail carrier. He delivered a letter to your mother, and according to our mother, he caught the flu there."

"Our mother fell ill next, and then it was everywhere," said Phil. "Our mother recovered, but she was never the same. She told everyone that my father had caught the disease from the Bergstroms, and that your family had broken the quarantine in order to buy and sell your horses. If not for the greed of the Bergstroms, she said, Waterford would have been spared. The hundreds who died here would never have suffered so much as a runny nose."

Sylvia clutched the arms of her chair. "I don't believe it," she managed to say. "My family never would have risked other people's lives for money."

"Of course not." Sarah reached out and touched her arm, frowning at the Schaeffers. "With all due respect, your mother wasn't a doctor, and no one knew about viruses back then. She couldn't have known for certain where your father contracted the disease, and unless she personally witnessed the Bergstroms crossing the quarantine line, she had no right to accuse them."

Edna held up her hands to calm them. "Please, boys, tell them the rest."

"I'm sorry I upset you," said Howard. "We just wanted you to hear the story we grew up with."

"We know your family didn't bring the flu to Waterford," said Phil. "Our father did."

"He was delivering the town's mail to the postal center in Grangerville when the quarantine signs went up," said Howard. "He stayed in Grangerville, but when people began dying right and left, he got scared and beat it out of town. He holed up in a hunting shack for a while, but when he ran out of food, he came home."

"Mother was so glad to see him that she cried," said Phil, "but she knew he had endangered the town. She came and went as usual rather than arouse suspicions, but she made him stay indoors with the curtains drawn for four days until they were both certain he wasn't sick."

"After that, they figured he was safe, so he acted as if he had never left Waterford," said Howard. "A few close friends knew he had been away, but my parents invented some story about him being laid up with a sprained ankle at an outlying farm, and that in all the confusion, Gloria never received word. Only one other person knew he had knowingly crossed the quarantine line."

"Sylvia's mother," said Sarah.

"Exactly."

"Our mother was horrified that she and our father had infected the town," said Phil. "Frankly, I think it would have come anyway. The Spanish flu was so contagious and the quarantine so easily breached that it was only a matter of time. The fact is, however, that our parents introduced it into Waterford, and my mother couldn't handle the shame. She was terrified that people would find out and condemn her."

"So instead she condemned my family," said Sylvia.

The two men nodded.

"She regretted that all her life," said Howard. "But once she started the lie, it got out of her control. She told herself that people would forget, but although they didn't talk much about the flu itself, everyone remembered to mistrust the Bergstroms long after they forgot the reason why."

"We knew nothing of this until the week before she died," said Edna. "The guilt of what she had done ate away at her for the better part of fifty years. She had bought your mother's quilt as a way to help your sister financially, and at the end of her life, her greatest concern was that we return the quilt to you."

"She wasn't content to return it to Claudia because she was afraid your sister would just sell it again," said Howard.

"If the secret bothered your mother for roughly fifty years, she must have passed away in the 1960s," said Sarah. "Why didn't you return the quilt to Sylvia as your mother requested?"

Sylvia thought she knew the answer, and Phil confirmed it. "No one knew where Sylvia was. Claudia didn't know, and the rest of the Bergstrom family had either moved away or passed on. We always assumed she would return to Elm Creek Manor some day, and we planned to return the quilt to her then."

"As the years went by, we all sort of forgot about it," said Edna apologetically.

"Then I moved away to Iowa." Howard frowned and shook his head. "I should have left the quilt here, but it was packed away with other things my mother had left me, and I never gave it a second thought. I found it when I was clearing out the basement after my wife passed away. I knew it ought to be in Waterford in case you came home, but I didn't want to ship it, so I decided to bring it the next time I came to visit."

And yet here he was, without the quilt. "What happened to it?" asked Sylvia.

Edna said, "I'm sure you heard about all that terrible flooding in the Midwest a few years back."

Sylvia could guess the rest, but she nodded.

"I lost nearly everything when the Mississippi crested," said Howard. "I'm sorry, Sylvia, but your mother's quilt couldn't be salvaged."

✻

"It was so waterlogged and encrusted with mud that they didn't recognize it as a quilt," Sylvia told Andrew when she and Sarah returned home. "They discarded it with the rest of the soiled clothes and bedding."

"There probably wasn't anything you could have done to restore it even if they hadn't thrown it away," said Andrew.

"Probably not," she admitted, but she still wished they had saved it. Soiled or not, it was still the work of her mother's hands, rare and precious, if only to her.

On the Monday after Thanksgiving, Sylvia and Andrew drove west in the Elm Creek Quilts minivan, which they favored over the motor home when the twists and turns of the Pennsylvania roadways were dusted with snow. Sylvia preferred not to travel in foul weather at all, but she was impatient to pursue this lead, and the owner of the Horsefeathers Boutique had not returned her calls. Sylvia wanted to believe that the owner either never received the messages or had been too swamped by the Christmas sales rush to call her back, but it was equally likely the owner had not called because she no longer had the quilt. Sylvia would have waited another week before going to see the shop in person, but the drive to Sewickley was reasonable and her need for answers urgent.

Sylvia's anticipation grew as they approached Sewickley. She had lived there for nearly forty years, from the time she first accepted a teaching position in the Allegheny School District until the lawyer called with news of her sister's death. When Sylvia went to Waterford to settle her sister's affairs, she had planned to sell Elm Creek Manor, return to Sewickley, and live out her days there. She never imagined she would return to Sewickley only to sell her house.

She happily pointed out her former home as they passed by it on Camp Meeting Road. "Goodness, they painted it robin's egg blue," she said, twisting in her seat and staring out the window. "When I lived there, the house was a deep brick red, with black shutters. It used to disappear into the trees."

"No danger of that now," said Andrew, carefully maneuvering the motor home down a steep, curving hill. Sylvia directed him to turn left on Beaver Street and into the downtown area, where several blocks of Victorian homes, shops, and restaurants were already decorated for Christmas, with colored lights in the storefronts and holly twined about the lampposts.

The familiarity of the sight warmed her, which was why the changes to her former hometown struck with unexpected surprise.

Her favorite café had become a men's clothing store, she saw as they passed, and the old Thrift Drug store was now a Starbucks. "The quilt shop is gone," she exclaimed with dismay, staring in disbelief as they passed a shoe store.

"They probably went under after you moved away," said Andrew. "What you spend on fabric could keep three or four quilt shops in the black."

"Just for that, I'm not treating you to lunch," Sylvia teased. "And I know all the best places around here."

They parked the motor home in a public lot and put on their coats and gloves, for although Horsefeathers was just around the corner, the wind blew cold and the air smelled of snow.

"I'm surprised they're allowed to use that color," Sylvia remarked as they approached the fuchsia storefront.

"I'm surprised anyone would want to."

"No, I mean I believe they have a board that regulates those sorts of things. At least they did when I lived here. The downtown district tries to maintain a certain aesthetic. You should have seen the uproar when McDonald's tried to move in."

By then they were close enough to read the bright gold letters painted on the storefront window. "HORSEFEATHERS BOUTIQUE. ART FROM FOUND OBJECTS," read Andrew. "That disqualifies your mother's quilt, since it's a lost object."

"One person's lost is another person's found," said Sylvia absently. Her hand was on the doorknob, but the assortment of oddities displayed in the window had captured her attention. A chandelier made of antique doorknobs. A men's trench coat pieced from velvet Elvises. Several picture frames embellished with everything from coins to insects trapped in amber. The whimsical collection had been arranged to set off each piece to its best advantage, obviously by someone quite fond of her creations.

"Whoever the owner is," said Sylvia, pulling open the door, "she must have a sense of humor."

Inside, the shop was almost too warm, but the heat was a welcome respite from the cold wind. Sylvia removed her hat and tucked it into her pocket, looking around in amazement. The aisles were stuffed with items that defied description—a sculpture made from stacks of old newspapers, a refrigerator transformed into a grandfather clock, a dress sewn from small, white rectangles of fabric that appeared to have printing on them. Sylvia leaned closer for a better look, and laughed. "'Under penalty of law this tag is not to be removed except by the consumer.'"

"That doesn't look very comfortable."

"I don't think that's the point, do you? I'm sure the artist was making a statement." She paused. "What sort of statement, I honestly couldn't say."

Andrew found the price tag. "An expensive one. This will set you back six hundred bucks."

"And here I was going to put it on my Christmas list." Sylvia looked around the shop. She didn't see any quilts amid the clutter, but a stout woman in a purple caftan had emerged from a backroom and was making her way toward them. Her dark brown hair hung nearly to her waist and, unless Sylvia's eyes were deceiving her, her earrings were made from pasta embellished with silver paint and glitter.

"Can I help you find something?" the woman asked.

"I hope so," said Sylvia. "Are you Charlene Murray? My name is Sylvia Compson. I left a message—several messages, actually—about an antique quilt that I believe may be in your possession."

"A quilt?" The woman's brow furrowed, and then she brightened. "Wait. Are you the woman from Waterford?"

"Yes, that's right."

"I'm so glad you stopped by," exclaimed Charlene. "I meant to call you back, but I lost the sticky note with your phone number."

"Maybe you sewed it into a pair of pants," offered Andrew.

Sylvia nudged him. "Your associate said that the quilt sounded familiar. Did she tell you about it? It was made in the medallion style, with appliquéd elm leaves, lilacs, and intertwining vines. The hand quilting is quite superior, fourteen stitches to the inch, except in a few places where my sister and I helped." She tried not to, but she couldn't help adding, "My stitches were nine to the inch back then. Any larger than that were my sister's."

"I know exactly the piece you mean." Charlene beckoned for Sylvia to follow her deeper into the shop. "It wasn't in the best condition when I took it on, but it was fabulous material, and it cleaned up nicely in the washing machine."

Sylvia winced. "I hope you used the gentle cycle. It *is* an antique."

"No, I just threw it in with the rest of my laundry," said Charlene airily. "I had to treat it as I know my customers would to see if it would hold up. No one hand washes anymore, no matter how many times I tell them this is wearable art and not something they picked up at the Gap."

"But you do have the quilt, right?" asked Andrew.

Charlene beamed. "I do, and wait until you see what I've done with it." She stopped at a clothing rack, pushed aside a few hangers, and gestured proudly to a quilted jacket. "You're in luck. This is the last one."

Sylvia took in appliquéd flowers and leaves, exquisite quilting— "Good heavens."

"Thank you. It's absolutely one of my favorites. I already sold one size small, two larges, and an extra-large." She removed the jacket from the hanger and held it up to Sylvia. "I was tempted to keep this one for myself, but it's a medium, and as you can see, I'm not. It should fit you, though."

Sylvia closed her arms around what remained of her mother's quilt and tried to think of something to say. All she could manage was, "Why?"

Charlene's laughed tinkled. "I get that question all the time. I take my inspiration from many sources, but I admit this one is a little more pragmatic. I had a friend who fought with her sisters over a quilt their late mother had made. Since they all wanted it and no one was willing to let the others have it, they took a pair of scissors and cut it into four pieces. My friend doesn't sew, so she asked me to repair the edges of hers so the filling wouldn't fall out. But since her little quarter of a quilt wasn't big enough for a bed anymore, I made her a vest instead."

Sylvia wanted to bury her face in the jacket and weep. "She let you do that?"

"Are you kidding? She was thrilled. Two of her sisters had me do the same thing to their pieces." Charlene peered at her inquisitively. "Do you want to try it on?"

Sylvia shook her head, but Charlene pretended not to notice and within moments had Sylvia out of her winter coat and into the jacket. She led Sylvia to a full-length mirror, where she gushed about how much the jacket suited her. Sylvia ran her hands over the jacket. It fit her well, and her mother's handiwork had retained much of its beauty despite its transformation. But the jacket was less than what the quilt had been, and Sylvia could not speak for the ache in her heart.

Charlene's chatter had ceased, and she regarded Sylvia with perplexed worry that deepened as the awkward silence dragged on. Finally, Sylvia took a deep breath. "Did you save the rest of it?"

"You mean the scraps from my sewing?" Charlene shrugged. "I saved all of the filling and some of the fabric, but it's long gone now, used up in other projects."

"And the other jackets—do you know where they might be?"

Charlene chuckled, flattered but bemused. "Why, are you planning to outfit a basketball team?"

"Please, do you know how I might find them?"

She shook her head. "My records aren't that detailed. I could ask my assistants if they remember, but we get mostly tourist traffic in here. The jackets most likely weren't purchased by anyone from Sewickley."

Sylvia's hopes of reassembling the quilt faded.

"What do you want for it?" asked Andrew.

Sylvia fumbled for the price tag dangling from her sleeve. "Four hundred." She shrugged off the jacket and handed it to Charlene. "Quite a return on your investment."

"It might seem expensive, but it *is* a one-of-a-kind work of art."

Andrew regarded her, stern. "By my count you made four others."

"Not in size medium, and the appliqués are arranged differently on each jacket," countered Charlene, but she looked sheepish. "Okay, I'll tell you what. Since you came such a long way, I'll give you ten percent off."

"I'll take it," said Andrew.

"No, Andrew," said Sylvia, thinking of his pension. "Let me get it."

But he insisted, and within minutes she was on her way back to the minivan, one arm tucked in Andrew's, the other clutching the handles of a shopping bag with the quilted jacket inside. A light snow had begun to fall. Andrew steadied her so she would not slip on the pavement, and she burrowed her chin into her coat when a sudden gust of wind drove icy crystals into her face.

Once they were in the car, Andrew asked, "Do you want to head home or find a place to stay overnight?"

Sylvia had lost all interest in Christmas shopping. "Would you mind if we went home, or is that too much driving for one day?"

He assured her he was up to the trip if she was, and as he pulled out of the parking lot, she spread the jacket on her lap and sighed, running her hand over lavender lilac petals and faded green elm leaves, tracing a quilted feathered wreath with a fingertip. Considering the fate of the whole cloth quilt and the Ocean Waves, she was fortunate to find any part of the Elms and Lilacs. "I suppose a mutilated remnant of my mother's quilt is better than nothing at all."

"Hey," protested Andrew. "Is that any way to talk about a man's Christmas present?"

"I'm sorry, dear." Sylvia hugged the quilt to her chest and managed a smile. "I am glad to have it, and it was good of you to get it for me."

"That's more like it." He glanced at her for a moment before returning his gaze to the road. "What's that writing on the inside?"

"This? It's just the size tag."

"Not that. On the left front, where the chest pocket would be."

Sylvia opened the jacket and gasped at the sight of a faded bit of embroidery. "It's my mother's initials, and two numbers, a nine and a two. That must be part of the date. I know my mother completed this quilt in 1927." She hugged the quilt, then leaned over and kissed Andrew. "Charlene was right; I am lucky. I would have purchased any one she had in the shop, but only this one had the embroidery."

"That's lucky."

"It is, indeed. And you know what else? I think it's a very good sign. I believe I will find the New York Beauty quilt before long."

She settled back into her seat, content for the first time in days.

"Maybe it's a sign for something else, too," said Andrew.

"Oh?" She raised her eyebrows at him. "Such as?"

"Maybe we should get married here."

"Instead of Waterford?" She frowned. "Then all our friends would have to travel—"

"No, they won't. I mean here and now."

Sylvia stared at him. "Now? As in right now?"

"As soon as we can find a minister or a judge or a justice of the peace. Come on, Sylvia, what do you say? We already have our marriage license. This way we could avoid all the conflict with the kids. They'll have to stop complaining and start getting used to the idea if we just go ahead and do it."

"That would put an end to my friends' plans for an extravagant wedding," mused Sylvia.

"We can still have a party. That way our friends can't say we cheated them out of their celebration."

Sylvia laughed. "I don't know if that will be good enough, but I suppose they'll forgive us eventually." She paused, considering. "Very well. Let's do it."

Andrew turned the minivan around.

They drove to the county clerk's office, where they learned a justice of the peace could marry them, but not until the following day. They made an appointment for ten o'clock the next morning and set about finding a place to stay for the night. Sylvia remembered a charming bed-and-breakfast on Main Street, and since it happened to have a rare vacancy, Sylvia and Andrew checked in and concluded this was another happy omen.

They unpacked their overnight bags and, disregarding the chill in the air, ventured back toward the shops. Sylvia didn't want a fancy wedding gown, but she certainly wouldn't marry in the casual travel clothes she had brought for the ride home, and she could only laugh at Andrew's suggestion that she wear the Elms and Lilacs jacket. To her delight, she found a lovely plum suit on sale, suitable for a wedding and yet something she could wear again, at Christmas. She insisted Andrew pick out something nice for himself as well and steered him toward a charcoal gray suit in which he looked quite distinguished. "This is your Christmas present," she retorted when he protested about the price, and bought him a pair of shoes to go with it.

Afterward, they hurried through the falling snow to a jewelry store, where they selected their wedding bands. They told the bemused jeweler that they needed the rings right away and would wait while he engraved them.

They celebrated their wedding eve supper at the finest restaurant in downtown Sewickley, and strolled hand in hand back to their bed-and-breakfast, full of anticipation for the morning. They kissed good night and teased each other about oversleeping and missing their important date, but each knew the other would not miss it for the world.

Sylvia hummed to herself as she hung up her new suit and got ready for bed, but just before she turned out the light, her glance fell upon the telephone, and she wondered if she ought to call Sarah, at least, and ask her and Matt to witness the ceremony. She could hardly invite them and ignore Andrew's children, however, so she turned out the light and went to sleep.

The next morning she woke before the alarm and lay in bed, listening to the wind blow ice against the windowpane. The dim light made the day seem younger than it was, but she heard Andrew stirring on the other side of the wall, and she knew she could not linger on such an important day.

Andrew had risen early, and he met her at breakfast with a small bouquet of flowers. It was lovely, and his face beamed with happiness as he kissed her and pulled her out of her chair. Their host and hostess were thrilled to discover they had a bride and groom at the table, and soon all the other guests were offering them congratulations and toasts of coffee and orange juice.

Andrew enjoyed every moment, but Sylvia found she had no appetite. When Andrew asked her if she felt ill, she assured him she was fine, just a little nervous from all the excitement. Andrew closed his hand around hers and held it while he ate, and by the time he finished, she felt much better. She even managed to swallow a few bites of her scrambled egg and drink most of her tea.

The sun had come out, chasing away the unseasonable cold, and nearly all the snow from the previous day had melted. They found a parking place right in front of the city clerk's office. "Another good sign," said Andrew, as he helped her from the minivan.

She clutched her bouquet and took his arm. "Do you have the wedding license?"

He touched his coat pocket. "Right here."

"And the rings?"

He stopped, frowned, and patted all his pockets in turn until he smiled and withdrew the two small velvet boxes from his front suit pocket. "They're here, too."

"Good. I have the strangest feeling we're forgetting something." Sylvia felt breathless. "Should I hold your ring?"

He smiled. "As long as you promise to give it back."

He gave her the ring box and offered her his arm again. She took it, smiled up at him, and allowed him to escort her inside.

Her heart pounded as they walked down the corridor toward the city clerk's office. People they passed spied her bouquet and grinned. Sylvia flushed and smiled back at them, then held her head higher and strode purposefully forward. She loved Andrew. She wanted to marry him. And yet . . .

She stopped short in the corridor, bring him to a halt. "Andrew—"

He looked down at her, his dear face full of concern. "What's wrong?"

"We can't do this. We shouldn't marry here, far from home, with strangers as witnesses." His face fell, but she knew in her heart what she said was true. "We should marry surrounded by people we love, or not at all."

He stared at her for a long, silent moment. He released her hands, turned away, and stood, head bowed, his back to her.

Hesitantly, she reached out and touched him softly on the shoulder. "Andrew?"

"You're right." He inhaled deeply, then turned to face her. She had never seen him more full of regret or resolve. "You're right. Let's go home."

Chapter Ten

1927

The weight and thickness of the envelope told Eleanor that it contained more than a simple news clipping. Her mother's mailings had grown less frequent since Father's death; six months had passed since the last. If the return address of the Manhattan brownstone had not been written in her mother's own hand, Eleanor would have assumed the elderly cousin with whom she lived had sent notice of her mother's death.

Inside the envelope was a sheet of ivory writing paper edged with a quarter-inch black border. Her mother's note took up barely half the page.

May 8, 1927

Dear Eleanor,

Cousin Claire has died and her late husband's property now belongs to his brother's children. They intend to live here themselves and would not keep me among them even if I wished to stay, which I do not. I do not expect you to take me in. If you felt for me the respect and concern a daughter owes her mother, you never would have left us. However, I have no one else, so I must turn to you and hope that time has softened your selfish heart. I am to be evicted at month's end, and unless I do not hear from you, I will have no choice but to take up residence in an asylum for destitute women. If you wish to spare me from that disgrace, respond promptly to

Your Mother,
Gertrude Drayton-Smith Lockwood

Eleanor kept the letter in a bureau drawer for a day before showing it to Fred and Lucinda. She would have consulted Elizabeth first, as the eldest and nominal leader of the family, but since her husband's death five years before, Elizabeth did little but rock in her chair and quilt and murmur bleak predictions about the future. Claudia laughed at her behind her back, but seven-year-old Sylvia would turn her dark eyes from her grandmother and lead Richard away by the hand as if the mournful words could not hurt him if he did not hear. The solemn girl seemed to believe it was her responsibility to protect her younger brother from all dangers, real and imaginary.

Her darling boy was little more than a year old but already as headstrong and spirited as his father. If she could have given Fred another son, she would have named him after the other brother he had lost in the war, but she knew her heart could not withstand another pregnancy. When she first thought she might be pregnant again, Dr. Granger had scolded her when she went to him, glowing with joy, to confirm her secret hope. After she nearly died in childbirth, he had exhorted her—and Fred, too—not to risk another. But Eleanor did not need the doctor's warnings or her husband's white-faced pleading to convince her. She had not recovered from Richard's birth the way she had with the girls. She had lost something she could not define, and she knew another baby would kill her. She had been blessed with three beautiful, beloved children, and she so wanted to see them grow up that she would cling to life with her fingernails for one more day with them.

Fred read the letter, snorted, and handed it to his aunt. Lucinda scanned the lines and barked out a laugh. "Dear Eleanor," she paraphrased, holding out the page to Eleanor. "I am so sorry that for almost forty years I was a hateful old hag to you instead of a loving mother. Now that I am impoverished in my dotage, won't you please take care of me?"

"I know better than to expect an apology," said Eleanor, returning the letter to its envelope. "She thinks I owe her one."

"We'll send her money," said Fred. "A monthly allowance so she can maintain her own household in New York. We don't have to bring her here."

"I don't think she will accept charity."

"Isn't inviting her to live with us charity?" asked Fred. "I can't forget how she mistreated you. I won't allow her to hurt you in your own home."

Eleanor touched his cheek. "I have you. I have the children. She has lost the power to injure me."

She smiled at him, and he placed his hand over hers and regarded her fondly, but there was a tightness around his eyes that none of her reassurances could ease. She had tried to hide her increasing weakness, but he knew her heart labored to sustain her life. He would fight against anything that would sap her remaining strength, even if it meant abandoning his mother-in-law to her own fate.

Nevertheless, she was Eleanor's mother, and Eleanor did have a duty toward her. If her mother-in-law agreed, Eleanor would invite her mother to Elm Creek Manor.

Elizabeth gave her permission, but not without misgivings. "I admire your willingness to forgive," she said, shaking her head, "but if she says one cruel word against you or my son, I will slap her."

Lucinda laughed, but Fred grimaced and Eleanor wondered if she had made a mistake. She could not bear it if her mother's presence brought more grief to a family that had seen too much mourning.

Before writing back to her mother, she told the children. Claudia clapped her hands, delighted that she would be able to meet Grandmother Lockwood at last. Eleanor forced a smile and stroked her eldest daughter's glossy curls. She had told Claudia stories of her childhood in New York, of pretty dresses, glamorous balls, beautiful horses, and the summer house. She had allowed Claudia to believe the fairy tale, reserving the truth for when she was older. Even after so many years, the thought of telling those stories pained her. Now, perhaps, she would not need to. Once Claudia met Grandmother Lockwood, she could decide for herself.

Sylvia, apparently, already had. "Why is she coming now, after so many years?"

"Someone else owns her home now, and she has to move," said Eleanor, knowing better than to dissemble with Sylvia, who would reproach her with dark, silent looks when she discovered the truth. "Naturally she would turn to family at such a time."

Sylvia looked dubious, and Eleanor held her breath, certain Sylvia would ask why Grandmother Lockwood had not turned to them before, such as when Grandfather Lockwood died, but Sylvia said only, "When is she coming?"

"I don't know," said Eleanor. "I will ask her. Now, off you go to the nursery. I have letters to write."

Sylvia gave her a curious look, but she picked up Richard and went off after her sister. Eleanor watched them climb the stairs, longing to run after them as she once had. Lately climbing the stairs tired her so much that she remained on the first floor from breakfast until retiring for the night. Fred had to help her, and more often than not, he simply lifted her into his arms and carried her upstairs, effortlessly, as if she were one of the children.

After she had transformed her study into a nursery, the library had become her favorite place to linger over a book or compose a letter, but over the past year she had moved her favorite books and writing papers to the parlor. She was not surprised to find the room empty at that time of day, since Elizabeth preferred the sitting room off the kitchen and everyone else was working outside, tending to the horses, absorbing her former duties into their own. She had not ridden in ages. Even the walk to the stables exhausted her now.

At the bottom of her stationery case, Eleanor found a few sheets of black-edged paper left over from when Fred's father passed away. She would observe the rituals out of respect for her mother. Mother would expect it.

She rehearsed her words in her head rather than waste paper and ink searching for the appropriate phrases. Mother was easily offended, and her present circumstances would render her even more sensitive. But after twenty unproductive minutes, Eleanor steeled herself and wrote the first words that came to mind, as quickly as she could.

May 14, 1927

Dear Mother,

The Bergstrom family is honored that you would consider coming to reside at Elm Creek Manor. You will have a comfortable room and bath of your own and all the privacy you wish. Your three grandchildren will be thrilled to finally meet you.

I have indicated the nearest train station on the enclosed schedule. Please let us know when you shall arrive so Fred and I may meet you.

I would be grateful if you would extend our sincere condolences to Cousin Claire's family.

Your Daughter,
Eleanor Lockwood Bergstrom

She read the letter over as the ink dried. Despite her attempts to sound cordial and welcoming, the words were as stiff and remote as anything her mother could have written.

The second letter was easier to write, for all Eleanor regretted the need to do so.

May 14, 1927

Dear Mrs. Davis,

Now it is my turn to instruct you to sit before reading on. I believe I have news that will give you one shock to equal all those you have sent me throughout the years.

My mother is coming to Elm Creek Manor, not merely to visit, but to live. I still cannot quite believe it, but she would not have asked unless she was in earnest, and I have her request written in her own hand.

She must vacate her current residence by the end of the month, so I suppose she will be among us by June. I tell you this not to warn you away but to prepare you. Promise me you will not cancel your visit on her account. You would not visit me at my parents' house because of her, but this is my home, not hers, and you will always be welcome in it. I will lock her in the attic if you cannot bear the sight of her, but please do not deny me the pleasure of your company. With my mother in the house, I am certain I will need you more than ever.

My children do not believe you are real and never will unless they finally meet the former nanny of

Your Affectionate Friend,
Eleanor

PS: If you simply cannot bring yourself to visit with my mother here, please consider coming before her arrival. We still have two weeks left in May. What more can I say to persuade you? Tell me and I will say it.

Eleanor sent off her letters, hoping for the best. When Mother arrived, everything would change. She would have to shield the children from Mother's cutting tongue. Claudia was lovely and usually obedient and thus might earn her grandmother's grudging approval, but Mother would shudder at Richard's noisy play and proclaim him incorrigible within minutes of meeting him. As for Sylvia, she stood little chance of earning her grandmother's favor. Bright and moody and perceptive, she was everything her grandmother disliked in a young lady, and her appearance was unlikely to help. Her hair always seemed a tangle no matter how often Eleanor instructed her to comb it, and she could not step out of doors without getting grass stains on her dress and dirt on her face.

She was seeing them through her mother's eyes, Eleanor realized, but those very things that her mother would find so offensive were what endeared them to Eleanor most.

All that week, she waited anxiously for replies to her letters. As before, as always, she found solace in quilting. Not in the way Elizabeth did, numbing her pain with the repetitive motions of the needle, but in the act of creation, in piecing together beauty and harmony from what had been left over and cast aside. Her art would not endure as long as painting or sculpture, but it would outlive her, and every time her descendants wrapped themselves in one of her quilts, she would be with them, embracing them.

Months ago, Fred and William had moved the quilt frame into the nursery so that she might quilt while she looked after the children. That was the excuse she made, but in truth, she did not want Fred to see the quilt she worked upon, a gift for their twentieth anniversary. Once she had not thought it possible she would live twenty years, and in a few weeks, she would have been married that long, more than half her life. It was a miracle, and she had Fred's love and God's grace to thank for it. She did not have the words to tell her Freddy what those twenty years had meant to her, so she stitched her love, her passion, her longing into the soft fabric, which was as yielding as they had learned to be with each other, and as strong, as closely woven together. She was the warp and he the weft of their married life, two souls who had chosen each other, not knowing the pattern their lives would form.

One morning she climbed the stairs to the nursery, resting every three steps before continuing upward. The children were surprised to see her; the girls ran to hug her, and Richard toddled after them, crowing with joy. Sylvia begged Eleanor to read them a story, which she did, then gathered them all into her arms for one big hug and asked them to play without her for a while. They were so glad to have her in the nursery again that they did not complain.

Eleanor removed the sheet she had placed over the quilt to keep off dust and sticky fingers. Two years in the making, the Elms and Lilacs quilt was truly her finest work. She had appliquéd each lilac petal and elm leaf by hand, using fabrics in the new lighter hues that were coming into fashion. She had quilted around the floral motifs in an echo pattern, as if the leaves and petals had fallen into a pond and sent out gentle ripples. In the open background fabric, she had quilted feathered plumes over a crosshatch. Every stitch and scrap of fabric she had put into that quilt had a meaning she knew Fred would understand. The elms came from Elm Creek Manor, of course, but everything else symbolized the cornerstone patio. As Freddy had given it to her, so would she share it with him.

Only the last corner of the quilt, a square less than a foot wide, remained unquilted. When it was complete, she would need to finish the scalloped edge with binding. A straight edge would take less time, but in such situations she preferred to sacrifice her deadline to her design.

She threaded a needle, slipped her thimble on her finger, and soon was engrossed in her work, the children's play a happy murmur in the background. Then Richard toddled over and demanded to be picked up. She laughed and settled him on her lap, but she put only two more stitches into the quilt before he began to squirm. "Richard, darling," said Eleanor, sliding the heron-shaped scissors out of his reach, "this will work only if you hold still."

"Let Mama quilt," said Claudia. "Don't be naughty."

"He's not being naughty," said Sylvia. "He's just being a baby. That's what babies do."

"But Mama needs to finish her quilt."

"I need to play with Richard, too," said Eleanor quickly, before the fight could escalate. Claudia could be as imperious as Abigail had once been, but Eleanor had known to ignore Abigail's bluster and let her have her way. Sylvia ought to do the same with her sister, but she would rather be right than give in to get along.

"We could take turns," said Sylvia, brightening. "One of us could quilt while the other two play with Richard. This way he gets to play with everybody and the quilt still gets finished."

Claudia regarded her with scorn. "You just want to work on Mama's quilt."

"So what if I do? As long as Richard's happy and the work gets done—"

"That is the point, isn't it?" interrupted Eleanor. "I think it's a fine idea. I've already taken my turn, so Claudia, would you like to quilt next?" Claudia nodded, and Sylvia, who had already reached for the spool of thread, snatched her hand back. She shot Eleanor a look of protest, but Eleanor shook her head to remind Sylvia she did not reward bickering.

"Mama, *pay*," beseeched Richard, tugging on her hand. "Pay bock."

"Very well." Eleanor allowed herself to be led away, with only one glance back at Claudia and her quilt. "Let's go play with your blocks."

Sylvia joined her, helping Richard stack his wooden blocks and building towers for him to knock over. Sylvia threw herself into their play, pretending to have forgotten her sister, but after ten minutes she looked up at Eleanor with such woebegone hope that Eleanor agreed she could take her turn. Claudia relinquished the needle with only a small pout, and though she dragged her heels a little, she brought over one of Richard's favorite storybooks and offered to read it to him. He climbed into her lap, stuck a finger in his mouth, and stared at the pictures while Claudia told him the story. Eleanor sat back and watched, grateful for the chance to rest. The tranquil scene made her forget the time until Claudia set the book aside and reminded her Sylvia's turn was over.

Sylvia traded her place at the quilt frame for Richard's story-book, and she continued reading from where Claudia had left off. Eleanor studied her daughters' handiwork, pleased to discover that both girls had used their very best quilting. Claudia, especially, had far surpassed her usual efforts, so that her stitches were virtually indistinguishable from her sister's, even though Sylvia's work was ordinarily finer. Freddy wouldn't care even if their stitches were an inch long and uneven, of course; he would be prouder of a quilt bearing his daughters' imperfect stitches than a flawless quilt they had no part in making.

The climb upstairs to the nursery must have taxed her more than she had realized, for she was ready for a rest when Claudia's turn came again. Claudia took the needle eagerly and set herself to work with enthusiasm, the tip of her tongue visible in the corner of her mouth.

Sylvia's turn came once more, and then Eleanor's, and then Claudia's again. The girls no longer made faces when Sylvia took over for Claudia, and Richard was content, enjoying play time with all three of them. Eleanor was congratulating herself for resolving the latest in her daughters' long series of disagreements when Claudia suddenly shrilled, "What is she doing?"

"Hmm?" Eleanor looked up from Richard's wooden train in time to see Sylvia quickly set down the scissors. "What's wrong?"

Claudia stormed over to the quilt frame. Sylvia folded her arms over her work, but Claudia shoved her aside. "She's ruining my work," cried Claudia. "She picked out all my stitches."

Sylvia thrust out her lower lip. "I didn't ruin her work."

"Liar! She did!" Claudia pointed at the quilt. "Come and see for yourself."

Suddenly Eleanor felt too exhausted to do anything more than pull Richard onto her lap. "Sylvia, did you remove Claudia's stitches from the quilt?"

"Only the bad ones," said Sylvia. She glared at her sister. "I can't help it that most of them were bad."

Claudia shrieked and Sylvia shouted back. Eleanor closed her eyes and kissed the top of Richard's head. "Stop it." She covered the baby's ears and raised her voice. "Girls! Stop it. Sylvia, that was a very naughty thing to do—"

"But it's a present for Daddy," said Sylvia, chin trembling. "It should be just right."

"My quilting is just as good as yours," said Claudia.

"Now who's the liar?"

"Sylvia," said Eleanor, stern. "What you did was wrong, and being saucy about it only makes matters worse. Apologize to your sister, and go to your room."

Sylvia shot her a look of shame and frustration before mumbling something that might have been an apology and fleeing from the nursery. Eleanor sighed and sank back into her chair, patting Richard to soothe him, although he seemed not half as troubled as she.

The room fell silent. Eleanor closed her eyes and felt weariness overtake her. She had almost fallen asleep when she heard Claudia say, "I'm finished now. Do you want a turn?"

"No, thank you, darling."

She heard Claudia's chair scrape the floor and soft footsteps. Then, near her ear, Claudia whispered, "Richard's asleep."

Eleanor nodded. Even with her eyes closed she had known, not only by the sound of his breathing, but because only when asleep did her son hold still for so long.

"Shall I take him downstairs to his crib?"

"Would you, please?" Eleanor opened her eyes and allowed Claudia to take him. "Be careful on the stairs."

"I will." Claudia regarded her curiously. "Mama, are you all right?"

Eleanor smiled. "I'm just tired."

"Why don't you go to bed and take a nap? I'll get Richard if he cries."

She was tempted, but the thought of all those stairs was too daunting. "I think I'll just rest here for a moment and then quilt some more."

Claudia looked dubious, but she nodded and carried Richard away, sleeping on her shoulder.

When the door closed behind them, Eleanor curled up on the sofa, pulled an old scrap quilt over herself, and drifted off to sleep.

Eleanor's mother sent a telegram: "June 2, 3:15 PM."

From the moment the terse reply arrived until the hour Eleanor and Fred went to meet her at the station, Eleanor felt an urgent need to warn her family about her mother, to instruct them how to behave in order to divert her wrath. In the end, she said nothing. She could not find the words.

Fred held her hand as they waited on the platform. As the passengers began to disembark, Eleanor scanned the faces and wondered how she would recognize her mother after twenty years, how Mother would recognize her. Then Fred squeezed her hand.

"There," he said, and nodded. Eleanor looked, her throat constricting with emotion—apprehension, anticipation. Hope. Her eyes met her mother's, and hope faltered.

Gertrude Drayton-Smith Lockwood wore black from head to toe; even the ostrich feathers bobbing on her hat had been dyed black to match the black wool of her coat. Her mouth hardened into a thin line as she descended from the train and gestured for the porter to fetch her trunk and satchel. The soft plumpness that had given her girlish beauty had been burned away, so that her features and dark eyes stood out sharp and prominent against her pale skin. She clasped her gloved hands and waited for Eleanor and Fred to come to her, her mouth displeased, her shoulders squared in long-suffering resignation.

Eleanor could not move until Fred gently guided her forward. Should she embrace her? Apologize in advance for everything Mother would find wanting in her new home? The crowd parted, and before Eleanor could force a smile, she found herself face to face with her mother.

"So." Mother eyed her, ignoring Fred. "I can see you're not well."

"It's good to see you, Mother." Eleanor kissed the air near her mother's cheek. She smelled of rose water. "I trust you had a pleasant journey."

"I abhor trains, and this one in particular was crowded and uncomfortable and unsanitary, but since you could not be troubled to come to New York for me yourself, I had little choice."

An icy smile played on Eleanor's lips. Her mother had had a choice: Elm Creek Manor by train or the asylum for destitute women on foot. That choice remained.

"The rest of the way will be more comfortable," said Fred

Mother grunted as if she certainly hoped so but doubted it. She bent stiffly and reached for her satchel, but Eleanor picked it up first. Fred moved to lift her trunk, but Mother pretended not to see him and waved for a porter. Fred wisely said nothing, but dismissed the porter with a shake of his head and carried the trunk himself.

Mother sniffed at the sight of their car and refused the front seat beside Fred to sit in the back with Eleanor. "My goodness, this is provincial," she muttered, peering out the window at the passing scenery.

"It is, isn't it?" responded Eleanor, ignoring the insult. "It's very restful after the noise of the city. You'll adore the town. It's quaint, very charming."

"I doubt I'll find much charm in it." Her mother folded her hands in her lap and turned her head away from the window, but glanced back again as if forcing herself to accept her new, diminished circumstances. Her frown deepened as they left the town behind, and she drew in a sharp breath at the sight of a herd of cows grazing in a pasture. Eleanor wanted to assure her Elm Creek Manor was not some mean farmhouse, but even more, she wanted to shake her mother and ask her how she could be so blind to the amaranthine sky, the rolling green hills, the lush forests that in autumn would be ablaze with color, breathtaking in their beauty.

Instead she sat back in her seat and watched the landscape roll by.

When Elm Creek Manor came into view, Mother straightened in her seat for a better look. She sat perfectly still, then she arched her brows and gave a derisive sniff that somehow lacked conviction. Fred parked the car, opened the door, and offered her his arm, which she ignored, or perhaps this time she truly did not see him, for her gaze was fixed on the manor.

Eleanor led her inside, and only then did Mother speak. "Well, Eleanor," she said, inspecting the grand front foyer. "I see you did not entirely come down in the world after all. Perhaps there was more calculation than romance in your choice."

Eleanor stiffened, and she was about to snap back with all the anger she had kept in check since leaving the train station when she heard footsteps pattering on the black marble. Lucinda and Elizabeth ushered in the children, freshly scrubbed and dressed in their second-best. Eleanor hid a smile, imagining Elizabeth and Claudia debating their wardrobe and deciding that their very best might seem too formal and off-putting, while second-best would acknowledge Mother as a member of the family while still marking the significance of the day.

Elizabeth came forward, smiling warmly, and kissed Mother on both cheeks. She had shed her mourning clothes for the day, and in her dark blue appeared almost festive next to Mother. "Mrs. Lockwood, how good it is to meet you at last," she said. "I'm Elizabeth Bergstrom, Fred's mother. I cannot tell you how grateful we are that you let us keep Eleanor to ourselves so selfishly all these years. We hope you will let us make it up to you by making our home your home."

With some satisfaction, Eleanor noted that Elizabeth's graciousness had utterly confounded Mother. "Thank you," Mother managed to say, and nodded to Aunt Lucinda as Elizabeth introduced her sister-in-law.

Claudia, who had been shifting her weight from foot to foot, could wait no longer. "Welcome to Elm Creek Manor, Grandmother," she said, throwing her arms around her. "I'm Claudia. I'm the oldest. I'm so glad you're going to live with us. Mama's told me all about you."

Mother started and patted Claudia awkwardly. "Has she, indeed?"

Sylvia hung back, holding Richard by the hand, until Eleanor surreptitiously beckoned her forward. "Welcome to Elm Creek Manor, Grandmother," said Sylvia, her voice a hollow echo of her sister's. "I'm Sylvia, and this is Richard."

"Yes. Well." Mother pried herself free from Claudia and caught Eleanor's eye. "I believe I would like to be shown to my room now."

At least Mother did not complain about her rooms, not even at the sight of a patchwork quilt on the bed. Perhaps hard times had forced her to reconsider her disdain for the beauty of thrift.

Eleanor oversaw dinner preparations with care, supervising the reproduction of her mother's favorite French recipes while Elizabeth and Lucinda attended to the best table linens and silver. William snatched an éclair on his way through the kitchen and remarked that he hoped that they ate like this every night of her mother's visit.

Elizabeth shooed him away with a wooden spoon. "It's not a visit. She's here for good, and those are for dessert," she added in a shout as he grabbed a second éclair and ran.

"Please tell me we aren't going to eat like this every night," said Lucinda, frowning at a spot of tarnish on a salad fork.

"Just tonight," promised Eleanor. Tonight, and then perhaps tomorrow, at breakfast. By then, first impressions would be over and Mother would have made up her mind how she felt about them. Little could alter her opinions after she had formed them, so these first few hours were crucial. Elizabeth seemed to be faring well, as did Claudia, but Fred might as well not exist as far as Mother was concerned.

Claudia offered to call Mother for dinner, and Eleanor gratefully accepted, wanting a few moments to freshen up. All was ready in the formal dining hall, which Eleanor usually regarded as cold and imposing, but tonight it seemed just the thing. If Mother's favorite foods failed to impress her, the china and silver and crystal would not.

But when Mother entered on Claudia's arm, carrying her satchel, she did not seem to notice the tokens of wealth she once thought she could not live without. Fred rose to pull out her chair, but she waved him off and gestured for Claudia to assist her. An uncertain smile flickered on Claudia's face, as if she was proud to be chosen but dismayed that her father had been slighted.

Conversation was careful, polite, and stilted. Only Richard seemed perfectly content, banging his spoon on his high chair and stuffing his mouth with potato and sweet peas. Suddenly he reached into his mouth, scooped out a handful of chewed vegetables, and dropped them on the floor. "All done!"

"Yes, darling, I see that," said Eleanor, bending over to wipe up the splatter. Sylvia giggled.

"Disgraceful," said Mother.

Eleanor sat up quickly. For that moment, she had forgotten her mother's presence. "What is?"

"That urchin of yours, wasting good food when so many in the world go hungry." Mother set down her fork and pushed her plate away. "I cannot abide such rich dishes. A clear broth would have been much better."

"That's easily granted," said Elizabeth, smiling. She rose and left the room to speak to the cook.

"I thought you loved French cuisine," said Eleanor, wiping Richard's face.

"I did, once, before we had to let our cook go after we lost the business." Mother sighed and dabbed at her lips with her napkin. "We lost everything, but I suppose you knew that."

"I did not," said Eleanor. "I thought Father became Mr. Drury's partner."

"In name only, but I am not talking about the merger. This happened later, after Mr. Drury died and his children inherited the company."

"The entire company?" asked Fred.

This time it suited Mother to acknowledge him. "Of course. After all, Mr. Drury owned the entire company, for all that he retained the Lockwood name at the stores. He only did that to profit from our good reputation, since he had ruined his own by seducing an innocent young girl into betraying her family."

Her words were met with silence.

"Well?" inquired Mother, eyebrows raised. "What did you think would happen? Did you think ownership of the company reverted to your father?"

"That is what I assumed," said Eleanor.

Elizabeth returned with Mother's broth. Mother tasted it and set down her spoon. "Even if your sister had lived to bear Mr. Drury a child, the children from his first marriage still would have been the primary beneficiaries of his estate, since he failed to make a new will. If he had preceded her in death, she would have been left destitute unless his children were generous enough to provide for her, which, considering how they treated us, seems unlikely." She took another sip of broth. "So as you can see, Mr. Drury betrayed Abigail in the end, just as he betrayed us."

"He did not betray her." Eleanor's voice shook with anger. "He would have seen she was provided for. How could he have been expected to predict such a disaster?"

"He did not have to. All he had to do was take stock of his own mortality, as every responsible husband should. Five years they were married before they died, and yet he could not spare one day to change his will. Either he was shamefully negligent or he never intended to change it."

"He must have made other arrangements."

"Nonsense. You simply can't bear to see the romance tarnished. You ought instead to take heed of his poor example and see to your own affairs. If I am not mistaken, you have little time to waste, for all you have exceeded the doctors' expectations until now."

Someone gasped. Claudia blanched, and Sylvia turned to Eleanor, stricken and confused. Eleanor felt the blood rushing to her head. She tried to speak, but could not.

"That's enough," said Fred, his dark eyes glimmering with anger. "You've said enough for one evening."

Mother looked incredulous. "You haven't told them?"

"Told us what?" asked Sylvia in a whisper.

"The children may be excused," said Elizabeth. "Eleanor?"

"Yes—yes, of course. The children may be excused." Clumsily, she lifted Richard from his high chair and handed him to Claudia, but Sylvia had not left her seat. Her dark eyes went from Eleanor to her grandmother and back, questioning and afraid.

"Don't send them away before dessert," said Mother. "I brought presents."

"We don't want any presents," said Claudia in a small voice.

"Nonsense. What child doesn't want presents? Give the baby back to your mother like a good girl and come here."

Obediently, Claudia returned Richard to her mother's arms, but before she could take a single step, Fred spoke. "There's a little matter to clear up first. You made a careless remark that obviously frightened the girls. Why don't you explain to them what you meant?"

Mother's hand flew to her bosom. "You want me to be the one to tell them?"

"You're the one who misspoke." Fred's voice was ice. "In this family, whoever makes the mess cleans it up."

Mother's eyebrows arched. "Misspoke?" She forced out a brittle laugh, but she could not hold Fred's gaze long. She glanced at Eleanor, but just as quickly looked away. Perhaps something in their expressions reminded her that the train ran east as well as west.

"What I meant to say, children, was that we all have our time," said Mother. "We—we—sometimes we pass on before we are prepared. That's all I meant to say, that your parents should be prepared."

Claudia was visibly relieved, but Sylvia's eyes remained steadily fixed on her grandmother. "Who is Mr. Drury?" she asked. "What did he do to our grandfather?"

"Goodness, don't they know anything about our family?" asked Mother. Eleanor could see Claudia wanted to assure her that she, at least, knew something, but whatever stories Claudia repeated would only reveal her ignorance of the truth.

When no one answered her, Mother waved her hand impatiently. "Never mind. Now that I am here, I will remedy that. You will learn all I can teach you about the Lockwoods, and my gifts will be a fine start."

Claudia almost smiled, but Sylvia's expression hardened, a reflection of her father that seemed too old for such a little girl. Eleanor knew at once that Sylvia had resolved never to listen to her grandmother's stories, never to learn about the Lockwood family history. Eleanor felt a twinge of grief, but she had turned her back on the Lockwood family, and she could not expect Sylvia to embrace it.

"Ah." From her satchel, Mother withdrew a small, white box. "Come, Claudia. This is for you."

Claudia left her mother's side and took the box from her grandmother. When she lifted the lid, her eyes widened in surprise and admiration.

Mother smiled. "Do you like it?" Claudia nodded and reached tentatively into the box, glancing up at her grandmother for permission. "Of course you may pick it up, silly girl, it's yours." Eleanor caught a glimpse of silver flashing in her daughter's hand. It was her mother's silver locket, an heirloom passed down to her from her own mother.

Claudia opened the locket. "Who are these people?"

"The woman is my mother, and the man, my father. I will tell you all about them. Would you like to try it on?" When Claudia nodded, Mother fastened the locket about her neck. "There. It suits you."

Claudia fingered the locket and smiled. "Thank you, Grandmother."

"You're quite welcome." Mother reached into her satchel and produced a small parcel wrapped in brown paper and tied with string. "Be sure you take good care of it. Sylvia, this is for you."

When Sylvia did not leave her chair, Mother handed the parcel to Claudia and gestured for her to take it to her sister. Sylvia slowly unwrapped the gift, and when the paper fell away, Eleanor saw a fine porcelain doll with golden hair, dressed in a gown of blue velvet. It was a beautiful doll, but Sylvia did not care for dolls. She never had.

"Thank you, Grandmother," said Sylvia, solemn, and hugged the doll.

"She was your mother's. They were inseparable until she decided she was too old for dolls. Then she sat on a shelf in the nursery gathering dust, the poor, neglected thing."

"I didn't neglect it," said Eleanor. "You're thinking of Abigail. That was her doll, not mine."

"That's not so," said Mother. "I recall very clearly giving it to you for Christmas when you were four."

"That was Abigail. She said Santa brought it." Eleanor could still see Abigail cradling the doll, brushing her fine hair, dressing her in the frocks Miss Langley sewed. "When Abigail no longer wanted her, she gave her to me, but by then I was not interested in dolls, either."

"You would have liked them still if Abigail had." Mother turned her gaze on Sylvia. "Well, my dear, it seems I've given you the doll no one wanted. I suppose you, too, will abandon her."

Sylvia shook her head.

Mother studied her for a moment, assessing her, then frowned and reached into her satchel. "This is for you, Eleanor, if you want it." Mother placed a black, leather-bound book on the table. "It was to go to Abigail, as the eldest girl . . ."

She left the sentence unfinished. Eleanor knew what the book was, but she was immobile, unable to rise from her chair. It was Claudia who, unasked, brought it to her.

"What is it, Mama?" asked Sylvia, who always took interest in a new book.

"It's the Lockwood family Bible." Eleanor traced the gilded letters on the cover, then turned to the first few pages, to the records of births, baptisms, marriages, and deaths her father's mother had begun. With a pang of sorrow, she noticed that her mother had not written in either of her daughters' marriages, or Abigail's death.

"I leave it up to you to complete the record," said Mother. "You are the only one who can."

She meant, You are my only surviving child. There is no one else. But Eleanor understood that, and what it meant that her mother had given her this inheritance now. "I will not complete it, merely continue it," she said, closing the Bible. "As Claudia will continue it after me."

"Why Claudia?" asked Sylvia. She had placed the doll on the table and had leaned closer to her mother for a better look at the Bible, but at the mention of Claudia's name, she sat up.

"That's the tradition," explained Eleanor. "The family Bible always goes to the eldest daughter."

She regretted the words when she saw the smug look Claudia gave her sister, and the resentful glare Sylvia gave her in return. She remembered how the unfairness of the custom had stung when she realized the Bible would belong to Abigail one day, and not herself. Now she would give almost anything to be able to place it in her sister's hands, and sit by her side as she wrote down the names of all of their children in her round, girlish script.

"I have no gift for you, Fred," said Mother. "But I have already given you my daughter, and my children were always my greatest treasures."

Fred inclined his head, a gesture of respect, of recognition. Eleanor wondered if Mother had prepared her remarks on the train or if she had spoken them as an afterthought, a token of gratitude for Elizabeth's generosity.

The rest of the meal was subdued, but Eleanor was thankful enough that the hostility had passed, and that the girls had apparently forgotten their grandmother's cryptic references to her health. Mother retired immediately afterward, without a good night to anyone, much less the thanks anyone else in her position would have gratefully offered. Elizabeth made the excuse that she was surely exhausted from her long day of traveling, but they all knew better, and Lucinda told Eleanor that her rudeness was the first of many bad habits they would rid her of for the sake of family harmony.

"I forgot something," Lucinda added, handing Eleanor an envelope. "This came for you while you were at the station."

Its postmark read Lowell, Massachusetts, where Miss Langley had resided for the past six years.

September 28, 1927

My Dear Eleanor,

I am so sorry I did not respond sooner, but your letter arrived while I was traveling, and I only just received it. Please accept my heartfelt apologies, but I must decline your kind invitation. I will come to visit you as soon as your mother departs, for New York or the great hereafter, whichever comes first.

All the reasons that delayed my travels in the past seem trivial now that our separation has been extended indefinitely. I regret all the missed opportunities, all the postponements, as I am sure you do, but we must not dwell on them. I am resolved to see you again, Eleanor, or I am not

Your Affectionate Friend,
Amelia

She was not coming. Eleanor crumpled up the letter and put it in her pocket. If Miss Langley would not come now, when Eleanor needed her the most, she would never come.

The next morning, Eleanor served her mother a delicious breakfast she barely touched. Eleanor offered to show Mother the estate, but she declined, saying that she would spend the morning finishing her unpacking.

"When do you expect the rest of your things to arrive?" asked Eleanor, accompanying her mother upstairs, fighting to conceal how the effort drained her.

Mother fixed her with a withering glare. "There are no other things."

Eleanor flushed. "I didn't realize—"

"What? That I did not exaggerate when I said we lost everything?" Mother reached the top of the stairs and waited for Eleanor to join her. "You grew up in a beautiful house full of lovely things, and if you had married Edwin Corville, you would have inherited them all one day."

"Instead I married the man I loved, and now I have my own house full of lovely things." Eleanor spoke coolly, but felt a sudden stab of sympathy for her mother as she imagined her selling off the accumulated treasures of generations of her family. The sympathy faded, however, when she recalled all that Mother and Father had been prepared to do to hold on to that way of life rather than accept the limits of their fortune and live within their means.

They walked down the hallway in silence. "Obviously your marriage, or this climate, or something out here in the country agrees with you," Mother said when they reached her door. "You lived much longer than anyone expected."

Eleanor gave her a tight smile, but would not acknowledge the question in her eyes.

Mother dropped her gaze and reached for the doorknob. "In any event, you are surely more fortunate than Mrs. Edwin Corville. I'm sure you heard how she caught her husband in bed with that opera singer."

"That is one news clipping you neglected to send me," said Eleanor. "Are you saying you admit I made the right choice?"

"I will not say that, and I will never say that," declared Mother. "Abigail certainly did not, for look where it got her. Dead, at the bottom of the sea. You, on the other hand, have done quite well for yourself."

"Please don't speak of Abigail that way."

"You always were afraid of the hard truths of life. You know you are more ill than anyone in your family perceives. And that Abigail sealed her own fate by betraying her father and me. And that you resent her for abandoning you to a choice that never should have been yours to make."

"I don't resent her."

"Of course you do. That's why you treat your daughters so differently."

Eleanor stared at her. "What on earth do you mean? I love my daughters equally."

"I said nothing of how you love them, only how you treat them. You prefer Claudia, and while Sylvia seems to be made of strong enough stuff to bear it—"

"You met them for the first time less than a day ago," snapped Eleanor. "I don't see how after twenty years you can presume to know anything about me or my children."

"I simply say what I observe. It is for your own good, and theirs. I do not want you to repeat my mistakes."

"See to it first that *you* do not repeat them." Eleanor paused to catch her breath. Her heart was racing. "If you intend to live in this house, you will treat everyone in it with respect, including my husband, including me. If you ever criticize my children again, call my son an urchin or say he is a disgrace, I will put you on the next train east if I have to carry you to the station on my back. Do you understand?"

Mother studied her, mouth pursed. "This is your home, not

mine. I assure you I will show you and your family all the respect you showed me when you lived under my roof."

She went inside her room and shut the door.

Mother did not come down for lunch. Lucinda left a tray outside her door, and half an hour later, she went upstairs to retrieve it. "So she does eat," she said with satisfaction, placing the empty dishes in the sink. "That will give us some leverage over her."

"We are not going to starve Eleanor's mother into being more sociable," scolded Elizabeth. "Be patient. She needs time to adjust to us."

After Eleanor put Richard down for his afternoon nap, the thought of her own bed tempted her, but she had too much work to do before the girls came home from school, even if her churning thoughts would allow it. Twenty years before, in her mother's house, Eleanor would have sought comfort in the solitude of her study. Now she climbed the stairs to the nursery, but by the time she reached the third floor, she felt light-headed and nauseous from exertion.

Eleanor seated herself in the chair by the window, where she had left the Elms and Lilacs quilt the last time she worked upon it. She had finished the quilting and had begun binding the three layers, but more than half the binding remained to be sewn in place, and tomorrow was their anniversary. If she worked on it for the rest of the day, she might finish by evening, but while Elizabeth and Lucinda would gladly give her that time to work, she did not have the strength to quilt for hours on end as she once had.

Freddy would not mind sleeping beneath an incomplete quilt, Eleanor told herself as she slipped her thimble on her finger. In fact, it would be more fitting that way, as the first quilt they had shared had also been a work in progress. So much had happened since that night on the train when they dreamed beneath the Rocky Mountain quilt together.

She sewed until her eyes grew too tired to see the stitches clearly, then rested before resuming her work. An hour passed. Richard would be waking soon, the girls were due home from school. They would be expecting her to chat with them as they had their afternoon snack. She knew she should join them, but if she descended those stairs she doubted she would be able to climb them again until Freddy carried her upstairs for bed.

That she would not let her mother see.

"Mama?"

Eleanor lifted her head to find Sylvia in the doorway. "Yes?"

"Were you sleeping?"

"No, just resting."

Sylvia crossed the floor and leaned against the armrest of Eleanor's chair. "Why didn't you come down for a snack? Weren't you hungry?"

"No, dear. I'm sorry I didn't keep you company. But as you can see . . ." She smiled ruefully and lifted the quilt. "I'm running out of time."

Sylvia studied it. "It looks like you're almost done."

"It might seem so, but I have to complete the binding, and then embroider my initials and the date." Eleanor sighed and adjusted the folds of fabric on her lap. "I often feel like a quilt is never truly finished, that there's always a little something more I ought to do. Your great-aunt Maude used to say I was too fussy."

"That's not true. You're not the least bit fussy." Sylvia hated to hear anyone she loved criticized, unless she herself was doing the criticizing. She watched Eleanor work for a moment. "Can I help?"

"'May I.'"

"May I help?"

"Of course you may."

Sylvia pulled up the footstool, threaded a needle, and began sewing the unattached end of the binding opposite her mother. They sewed toward the middle in silence. Sylvia looked up the first time Eleanor paused to rest, but she resumed her work without questioning her. Eleanor watched her small dark head bent over the quilt and wondered if any of her children would ever understand how deep, enduring, and profound was her love for them.

"Why did you give the Bible to Claudia?" asked Sylvia, without looking up.

"I have not given it to her yet," said Eleanor gently. "It belongs to the whole family."

"But Claudia will get it someday."

"Someday. Years from now."

"Why Claudia? Why not me?"

"Because she is the eldest daughter. That is the tradition."

"You weren't the eldest daughter," Sylvia pointed out. "Neither was your father."

Eleanor had to laugh. "No, he certainly was not, but he was an only child, so his mother had no daughters to leave it to. In my case, the Bible would have gone to my sister if she had not died."

"Why don't you ever talk about her?"

"I don't know." Eleanor sat back and thought. "I suppose because I miss her very much."

"Maybe if you talked about her, you wouldn't miss her so much."

Eleanor smiled. "Perhaps."

"Mama?"

"Yes?"

Sylvia set down her needle and took a deep breath, and, in a flash of panic, Eleanor realized she was going to ask if Eleanor was going to die. She dreaded the question, but she would not lie.

Sylvia's eyes were on her face, searching.

"What did you want to ask me, Sylvia?"

"Nothing." Sylvia picked up her needle and bent over her work. "Will you tell me about your sister?"

Eleanor took a deep, shaky breath. "Of course.

"Your aunt Abigail was four years older than I," she began, and as she spoke, she recalled what her mother had said earlier that morning. Mother was wrong. Eleanor did not favor Claudia out of guilt for any long-buried resentment, but because she had almost lost her. The image of her darling baby suffering from influenza made her choke back reprimands and punishments even when they were deserved.

If there was a grain of truth in Mother's accusation, it was that Claudia did remind Eleanor of Abigail, with the gifts their parents had not nurtured and the faults they had allowed to flourish. Claudia needed Eleanor's guidance more than her younger sister, who reminded Eleanor of herself, except that Sylvia was strong and resilient and beautiful.

With Sylvia's help, Eleanor finished the Elms and Lilacs quilt by late afternoon.

They hurried downstairs, late for supper, to hide the quilt in Eleanor's bedroom closet. Later that night, while Fred slept beside her, Eleanor stole from bed, carefully lifted away the light coverlet they slept beneath on warm summer nights, and tucked in her beloved husband beneath his anniversary gift.

Something woke her before dawn—a noise, a stillness, a touch on her hair. She opened her eyes to find Fred sitting up and gazing at the quilt with shining eyes.

"Happy anniversary," she whispered, and reached out for him.

He brought her hand to his lips. "It's beautiful."

"The girls helped."

He grinned. "I'm sure they did."

He lay down beside her again and held her. They reminisced about their first years together as husband and wife, marveling at how swiftly twenty years had passed. They talked about the children, the funny and heartbreaking things they had done, muffling their voices so their family would sleep on, undisturbed, leaving them this time to themselves. They left other memories unspoken— their arguments, their angry bursts of pride, the demands that had seemed so important once but now stood plain and bare for what they were, a senseless squandering of precious time, moments they longed to go back and collect and spend more wisely, like shining silver coins fallen from a tear in a pocket.

They talked until the sun began to pink the sky. Then Fred kissed Eleanor and told her to get dressed so he could give her his gift.

She did, quickly, and though she was not tired, he lifted her up and carried her downstairs, across the marble foyer she thought too grand, into the older west wing of the manor and out the door to the cornerstone patio, and on, until they reached the stables.

With the sure skill of a man who loved horses, he saddled his own stallion and a mare Eleanor had long admired but had never ridden. Her heart quickened, but she hesitated. "Freddy—"

"Have you forgotten how to ride?"

"Of course not."

"Do you want to ride again?"

"Of course I do," she said. "I long for it. I dream of it."

He held out a hand to assist her. "Then what's stopping you?"

"I shouldn't. The doctors say—"

"Eleanor, if you and I did no more than what was allowed, then right now you would be Mrs. Edwin Corville of New York and I would be an old lonely bachelor with only these horses to keep me company."

Eleanor smiled, but her heart ached with sorrow. "You would have married someone else."

"That's where you're wrong. You are the only woman I ever could have loved, Eleanor. I knew that from the time I was fourteen and I saw you tearing around the corral on a horse."

She felt tears spring into her eyes. "You could have loved someone else." She took a deep breath, and, instinctively, placed a hand on her heart to calm it. "You still could love someone else."

His face darkened. "No, Eleanor. Not on our anniversary."

"You are still a young man, Fred. The children will need a mother."

"They have a mother. You."

"I heard you talking to Dr. Granger."

He held perfectly still, and when he spoke, his voice was quiet. "What did you hear?"

"That I will be lucky to live another year."

Fred busied himself adjusting her horse's bridle. "Doctors," he said gruffly. "According to your doctors, you've been at death's door for almost thirty-eight years."

"We have to talk about this. We have to prepare the children."

"Nothing will prepare them. How could anything prepare them for life in a world without you?"

His voice broke, his pain was laid bare, but she knew she must say what she needed to say, for they might never broach this subject again. She had tried too often to tell him what he would not hear. "I want you to know you have my blessing if you should choose to remarry."

"I don't want your blessing," he said helplessly. "I want you. Twenty years is not enough. It went too fast."

He bowed his head and turned away. She went to him and brushed away the tears he had not wanted her to see.

He pulled her into an embrace. The time for words had passed, she thought, but it would come again. She would make him hear her, and if it could not prepare him it would at least ease her own passing. She would tell him that twenty years had not been enough. She would tell him that she would not have traded these twenty years with him for a hundred lifetimes without him. She would tell him she was grateful for every single moment of her life.

She blinked away her tears, smiled, and reached for the mare's reins.

In the meantime, she was going to live.

Chapter Eleven

Sylvia and Andrew did their utmost to convince Amy and Bob to bring their families to Elm Creek Manor for Christmas. It was the most central location, they argued. They had plenty of room for everyone. The snowfall was particularly excellent that year for cross-country skiing and tobogganing, and if that didn't interest the older grandchildren, Waterford had plenty of theaters and clubs that would be open even while the college was on semester break. More important, if Andrew and his children did not spend the holidays together, it would be the end of a tradition that had endured since Amy and Bob were babies. The Coopers always celebrated Christmas as a family, no matter what distances separated them, no matter the demands of their jobs and school. Until this year, it had been a tradition each of them had been happy to keep.

By the second week in December, their persistent invitations had worn away at Bob and Cathy's resolve, and they promised to come if Amy would. When Amy's resistance seemed to weaken at this announcement, Andrew appealed to her husband, Paul, for help. He seemed a likely ally, since he had added a note beneath Amy's signature on their Christmas card congratulating Sylvia and Andrew on their engagement. Moreover, the last time Andrew spoke to him on the phone, Paul had told him he wished his late father, a longtime widower, had found a "neat lady" like Sylvia with whom to spend his golden years.

Andrew called Paul to find out how close Amy was to changing her mind, and what, if anything, they could say to bring her around. Paul confided that she had been very unhappy on Thanksgiving without them, and that as recently as two days ago, she had told him she regretted giving her father an ultimatum. Unfortunately, he added, "You know Amy. Once she thinks she's right, she refuses to back down. She's afraid that if she agrees to see you, you'll think she approves of your marriage."

"We respect her right to disapprove of us," said Andrew. "We don't understand it, but we accept it. What I can't accept is being shut out of her life, especially when she admits she wants to see us."

"She won't be able to keep this up for long," Paul consoled him. "No one in your family has the stomach for a long-drawn-out fight. Give her more time. She'll come around long before June. I hate to give up on Christmas, but I don't see any way to convince her by then."

"It's not just about Christmas," said Andrew. He glanced helplessly at Sylvia, who stood nearby, listening in on the cordless extension. She nodded, and as they had arranged beforehand, Andrew asked Paul how he and Amy would feel about having the family gather at their home in Connecticut instead. It would throw their arrangements into an uproar, but it was their plan of last resort, and they were running out of time.

Paul asked them to hold on, and they waited anxiously throughout the long silence until he returned. They were not surprised to learn that Amy had refused. Not only that, she came to the phone herself to tell them that she, Paul, and their children had decided to spend a quiet family Christmas at home, and she would appreciate it if they would accept this as the last word on the subject.

"Maybe next year," said Andrew.

"Maybe," said Amy softly, and hung up.

"She's as unhappy about this conflict as we are," Sylvia told Andrew afterward.

"Then why doesn't she just bury the hatchet?" grumbled Andrew. "Honestly, Sylvia, she's so stubborn, you'd think she was your daughter instead of mine."

"Who are you calling stubborn?" asked Sylvia indignantly, then added, "Well, I suppose I am—stubborn enough to insist that we have a merry Christmas anyway. I have no intention of altering our plans, as long as you don't."

"I don't," Andrew assured her. "I just wish the kids would be here to celebrate with us."

Sylvia did, too, but what could not be changed had to be endured. On Christmas Eve, at least, they would not be alone. Sarah and Matt as well as all the Elm Creek Quilters and their families would celebrate at Elm Creek Manor, as they did every year.

On the morning of Christmas Eve, Sylvia and Sarah rose early to finish their preparations for the party. At times like these, Sylvia was especially grateful for Sarah's business skills; a week before, when Sylvia told her how important this particular party would be, Sarah had made up lists and menus and schedules so that they could accomplish everything and still have a little energy left over to enjoy the party themselves. Only once did Sarah grumble that Sylvia could have given her a little more notice, but she soon got so caught up in organizing and planning that she forgot Sylvia's small offense.

By late afternoon, a light snow had begun to fall, but there was no sign of the roaring blizzard Sylvia had feared would keep their friends at home. A half hour before the first guests were to arrive, Sarah ordered Sylvia out of the kitchen and upstairs to put on the plum suit she had purchased in Sewickley. "Matt and I can take care of the rest," said Sarah, who had somehow found time to change earlier, and now wore a green-and-red plaid apron over her dress.

Sylvia complied, and as she hurried upstairs, she met Andrew coming down, wearing his new suit. "You look very handsome," she told him in passing.

He laughed. "No time for a kiss?"

"You'll get your kiss later," she promised, and hurried off to her room.

Her suit lay on the bed, freshly pressed and waiting. Beside it sat a small bouquet of ivory roses tied with a plum velvet ribbon. "Oh, Andrew," she said, smiling. He had not left a card, but only Andrew would have thought to give her flowers.

She dressed quickly, but took time for powder and lipstick. She put on earrings and a pearl necklace that had once belonged to her mother, and fussed with her hair longer than usual. She was not vain, but tonight she wanted to look her best. She scrutinized herself in the mirror, frowning critically. "That will have to do," she said, but she gave her reflection a nod of approval. She thought she looked rather nice, if a trifle flushed from the excitement.

She returned downstairs, smiling with delight when she saw the Christmas tree lit up in all its splendor. Sixteen feet high, it would have seemed enormous in any other room but the grand foyer. Andrew and Matt had needed a day to string the small white lights upon it, and the better part of another to decorate the boughs with ornaments. Ordinarily Sylvia preferred a smaller tree, just the right size for the parlor, but this year called for something special.

At that moment the front door opened. Matt appeared in the doorway, stomping his feet to clear the snow from his boots. He spotted Sylvia and grinned. "There's still time to put up the blinking colored lights if you like."

"Not on your life," retorted Sylvia, taking his coat as he came inside. "How's the driveway?"

"It's clear. The snow wasn't too deep," said Matt. "Don't worry, Sylvia. The weather's fine. Everyone will be here."

"Not quite everyone," said Sylvia, rueful. But it could not be helped.

Matt had other chores to attend to before the guests arrived, so Sylvia left his coat in the cloakroom and went alone to the ballroom, where Sarah had just finished lighting the last hurricane lamp centerpiece, blowing out the match as she inspected her work.

Sylvia took a few steps toward her and stopped short, enchanted by the transformation candles, poinsettias, ribbon, and evergreen boughs had wrought on the ballroom. Andrew had built a fire in the large fireplace at the far side of the room, and nearby was the Nativity scene her father had brought back from a visit to the Bergstroms' ancestral home in Baden-Baden, Germany. Earlier that day, Summer had stopped by to set up her CD player at one end of the dance floor, and Christmas carols wafted on air fragrant with the scents of pine and cinnamon and roasted apples. Just across the dance floor, the cook and two assistants—his daughter and her best friend, or so Sylvia had overheard—were placing silver trays of hors d'oeuvres and cookies on a long table, and preparing the buffet for hot dishes still simmering in the kitchen. Someone had opened the curtains covering the floor-to-ceiling windows on the south wall, and snowflakes fell gently against the window panes.

Sarah joined her as Sylvia took in the sight. "What do you think?" she asked.

"It's absolutely splendid," declared Sylvia, putting her arm around her young friend. "I can't imagine a lovelier or more festive place to spend a Christmas Eve."

"If you had given me more time, I could have done more."

"Nonsense. It's perfect the way it is." Sylvia hugged her. "Thank you, dear."

Sylvia had Sarah show her to her seat so she could leave her flowers at her place. She wanted to seek out Andrew so they could share a moment alone before the festivities began, but just then, the front bell rang, and a few moments later, their guests began to fill the ballroom. First Summer arrived with her boyfriend and her mother, Gwen, and then Judy entered with her husband and young daughter. Next came Diane, stunning in a black crushed velvet dress, accompanied by her husband and two teenage sons. Bonnie and her husband followed close behind; with them were a number of young men and women Sylvia recognized as their adult children and their spouses. The precious bundle cradled in the pink-and-white Tumbling Blocks quilt was surely Bonnie's new granddaughter, and in her eagerness to meet the baby, Sylvia forgot all about finding Andrew.

More guests arrived, including the rest of the Elm Creek Quilts staff and faculty and their families, other friends from Waterford, college students Sylvia had befriended while participating in various research projects, and Katherine Quigley, a prominent local judge. As soon as Katherine and her husband arrived, Sylvia made a point of welcoming them to Elm Creek Manor and thanking them for coming. Since the Quigleys were not a usual part of Sylvia's circle of friends, Sylvia had been concerned about making them feel comfortable, but when nearly a dozen people called out greetings the moment Katherine entered, Sylvia had to laugh at her worries.

Cocktails were served, and then a delicious meal of roasted Cornish game hen with cranberry walnut dressing that reminded Sylvia all over again why some quilters claimed they came to Elm Creek Quilt camp for the food alone. Afterward, Summer put some big band tunes on the CD player and led her boyfriend, Jeremy, onto the dance floor. Other couples joined them, and soon the room was alive with laughter, music, and the warmth of friendship.

As the first notes of "Moon River" played, Andrew found Sylvia chatting with a few of the Elm Creek Quilters and asked her to dance. "You're so popular, I've hardly had a moment alone with you," he teased.

Sylvia laughed. "You've never been the jealous type. I certainly hope you don't plan to start now."

He promised he wouldn't, and she closed her eyes and touched her cheek to his as they danced. He had become quite a fine dancer since the previous summer, when he had promised to learn to dance if she would learn how to fish. She still hadn't caught anything, but Andrew said, "Fishing isn't just about having a trout on the fire at the end of the day." She replied that she felt exactly the same about quilting.

"I don't think I've ever had a happier Christmas Eve," said Sylvia. "I hate to see it end."

"Is that so?" He regarded her, eyebrows raised. "Does that mean you've changed your mind?"

"Of course not," she said, lowering her voice as the song ended. "In fact, I was just about to suggest we get started."

He brought her hands to his lips. "I was hoping you'd say that."

Sylvia signaled to Sarah, and while her young friend found Judge Quigley in the crowd, Sylvia picked up her bouquet and met Andrew at the opposite end of the dance floor from where the mayor waited with Sarah and Matt. Sylvia took a deep breath and swallowed.

"Nervous?" asked Andrew, smiling.

"Not at all," she said, and cleared her throat. "I just hope our friends will forgive us."

Andrew chuckled. "They'll have to, once we remind them that you and I never said anything about waiting until June."

"May I have everyone's attention, please?" called Sarah over the noise of the crowd. Summer turned down the volume on the stereo. "On behalf of Sylvia and Andrew and everyone who considers Elm Creek Manor a home away from home, thank you for joining us on this very special Christmas Eve."

Everyone applauded, except Andrew, who straightened his tie, and Sylvia, who took his arm.

"It is also my honor and great pleasure," said Sarah, "to inform you that you are here not only to celebrate Christmas, but also the wedding of our two dear friends, Sylvia Compson and Andrew Cooper."

Gasps of surprise and excitement quickly gave way to cheers. Sylvia felt her cheeks growing hot as their many friends turned to them, applauding and calling their names.

"You said June," said Diane, her voice carrying over the celebration.

"No, *you* said June," retorted Sylvia.

"But I already bought my dress," wailed Diane, "and picked out your gown!"

The gathering of friends burst into laughter, and, joining in as loud as anyone, Sarah held up her hands for quiet. "If you would all gather around, Andrew would like to escort his beautiful bride down the aisle."

The crowd parted to make way for them, and Summer slipped away to the stereo. As the first strains of Bach's "Jesu, Joy of Man's Desiring" filled the air, Sylvia nodded to Andrew, and they walked among their friends to where the judge waited.

To Sylvia, every moment of the simple ceremony rang as true as a crystal chime. They pledged to be true, faithful, respectful, and loving to each other until the end of their days. They listened, hand in hand, as the judge reminded them of the significance and irrevocability of their promises. They exchanged rings, and when they kissed, the room erupted in cheers and applause. As Sarah and Matt came forward to sign the marriage license, Sylvia looked out upon the gathered friends wiping their eyes and smiling and knew that she and Andrew had wed surrounded by love, exactly as they knew they should.

If only Andrew's children and grandchildren were there to share this moment. If only they were as happy for Sylvia and Andrew as their friends were. Sylvia looked up at her new husband and saw in his eyes that he shared her wistful thoughts.

She reached up to touch his cheek. He put his hand over hers and smiled.

Sylvia woke Christmas morning in the arms of her new husband.

She watched him as he slept, reminiscing about the previous night. It had truly been a marvelous wedding, exactly the sort of celebration she and Andrew had wanted. Even the Elm Creek Quilters had enjoyed themselves too much to complain that their own plans for the wedding would now have to be abandoned. "I feel sorry for Judy's daughter," Summer had confided to Sylvia as the celebration wound down. "The Elm Creek Quilters are going to do the same thing to her that they did to you, and they won't be fooled by a surprise early wedding twice."

"Emily?" echoed Sylvia. "I'd be more concerned about yourself."

"I think I'll elope," said Summer, blanching. "Or stay single."

"Good luck, dear," Sylvia had told her, knowing Summer was unlikely to escape that easily.

Sylvia muffled a laugh at the memory and carefully sat up in bed. Andrew slept on, undisturbed, warm and snug beneath her old Lone Star quilt. It suited the master suite perfectly, just as Sarah had assured her it would. Except for moving their clothing and other personal items into the suite they would share, Sylvia and Andrew had decided to keep their old rooms as they were. Everyone needed a private retreat every now and then, even newly married sweethearts.

She put on her glasses, slipped on her flannel robe and slippers, and seated herself at the desk near the window. More snow had fallen overnight, but the flakes were fluffy and light, and once the snowplows made their rounds, the roads ought to be safe for travelers.

The family Bible lay on the desktop where she had left it the previous afternoon after moving her things into the new room. First, she read the story of the Nativity from Luke, a Christmas tradition of her own.

She reflected on the words, then glanced at Andrew, smiled, and retrieved a pen from one of the desk drawers. She turned back to the front of the Bible, to the record of important milestones in the Lockwood family written in several different hands. The last entries were in her mother's small, elegant script. She had recorded her own marriage to Sylvia's father, her sister's marriage and death, her parents' passings, and the births of all three of her children. No one had written in the date of Sylvia's mother's death, nor those of the loved ones who had followed.

The familiar melancholy that stole over Sylvia whenever she contemplated the record touched her only lightly that morning— and then, as she took a second look at a name that had caught her eye, it vanished entirely.

"Herbert Drury?" she exclaimed. "Abigail Drury is Aunt Abigail?"

"Who's what?" asked Andrew sleepily, sitting up in bed with a yawn.

"The quilt designer, the one from the magazine. The woman whose name seemed so familiar. My goodness, she was my aunt. My mother's sister. I didn't recognize her married name."

Andrew grinned and put on his robe. "You forgot your own aunt's name?"

"I did, and I'm not ashamed to admit it. She died long before I was born, and my mother always referred to her as her sister, or Abigail, but never Abigail Drury."

"So your Aunt Abigail designed the whole cloth quilt." Andrew pulled up a chair and stroked her back as he read over her shoulder. "That's one more mystery solved."

"No, I don't think so," said Sylvia. "My mother told me on several occasions that she was the only quilter in her immediate family.

An aunt or a family friend taught her. I can't recall which." Sylvia thought for a moment. "I'll bet half my fabric stash my mother designed that quilt and gave her sister the credit."

"Why?"

"Well . . ." Sylvia considered, then indicated the record of her aunt's death. "I suppose because Aunt Abigail had died only a few months before the pattern's publication. Perhaps my mother used her sister's name in tribute, to immortalize her, in a sense."

Andrew leaned closer for a better look. "April fifteenth, 1912. Did you know that's the same date the *Titanic* sank?"

"Of course I know. No one in my family could ever forget. Of course, we're not sure whether Aunt Abigail died on the night of the fourteenth or the morning of the fifteenth."

Andrew stared at her. "Your aunt died aboard the *Titanic*?"

"She and her husband, yes."

He shook his head in amazement. "Now, that's a Bergstrom family story I haven't heard."

Sylvia supposed it was, but since her mother had told her only those few spare details, she had little more to share with Andrew.

Andrew touched the page where the date of Aunt Abigail's death was written. "This is your mother's handwriting?"

"Yes."

"Your grandmother didn't pass on until several years later. Why didn't she make this entry? Come to think of it, she should have put down your mother's and aunt's weddings, and the births of you and your siblings, but it looks like your mother did those, too."

"My grandmother abandoned the record after both of her daughters ran off to marry against her wishes," said Sylvia lightly.

"Your grandmother didn't approve of your father?" asked Andrew, incredulous. He had admired Sylvia's father since childhood. "Why not?"

"I don't know. My grandmother never spoke an ill word about him in my presence. Of course, I know little more about her than about Aunt Abigail. I met her for the first time when I was seven years old and she came to live with us. She died less than two months after her arrival."

"All this talk about death, marriages the family doesn't approve of . . ." Andrew shook his head and gave her a rueful smile. "This isn't a very cheerful project for the first morning of your honeymoon."

"Don't you worry," she told him, smiling. "I believe it will have a happy ending."

She took up her pen and finished the record her mother's great-grandmother had begun. Her mother's death, a date she would never forget. Her marriage to her first husband, James. The death of James and her beloved little brother, on the same day in the same tragic accident far from home. Claudia's marriage and passing, which she should have witnessed, but learned of through letters from mutual friends.

She concluded her entry by recording her marriage to Andrew. Then she set the pen aside. She did not know who, if anyone, would continue the record after her. She would not be dismayed if no one did. It would not bother her in the least if the record ended on a note of joy and promise, the union of two dear friends.

When Sylvia and Andrew finished packing, they went downstairs for breakfast. Sarah and Matt were lingering over coffee in the kitchen, waiting to wish them a Merry Christmas and safe journey before leaving for Sarah's mother's house. Sarah and Matt had prepared the newlyweds a special breakfast: blueberry pancakes with maple syrup, a pot of lemon tea for Sylvia, and good strong coffee for Andrew. And as they sat down to eat, Sarah placed a brightly wrapped box on the table. "Your Christmas present," she explained. "It's a wedding gift, too."

Inside Sylvia discovered a digital camcorder. "My goodness," she exclaimed.

"It's to record all your honeymoon memories," said Sarah.

"Maybe not all of them," said Matt, winking at Andrew. Sarah rolled her eyes. "What? The poor man didn't even get a bachelor party. I think I'm allowed one tasteless joke."

"That's the best you can do?" inquired Sylvia. "I've heard worse at your average quilting bee."

They all laughed, and Andrew, who loved gadgets, eagerly opened the box. "This is great, kids. Thanks."

"Yes, thank you," added Sylvia, though the device looked so complicated she decided not to touch it until she read the manual. "We'll enjoy documenting our travels for you."

"Will you spend your whole honeymoon in the Poconos?" asked Matt.

"No, just tonight," said Sylvia. "Tomorrow morning we're continuing on to New York."

Sarah's face lit up. "To see some Broadway shows? To go shopping?"

"That, and we're going to visit my mother's childhood home. I've never seen it. I wrote to the current residents, and they graciously offered to give us a tour."

Andrew caught Sylvia's eye and smiled. "After that, we're going to Connecticut."

Sylvia smiled back at him. If Amy wouldn't come to them, they would go to her.

When the last bite of Sarah's delicious pancakes was gone and the dishes were washed and put away, they exchanged the rest of their gifts. Then, to put their young friends' minds at ease, Sylvia wrote down their itinerary, including the number of her new cellular phone, a Christmas present from Andrew.

Sarah and Matt helped them carry their luggage to the Elm Creek Quilts minivan. "Will you call me at my mother's house when you get to the inn?" asked Sarah.

"If you promise to stop worrying," said Sylvia, climbing into the passenger's seat and shutting the door. Andrew started the engine, and Sylvia waved good-bye through the window.

"Get a shot of us pulling away from the manor," said Andrew as they crossed the bridge over Elm Creek.

"Oh, for heaven's sake," grumbled Sylvia cheerfully, but she took the camera from its case. "I hope you won't have me doing this the whole way there."

"Of course not," said Andrew. "The batteries will run down."

Even so, she did spend quite a bit of time behind the camera as they traveled, sometimes at Andrew's request, sometimes on her own initiative, when a particularly lovely valley or snow-covered mountainscape inspired her. When they stopped for lunch or to stretch their legs, Andrew took his turn, and to Sylvia's amusement, he spent more time training the camera on her than on the sights of the journey.

"I'm coming with you," she teased when he had her stand right in front of a historical marker, so that no one watching the video would be able to read why it was so important. "You don't need a picture of me."

He replied that he was capturing their honeymoon memories, as instructed, and whenever she tried to step out of the way, he followed her with the camera. She eventually gave in, realizing that if she didn't play along, their entire vacation video would consist of her complaining and ducking out of camera range.

They arrived at the Bear's Paw Inn by early afternoon. The proprietors, Jean and Daniel, were pleased to see them again, and were thrilled to discover that they were on their honeymoon. They showed Sylvia and Andrew to their usual room, where they relaxed until suppertime.

They joined their hosts and two other vacationing couples in the dining room, and Daniel began the meal by offering a toast to the newlyweds. The food was delicious, the company pleasant, and eventually the conversation turned to quilting when a new guest inquired about the quilts displayed throughout the inn. Jean, an avid collector, was pleased to entertain them with stories of how she had acquired her favorite pieces and what she knew of their history. For Sylvia, the details of the quilts' makers and prior owners called to mind her own quest to find her mother's quilts. Thinking of what those fragile heirlooms had endured reminded her how fortunate she was to have found the Crazy Quilt whole and sound, and how generous Mona Niehaus had been to part with it. She was grateful to have the Elms and Lilacs quilt, too, for despite its altered condition, her mother's love for her family and willingness to endure any hardship for their sake was still evident in every stitch. While the Ocean Waves quilt had been lost forever, its beauty would survive in her memory, and she would learn from the example of Gloria Schaeffer's sons and not put off acts of healing and forgiveness. The whole cloth quilt, too, was beyond her reach, but knowing her mother had created it after all, and that she had lovingly offered it to the world in her sister's name, brought her as much comfort as the quilt itself would have done. And while the New York Beauty quilt still eluded her, she would continue to search. That was one lesson her mother had taught her well: Persevere, hope, and do all things with love, for then the attempt would be successful even if it fell short of the goal.

"Have you ever been to the New England Quilt Museum?" one of the new guests asked Sylvia.

"Indeed I have," said Sylvia. "Although not recently."

"If you have a chance to visit again soon, you should," said Jean. "We spent Thanksgiving with our son in Boston, and we made a day trip out to Lowell. The museum had just set up the most beautiful exhibit of Christmas quilts. If you're heading east, it's definitely worth going out of your way."

"Lowell's only about two hours northeast of Amy's house," said Andrew.

"Some of their quilts are even closer than that," said another guest, an avid quilter who had come running into the inn when she returned from a day of skiing to discover the Elm Creek Quilts minivan in the parking lot. "The Penn State branch campus in Hazleton has some pieces from the New England Quilt Museum in their library gallery. It was a special themed exhibit called—oh, what was the name again?"

"The Art of Women Pioneers," offered her husband.

"Yes, something like that. There were quilts, of course, but also other needlework, pottery, weaving, and other media, all on loan from museums across the country. The stories of the women who made those pieces were fascinating. I highly recommend it."

Sylvia nudged Andrew. "Not only recommended, but highly recommended. Surely you don't expect me to resist that."

"I don't, but we already passed Hazleton. Should we see it on our way home?"

"That sounds like a fine idea."

"I wish my film wasn't still in the camera," the other guest lamented. "I took a picture of an absolutely stunning quilt in a pattern I had never seen before. I'm sure you would be able to identify it."

"Perhaps I still can," said Sylvia. "Describe it for me."

"Well, it looked to me like a cross between the Sunflower and the Grandmother's Fan pattern. Imagine a quarter circle with narrow spires branching out from it like sunbeams—"

"Were the blocks separated by sashing?" interrupted Sylvia.

"Very distinctive sashing, as a matter of fact. The strips had spires similar to those in the blocks, and at the junction of the sashing strips were small pieced stars. Do you know the pattern?"

"I do," said Sylvia, nearly breathless from excitement. "In fact, I think I may know the very quilt. Do you recall how long the exhibit will be there?"

She shook her head. "I don't, sorry. We just stopped by on our way north from Harrisburg."

"I would hate to miss it," said Sylvia, giving Andrew a significant look. "I simply can't miss it. By the time we come home, the pieces in the exhibit might have been returned to their owners."

"I don't mind a detour if you don't," said Andrew, with a good-natured grin. "After all, you are the bride."

❧

The next morning, they bid their hosts good-bye and backtracked west for an hour through a light flurry of snow, then turned south. As they drove, Sylvia mulled over the other guest's words. A special themed exhibit, she had called it, comprised of pieces from several different museums. While Grace Daniels's contact at the New England Quilt Museum had confirmed that there were no New York Beauty quilts on display or in storage, Sylvia had not thought to have Grace specifically inquire about pieces on loan to other galleries.

Sylvia laughed, and when Andrew asked her why, she said, "I couldn't find the New York Beauty quilt among large quilt collections or even on the entire Internet, and yet here I am hoping it will be among these few quilts."

"You never know," said Andrew. "Stranger things have happened."

"Not this strange," retorted Sylvia, and yet she could not shake a sense of hope that ran contrary to all common sense. Her mother was not a pioneer, so her work would not even fit the exhibit's theme. It was too much of a coincidence that Sylvia would happen to stay at the same inn as a woman who happened to see her mother's quilt, and who just happened to mention it in passing conversation. And yet it might not be such a coincidence after all. The other guest had sought out the Hazleton exhibit because she loved quilts, and she and Sylvia had both selected the Bear's Paw Inn for that same reason. Indeed, tracking down her mother's quilt by chatting with other quilters was similar to Summer's search on the Internet, only on a much smaller scale. Was it really so wrong for Sylvia to hope, as long as she didn't set her expectations so high that she forgot to enjoy what was right before her?

"It will be a lovely exhibit either way," she said firmly. Andrew grinned and shook his head as if she had spoken her entire argument with herself aloud.

Following the directions the couple from the inn had provided, Andrew drove on to the campus and found the library with the help of a graduate student trudging along the snow-dusted sidewalk, bent over from the weight of his backpack. They parked in an empty lot just as the wind began to pick up and the flurries turned into a light but steady snow shower. Sylvia pulled up the hood of her coat and put on her gloves as Andrew came around to her side to help her from the minivan.

They spotted the sign posted on the glass door from the sidewalk. "That can't be good," said Sylvia, glancing over her shoulder at the empty parking lot. Sure enough, when they drew closer to the sign, they learned that the library would be closed for another week for the semester break.

"That's too bad," said Andrew. "We can still visit the museum in Lowell, though."

"That New York Beauty quilt won't be in the museum," Sylvia reminded him. "I'm not giving up yet, not after turning back especially to see this exhibit. I had my heart set on seeing some quilts today, and I'm determined to do so."

"We could drive around town until we found a quilt shop," suggested Andrew, but Sylvia cupped her hands around her eyes and pressed them against the glass. She thought she saw a light coming from one of the rooms on the other side of the front desk.

"Come on," she said. She made her way along the sidewalk for a few paces, then stepped off into ankle-deep snow.

"Careful," Andrew said, and gave her his arm.

They circled the building, stopping to look in each window. Andrew worried aloud that a security guard might haul them off for trespassing, but Sylvia figured the risk was worth it. "Who would pick on two senior citizens on their honeymoon?" she teased, peering into what must have been a staff lounge. "Aha! Look on the counter, beside the refrigerator. See that red light? Someone made coffee this morning."

"Or they left the pot on from the end of the semester."

Sylvia knew he could be right, but was unwilling to admit it. The next two windows looked in upon shelves of books, but the third revealed a large cluttered office containing several computers, carts of tagged books, and one young woman sipping from a coffee mug as she collected sheets of paper emerging from a printer.

Sylvia tapped on the window. The woman jerked her head up, her long blond braid slipping over her shoulder. Sylvia smiled and waved, but the woman shook her head, mouthed some words, and turned back to the printer.

"I think she said they're closed," said Andrew.

"That would be my guess, too." Sylvia rapped on the glass again, and when the woman looked up, Sylvia beckoned her to come closer.

The woman sighed and came over to the window. "We're closed," she called, her words barely audible through the glass but her meaning unmistakable.

"Please?" shouted Sylvia. "We won't take but a moment of your time."

Sylvia wasn't sure if the woman understood, but after a moment, she nodded and pointed toward the front of the building. "Hurry," said Sylvia, taking Andrew's arm again. "Before she changes her mind."

The woman was waiting for them inside the front foyer. As they stomped their feet to shake off the snow, she unlocked the door and held it open. "May I help you with something?"

"We understand you have an art exhibit here," said Sylvia, breathless from racing around the building. "May we please see it?"

"I was hoping you just wanted to use the bathroom," said the woman. "I'm afraid the library's closed until next week."

"We won't be here next week," said Andrew. "We're just passing through on our way to New York."

"We heard your exhibit is not to be missed," said Sylvia. "May we just take a brief look at the quilts, if nothing else? We won't disturb your work."

"We're on our honeymoon," said Andrew.

The woman blinked at him. "You're what?"

"We're on our honeymoon," he repeated, and Sylvia nodded.

"No kidding." The young woman eyed them. "Congratulations."

"Thank you, dear," said Sylvia. "Now, I'm sure it's against the rules, but it's cold out here and we've come a long way. May we please come inside?"

"We promise we won't touch anything," said Andrew.

The woman hesitated, then pushed the door open wider. "Oh, all right," she said. "I can give you fifteen minutes. But if anyone catches us, I only let you in to use the bathroom."

They thanked her and wiped their feet thoroughly on the foyer mat so that they would leave no trace of their visit. The young woman introduced herself as Claire and led them into the library gallery.

Sylvia glimpsed paintings, woven baskets, silk embroidery, pottery, but mindful of the limited time, she continued to search the room instead of admiring them. "The quilts are along that wall," said Claire, pointing, at the same moment Sylvia spotted them.

Sylvia could only nod in reply.

The Crazy Quilt had caught her eye first, for it was so like her mother's, composed of unusual diamond-shaped blocks. It had held her attention for only a moment, though, for beside it hung a New York Beauty quilt.

The colors were right. That much registered as Sylvia crossed the floor, slowly, as if in a dream. The number and arrangement of blocks were right. So was the pattern of hand-quilted stitches flowing in feathered wreaths and plumes as only her mother could have worked them.

She felt Andrew's hand on her elbow just before she ran into the velvet rope stretched before the display. "That's the one, isn't it?" he asked softly.

Sylvia nodded.

Claire had followed them across the room. "Isn't it beautiful?"

"Yes." Sylvia cleared her throat. "It is indeed. What do you know about it?"

Claire shrugged. "Only what I read in the brochure and heard from the art professor who arranged the exhibit."

"I'm afraid I have bad news for your professor," said Sylvia. "I know for a fact that this is not a pioneer-era quilt."

"Oh, he knows that," said Claire, with a laugh. "We use the term 'pioneer' metaphorically. All of the artists featured here were pioneers in their fields—medicine, psychology, child development, politics, and in this woman's case, social reform."

Sylvia's eyebrows shot up. "I beg your pardon?"

"Social reform. She was a key figure in the women's suffrage and labor rights movements. Hold on a moment. Let me get an exhibit guide." Claire hurried off and returned holding a small booklet, which she handed to Sylvia. "Her name was Amelia Langley Davis."

Sylvia accepted the guide, shaking her head at the unfamiliar name. She turned the pages until she came to a brief biography of the artist credited with her mother's work. Amelia Langley Davis was born in England, immigrated to the United States, and worked as a nanny for several years in New York, where she became involved in the workers' rights movement. Upon moving to Boston, and later, to Lowell, Massachusetts, she played a key role in the labor union organizing among garment workers. After serving a prison sentence for "seditious utterings" at a labor rally, she devoted herself to improving the conditions for incarcerated women, including the establishment of several "residential work-houses," where recently released female convicts lived and learned a trade as they adjusted to life outside prison walls.

"She sounds like a remarkable woman," said Sylvia when she finished reading, "but I assure you, she did not make this quilt."

"I know," said Claire, regarding her curiously. "I guess you heard. Well, you're not the only person to think this quilt doesn't belong in this exhibit. I thought so, too, until I heard the story behind it and had some time to think it over."

She turned the page in the exhibit guide and indicated that Sylvia should read on.

New York Beauty Quilt
Pieced, cotton and wool c. 1920–1930

This item is unique among those selected for The Art of Women Pioneers exhibit in that it was not made by the artist, but is instead a piece that she owned and treasured. While the identity of the actual quiltmaker is not known, she is believed to have been one of Amelia Langley Davis's earliest students, most likely a former convict who resided in the first residential workhouse Davis established in Lowell, Massachusetts. It is not certain if Davis supervised the making of this quilt, but the style, pattern, color design, and material selection suggest that she was influential in the quiltmaker's development, almost certainly as her teacher.

According to Davis's journal for April 4, 1950, she acquired the quilt in the town of Waterford, Pennsylvania, from the quiltmaker's daughter. Only one cryptic reference confirms that Davis and the artist knew each other: "It was with a heavy heart that I at last traveled to Waterford, knowing I had delayed my journey too long. I came too late to see her, but I did meet one of her daughters, the eldest. The brother was killed overseas and the other sister's whereabouts are unknown. The eldest sells off her family's possessions. I managed to purchase the New York Beauty, which I knew at once from her letters, although she called the pattern Rocky Mountain. I would have rescued more but her daughter had none left to sell me. It is a cold comfort that at least my dear friend did not live to see her children estranged, her handiwork scattered."

It is known that Davis kept the New York Beauty quilt with her throughout the rest of her life, but the story of its creation has been lost. This piece was included in this collection not because it was precious to her, however, but because it represents Davis's commitment to her students, a crucial facet of the art in which she was a pioneer.

Sylvia looked up from the guide, her gaze fixed on the New York Beauty quilt, but her thoughts far away. Whoever this Amelia Langley Davis was, she must have known Sylvia's mother. The details from her journal could not possibly have referred to any family but the Bergstroms. But if she was such a "dear friend," why had Sylvia's mother never mentioned her—or had she, and had Sylvia carelessly allowed the stories to pass by unheard?

Her mother had confided little about her life before coming to Elm Creek Manor—but Amelia Langley Davis had also lived and worked in New York. Could she have been Sylvia's mother's nanny? Could she have been that distant relative or family friend who had taught her to quilt?

Grief came over Sylvia, for the stories lost, for those pieces of her mother's life she would never know. Now only her quilts remained, silent and steadfast testaments to the woman she had been.

And yet one other part of her legacy remained: Sylvia herself, and all that she recalled, and all that she had yet to discover.

Gazing at the quilt that had so long eluded her, Sylvia resolved to gather the precious scraps of her mother's history and piece them together until a pattern emerged, until she understood as well as any daughter could the choices her mother had made. She had no daughter to pass those stories along to, but she had Sarah, and she had Andrew's children, and among them she would surely find one who would listen, so that her mother's memory would endure.

She would begin by setting the record straight.

"Your booklet is incorrect," Sylvia told Claire. "I don't know for certain how your Amelia Langley Davis knew the quiltmaker, but I do know who she was."

She turned back to face the quilt, her grief forgotten. She had found the New York Beauty at last, and with it, a small portion of her mother's history. For years and years to come, the New England Quilt Museum would share her mother's quilt with the world, and soon, also, the story of the woman whose hopes and dreams and longings still lingered in the soft fabric, in the gentle colors, in the intricate stitches, like the last fading notes of a song.

"My mother made this quilt," said Sylvia, and though Claire regarded her skeptically, Sylvia smiled, knowing that in a moment, Claire would turn over the quilt to reveal the initials and date Eleanor Lockwood Bergstrom had embroidered so many years ago, as if she had known this day would come.

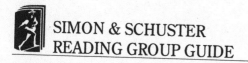

SIMON & SCHUSTER
READING GROUP GUIDE

The Quilter's Legacy

INTRODUCTION

Newly engaged Sylvia Bergstrom Compson has her hands full running Elm Creek Manor and preparing for the holidays. But a more urgent matter trumps everything when she discovers that several of her late mother's beautiful handmade quilts have gone missing from the attic of Elm Creek Manor. Using journal entries, receipts, quilting websites, and other clues, Sylvia and her fiancé, Andrew, embark on a cross-country road trip to track down the precious heirlooms. During her journey Sylvia realizes how little she knows about her mother, who died when Sylvia was a young child. Through flashbacks and alternating narratives, readers learn more about Sylvia's mother, Eleanor, and her fascinating life—her wealthy childhood in New York, the tragedies that tore her family apart, and her greatest loves. As Sylvia tracks down the lost quilts and their stories, she begins to piece together her family history and the secrets of her past.

QUESTIONS FOR DISCUSSION

1. Based on what you know of Sylvia, why might she have initially been so hesitant to marry Andrew? Why does she have reservations about permanently moving in with him?

2. Eleanor and Sylvia both encounter difficulties as they prepare to marry. Despite their vastly different circumstances, how do their struggles parallel each other?

3. How does Chiaverini build suspense by alternating between Sylvia's and Eleanor's points of view? Discuss some of the sections where she provides clues to the novel's final outcome.

4. Discuss Eleanor's relationship with Miss Langley. How is Miss Langley both a positive and a negative influence on Eleanor? How do both their actions dramatically affect the course of each other's lives?

5. What did you think about Andrew's children's reaction to the news of Sylvia and Andrew's engagement? Were they completely overreacting or could you understand their reservations based on their family's history?

6. Discuss the social and political events that Chiaverini weaves into the narrative of *The Quilter's Legacy*, from the voyage of the *Titanic* to the women's suffrage movement. How does Chiaverini integrate these historical elements into the

framework of the story? How does the novel's inclusion of real events enhance your reading experience?

7. When Eleanor's parents attempt to force her to marry Edwin, Eleanor's mother tells her she should "never marry for love. Marry for position and security, as your father did. As I should have done. That is the only way you will not be disappointed. That is the only way you will receive exactly what you were promised." (p. 110–11) What do we learn about Eleanor's mother in this passage? What is ironic about this advice?

8. How might Eleanor have avoided developing influenza when everyone else around her had it?

9. Discuss the scene where Sylvia visits the Schaeffers and discovers their long-buried secret. In some ways her visit is both successful and unsuccessful. What does this section say about the turns life can take? Does it reinforce any other common themes in the novel?

10. Discuss the following passage: "Mother was wrong. Eleanor did not favor Claudia out of guilt for any long-buried resentment, but because she had almost lost her. . . . If there was a grain of truth in Mother's accusation, it was that Claudia did remind Eleanor of Abigail, with the gifts their parents had not nurtured and the faults they had allowed to flourish." (p. 283) Can you elaborate more on what both Eleanor and her mother mean? What other circumstances might lead parents to inadvertently favor one child over another?

11. Do you think that Eleanor made the right decision in allowing her mother to live at Elm Creek Manor? Could you have forgiven her if you were Eleanor?

12. Why was Miss Langley never able to visit Eleanor? Do you believe she was truly too busy, or were there other reasons behind her decision? Based on what Sylvia and Andrew learn at the end of the novel, what else might have motivated Miss Langley's actions aside from the reasons she gave Eleanor?

13. When Sylvia makes her final discovery at the Pioneer exhibit she is overcome with grief "for the stories lost, for those pieces of her mother's life she would never know. Now only her quilts remained. . . . And yet one other part of her legacy remained: Sylvia herself, and all that she recalled, and all that she had yet to discover." (p. 309) Discuss the various meanings of the word *legacy* in the novel. How does the title have a double meaning? Where else does this theme occur?

14. How did Chiaverini's inclusion of the family tree from the Lockwood family Bible help you piece together parts of the family's history on your own? Did seeing some of the dates before finishing the novel create an element of suspense? Were you surprised by the dates listed for Eleanor's lifespan?

15. Discuss any other passages or themes in the novel that were of particular interest to you. What did you take away from the novel? Which parts resonated most strongly with you? Why?

ENHANCE YOUR BOOK CLUB

1. If this is your first time reading an Elm Creek Quilts novel, try one of the other numerous books in the series. Jennifer Chiaverini's website, elmcreek.net, contains an FAQ page that lists the novels in order of publication and chronology. The beautifully designed site is also full of information on all of Chiaverini's books, galleries of fabrics, quilts and patterns, and upcoming events.

2. Gatherings of friends, food, and family are a huge part of life at Elm Creek Manor. Take a cue from Sylvia and Sarah and throw a holiday party. (If there's no holiday coming up, throw a party just because, or make up your own holiday!) Ask each person to bring a favorite traditional family dish to add a bit of history to the table. Try adding an element of surprise, the way Sylvia does at her Christmas party.

3. Chiaverini writes, "That was one lesson [Sylvia's] mother had taught her well: Persevere, hope, and do all things with love, for then the attempt would be successful even if it fell short of the goal." Make a list of five things you would like to pursue purely out of love, regardless of how likely or unlikely it is that you'll achieve them.

4. Visit www.quilthistory.com/museums.htm for an extensive list of museums around the country that contain outstanding quilt exhibits. Plan a group trip to the one nearest you.

QUESTIONS FOR THE AUTHOR

As does *The Runaway Quilt*, the previous installment in your popular Elm Creek Quilts series, *The Quilter's Legacy* offers fascinating lessons in American history. What inspired you to continue exploring our nation's past through the lens of fiction?

I'm fascinated by history, especially women's roles in American history, and writing the Elm Creek Quilts series has given me the opportunity to study and write about a variety of historic periods and places. As I was writing *The Runaway Quilt,* it occurred to me that I had explored Sylvia Compson's paternal heritage thoroughly in the course of four books, but I had offered relatively little information about Sylvia's maternal ancestors. I decided to devote *The Quilter's Legacy* to Sylvia's mother and her history, a story Sylvia herself did not know well. In the course of my research, I realized that Sylvia's mother would have lived through a very turbulent period in our nation's history. Although she died young, she witnessed the women's suffrage movement, the struggle for labor rights, World War I, the influenza pandemic of 1918, and other pivotal events.

Since Eleanor was a quilter, I also wove in quilting lore from her day. The quilts Eleanor creates and the fabrics and tools she works with were typical of the times. Quilting lore was an especially useful creative device for understanding Eleanor, since trends in quilting have reflected trends in American life. Social and political events of each period influenced everything from the materials quilters used to the subjects they depicted. I have found that quilts and other examples of the "domestic arts" can teach us a great deal about everyday life in these bygone eras.

In *The Quilter's Legacy*, Sylvia Bergstrom Compson embarks on a nationwide search for five quilts her mother made, with hopes of learning more about the woman who made them. Why did you decide to keep so much about the life and character of Eleanor Lockwood Bergstrom a mystery to her daughter?

In the first Elm Creek Quilts novel I established that Eleanor died when Sylvia was only ten years old, so I had to reflect carefully on what Sylvia would have known about her mother. Although the book would have been easier to write had Sylvia known her mother well, Eleanor would not have told a young child about certain memories she probably would have shared readily with a grown daughter. Ultimately the reader comes to know Eleanor far better than Sylvia does, which I hope will make readers reflect upon how much is lost when stories aren't shared among generations.

What makes Eleanor a remarkable woman for her time and circumstances?

Strong, independent women have existed in every generation, but perhaps what sets Eleanor apart is that she was courageous enough to risk everything for the chance of a more fulfilling life. At the time she decided to marry Sylvia's father, Eleanor knew her family would disown her, and she also believed she was risking her very life by giving up her inheritance. A childhood bout of rheumatic fever had left her with a weakened heart, and Eleanor believed that Sylvia's father would be unable to afford the medical care she needed. She decided that a few years with the man she loved would be far better than decades without him.

Who was your inspiration for the extraordinary Amelia Langley? How does she stand as a role model for women in the twenty-first century?

I drew upon many historical figures in creating Amelia Langley, each of them a pioneering woman involved in the causes of equal rights and social justice, including Susan B. Anthony and Dorothy Day. Amelia Langley is a strong role model for contemporary women regardless of their political beliefs because she stands up for what she believes in and accepts the consequences of her actions.

Do you think women today understand the importance of the suffragist movement—or the price paid by pioneering feminists?

It depends upon the generation; women who lived through the women's rights movement of the sixties and seventies seem far more aware than younger women are of the sacrifices past generations made in order to achieve the rights we enjoy today. This is another reason why it is so important for older generations to tell their stories, so that their struggles and sacrifices are neither taken for granted nor forgotten.

What took Sylvia so long to agree to marry Andrew Cooper, a man she deeply loves? Why did Andrew's grown children object to their match? Is there a message in this fictional love story for real-life widows and widowers of a certain age?

Sylvia put off Andrew's proposals because still grieved for her first husband, her first love, even though he had passed away many years before. Also, after many lonely and unhappy years she had finally made peace with her past and found some contentment for herself, and she was reluctant to jeopardize that.

Andrew's grown children never expected their father to marry again, and so the announcement of his engagement catches them completely off guard. They like Sylvia, but she's several years older than their father and has had some health problems, including a stroke. They're afraid that before long, their father will again have to suffer the grief of losing a beloved wife, and they want to spare him that.

The Elm Creek Quilts series moves effortlessly between the past and present from one book to the next. Tell us how that feels creatively. How do you come up with so many different story lines spanning different generations? Did you plan to take this approach from the beginning of the series?

I enjoy writing both contemporary and historical stories, and I'm pleased that my readers—and my publishers—have embraced my more flexible definition of a series so that I can continue to write in both genres. When I wrote my first novel, *The Quilter's Apprentice*, I had no idea it would be the first of many intertwined books, so I didn't map out an extended storyline that would be spread out over a certain number of volumes. In hindsight, I think it's fortunate that I launched the Elm Creek Quilts series this way. Instead of proceeding in a strict linear fashion, following the same thread of the same character's life in perfect chronological order, I've been able to take secondary characters from earlier stories and make them the protagonists of new books. In other novels, I've delved into a familiar character's past, exploring entirely new settings and characters that are still tied in some way to the Elm Creek Valley. Because I'm not stuck in the traditional series format, I've enjoyed the creative freedom to write novels that explore new characters and settings while still satisfying readers who want to see the people and places they have already come to know and love.

What do you say to people who assume your books are only about quilts?

People who assume my books are only about quilts obviously haven't read them! I've always known that my books are about quilters—in other words, people—rather than quilts or quilting. That said, the quilts my characters make are never arbitrary. They aren't included as an afterthought or as set decoration, but are as important to my characters as real quilts are to the quilters who make them.

Often I'll use a quilt to provide insight into a particular character's personality or past. You can learn a great deal about quilters from the style of quilts they make, the techniques they use, their color and fabric palettes, and whether they finish quilts or have a closet full of abandoned projects. Sometimes a quilt will play an important role as a narrative device. In *The Quilter's Apprentice,* a sampler quilt serves as a useful instructional project as a master quilter teaches her young friend how to quilt, but the patterns also evoke stories from the older woman's childhood and life as a young bride on the World War II home front. In *Round Robin,* a collaborative project allowed me to tell the story from different characters' perspectives as the central block was passed around the circle of friends and each contributed her border.

Ultimately, however, my novels are character-driven stories of friendship, history, moral courage, and ordinary people's struggle to overcome adversity—and you don't need to know anything about quilts or quilting to enjoy them.

About the Author

Jennifer Chiaverini is the author of the Elm Creek Quilts series, as well as four collections of quilt projects inspired by the series, and is the designer of the Elm Creek Quilts fabric lines from Red Rooster Fabrics. She lives with her husband and sons in Madison, Wisconsin. Visit her at www.elmcreek.net.

> **"An outstanding series of novels** about a fascinating craft. Quilting, in the hands of Chiaverini, allows us to explore human relationships in all their complexity."
>
> —*Booklist*

Also available from Simon & Schuster

Available wherever books are sold or at www.simonandschuster.com